Praise for *The End of the Story*

"Passion and regret, writing and revision, the impossibility of describing, or even remembering, love—these themes animate Lydia Davis's brilliantly original, funny, wise, and quietly brave new novel."

—Francine Prose

"Self-consciousness is one of the noblest literary virtues, especially as so exquisitely practiced by Lydia Davis in *The End of the Story*. This modular—modulating—novel is about the taste of memory and the awkwardness of lovesickness. Davis explores the decomposition of a relationship and, beyond that, an obscurer object of desire, the composition of her story. A fascinating, piercingly told, smoldering tale."

—Charles Bernstein

"It is Davis's style that makes the novel come alive. Evocative physical description and somberly beautiful language are among her considerable gifts . . . some descriptions will lodge in your mind forever."

—*The Boston Globe*

"Brilliant . . . The palette of Davis's novel reminds me of green tea, bone, quartz light, and dried apricots, and its French room tone buzzes with the obsessiveness of Michel Leiris, the saltwater air of Jane Bowles, and the grouchy who-cares-a-damn silence of Jean Rhys. No contemporary writer has so bravely explored the grisaille of solitude, boredom, pique, and discontent in the midst of desire, or the severe elegance of a thinking woman."

—*The Village Voice*

"An aching love story recollected in tranquility."

—*Publishers Weekly*

The End of the Story

Lydia Davis

Picador
Farrar, Straus and Giroux
New York

The author wishes to thank the Ingram Merrill Foundation, the Mrs. Giles Whiting Foundation, the National Endowment for the Arts, and the Fund for Poetry for their generous support.

www.picadorusa.com

Picador® is a U.S. registered trademark and is used by Farrar, Straus and Giroux under license from Pan Books Limited.

For information on Picador Reading Group Guides, as well as ordering, please contact the Trade Marketing department at St. Martin's Press.
Phone: 1-800-221-7945 extension 763
Fax: 212-677-7456
E-mail: trademarketing@stmartins.com

ISBN 0-312-42371-3
EAN 978-0312-42371-1

Library of Congress Catalog Card Number 96-72969

First published in the United States by Farrar, Straus and Giroux

First Picador Edition: July 2004

D 20 19 18 17 16

The End of the Story

The last time I saw him, though I did not know it would be the last, I was sitting on the terrace with a friend and he came through the gate sweating, his face and chest pink, his hair damp, and stopped politely to talk to us. He crouched on the red-painted concrete or rested on the edge of a slatted wooden bench.

It was a hot day in June. He had been moving his things out of my garage and into the back of a pickup truck. I think he was going to take them to another garage. I remember how flushed his skin was, but I have to imagine his boots, his broad white thighs as he crouched or sat, and the open, friendly expression he must have worn on his face, talking to these women who were not demanding anything of him. I know I was conscious of how my friend and I looked, the two of us sitting with our feet up on our deck chairs, and that in my friend's presence I might seem even older to him than I was, but also that he might find this attractive. He went into the house to get a drink of water, then came back out and told me he was finished and would be on his way.

A year later, when I thought he had forgotten me altogether, he sent me a poem in French, copied out in his handwriting. There was no letter with the poem, though he addressed it to me, using my name, as though beginning a letter, and closed it with his name, as though closing a letter. At first, when I saw the envelope with his handwriting on it, I thought he might be returning the money he owed me, over $300. I had not forgotten that money because things had changed for me and I needed it. Although the poem was addressed to me from him, I wasn't sure what he meant to say to me with that poem, or what I was meant to think he was saying, or how he was using it. He had put his return address on the envelope, so I knew he might expect an answer, but I didn't know how to answer it. I didn't think I could send another poem, and I didn't know what kind of letter would answer that poem. After a few weeks had passed, I found a way to answer it, telling him what I thought when I received what he sent, what I thought it was and how I discovered it was not that, how I read it and what I thought he might mean by sending me a poem about absence, death, and rejoining. I wrote all this in the form of a story because that seemed as impersonal as his poem. I included a note saying the story had been hard for me to write. I sent my answer to the address on the envelope, but I didn't hear from him again. I copied the address into my address book, erasing an earlier one that had not been good for very long. No address of his was good for very long and the paper in my address book where his address is written is thin and soft from being erased so often.

The End of the Story

Another year went by. I was touring in the desert with a friend, not far from the city where he had lived, and I decided to look for him at his last address. The trip had been uncomfortable so far, because I felt oddly estranged from the man I was with. The first night I drank too much, lost my sense of distance in the moonlit landscape, and tried drunkenly to dive into the white hollows of the rocks, which appeared as soft as pillows to me, while he tried to hold me back. The second night I lay on my bed in the motel room drinking Coca-Cola and barely spoke to him. I spent all the next morning on the back of an old horse at the end of a long line of horses, riding slowly up into a single cleft in the hills and down again while he, annoyed with me, drove the rented car from one rock formation to another.

Out of the desert, our relations grew more comfortable again, and as he drove I read aloud to him from a book about Christopher Columbus, but the closer we came to the city, the more preoccupied I was. I stopped reading and looked out the window, but I noticed only isolated pieces of what I saw as we approached the sea: a ravine full of eucalyptus trees descending to the water; a black cormorant sitting on a monolith of pitted white limestone that had weathered into an hourglass shape; a pier with a roller coaster; a cupolaed house high above the rest of the town beside a queen palm; a bridge over railroad tracks that wheeled away ahead of us and behind us. When we headed north toward the city, we went along next to the tracks, sometimes within sight of them and sometimes away from them, when they veered inland and our road continued along the top of the cliff by the water.

I went off by myself the next afternoon and bought a street map. I examined it sitting on a stone wall that was cold under me though the sun was warm. A stranger told me the street I wanted was too far away to reach on foot, but I set off on foot anyway. Every time I came to the top of a hill, I looked out over the water and saw bridges and sailboats. Every time I descended into another small valley, the white houses closed in around me again.

I had not known how large the city would seem to me as I walked or how tired my legs would become. I had not known how the sun on the white housefronts would dazzle me after a time, how it would beat down hour after hour on housefronts that grew whiter and then less white as the hours passed and my eyes began to ache. I got on a bus and rode for a while, and then got off and walked again. Though the sun had shone all day, by late afternoon the shadows were chilly. I passed some hotels. I did not know exactly where I was, though later, when I left the neighborhood, I saw where I had been.

At last, after walking sometimes in the right direction and sometimes in the wrong one, I reached his street. It was the evening rush hour. Men and women in business clothes walked up and down the street past me. The traffic moved slowly. The sun was low and the light on the buildings was dark yellow. I was surprised. I had not imagined that his part of town would look like this. I hadn't even believed this address existed. But the building was there, three stories high, painted light blue, a little shabby. I studied it from across the street, standing on a step in which was embedded a row of tiles spelling out the name of a pharmacy, though the door behind me opened into a bar.

The End of the Story

For more than a year now, since I had written that address in my address book, I had imagined very precisely, as though I had dreamed it, a small sunny street of two-storied yellow houses with people going in and out of them, up and down front stoops, and I had also imagined myself sitting in a car diagonally across the street from his house, watching his front door and his windows. I had seen him coming out of the house, thinking of other things, his head bowed, running down the steps briskly. Or coming more slowly down the steps with his wife, as I had seen him twice before with his wife when he did not know I was watching him, once from a distance as they stood on a sidewalk near a movie theater and once through his apartment window in the rain.

I wasn't sure I would speak to him, because when I imagined it I was disturbed by the anger I saw in his face. Surprise, then anger, and then dread, because he was afraid of me. His face was blank, and stiff, his eyelids lowered and his head thrown back a little: what was I going to do to him now? And he would move back a step as though that really took him out of my range.

Though I saw that his building existed, I did not believe his apartment would exist. And if his apartment existed, I did not believe I would find his name taped up beside the bell. Now I crossed the street and went inside the same building where he had lived, perhaps very recently, certainly within a year, and read the names ARD and PRUETT on a white card next to the bell of his apartment, number 6.

I realized later that this strange, genderless pair, Ard and Pruett, must have been the ones who discovered whatever he left behind: the bits of tape stuck to things, the paper clips and pins between the floorboards, the pot holders or spice bottles or pot lids behind the stove, the dust and crumbs in the corners of drawers, the hard, stained sponges under the bathtub and under the kitchen sink that he once used in his energetic way to clean a basin or counter, the stray pieces of clothing hanging in dark parts of the closet, fragments of splintered wood, nail holes in the plaster with smudges or scrapes around them or near them that would seem random just because Ard and Pruett wouldn't know what their purpose had been. I felt an unexpected relation to these two people, though they did not know me and I had never seen them, because they, too, had lived in a sort of intimacy with him. Of course it could have been the tenants before them who found what he left, and maybe Ard and Pruett had found the marks of another person altogether.

Because I had to go as far as I could toward finding him, I rang their bell. If I did not find him this time, I would stop trying. I rang, and rang again, and yet again, but there was no answer. I stood outside on the street just long enough to feel I had arrived, at last, at the final point of some necessary journey.

I had set out to walk to a place that was too far to reach on foot. I had gone on even when it became too late in the day, and when I was at the limit of my strength. Some of my strength had returned when I came near the place where he had lived. Now I walked on past his house, toward Chinatown and the red-light district, the warehouses by the bay, and the water, as I thought, trying to remember the city, and even though he no longer lived in that house, and I was so tired, and I had to go on walking, and there were more hills to climb on all sides of me, I felt calmed by having been there, as I had not felt since he left me, as if, even though he was not there, I had found him again.

Maybe the fact that he wasn't there made this return possible, and made an end possible. Because if he had been there, everything would have had to continue. I would have had to do something about it, if only to go away and think about it from a great distance. Now I would be able to stop looking for him.

But the moment when I knew I had given up, when I knew I had ended the search, came a little later, as I was sitting in a bookstore in that city, with the taste in my mouth of some cheap, bitter tea brought to me by a stranger.

I had come to rest there, in an old building with floors of creaking wood, a narrow stairway leading downstairs, dim lighting in the basement, and a cleaner and brighter upper level. I had walked through the bookstore, downstairs and back upstairs and around the corner of every bookcase. I sat down to look at a book, but was so tired and thirsty I couldn't read.

I went to the front counter, next to the door. A somber man in a cardigan sweater stood behind it sorting books into piles. I asked him if there was any water, if I might have a glass of water, though I knew there probably wasn't any water here, in a bookstore. He said there was no water, but that I could perhaps go to a bar nearby. I said nothing, turned away, and went a few steps up into the front room that overlooked the street. There I sat down again on a chair to rest while people moved quietly around me.

I hadn't intended to be rude to the man, I simply couldn't open my mouth and speak. It would have taken all my strength to push the air out of my lungs and make a sound with it, and it would have hurt me to do it, or taken something from me that I couldn't spare just then.

I opened a book and looked at one page without reading it, then leafed through another book from beginning to end without understanding what I saw. I thought the man behind the counter probably mistook me for a vagrant, since the city was full of vagrants, particularly the sort who would like to sit in a bookstore as the afternoon grew darker and colder, and might ask him for a glass of water, and might even be rude if he did not give it to her. And because I thought, from his expression of surprise, and perhaps concern, when I turned away without answering him, that he mistook me for a vagrant, I suddenly felt I might be what he thought I was. There had been other times when I felt nameless and faceless, walking through city streets at night or in the rain when no one knew where I was, and now this feeling had unexpectedly been confirmed by the man standing across the counter from me. As he looked at me, I floated away from what I thought I was, and became neutral, colorless, without feeling: there was an equal choice between what I thought I was, this tired woman asking him for water, and what he thought I was, and there might not be any such thing as the truth anymore, to bind us together, so that he and I, facing each other across the counter, were more separate than two strangers usually are, isolated as though in a bank of fog, the voices and footsteps near us silenced, a little well of clarity around us, before I, in my new character as vagrant, too tired and disoriented to speak, looked away without answering and went into the next room.

But as I thought this, he walked up to me where I sat

close by a tall bookcase. He leaned down to me and gently asked me if I would like a cup of tea, and when he brought it to me I thanked him and drank it. It was strong and hot, though so bitter it parched my tongue.

This seemed to be the end of the story, and for a while it was also the end of the novel—there was something so final about the bitter cup of tea. Then, although it was still the end of the story, I put it at the beginning of the novel, as if I needed to tell the end first in order to go on and tell the rest. It would have been simpler to begin at the beginning, but the beginning didn't mean much without what came after, and what came after didn't mean much without the end. Maybe I did not want to have to choose a place to start, maybe I wanted all the parts of the story to be told at the same time. As Vincent says, I often want more than is possible.

If someone asks me what the novel is about, I say it's about a lost man, because I don't know what to say. But it is true that for a long time now I have not known where he is, after first knowing and then not knowing, knowing again and then losing him again. He once lived on the outskirts of a small city a few hundred miles from here. He once worked for his father, a physicist. Now he may be teaching English to foreigners, or teaching writing to businessmen, or managing a hotel. He may be in a different city, or not in a city at all, though a city is more likely than a town. He may still be married. I was told that he and his wife had a daughter and that they named her after a European city.

When I moved to this town five years ago I stopped imagining that he would appear suddenly in front of me, because it was too unlikely. It had not been so unlikely in other places I lived. In at least three cities and two towns, I kept expecting him: if I was walking down a street, I imagined him coming toward me. If I was walking through a museum, I was sure he would be in the next room. Yet I never saw him. He might have been there, in the same street or even the same room, watching me from a short distance. He might have slipped away before I noticed him.

I knew he was alive somewhere, and for several years I lived in a city he would almost surely visit, though my neighborhood was a dirty, run-down area by the harbor. The closer I went to the center of the city, in fact, the more I expected to see him. I would find myself walking behind a familiar figure, broad, muscular, not much taller than I was, with straight, fair hair. But the head would turn and the face would be so unlike his, the forehead wrong, the nose wrong, the cheeks wrong, that it would become ugly just because it could have been his and was not. Or a man would come toward me from a distance with his arrogant, tense bearing. Or, close by, in a crowded subway car, I would see the same pale blue eyes, pink skin with freckles, or high, prominent cheekbones. Once, the features were his but exaggerated, so that the head was like a rubber mask: hair the same color but thicker, eyes so light they were almost white, forehead and cheekbones jutting out grotesquely, red flesh hanging from the bones, lips pressed together as though in a rage, body absurdly wide. Another time, the version of his face was so lacking in definition, so smooth and open, that I easily saw how, in time, it would develop into that other face I had loved so much.

I saw his clothes on many people: of good but coarse

material, often threadbare or faded, always clean. And I couldn't help believing, though I knew it made no sense, that if enough men were to wear these clothes in the same place, he would be forced to appear by a sort of magnetism. Or I imagined that one day I would see a man wearing exactly what he wore, a red plaid lumber jacket, or a light blue flannel shirt, and white painter's pants, or blue jeans torn at the cuffs, and this man would also have straight reddish-gold hair combed to one side of his broad forehead, blue eyes, prominent cheekbones, tight lips, a broad strong body, a manner that was both shy and arrogant, and the resemblance would be complete, down to the last detail, the pink in the whites of his eyes, or the freckles on his lips, or the chip in his front tooth, as though all his elements had come together and the only thing needed, to change this man into him, was the right word.

Although I remember it was on a sunny late afternoon in October, on the top floor of a tall public building, I can't remember the reason for the reception. Surrounded by other people, in a sort of atrium, either circular or octagonal and flooded with sunlight, with doorways opening out from it, I was taken up to him by Mitchell, who told me his name. I forgot his name immediately, as I almost always did when I was introduced to someone. He already knew who I was, so he didn't forget my name. Mitchell went away, leaving us alone. We stood there in the midst of women moving slowly and tentatively through the rooms singly and in pairs, in and out of the strong sunlight. He told me he had imagined I would be older. I was surprised that he had imagined anything. I was surprised by several things: his frankness, the way he was dressed, in what seemed to me a hiking outfit, and, more than that, the fact that he existed at all, standing here talking to me, since no one had mentioned him to me before. I did not think about him after I left the place, maybe because he was so young.

Later that day, I went up to a shabby café on the coast road to the north of my town where he and a few friends, along with other people I didn't know, had come to watch a performance of some kind that included primitive tribal chants. When I came in, the room was already darkened except for the spotlights on the stage. The only empty chair I could see at the long table was the one next to him, though a piece of clothing and maybe a purse were hanging from the back of it. When he saw me hesitate over the empty chair, he stood up and removed these things, taking them down to the other end of the table. In fact, another woman came to the chair soon after the performance began, in the dim light, and with irritation walked away to another seat. I don't know who this woman was.

He was sitting at one end of the table, looking down the length of it, his back to the door I had come in by, and I was sitting to his left, facing a small stage where two men were performing, one chanting and singing, the other plucking a bass fiddle. Across from me was Ellie. I didn't know her very well then. He kept leaning over to her during the performance, which was so noisy and close to us in the crowded room that no one could talk during it except by speaking directly into another person's ear.

At that time I liked to drink. I always needed a drink if I was going to sit and talk to someone. If I had to sit in a public place that did not serve alcohol, I was uncomfortable and could not enjoy the time, just as, if I was invited to someone's house for the evening, I liked to be offered a drink as soon as I walked in.

At the first intermission, I asked him and Ellie if the café served alcohol, and they said it did not. I asked them where I could go to buy something to drink. They said there was a little grocery a short walk away where I could buy beer, and he offered to go with me, and again quickly stood up from his chair.

Outdoors, he walked along beside me over the beaten dirt at the edge of the road, through the litter of dry leaves and wood buttons from the eucalyptus trees.

I can't remember what we talked about, but in those days I almost never remembered what I had talked about with a person I had just met because I had so many other things on my mind. I was worried not only about whether there was something wrong with my clothes or hair, but also about how I was standing, walking, or holding my head and neck, and where I was putting my feet. And if I was not walking but trying to eat and drink as I talked, I worried about how to swallow the food and drink in such a way that I wouldn't choke, and sometimes I did choke. All of this kept me so busy that although I remembered a sentence long enough to answer it, I didn't think about it long enough to remember it later.

The road was dark by the time we went out, at seven-thirty or eight. Or rather, the side of the road where we were walking was lit by streetlights and floodlights around the café and the stores near it, and the other side of the road was dark, lined by eucalyptus trees shading the road from the electric lights. A sign or two hung among the trees, and beyond the trees lay two pairs of railroad tracks, also dark, and across the tracks a small streambed, not visible itself but marked by the tall grasses that bordered it, and then another road, smaller and not much traveled, but well lit, at the foot of a bare hillside. In the other direction, in back of the café and the stores, the ocean was a few hundred yards away at the base of a hill or cliff, so large and dark that even though I couldn't see it, its darkness hovered over the road and the electric lights fought against it.

I'm not sure whether we walked on dirt or asphalt, what we passed, or how he walked next to me, whether awkwardly or gracefully, quickly or slowly, close to me or a few feet away. I think he was bending toward me in his eagerness to talk and hear what I was saying, which was difficult, since I spoke very quietly. I'm not sure what brand of beer we bought, just what the confusion was about the money and the brand of beer, whether he paid for my beer as well as his own. Maybe I wanted a more expensive brand and bought two bottles of that, while he had only enough money for two bottles of a cheaper brand and spent the last money he had on them. I know he spent his last money on something because much later in the night or the early hours of the morning he ran out of gas and having no money at all, asked a stranger on the street for a dollar. He told this to Ellie in the library the next day and she told it to me, though long after.

There was his invitation, once we were back in the café, my hesitation, his boldness, my misunderstanding, then the noise of his car, my fear, the coast at night, my town at night, my yard and the rosebush, the jade bushes and my fence, my house, my room, the metal chairs, our beer, our conversation, his misstatements of fact, his boldness again, and so forth.

The End of the Story

When he asked me to go out for a drink with him, and the first thing I said was that I really should be home working, I felt like a dull translator, or a cautious professor, much older than he was. I had been feeling older and older anyway at that time, maybe because I was in a new place and a new situation, and had to see myself freshly and size myself up as though I was not as familiar to myself as I had thought. I was not really so old, but I was still many years older than he was.

There is more that I don't like remembering: my hesitation, my sudden worry, my anxiety as I hurried after him, the embarrassment of having run after him, my lack of grace, feeling older but not acting my age, I thought.

He walked with such determined steps out of the café after the performance was over, without saying anything to me, that I thought he was hurt by my hesitation. We had not spoken more than a dozen sentences to each other and already I thought I had hurt his feelings, which isn't surprising since I often thought he was hurt, and angry, even when I had known him much longer than just a few hours. Of course, the fact that I rushed out after him must have shown how much I wanted to go off somewhere with him, despite my hesitation. When I went out after him he told me he was only removing some things from his car. It was his own awkwardness that had made him leave so abruptly.

As we stood by our cars outside the café, he asked me where we might go. Then, bolder again than I expected, he asked me if we might go to my house. I hesitated again, and this time he apologized. I liked his modesty in doing that. I knew almost nothing about him, so each thing he did and said showed me an entirely new aspect of him, as though he were unfolding in front of me. I did not mind going straight home, because I was tired. I got into my car, and he got into his. I waited for him so that he could follow me, and when he turned on his engine, his large, old, white car roared. It continued to roar so loudly, as it followed just behind me, that my teeth began to chatter and my hands shook on the steering wheel, which I gripped until my knuckles hurt.

With his headlights filling my rearview mirror, and my hands tight on the wheel, we drove down the coast through another town where a movie theater was emptying out, on down by the water, across some marshland, and up a dry hillside into my town, past the traffic lights and the outdoor café on the corner, and after a left turn, up the hill to my house.

It seems to me that he stumbled in the dark as he crossed the rutted dirt driveway under the cedar tree, but I may be confused about that, because I myself fell backward off the bank of sea fig into the driveway a few days later, as he was leaving. I was waving goodbye to him. I did not actually fall, but stumbled back off the high bank in front of the house on which the cedar grew. I was always awkward with him, I had trouble controlling my arms and legs when I walked through the room, when I sat down in a chair. He said I was awkward because I was so eager, and moved too fast for my own body.

Now I walked ahead of him, and by the front wall he lifted a stem of thorns that hung down from an overgrown climbing rose so that I could pass without scratching myself. Or maybe he couldn't have done this in the dark, and it was on another day, in the daylight. Or it was that night, but the night was not entirely dark. In fact, it is only dark in my memory of that particular night, because I know there were two bright streetlamps nearby: one of them shone into my room.

We made our way across the circular drive and past the untidy rosebush, which grew by the window where I sat so much of the time staring out, and around the side of the house past the jade bushes. We followed a brick path to a gate of white painted wood set in a fence of white painted wood, and through the gate into the arcaded walkway past the windows of my room to the door of my room. An electric light shone from inside a lantern fixed to the white stucco wall next to the door.

Inside, we sat down on two folding metal chairs between the green card table where I worked and a rented upright piano. I brought back from the kitchen two beers, which we drank on the uncomfortably hard chairs.

He told me he had just finished writing a novel, but later this turned out not to be true. What he had just finished was not a novel but a story twenty pages long that he then cut down to six pages. Either I had not heard him right or he was so nervous that he said the word "novel" by mistake and did not hear it.

Because I did not know his name, he seemed only half real, and a stranger to me, though I was not afraid of him. I was startled by him a third time, after a couple of hours had gone by during which we sat talking politely, distantly and carefully about one thing and another, on our separate, hard chairs, when he asked me if he could take his boots off.

.

The fact that I must be mistaken about some of this doesn't bother me. But I'm not sure what to include. There is my hesitation in the café and his persistence. The way I followed him out of the café and back in again. The roar of his car when he started it. The way the headlights and grille of his old white car filled my rearview mirror. The gentleness with which, next to my house, he lifted the strand of rose thorn out of my way so that I would not scratch myself. The hard metal chairs. Then the awkwardness of the bright light by my bed. The way my mind hovered like a little professor in glasses in the air above what was happening down below, and judged this and then judged that.

At dawn, I was asleep, and I woke up because he was saying something to me before he left. I woke up further to understand what he was saying. He was quoting some poetry to me as a way of leaving, and I understood why he was doing it, but it bothered me.

Then there was the roar of his car again when he drove away from my house, disturbing the peace of the wealthy neighborhood. Even if no one could see or hear him, I was embarrassed to have such a young man leave my house at dawn in a car that roared through the stillness of the elegant seaside town, going down the hill past the fenced and hedged properties of my neighbors: the people across the street in their pagoda-style house who owned a large part of the town and who later invited Madeleine and me, along with many others in the town, to a party in celebration of a new acquisition or construction, maybe their swimming pool; the elderly couple down the hill from them whose elaborate cactus garden bordered the small lane that led to the convenience store where I went to buy such things as cigarettes and cat food; the young couple next door to us down the hill in a little white cottage which they did not own but were renting, though I did not know it then, as I did not know that the young woman, who worked in a clothing store down on the main street and sold me something now and then, would be killed on the highway a few years later when a large truck ran into her from behind as she slowed approaching the exit ramp near our town; then past the Norwegian church of dark brown wood, with its line of eucalyptus trees in front, turning right at the bottom of the hill and roaring at a greater and greater distance, until I couldn't hear it anymore.

·

I am close enough to the ocean here, too, so that now and then a seagull flies overhead. There is a creek not far away, so wide I used to call it a river before Vincent corrected me. It flows into a very broad tidal river which Vincent told me should not be called a river either, but an estuary. This village lies on a ridge between the two bodies of water.

But it is a different ocean. And I wouldn't be able to get to it without passing through miles and miles of the city, because the city is built right out to its shores. There are no sea figs, no jade bushes, and no palms here. The rocks are not sandstone but granite and lime. The soil is not sandy and not reddish but dark brown and loamy.

It is March, and cold. Vincent's thick cotton socks hang on the line, still damp after several hours in the sunshine. There is an inch of snow on the ground, but some migrating birds have already come back and are singing and looking for nesting spots. Finches flutter around the eaves of the back porch and we track mud into the kitchen.

I have just finished translating a long autobiography written in a difficult style by a French ethnographer. It is a good thing I am done, because the longer I spend on a book, the less money I have. I will send it off to the publisher along with my bill, and wait for my check to arrive.

Earlier today I was reading about a Japanese writer who lives in England and writes in English. His novels are meticulously constructed, have very little plot, and present information in a fragmentary, offhand way. The article seemed important to me for a reason I couldn't identify, and I intended to save it and reread it, but I have lost the magazine. I am inefficient in the way I work on the novel, and that inefficiency infects other things I try to do. This was more understandable when I had to keep leaving the novel and coming back to it. Now, even though I work on it almost every day, I still become confused and forget what I was doing when I left off the day before. I have to write instructions to myself on little cards with an arrow in front of each. I look for the arrow, read the instruction, follow it, then gradually remember what I was doing and know where I am until I stop for the day, when I write myself another instruction. But on my worst days I just sit here in my nightgown, my own warm smell rising from the opening of my collar. I listen to the cars go by in an endless stream on the road below my window and think something is happening just because time is passing. I won't get dressed until I have sat here half the day. I won't always shower first, only at a point when I feel I have thoroughly ripened.

I used to like to go over every moment of that first evening, when he and I sat there at the table with friends on one side of me, friends on the other side of him, the noise of the performance so loud that no one could talk, when we walked out together, not knowing each other, and bought two bottles of beer each to bring back in, had drunk one bottle each, and had still one bottle unopened in its brown paper bag by our feet, and sat without opening it, saving it for a little while. This seemed to me, in a way, the best moment of all, when it had hardly begun. When we opened the second bottle of beer we would also be opening everything that came after, through the late fall and the winter, but as long as we sat without opening it we were on a sort of island, and all the happiness lay ahead of us, and would not begin until we opened the second bottle of beer. I couldn't see this at the time, because I didn't know what was going to follow, but later I could look back and see it.

Looking back at that evening was almost better than experiencing it the first time, because it did not go faster than I could manage it, I did not have to worry about my part, and I was not distracted by doubt, because I knew how it would come out. I relived it so often, it might have happened just so that I could relive it later.

Then, after he left me, the beginning was not only the first, happy occasion, opening into an infinite number of happy occasions, it also contained the end, as though the very air of that room where we sat together, in that public place, where he leaned over, barely knowing me, and whispered to me, were already permeated with the end of it, as though the walls of that room were already made of the end of it.

·

I had arrived in town a few weeks before I met him. I had a job but no place to live. I was staying in a tidy apartment belonging to a couple of graduate students who were out of town. I had come there to teach, but I had never taught before and I was frightened. Alone in that apartment I took books down from the bookshelves and read things I thought might help me answer the questions of the students. I imagined that the students would be smart and already know more than I did. But I read so hastily and so randomly that I did not remember anything.

Mitchell was the only person I knew, and he showed me around the city and the nearby towns, walked with me through the campus, answered my questions, and introduced me to people, though he often forgot the names of even his oldest colleagues because of his own shyness. There were two places where he thought I might want to live, a small furnished apartment I would have to myself and an unfurnished room in a large house that I would be sharing with another woman. He took me to see the house first and I never went to see the apartment.

The house was beautiful and nearly empty, the rooms in its two wings opening onto a terrace enclosed by a fence and old shrubs. I thought it was like a Spanish hacienda, though I was not sure what a Spanish hacienda was. The woman lived there with her dog and her kitten. No one knew her very well, but they had formed opinions of her. Mitchell led me through the gate onto the terrace, and the woman, Madeleine, came out of her rooms on the other side of the terrace to meet us. She was tall, with long reddish-blond hair tied back and a wide, tense, unchanging smile on her face, nervous, I could see, about meeting me, so nervous she was almost rigid with fear. It was midday, and the sun shone down on us brilliantly.

Besides the dog and the cat, the only things I saw on that first visit were some electronic equipment and some large unpainted cord pots that Madeleine had made. They were probably standing out in the sun. I never saw the electronic equipment again.

The End of the Story

I was nervous, too, at the thought of living with a woman I did not know, whom no one knew very well, in that house with its musty smell of garlic, stale incense, millet, tea, dog, cat, and rug shampoo. Though Madeleine kept her part of the house very clean, it was infested with fleas from the animals. My room had no fleas in it but was covered with a layer of old dirt.

All I had in my room, at first, besides a box spring and mattress which Madeleine and I brought up out of a basement storeroom at the far end of the house, was the contents of my car, what I had brought with me across the country. Then we found, maybe also in the storeroom, the card table and the metal chairs.

Living in the same house together, we continued to act as though we were living alone. We went on talking to ourselves in our separate rooms. From one room, on a bad day, would come the word "shit," from another the word "bitch." Or there would be confusion: in the middle of the night Madeleine would remember that a half-finished pie had been left out and get up to put it away, but I had already put it away. She would think she had done it herself and forgotten.

Madeleine did not have the money for either a car or a telephone. I had a telephone installed and rented a piano. When I was out of the house Madeleine would bring into my room the only music she had, a tattered Schirmer's edition of Chopin's *Nocturnes* with rings of coffee stain on its yellow cover, and play the same pieces over and over in a languid style. Often enough, when I came home, I would find her there playing, sitting very straight, and I would be either pleased or irritated, depending on my mood and the state of our relations, which fluctuated constantly. In the evening after supper I would play Haydn sonatas. My style was monotonous, harsh, and mechanical.

But when she played the piano, and played badly, she did it with such grace and dedication that even though I knew her performance was imprecise and romantic, I was still convinced that it was somehow right. Because she did not doubt herself, because she did each thing with such conviction, I always believed her despite myself. I often felt clumsy next to her, or innocent to the point of stupidity. And yet I was not innocent. Later, when he was with us, he seemed even more innocent.

When I moved into the house, it was the dry season, and the skies were slow to grow heavy, slow to rain, letting go only a few drops at a time now and then. I taught one class each day. Driving home by the beaches I would look at the curling waves and think of the first beer I would drink when I got home. I would not eat right away but have a cold beer or a glass of wine. I was too worried about the next day's class to see anyone in the evening, most evenings. I corrected papers and wrote down ideas for the class. Even after I had gone to bed, I went on teaching in the dark, sometimes for several hours. I expressed things better there in bed than I would the next day.

If I did spend the evening with other people, I liked the wine or beer to be poured freely. I would take off my glasses and put them in my lap, where they kept sliding down onto the floor. At last I would let them lie there, covering them with my bare feet. Outlines softened, features became illegible, and I slowly grew numb. If people around me stopped drinking, I did not like it, because it meant the evening was ending, real life was starting up again, and the next day loomed. I went on drinking alone,

The End of the Story

though I knew I shouldn't, since I would have trouble driving the car home, I would not notice stop signs, I would grimace in concentration as the road curved down by the beach and up again over the hills, as I waited out the changing traffic lights in the empty intersections. But it was hard to stop drinking, because in a part of myself I must have believed that if I went on and on, to the point where my fingers lost their coordination, even beyond that to the point where my head drooped to one side and my eyes closed briefly, and even beyond that to where I could speak coherently only by deliberately collecting my thoughts and my words, I would come out the other end into a new condition, into a new world. Looking in the mirror once I was home, I would see that there were small changes: my cheeks were flushed, my hair was limp and disordered, and my lips were pale.

Most of each day, I would sit at my card table and work. My room was very large, with a red tiled floor, a peaked ceiling, dark beams, deep embrasures, white stuccoed walls so thick the air in the room was always cool when the sun was shining and the air outside was hot. If I looked up from my work, I saw dark green pine branches waving slowly against the sky, a shrub of rich red roses beyond the trees, rubbery, arching spears of succulents with serrated edges, and the soft powdery dirt scattered with pinecones at the base of the tall cypress that leaned away from the house. Across the street was a latticework gate in an Oriental style. Now and then, in the sunlight, a young girl in loose blue clothing carrying a tennis racket would enter the gate, greeted by two small dogs. Cars drove by slowly, climbing or descending the hill. People out for a walk appeared suddenly with a soft patter of footsteps on the asphalt or a louder, brittle ring of voices, old women and old couples, nicely dressed, white-haired, walking carefully down to the ocean or down to the main street to shop or to look at the window displays, and back up to their houses. Roaming dogs trotted into view from the edge of the windowframe, sniffing.

I often heard a train going by at some distance, down the hill from me, close to the water. It was easier to hear at night. During the day, many other noises came between me and it: the voices of my pleasant neighbors with time on their hands talking in the street outside my window, the occasional cars winding their way slowly up and down the side of the hill, the constant traffic of cars and trucks two blocks down from me on the coast road, the engines of heavy machinery at construction sites a few blocks away, the sound of hammering and sawing from the same sites, and other noises I couldn't distinguish creating a general din that seemed benevolent because it went on under the steady, hot sun and in the midst of an orderly profusion of dark green, thick-leaved shrubs and trees and ground cover scattered with dark red and pale blue flowers.

At night, the air, soft and fragrant, was clear of most of these noises, as it was clear of the hot sun and the profuse colors, as the plants, in the dark, were only soft shapes against the walls of buildings or against the curb of the street, and through this emptier air I could hear the wheels of the train clattering along the track and the hoot of its whistle, as pure as its single yellow eye.

During the day I might leave my table to go outside, and if I had been inside for a long time, the warmth of the sun, the sweetness of the breeze, and the colors of the plants beyond the white fence were so intensified by the hours indoors that they seemed an almost unbearable assault. I would drive Madeleine to get clay or to shop for food. Or I would walk down to the main street past the fenced yard of cactuses and bare dirt, past an old man in a straw hat and overalls gardening very slowly with large leather pads strapped to his shins, past the Norwegian church, past the wooden medical offices with their spotless windows, sprinklers coming on and going off everywhere in the beds of sea fig, endless sunshine glinting off the chrome of the cars.

Or I walked on the beach or the hillside, alone or with Madeleine. When she was not busy making something out of clay or papier-mâché, in her room or out on the terrace, when she was not cooking or eating, when she was not meditating or watching television, all of which she did with the same serious, undivided attention, she would walk for hours at a time with a steady, restless energy, her dog by her side, stopping only to talk to someone she knew or to fend off small gangs of boys who teased her and called her by insulting names because she was not like the other people in the town. She walked up and down the main street, she walked beyond the shops to the park, she walked beyond the railroad station to the beach, by the water into the distance and then back to the point she had started from and into the distance again in the other direction.

If I walked with Madeleine, we walked on the beach or along the cliff overlooking the ocean, and if I walked alone, I went up the hill away from the house.

Because the town was built on a steep hill, and because all the towns along the coast were built on hillsides or on top of the cliff above the ocean, I always had the sense of living above something, of living on a small level spot, a ledge or a plateau, with steep slopes above and below. My house and its terrace were one level place. The coast road was another. The park below it was another, and a short drop below that the railroad tracks another, carved into the hillside above the beach. The roads above my house were now steep, now level for a moment, now rising gently, as I walked up past lush gardens hanging off the hillside, yards so thickly planted that it wasn't always easy to see that a grove of trees was part of a property, a private property, attached to a house that was often concealed. The properties were carefully tended, but on the edge of each there might be a single beer bottle or can, by the road, as though the road itself, running like a river through this place of private properties, carried on its back the life of the outside world, and had thrown up on its banks signs of the outside world that the owners of the properties would carefully remove, walking along the edges of their groves or lawns by day, and that the road with its flotillas of joyriding, fast-moving teenagers, a river rising and then falling again, would leave again by night. And almost every road tended to climb the hillside and descend again, whether it went straight up, steeply, when, as I walked, my back would be to the ocean, or went gently up, running across the hillside almost parallel to the ocean, when I would see the ocean from almost every point on the road, either a bit of blue sheeting behind the branches of a pine or a broad plain of blue, or silver, or black, where I had come out past a house and above any planting, so that if I followed it up far enough it always went down again, as though it could only resist the force of gravity for so long. At a distance ahead of me in the middle of the crossroads I might see a large pinecone, or it might be a mourning dove, dark and cone-shaped. The breath of the eucalyptus would be so heavy on the air it coated my open lips.

Because this landscape and this climate were new to me, I liked to study them, though less often on foot and more often through the windows of my room or my car. The coast road roughly followed the line of the coast, sometimes veering inland on the other side of the hill from the ocean and sometimes staying within sight of it, but high above, on a cliff. When it descended to run right alongside the beach and close to the water, I would look out at the waves, looming over my head, or up at the hang gliders in the air like great birds, or across the sand at the black-suited surfers coming back toward the road with their surfboards under their arms, all these people not only on the sand but also in the water, and in the air. In the air were also kites and once or twice a great, striped, hot-air balloon racing inland.

People on the beach were often in pairs, two divers in suits weighed down with gear occupied with buckling or unbuckling their things, or two hefty bearded men in shorts exercising side by side, or a middle-aged man and wife with straight brown legs and spotless sweatshirts and shorts walking at a brisk pace, or a muscular blond student, glasses pushed back on his head, in a chair reading a heavy leather-bound book while his blond girlfriend lay near him on a towel. If I was not in the car but down on the beach, from a certain spot I could look up and see the little seaside train station, trains coming in with ringing bells, thick crowds edging the platform.

There is a train near here, too, a freight train that takes so long to go by that I have forgotten all about it by the time it has passed. It, too, is easier to hear late at night, when the road is quiet and the rhythmic click of the wheels bounces off the hillside behind it. Or in wet weather, when the tracks seem so near they might lie just out of sight beyond the trees.

This morning I ache all over because I worked so hard yesterday cleaning the house and preparing a complicated meal for one guest, a lone man who seems all the more lone because he is so tall and thin and has such a simple name, Tom, and who, maybe for the same reason, always gives the impression of being a quiet man though he talks quite readily. The dinner went off fairly well despite the fact that Vincent's father was such a distraction to us, sitting in an armchair to my right and asking for pieces of my food.

So much time has gone by since I started working on this novel that first I left my city apartment and moved in with Vincent, and then his father moved in with us, causing extra work and bringing a succession of nurses into the house to care for him.

During the same time, a meadow I used to pass on my walks was replaced by a small townhouse development. The meadow had many wildflowers, and at least four different varieties of grasses. It had a small grove of spindly saplings at one end, and at the other a great oak tree set back against the rocky hillside near a trolley shed. Now the oak is gone, and the row of townhouses sits back against the hillside. In front of it, where the meadow lay, is only the fresh black asphalt of a new driveway and a considerable stretch of bare lawn.

On another empty lot outside our village, a car wash has been built. And only a few months ago, a large project of residential housing and offices was approved despite the opposition of almost everyone in the town. It will occupy some wild acres down the road from here where the chicken farmer used to roam around when he was a boy. The chicken farm has also closed down its operation and the farmer makes birdhouses to sell in his roadside store. These are only a few of the changes.

We have a new nurse for Vincent's father, and she is on duty downstairs now. She seems responsible and a hard worker, and more cheerful than the last, though something of a hypochondriac. She wears a tattoo on her upper arm that I haven't yet dared to examine. At the moment, the old man is demanding a different lunch from the lunch I wrote down for him. The whole time I am up here I am also listening to them with one ear. The old man accepted her very sweetly this morning, and put his arms around her when she came, though it is only her second day. She whispered to me, "I think he likes my hair." If she does not keep him distracted, though, he will begin asking for me.

I have had almost constant problems with these nurses. Although they like the old man, they don't last very long. One came only half the time, came late when she did come, and offered a different excuse each time—illness, car trouble, a heavy menstruation, the change to daylight saving time, etc. Another contracted to work the whole summer and then, after a few weeks, abruptly told me she was going off to the Caribbean Islands to teach cooking. When I protested, she became indignant and disappeared altogether without even coming to say goodbye to Vincent's father, who continued to be puzzled by this no matter what we told him.

In the living room below me now, the nurse is coughing

and picking out a tune on the piano, maybe to let me know it is time for me to stop work and relieve her. One of them used to come up and announce the time if I was five minutes late going down. Another just let the old man begin climbing the stairs, though it was so hard for him.

·

He told me, after several days had gone by, that he had left at daybreak after the first night because he did not know if I would want to wake up with him. Later that morning he went to see Ellie in the library. He wanted her advice. He wanted to know if she thought he should wait for me to come out of my class, if he should stand by the path to my classroom building and meet me. Ellie said of course he should. He wanted to know if it would make me uncomfortable. She said of course it would not. So it was with Ellie's encouragement that he waited for me later, carefully posed, holding or smoking his pipe. Ellie told me all this months after.

The second time he came, he stayed on into the morning and spent the day with me. We went walking on the beach. As he climbed down to the sand over the rocks I could not look at him, though I was not sure why. We walked a long way past the rocks and over the drifts of broken seashells without talking. I was uncomfortable. I thought he was silent out of timidity. I made efforts to talk to him, but it was hard. The silence between us was so thick that words were not so much spoken as forced through it. I stopped trying.

·

I did not know what his last name was, and I was not sure of his first name. If it was what I thought it was, it was unusual and I had never known anyone with such a name.

The End of the Story

I was embarrassed to ask him. I hoped I would see it or hear it somewhere.

I wonder, now, why I did not call someone up and ask. There were at least two people I could have called. But I did not know them very well, as I would later. It is easier for me to see why I did not ask him directly. The moment had passed long before when I could have done that without feeling foolish.

I did not find out what his name was for several days, because during these days I was almost always alone with him. And because I did not have a name for him, he continued to seem like a stranger, even though he was very quickly becoming so close to me. When I did learn his name, I was learning the name of someone like a husband, a brother, or a child to me. But because I learned it only after I knew him so well, his name also seemed strangely arbitrary, as though it did not have to be that one but could have been any other.

Two days after I met him, I came home late and went to bed and lay there in the dark, nervous, thinking about him, wishing he were with me, then sleeping lightly for only a moment or two before waking again to think about him. Suddenly, after two in the morning, a car roared up the hill past my window, headlights swam over the room, the engine died, and the headlights went off. I looked out the window by my bed and saw the white hood of a car parked beyond the big cedar in front of the house. I heard a voice speaking, and I could distinguish some of what it said: "I want you . . . I can't . . . this carousel . . . this old carousel . . . into the city . . ." I was sure he was the one talking to himself out there, because the car was white, it roared, and it had stopped outside my house. I thought that if he did this, it might mean he was a little crazy. But I did not yet know him very well. I did not know if he was crazy. I only knew he became distracted from time to time, and forgot what he was doing and where he was. At this point, I was willing to accept whatever I might learn next, though it frightened me a little.

I put on some clothes. I walked out by the side of the house and under the cedar tree along the driveway to the edge of the street. But now I saw that the car was smaller than his. It was not his car after all. Now I was frightened for a different reason—this was a stranger out of control, even more unpredictable. I turned back toward the house, the headlights came on again and caught me, and the voice said, "Are you all right?" I stopped walking and asked, "Who are you?" and the voice said something like "I'm just trying to sort myself out."

I went back in. I went down the hall to the bathroom. I sat down on the toilet and saw that my hands and legs were shaking.

Later that night I dreamed I had found a short piece of his writing on the hall floor. It had a title page and my name on it and my address at the university. Most of it was plainly written, but it contained a passage about Paris in which the writing became suddenly more lyrical, including a phrase about the "shudder of war." Then the style became plain again. The last sentence was briefer than the rest: "We are always surprising our bookkeepers." In the dream, I liked the piece and was relieved by that, although I did not like the last sentence. Once I was awake, I liked the last sentence, too, even more than the rest.

I see now that since I hadn't yet read anything by him at

the time of the dream, what I was doing was composing something by him that I would like. And although this was my dream and he did not write what I dreamed he wrote, the words I remember still seem to belong to him, not to me.

•

Three days after we met, a friend called him by his first name in my presence and then I knew I had been right. Another two days went by, and I learned his last name when I went into the special section of the library containing little magazines and saw his full name printed with his poems.

I had wondered what I would do if I did not like his poems. But I had not even thought about seeing his last name on the page and was not prepared for the shock I felt. The shock did not come from the name itself, dense with consonants and difficult to pronounce, and one I had never seen before and would never see again, so that it seemed to belong only to him. The shock came from something else I couldn't at first identify.

Knowing his name, after I had waited so many days to learn it, seemed to increase his reality. It gave him a place in the world that he had not had before, and it allowed him to belong more to the day than he had before. Until then, he had belonged to a time when I was tired and did not think as well as I did in the daytime, and did not see as well, when there was darkness on all sides of whatever light there was, and he came and went through darkness and shadow more than light.

Then, too, as long as he had only a first name, he might belong to a story told me by someone else, or he might be no more than a friend of someone else, he might be a person I did not know very well. In fact, I did not know him very well, at the same time that I had already become so close to him that not an inch separated us.

But even after I knew his name, even when I had known him for weeks, I never quite lost the feeling that he was someone I had never seen in the daylight, who came suddenly into my room with me in the middle of the night and had a name I was not sure of.

I had another shock after I was done reading his poems and went to find Ellie in the back of the Rare Books section, when she told me that his mother was only five years older than I was.

·

For a long time, I did not know what to call him in the novel, or what to call myself either. What I really wanted was a one-syllable English name for him, to match his own actual name, but as I searched for an equivalent, I found my mind playing the same trick it played on me when I came up against a difficult problem in translating—the only solution that really seemed to fit was the original word itself. Finally I decided to take the names for the two characters from the names of the man and woman in a story he had written. So at that point I called them Hank and Anna. Then I gave Ellie the beginning of the novel to read. I said there was no hurry, she did not have to read it right away, but I did not expect her to take as long as she did. At first I did not mind that she hadn't read it, because I did not want to think about it myself. I wanted to rest from the novel. But finally I became impatient to hear what she had to say.

The reason she did not want to read it right away was that the story was too much like an experience she was having at the time. She had become very attached to a man younger than she was. He had not left her, but she was afraid he would. By the time he did leave her, soon after, she had still not read what I had given her, and now it was even harder, though she told me she was trying to prepare herself to do it. She was so angry she wanted to move to a foreign country.

In the meantime, I thought of showing it to someone else, but no one seemed quite right. Several friends had offered to look at it, but some of them, I knew, would not be objective, and others would probably not be helpful for other reasons. I could think of two who would be helpful, but I wanted to wait until I had more to show them.

Vincent asked me why I didn't show it to him. He seemed eager to read it, maybe in order to find out more about me, and about certain episodes in my life I have been hiding from him, he thinks, such as what he calls my "fling" in Europe. I would not call it a "fling" to be lying in a hotel bed for four nights next to a thin, nervous man, trying not to wake him up, and then, when I couldn't sleep, sitting on the tiles of the bathroom floor trying to read but too drunk to make sense of what I was looking at. This man had terrible trouble sleeping when he was away from home. He was often away on trips, and when he returned to his wife in the Jura Mountains he slept for several weeks. This was what he told me. His face white and tense with fatigue, he would creep through the darkened hotel room saying he had to sleep. He would crawl under the covers, curl up at my back, start talking into my neck, and continue for an hour or more. Then he would doze off. If I couldn't sleep, I would go into the bathroom, turn on the light, and sit on the floor, or I would leave the hotel.

The first night, I got out of the hotel all right and back into my own hotel. The second time I tried to leave, it was dawn and the front door was locked. I didn't want to wake the tired man, since he was sleeping at last, so I rang for the night clerk, who came out in his bathrobe, his face very cross, and unlocked the door only after a lot of arguing. I went out through the steamy entryway past a tiled basin of goldfish and into a street where a group of workmen in the early morning sun were repainting a yellow line on the road and looked up at me curiously, since I was still dressed in my black evening clothes. The front door of my own hotel was locked, too, so I walked around the village for a while, watching as people set up stalls in the marketplace.

Later that day, when I went to the beach to swim, I did not feel very well. All I could do was stand waist-deep in the water for a long time looking out at the horizon and then back at the other bathers, who lay flat on their straw mats or sat in the strong wind shading their eyes from the stinging sand. I soon began to feel faint from the heat and the glare, made my way out of the water and up the sand toward the beach café, and spent the rest of the afternoon sitting there in my robe under the concerned gaze of the owner and the waitress, holding ice against my forehead and eating a little salt off my fingertip. When the sun was low in the sky, a tall Englishwoman helped me across the sand to a taxi and then settled me in my hotel room with some aspirin and a glass of water.

I don't want to show this to Vincent just yet, because he seems so skeptical already. He knows more or less what the book is about, though I haven't told him directly, and he tends to regard all the love affairs in my life as having been sordid. I admit there were other men before him.

The End of the Story

There was a painter who lived alone in an old boat shop, and an anthropologist who used to take me to the opera with his mother. There was another directly after that one, who smiled a great deal, and another directly before him, who drank a great deal, and the one who took me into the desert, and another before that, who became very jealous over things he only imagined. But none of these affairs lasted very long, a few were not even consummated, and all were with entirely respectable sorts of men, most of them college professors.

Ellie finally read the pages I had sent her. By then she was about to move to a foreign country after all, though only for one year and not because of her young lover, and my manuscript was part of the business she had to take care of before she left. She seemed to like it, but she said the names were wrong. She did not want the hero to be named Hank. She thought no one could fall in love with someone named Hank. She said it made her think of "handkerchief." Of course it isn't true that no one can fall in love with someone named Hank. But she meant I could choose any name I liked for my hero, while men named Hank, and the men and women who fall in love with them, are not free to choose.

After Ellie objected so much to Hank, I called the woman Laura and the man Garet for a while. But I did not really like the name Laura for this woman, since a woman named Laura feels to me like a peaceful woman, or at least a graceful one. Susan might have been better, but a woman named Susan would be too sensible to walk from one end of a town to the other and back again for an hour at a time, at night, looking for a man and his old white car even if he is with another woman, just because she is determined to have at least a glimpse of him. She would not drive to his house in the rain and walk up onto a balcony and look in the window of his apartment.

So then I called her Hannah, and then Mag, and then Anna again. I described my room, and how this woman, Anna, sat at the card table trying to work despite everything. In other versions it was Laura at my card table, or Hannah playing the piano, or Ann in my bed. For a long time I called him Stefan. I was even calling the novel *Stefan* at that point. Then Vincent said he did not like the name because it was too European. I agreed that it was European, though I thought it suited him. But I wasn't entirely satisfied with it anyway, so I tried to think of another name.

A friend of mine who has written several novels told me a few months ago that in one novel she went ahead so fast, looking back only a page or two each day, that she later discovered, when she reread the novel, that the name of one character changed twelve times in the course of the book.

•

What I saw, when I saw him standing by the path waiting for me, was not only his face, not only his hands, and not only the position of his body, but also his red plaid flannel shirt, frayed at the collar, his thready white sweatshirt, his khaki army pants, and his hiking boots. He had a pipe in his hand and a bag over his arm.

Each time I met him, in the beginning, I paid such close attention to what I saw when he appeared, and what was different about him from what I had last seen, that I remember his clothes with surprising clarity.

If I put my arms around him, what I felt under my

fingers, against my skin, was the material of his clothes, and only when I pressed harder did I feel the muscles and bones of his body. If I touched him on the arm I was actually touching the cotton sleeve of his shirt, and if I touched him on the leg, I was touching the worn denim of his pants, and if I put my hand on his lower back, I felt not only the two ridges of muscle, hard as bone, but also the soft wool of his sweater warming to the warmth of my hand, and if he was hugging me against his chest, what I would see, within an inch of my eye, was the weave of cotton threads of his shirt or woolen threads of his sweater or the fuzzy nap of his lumber jacket.

Just as he looked a little different to me each time I saw him, I also learned new things about him each time. Each thing I learned about him came as a small shock, and either pleased me or disturbed me, and disturbed me either a little or a good deal. When we sat in the bar later that day, the first day, he surprised me by saying angry things about some of my students and then about Mitchell. His tone was a tone of jealousy, though he had no reason to be jealous. And when he said these angry things, he abruptly seemed a stranger to me again, one I didn't like. Only when I knew him better did I understand that the anger I heard came from his disappointment, and he was often disappointed. Nearly everyone disappointed him and therefore angered him—nearly every man, anyway: he expected a great deal from men, and he wanted to admire them.

He was angry with certain men and he was indignant at certain great writers, and the two feelings came from the same sort of disappointment, I thought. He was always reading the great writers, as though determined to know all the best that had ever been written. He would read most of what one great writer had written, then he would become indignant. There was something wrong there, he would say. He respected the writer, but there was something wrong. He would read most of what another had written and again become indignant. There was something wrong there, too. It was as though these writers had failed him. To be great might mean to be perfect, in his eyes. When he pointed out how they failed, I couldn't disagree—his reasons were not bad. But in his determined reading he left behind one failed writer after another. Maybe he had to see how they failed if he was to find a place in that world for himself.

One of the things I learned, because I asked him directly, was that there had been not just a few but many women before me, and that I was not even the oldest. At the time, this startled me and seemed to diminish what there was between us. Then, as time passed, I became used to the idea and accepted it.

Later I could say to myself that at least I was the last woman, since he married after he left me. But maybe he hadn't even been telling me the whole truth. It was the slight pause before he answered me, and his look of embarrassment, that made me believe him. Maybe he was embarrassed by the crudeness of my question, and a false answer was the only answer to such a question.

•

The first time I told him I loved him he only looked at me thoughtfully without answering, as though considering what I had said. At the time, I did not understand his hesitation. The words were drawn out of me, almost despite me, and he did not answer. Now I think that if he could be so careful about saying the same thing to me, he probably loved me more deeply than I loved him. I had probably said what I said much too soon to mean it, and he knew that, though he couldn't help saying the same to me a few days later, since he probably really did love me, or thought he did.

I say at one point that I fell in love with him quite suddenly, and that it happened when we were staring at each other by candlelight. But this seems too easy, and I also can't remember just what candlelight I was talking about. There was no candlelight in the café the first evening, and there was no candlelight in my house later that night either, so I evidently don't mean that I fell in love with him the first night. And yet I do remember that even as soon as the next morning, when I saw him again, I felt a sudden, strong emotion. If I wasn't in love with him, I don't know what I was feeling. If I had already fallen in love with him by then, it must have happened sometime between the moment he left me in the early morning and the moment I saw him again, unless it happened the very instant I saw him again.

Did it have to happen when he wasn't present and when I wasn't aware of it? Maybe it didn't happen suddenly, after all, but gradually, so that what I felt when I saw him again was only a first degree of it, and there were further degrees—later that day, the next day, the next, and then two days after that, until it reached an extreme of intensity, not destined to go any further, and then wavered and fluctuated before declining gradually, so that the thing was always in motion? A candle may in fact have been burning in the room the first time I said I loved him, but that wasn't the moment I fell in love with him, I know, so I'm still not sure what candlelight I meant.

If the light was on, I saw every detail of him down to the grain of his skin, and if the room was dark, I saw the outline of him against the dim sky outside, but at the same time knew his face so well that I could see that, too, and even what his expression was, though without the light not all the detail of him was there.

I thought that in certain cases a person fell in love slowly and gradually, and in others very suddenly, but my experience was so limited I couldn't be sure. It seemed to me I had fallen in love only once before.

There were times when I felt I loved him, but other times when I did not, and because he was wary and intelligent he must have noticed exactly when I seemed to love him and when I did not, and maybe he did not quite believe me because of that. Maybe that was why he hesitated and let so many days go by, after I said I loved him, before he answered me.

I think that a certain hunger for him came first and was followed by a feeling of tenderness, gradually increasing, for a person who aroused such hunger and then satisfied it. Maybe that was what I felt for him that I thought was love.

The first feeling I had for him, though, even before that, was no more than a calm appreciation of him as I first saw him—an agreeable, intelligent, robust sort of person who found me attractive, too, so that in a simple way, that same night, like two hungry and thirsty people, we could decide we wanted to find a place to be alone together and remain together long enough to satisfy our appetite.

This appreciation, and this mild hunger that was not for him in particular but for any man who had some of the qualities I liked in him, did not grow stronger right away, and did not immediately become a particular hunger, a hunger that could be satisfied only by him. Another feeling came before, almost right away, within hours, certainly by the next day, the next time I saw him, and that was a kind of fascination, or a kind of distraction. He entered my mind as a distraction from what had been in my mind before. He took over a large part of my mind so that he was an obstruction to me: I had to think around him to think of anything else, and if I succeeded in thinking of something else, it was not long before the thought of him would push aside the other thought again, as though it had gained strength from being ignored a short time.

He was a distraction to me when I was not with him, and when I was with him, I was fascinated to look at him and listen to him. The sight of him, and the sound of him speaking, kept me still, or kept me near him. It was enough to be near him and watch and listen to him, half paralyzed, whereas just a day or two before I had not even known him.

It was the distraction that seemed to demand that I stop whatever I was doing and return to him, where I could see him, and then it was the fascination that made me need to be close to him, and then it was this need to be close to him that turned into a hunger that grew stronger and stronger in me and in him, too.

·

His room was in a town about a mile away from mine, past the racecourse and the fairgrounds and a long stretch of dirt used for parking during the races and fairs. When I drove there I followed a road that curved around the race-track parking lot, and on one side there was the dark expanse, at night, of that empty lot and on the other another empty stretch, of rutted dirt, going back to a channel of water and farther back to the hills that had no houses on the side overlooking the racetrack but were thick with houses, including mine, on the other, the side above the ocean. I then crossed a narrow bridge over the channel of water that flowed out of the hills, where it was a rocky stream surrounded by scrubby, weedy trees and filled in late May with soft-shelled crawdads, its muddy banks littered with watermelon rinds and beer bottles, down to the ocean, where it was wide and shallow and at ebb tide drawn out by strong currents, its banks of sand eaten away and falling piece by piece into the moving water. I then climbed the inland side of another hill.

The first time I went there, I found my own way, following his directions. Behind a row of garages he had a single, narrow room with no bed, not even a mattress on the floor, only a sleeping bag on the carpet, and no other furniture, only books and clothes standing or falling in piles along the walls, a typewriter, too, unless he kept the typewriter in his garage, and a set of Indian drums. There was a small kitchen adjoining the room, and in the kitchen there was only a hotplate on a table, next to a small refrigerator. The bathroom was off the kitchen. I stayed for a little while, drinking a cup of tea with him or a glass of water, sitting on the carpet. He apologized for the size of the room, probably because I looked so uncomfortable.

After we drank our tea or water, he showed me his garage. He was proud of it. The concrete room was filled with freestanding bookcases containing a large number of books. I was impressed by the number of books he owned. He did not tell me that most of them belonged to a friend. The friend became very angry at him later about something to do with the books, maybe that the books were confiscated by the landlord when he was forced out. There was a desk facing the garage door, with a lamp and a typewriter on it, and he worked here. He often worked for long hours alone at his writing, though it was hard for me to find out from him what he was writing. Either he wouldn't tell me when I asked or I didn't want to ask.

I said to myself that the reason I did not often go to his room was that it was so small and dark, but after he moved up the coast one or two towns to a light, airy apartment overlooking a cactus nursery, I did not want to go there either, very often, once, that I remember, when I helped him arrange books in a low bookcase, and another time when he made a very large pot of rather thin cabbage soup for us to eat for supper, but only a few times after that, so I had to admit that I simply preferred to see him in my own house. When he left the apartment overlooking the cactus nursery, I was no longer talking to him very much or very openly, and I knew he had moved but did not know where he had gone. After that, I moved, and I don't think he knew where I was living either.

He played the Indian drums, or at least he told me he did and I believed him. He told me he had lived in India when he was a child. He had returned to America on a boat with his mother and sister. He offered to play for me, but a long time went by before I would let him. At the thought of listening to him play this instrument, so strange to me, I felt the same embarrassment I felt some time later when another friend played his guitar and sang freedom songs. I asked him once to drum on my back, and he did, thumping me with his fingers and the heels of his palms. When at last he did play the drums for me, it was toward the end, when

I was uncomfortable with him and felt very little for him, and he was hurt by me, and we were doing things that we had not done before, as though to see if we would feel anything more for each other, but I felt only the same embarrassment I had expected to feel.

When I first started working on the novel, I thought I had to keep very close to the facts about certain things, including his life, as though the point of writing the book would be lost if something like the Indian drums were changed and he were to play another instrument instead. Because I had wanted to write these things for so long, I thought I had to tell the truth about them. But the surprising thing was that after I had written them the way they were, I found I could change them or take them out, as though by writing them once I had satisfied whatever it was I had to satisfy.

At times the truth seems to be enough, as long as I compress it and rearrange it a little. At other times it does not seem to be enough, but I'm not willing to invent very much. Most things are kept as they were. Maybe I can't think what to put in place of the truth. Maybe I just have a poor imagination.

One reason I kept going back to work on the novel was that I thought I would be able to write it almost without thinking about it, since I knew the story already. But the longer I tried to write it, the less I understood how to work on it. I could not decide which parts were important. I knew which ones interested me, but I thought I had to include everything, even the dull parts. So I tried to write my way through the dull parts and then enjoy the interesting parts when I came to them. But in each case I passed the interesting parts without noticing, so I had to think maybe they were not so interesting after all. I became discouraged.

Several times I was tempted to give up on it. There were other things I wanted to do instead, another novel I wanted to write and a few stories I wanted to finish. I would have been glad to let someone else write this one for me if I could have—as long as it was written, I thought I did not care who wrote it. A friend of mine said that if I didn't manage to write the novel I could at least save parts of it and make stories out of them, but I did not want to do that. In fact, I did not want to give it up, because I had spent so much time on it already by then. I'm not sure that is a good reason to go on with something, though in certain cases it must be. I once stayed with a man too long for the same reason, that there had already been so much between us. But maybe I had other, better reasons to keep on with this, even if I'm not sure what they were.

So I haven't been able to write it almost without thinking about it, after all. I tried chronological order and that didn't work, so I tried a random order. Then the problem was how to arrange a random order so that it made sense. I thought I could have one thing lead to another thing, each part grow out of the part that came before, and also include some relief from that. I tried the past tense, and then I put it in the present tense, even though I was tired of the present tense by then. After that, I left parts of it in the present tense and put the rest back in the past tense.

I kept stopping to translate. I told Vincent I was writing less than a page a week, and he laughed because he thought I was joking. But although it took me so long to write a page, I kept thinking the work would go more quickly. I always had a different reason for thinking it would go more quickly.

At times the novel seems to be a test of myself, both as I was then and as I am now. In the beginning, the woman was not like me, because if she had been, I could not have seen the story clearly. After a while, when I was more used to telling the story, I was able to make the woman more like me. I sometimes think that if there was enough goodness in me then, or enough depth or complexity, this will work, if I can make it work. But if I was simply too shallow or mean-spirited, it will not work, no matter what I do.

•

I was not the same with him as I was with other people. I tried not to be as determined, as busy, as hasty, as I was alone and with friends. I tried to be gentle and quiet, but it was hard, and it confused me. It also exhausted me. I had to leave him just to rest from it.

I had to leave him anyway, to work. I gave my students a great deal of work and that meant I had a great deal of work to do myself, reading their papers. I worked in my office and at home in the evenings, too.

My office, between two classics professors on the seventh floor of a new building, was roomy and full of bare shelves, with a row of tall, narrow windows looking out over tennis courts, groves of eucalyptus trees, and the ocean in the distance. The windows were sealed shut and soundproof. But through the walls, whenever I stopped work to listen, I would hear voices: the laughter of a student and teacher together, then the rhythmic chant of the teacher explaining, and then the drone of Latin conjugations—always, it seemed, the verb *laudare*, "to praise."

I would stop working, look out the window, and put my

hands and then my arms up to my nose and smell my skin. My own smell, of perfume and sweat, reminded me of him.

Another smell that made me think of him was the raw wool of the Mexican blanket on my bed. He would often leave early to let me sleep, but I would not be able to sleep. A few hours later he would come and find me in my office. When I was the first one up, and he got out of bed after I did, he would make the bed carefully and neatly. The first time he did this was the first morning he woke up there. Every time he did it, it seemed to me an act of tenderness, because he was arranging something of mine with such care, and taking part in the arrangements of my house.

I was waiting for him in a crowded room. He had not come to meet me and I decided he was not going to come. I thought he had left me already, before we had been together even a week. My disappointment was so acute that the room seemed to empty of whatever life it had had, and the air became thin. The people, chairs, sofas, windows, curtains, lectern, microphone, table, tape recorder, and sunlight were empty shells of what they had been before. When he actually left me, months after that, the world was not empty but worse than empty, as though the quality of emptiness had become so concentrated it turned into a kind of poison, as though each thing appeared alive and healthy but had been injected with a poisonous preserving agent.

This time he had not left me, he had only come late. He was there in the crowd by the door when I stood up to go. The life came back into everything in the room. He explained to me that he had lost track of the time. He occasionally lost track of the time and what he was doing, he did not always know what he was doing or how to plan what he had to do, and it was hard for him, at times, to do what he had to do.

We left the place together to go to a friend's house and we quarreled on the way.

There must have been at least seven readings that I went to while I knew him, or even more. It is hard to describe a reading in a way that is exciting, and it would be harder still to describe more than one in the same novel, even if some of the poetry I heard made me angry, which it did. I could change them to something else, like lectures, or dances, but I don't think I would have gone to more than one dance. The last reading was a reading of sound poetry, the most difficult one for me. Because I was forced to sit still while my mind had nothing much to hold on to, it wandered away from me and went through the plate-glass window searching yet again for him.

We were quarreling over his friend Kitty. We were sitting together in his car in a narrow, sunlit street. On either side of us were small patches of clipped green lawn that came right down to the white sidewalks. The houses set in these patches of lawn were small and white, of one story, with red-tiled roofs. A short palm tree grew beside one house, a shrub with rubbery leaves by another, a red-flowered vine by a third. Each house on this street seemed to have a lawn and just one other thing growing on the lawn, as if that were a rule. The sun shone down at an angle and reflected off the white sidewalk and the white walls of the houses, and because the houses were so low and small, with so few trees about, a great expanse of blue sky was visible. We were waiting to get out of the car and go into a friend's house. Either we were the first to arrive or we were simply trying to finish our quarrel.

He was going to give a reading himself in a few days. He was going to read a few of his poems and also a story. He told me he wanted to invite this woman Kitty to his reading because she had helped him to plan it.

The last time he had talked about her had been in my office. He had come up behind me in the hallway outside my office, and put his arms around me and kissed me there, publicly, which had made me nervous. Though the hallway ahead of me seemed to be empty, I thought someone appeared suddenly behind me and vanished again.

Sitting inside my office, first he complained about her, then he worried about her. I did not like hearing even this woman's name, because as soon as he mentioned it he seemed to move away from me, to go out of the room and leave me sitting there opposite his face, which was abstracted and preoccupied, with a slight frown of annoyance on it, and opposite his body, which had become very still. I felt I had been forgotten, or at least what I was to him now had been forgotten, as though he had suddenly mistaken me for an old friend to whom he could confide his worries or complaints about Kitty.

Kitty appeared in his room a few weeks later, and the reason he gave me for her visit did not make sense to me when I tried to understand it.

His reading was on a Sunday afternoon, in an elegant old house on a hill in a run-down part of the city. The house had heavy banisters and stained-glass windows in the stairwells, thick curtains drawn back from the doorways with velvet cords, alcoves and bay windows, high ceilings and chandeliers. He read with another poet, a man my age, but I can't remember who it was, and I also confuse this reading with another one in the same house months later, after he had left me, in which a woman read a story about Robinson Crusoe. I stood at the back of the room, where I could look away from the rows of people through an arched doorway into the next room, which was empty. I watched what I could see of him where he stood, the length of the room away from me, at a lectern. I could see only his head and shoulders above the heads of the audience. I was prepared to be embarrassed, for his sake, if he did not read well or if he read something that was not very good. But he read clearly and confidently, and nothing he read sounded bad, though I did not particularly like the story he read. Kitty did not come.

．

I could say more about the house where he read, but I'm not sure how much description to have in the novel. Another thing I could describe would be the landscape, the reddish, sandy earth spilling onto the edges of the sidewalks everywhere, the lines of cliffs above the ocean and the eroded sandy ravines descending to the water, the ocean so close I could hear the waves late at night, like a curtain coming down again and again, if the tide was high. It was not a lush landscape, because the climate was so dry. Part of each year, the hills were brown, and the only thick green vegetation grew up in the clefts of the hills where the dampness would gather, or in the towns where plants were watered and the succulent ground cover thrived and fat shrubs with glistening leaves hugged the shops.

Because I had not known the landscape before, it interested me. It was so difficult, with broad highways cutting through everything and always some new construction rising abruptly off a brown hill, houses stacked or piled on top of each other in the wide-open spaces as though anticipating future congestion, or in a small canyon a line of new houses along a new road, and at the end of the line the latest house under construction, a framework of raw wood, while the first houses were already occupied, with cars in the driveways. Only rarely did a vestige of something older remain like a vision, an old ranch house at a distance from the road, a weedy, dusty track leading to it and a grove of gnarled live-oak trees and eucalyptus around it.

Eucalyptus trees with their smoky, oily smell grew everywhere, very tall, the boles going far up before sending out a branch. They were untidy trees, with wood soft and weak. They kept losing branches, so that there were great gaps along the trunks. They kept dropping their narrow, tan, spear-shaped leaves, which littered the ground under them, and layers of bark fell from them in long strips, along with little wooden buttons, brown with crosses carved out of them on one side, powdery blue on the other. An old professor at the university often complained that as he lay in bed at night he was kept awake by the hooting of a nearby owl and by those wooden buttons which dropped onto the roof over his head and rolled down to the eave, one by one, dropping and rolling, dropping and rolling all night long.

•

After his reading, in the late afternoon, he and I went with a group of others to a friend's house on another hill nearby, directly under a flight path to the airport out in the bay. We spent most of the time in the back yard, and enormous airplanes flew low overhead frequently. Each time, we would stop talking and wait until they passed. The yard was weedy and a pretty lime tree grew near the house. Two little boys threw balls into the air over and over again, and the balls kept getting caught in the tree or landing on the roof of a shed at the back of the yard.

He had not read the story I knew already, the one he had described to me as a novel the first evening we met, a very clear, precise, and confident story about a man and a woman in their middle age who meet at the seaside where the woman is on vacation and the man works for a hotel, the setting vaguely European. It contained quiet, well-turned descriptions, including one about the effect of the sun on the woman's pale legs, that I liked each time I read them. I liked so many parts of the story that the rest of it also seemed good. Now I wonder if I was drawn to him because he had the sort of mind that would want to write that sort of story, the sort that I liked already, or if he was drawn to me because I had the sort of mind that would like the sort of story he liked to write. A friend of mine, after reading the story, said he did not like it, because the characters, so very silent and distant with each other, yet so firmly tied by their wordless understanding, were not people he would want to know. I did not think about that, but only about how the story was written.

Later he read me seven short poems that he had written for me. He told me he had made a rule for himself that each one had to contain a reference to a flower. He would not let me keep them because they were not finished. In the end, he never gave me a copy of the poems. Maybe he never finished them. So I don't have them here, where I could reread them and see what I think of them now, as I have the story. It is here in my room, in a folder by itself, though I have not looked at it often, in all these years, for fear of knowing it so well that I can't see it anymore for what it is. But every time I have read it, the phrases ring peacefully in my ears, the order and clarity still please me.

I remember a few lines from his poems, including one in which he said the coast had a mile in it. That was the mile between my house and his. I liked the poems, though they were more careful than the story, or rather the care he put into them was so evident they seemed cautious, whereas the care in the story seemed just right. I had heard those poems, and I heard others at his reading, and I had read still others in the library, or maybe the same ones he had read, and I knew one story well, and heard another at his reading, and later he would read to me from his notebook, and this was all I knew of his writing. He was always writing, and he told me from time to time that he was working on a story, or a play, or another play, and later a novel, but I never saw any of them because he never seemed to finish one thing before abandoning it or putting it aside temporarily, as he said, and starting another, and he wouldn't show me any work unless it was almost finished.

He wrote things in a notebook, and I wrote things in a notebook. Some of what we wrote was about each other, of course, and now and then we read aloud from our notebooks. The things we had written were often things we would not say to each other, though we would read them aloud. But we were not willing to say anything about them after we had read them either.

So that behind my silence, and behind his silence, there

was a good deal of talk, but that talk was in the pages of our notebooks, and was therefore silent, unless we chose to open the notebooks and read from them.

If he had been a bad writer, I think I could not have gone on with him. Or my lack of respect for the thing he did that was most important to him would have destroyed us before very long. But the fact that he wrote well did not help me to love him more deeply than I did. If I loved him at all, that had nothing to do with his writing, and when I talked to him about writing I felt I was not his lover and we were as distant as two people who did not know each other very well but respected and liked each other.

The distance between us at these times was not unlike the distance between us when we were with friends. We never gave any sign, in front of other people, of what was between us. It was evident to someone else only when we arrived together or left together, two moments I always savored, partly because they were in such contrast to all the other moments, when our closeness was unacknowledged. I wasn't ashamed of him, or embarrassed, but I often wanted to move away from him, so that although I knew he was near me, I did not touch him. In fact, I wanted to have him near me and at the same time move away from him.

Maybe we never stopped being conscious of our oddness, that some people might disapprove of us because he was so much younger, or because I was a teacher and he was a student, though he was not my student and many other teachers were his friends, and though he was older than most of the other students. But maybe we also sensed that if we had even simply held hands in front of our friends, they would have paid close attention to this, and it would have satisfied their lively curiosity about just how we behaved together, just what our relationship was—did I act as a mother toward him? Was he protective of me, like a son or a father? Or were we the same age in our behavior? Were we tense or relaxed? Were we violent together or gentle? Were we mean or kind?

I knew their curiosity was lively because in that place, as long as I lived there, and even after I left, all of us had a great deal of interest in the lives of our friends and our acquaintances and even people we had never met. There was a great hunger for stories, especially stories involving emotion and drama, especially love and betrayal, though this curiosity and interest was not unkind, usually.

Another reading was given by someone I identified in my notebook as "S.B." After that reading, where he sat behind me, we went out with a group of people to a Mexican restaurant. There were many meals in restaurants at that time, especially in Mexican restaurants, because groups of friends and groups hosting visitors to the university often went out to eat together. Later in the novel I mention a dinner in a Japanese restaurant during which I left the table and tried to call him from a phone booth by the restrooms. But I do not describe the meal or the friends, even though there were some interesting people present. In fact, throughout these months I was also seeing and meeting interesting people, so that everything surrounding the story, everything I am leaving out of it, would make another story, or even several others, quite different in character from this one.

Later, we stood alone in a friend's living room and he

was offended because I would not kiss him. He may have thought I was ashamed of him, but I simply did not want him to kiss me just then.

I can't remember who "S.B." is or what sort of reading it was. I also can't remember, though I try over and over again, what happened in the week before it, when he and I were just getting to know each other. There are only two entries in my notebook for that week, and only one has anything to do with him. In that entry I describe what seems to me an incident without any importance at all: I was having lunch at a café on campus with a person I identify as "L.H." We were sitting outdoors on the terrace. A skunk appeared in the concrete planter of a tree near us and caused some excitement among the students and faculty eating lunch. I happened to glance over at the doorway that led into the café, and I saw him standing there with a tray in his hands, looking displeased. I thought he was disappointed that so many people were sitting there in the sun, and all the seats were taken, but he could have been frowning because his eyes were not good, or because the sunlight was so bright, since he frowned often, especially in the sunlight. I don't know if he saw us and came over, if he sat with us, or if he simply turned around and left. If I hadn't written anything in my notebook about that week, and if I hadn't remembered the reading, I don't think I would be so acutely aware of those days about which I can't remember anything.

I am working from my memories and my notebook. There is a great deal I would have forgotten if I had not written it in my notebook, but my notebook also leaves out a great deal, only some of which I remember. There are also memories that have nothing to do with this story, and there are good friends who do not appear in it, or appear only indistinctly, because at the time they had nothing or little to do with him.

.

When I think of him frowning in the sunlight as he looked out at the café terrace, I wonder if I have been wrong, all this time, about another occasion on which he was frowning. The only photograph I have of him shows him frowning at me from a distance of about fifteen feet. He is on a sailboat belonging to a cousin of mine, he is bending over, his hands are busy, perhaps fastening a rope, and he is looking up sideways at me, frowning. The picture is not very sharp, probably taken with a poor camera. I have assumed all this time that he was frowning in annoyance at me for taking his picture at such a time, when he was trying to do something difficult on the boat of a man who made him uncomfortable because he barked orders at him to do things like fasten certain ropes and also because he clearly did not approve of this relationship. But now I realize he might have been frowning merely because he was looking up suddenly into the bright sunlight.

A year after this picture was taken I went sailing with the same cousin, on the same boat. Back home, I happened to take the picture out and look at it again. This time I had trouble reconciling what I saw with what I knew. He was there on the boat, in the picture, and I was looking at him, but he was not on that boat any longer: I had just been there the day before, and I knew he was not there. Within an hour after the picture was taken, in fact, he was no longer on the boat, because we were at the dock when I took it, preparing to go ashore. But as long as he and I were still together he was somehow still on the boat, he was not distinctly absent from it, as he was a year later.

●

I have been thinking about that photograph, because I mentioned it to Ellie recently on the phone. Except for her one year in England, Ellie has lived near me for a long time. But now she is about to move again, this time to the Southwest. She told me she had gone down to the basement of her apartment building the day before to look through her things. First she discovered that she couldn't open the padlock on her storage bin. Another tenant, believing the storage bin was his, had instructed his secretary to break off the lock Ellie had put on it many years before and replace it with a new one. The lock had belonged to Ellie's father. It had been the only thing of his she had left. Everything to do with this move was disturbing to her anyway. Now she was further disturbed because her father's lock had been destroyed and removed by a stranger, and she was shut out of her bin. Then, when she was able to get into it, she found that a flood had ruined some of her books and papers.

But she was calling to tell me she had discovered several photographs of him in one of her boxes, and she thought I might like to have them. She said there were two, but then, as she went on talking to me and at the same time looked through the pile of pictures in her hand, pictures of a party she couldn't remember, and more of people we both knew and people only she knew, she discovered another of him, although in this picture he was partly obscured by a cluster of people. She asked me if I wanted copies of them. I told her I did, though I also said that when the envelope arrived I might not open it right away.

The End of the Story

By now I am used to the version of his face that I have created from my own memory and the one snapshot I have. If I saw a clear picture of him or, even worse, several pictures from different angles and in different lights, I would have to get used to a new face. I don't want to be unsettled just now, and I know I will be tempted not to open the envelope at all. But I will also be curious.

·

The nurse, downstairs, is playing the piano to entertain Vincent's father. She is making mistakes just where I know she will. I listen for the mistakes and can't hear the words I am trying to write. The old man loves it when she plays, though.

These days, in the warm weather, spiders spin webs between the bottoms of the lampshades and the sides of the lamps. Many strange small black insects fly constantly about the lamp. We have screens on all the windows and doors, but the cat has torn holes in the bottom corners of some. Spiders also spin single strands of web across the paths in the yard at night, even in the time it takes me to walk out to the corner grocery store and back, so that when I come in from the street the soft threads collect on my bare legs.

Before the meadow was plowed over in preparation for building the townhouses, I began learning to identify the wildflowers that grew there, then the wild grasses. I had never thought of identifying kinds of grass before. Now I realize that I should be able to identify spiders, too, by their appearance, the forms of their webs, their habits, and where they choose to live, so that I can name them instead of calling them "big spider," "little spider," "little tan spider," etc.

At times I have the feeling someone else is working on this with me. I read a passage I haven't looked at in weeks and I don't recognize much of it, or only dimly, and I say to myself, Well, that's not bad, it's a reasonable solution to *that* problem. But I can't quite believe I was the one who found the solution. I don't remember finding it, and I am relieved, as though I expected the problem still to be there.

In the same way, I will decide to include a certain thought in a certain place in the novel and then discover that several months before, I made a note to include the same thought in the same place and then did not do it. I have the curious feeling that my decision of several months ago was made by someone else. Now there has been a consensus and I am suddenly more confident: if she had the same plan, it must be a good one.

But at other times I discover that this person working with me has been hasty or careless, and now my work is even more difficult, because I have to try to forget what she wrote. Not only do I have to erase it or cross it out but also forget the sound of it or I will write it again, as though from dictation. I should know better, because when I translate, I have to make the English as good as I can when I first write it down or the bad sound of a bad version will stay with me and make it harder for me to write a good version.

Another problem, on some pages, is that I keep putting a sentence in because it seems to belong there, and then I keep taking it out again. I have just figured out why this happens: I put the sentence in because it is interesting, believable, and clearly expressed. I take it out again because something about it is wrong. I put it in again because the sentence is good in itself and could be true. I take it out

The End of the Story

again because I have at last examined it closely enough to see that for this situation it is simply not true.

There is another reason why I will write a sentence and then immediately take it out: in certain cases I have to write a sentence on the page before I know it won't work in the novel, because it may be interesting when I say it to myself but no longer interesting when I write it down.

For a long time, there was the same pattern to our days and nights. I would work all day and sometimes into the evening, or spend the evening with other friends of mine, and he would go to his classes and study and write and see his friends, and then fairly late in the evening he would come by and we would have a beer together and talk and go to bed and get up in the morning and separate for the day. We rarely slept apart from each other, because I had such trouble sleeping if I was by myself and because during the first months, anyway, he had no bed in his room, only his sleeping bag on the floor. He told me he would not buy a bed as long as he could sleep in mine.

He had almost no money. He had no extra money for such a thing as a bed. He had less and less money the longer I knew him. He was waiting for a student loan that was put off from week to week. I had so much money, just then, and was so unused to having money, that I spent it without thinking, and twice I lent him a particular sum of money that he needed. Both times he was reluctant to take it, though the first time more reluctant than the second. The first time, I lent him a hundred dollars, though he was already a little uncomfortable about being twelve years younger and a student, without taking my money, too. He paid it back quickly, but the second sum, $300, which I lent him before I went East for the second time, he never paid back.

He also had great difficulty getting a job. It seems to me he worked in the university library for a while. At the time he left me he was working at a gas station.

Sometimes I played the piano for him. He liked me to play for him. He would sit very still, on the edge of the bed or on a hard chair on the bare floor, and watch me and listen. His face, as usual, gave me no hint of what he might be thinking. We played tennis together, until I did not seem to be able to improve any further and became discouraged. We saw friends together, but these were almost always friends of mine. Though they had known him longer, they were not close friends of his, either because he was so much younger or for some other reason, but they soon became close friends of mine. Once we had a drink with Ellie in a grand old bayside hotel. Ellie later told me she thought I had been rather unkind to him as the three of us sat there talking, side by side on a sofa, watching the guests of the hotel walk by and pause over an antique jigsaw puzzle laid out on a nearby table.

Not long after we met, we went together to visit Evelyn, a friend of Ellie's and mine who lived with her two young children in three rooms in the back half of a small house. The children were frantic the day we visited, they almost never stopped moving at high speed, laughing or bursting into tears or flailing each other or their mother with their fists. While we talked to Evelyn in the larger room, where she prepared meals, ate, slept, worked, and read books from the library, the children played wildly together, sometimes out in the grove of bamboo trees and around the trash cans in the alley behind the house, and sometimes in their

The End of the Story

bedroom, where they jumped off the windowsill onto the bed over and over again, or hid from their mother and called out to her, or took off their clothes and sat in large straw baskets. Evelyn kept getting up to scold the children in her gentle, ineffectual way, or to take a lightbulb from the bathroom, or a handful of toilet paper, because she never bought enough of any supply to have extra and was always borrowing something from one room to use in another. Each time Evelyn left the room, I would look over at him where he sat with me at the large, round dining table and feel how content I was with him, how content we were simply to sit there and look at each other, and it seemed to me easier and simpler to love him there than in any other place.

I think now this might have had something to do with Evelyn's nature. Evelyn did not see things the way most people saw them. Everything was always so fresh and interesting to her, she was so often amazed and pleased by what she saw, for certain peculiar and unpredictable reasons of her own, that she would stop short in the middle of what she was doing, marveling at it, incapable of going on to anything else very quickly, so that even her meals reflected this, and were either incomplete, because she had gotten no further than one amazing food or one amazing dish, or complete, but served hours later than she had said she would serve them because she stopped and spent so long contemplating each part of them. She did not judge things, or her judgments were not harsh, or they did not have anything to do with the judgments of other people. So that, in her presence, everything seemed to be full of wonderful possibilities, and that afternoon I felt that what we had just then was entirely satisfying and good.

His life apart from me was not very real to me. He did not force me to pay much attention to it, because he was too modest or, if not truly modest, spoke of himself only briefly and then left the subject as though something would be lost or harmed if he dwelled on it for too long.

I did not know exactly what he did when he was away from me. I could imagine him alone in his room. I could see him working at a job, and the job was always menial, and demeaning. I could see him in his garage. Then there were the tedious daily things he must have done some of the time he was not with me, such as shop for food, cook, clean his apartment, wash his clothes. I could form only a vague picture of him with his friends, who were unknown to me, who lived in rooms in unknown places in the city. Most of his friends were as young as he was, and because I did not regard people of that age as very interesting, even though I had been that age myself, they tended to merge for me into an undifferentiated group. When I pictured him in their company he seemed much younger, as though they were his playmates and I were his aunt—not quite his mother, though his actual mother was herself so young, as I had discovered, so young that she seemed, even to him, like an older sister.

I didn't know how much time he spent with his friends, since he didn't always tell me he had seen them or, if he told me, give me any idea how long he had been with them. I couldn't really believe that anything important took place when they were together. My impression was that he and his friends only sat somewhere and talked to each other in a way that didn't add anything to them or change them but only marked time while they grew a little older and perhaps more capable of undergoing interesting changes, and that

The End of the Story

this talk went on in a room, an apartment, a house, a campus bar, or a student center—in a private place or a university place, but not a public place in town, such as the café where he met his older friend.

This was the one friend who might have interested me, an eccentric, reclusive man vaguely associated in my mind with literature, who was nearly an old man or was an old man, to my way of thinking at the time, though I now realize that he was probably no older than sixty, and of course, as I begin to approach fifty myself, sixty seems younger and younger to me. He would meet this friend in the café or go see him where he lived in a mysterious part of town which I imagined to be the heart of the oldest part, a part even older, perhaps, than was possible in that town, most of which was not very old. Perhaps I imagined it older and older the more I thought of it, just because I had so little idea where it was.

This friend lived in a single, small room crowded with bookshelves and books, and permeated with the stale smell of unwashed clothing and the strong, bitter smell of tobacco—or, since I never went to visit him myself, did I only imagine this when I imagined an old man living alone? I also saw the old man as bearded and a little plump around the waist, thighs, arms, and cheeks, but I don't know if he told me this or if I instantly formed this picture of the man when he first told me he was visiting a bookish old man in a small room filled with books, and never questioned the picture, so that it registered in my mind as the truth.

Actually, many years before, I had known another bookish old man who was visited by another ardent young man, and maybe I simply applied the picture I knew to this old man.

Although this friend was more interesting to me than his young friends, and raised him a little in my estimation, while his young friends and what he might possibly be doing with them only lowered him, my interest in this friend was still very limited, because the friendship seemed not entirely innocent to me but contaminated, as I saw it, by his self-consciousness, as though he knew how touching it might be that an idealistic and ambitious and talented young man should have a friendship with a much older, poorer, better-educated man, in the presence of whom the younger man's vanity would drop away and he would become pure and even good, or at least feel pure and good. Because I was sure that alongside his real interest in the old man was his awareness of himself visiting the old man, himself at the knees of an old man who had set himself apart from society, the pleasure he might bring to an isolated old man as he freely shared his youth, his freshness, his quick mind, his gentle manners. And he shared these things freely, because there could be no danger of any lasting hold, since his youth itself gave him permission not only to forget the old man for weeks at a time, distracted by the enormous effort of making or beginning some kind of life for himself, but also to move on abruptly and permanently, leaving him behind when the time came to go. So, although there was real tenderness and happiness in his voice when he spoke of him, it was mixed with a naïve elation, a naïve pride in the fact that he owned such an unusual and precious jewel as this friendship with an eccentric, smelly old man awake in the night and asleep in the day, belonging more to the East or even to Europe than to the West, and certainly nothing like the people we saw around us on the palm-lined streets of these seaside towns.

The End of the Story

Now it comes back to me that several of the friends he saw were connected with the theater in town, although I'm not sure if they were students or professional actors, directors, or stagehands. I remember that when he talked to me about the theater and these friends, his tone was firmer, more confident, as though he hoped or expected that I would be impressed by this, at least, by the fact that friends of his, who evidently respected him, were involved in something as compelling as a theater performance. But I'm not sure my interest and respect could have been aroused by anything in his life except the very same things and people that aroused my interest and respect in my own life.

For instance, I know I respected him for having read certain books, and read them so closely and in such an orderly way, but these were always books that I myself intended to read. And I respected him for the way he wrote.

I would not have wanted to spend much time, anyway, or maybe any time at all, with his young friends, who were so much younger that I would have felt like an old woman or their teacher and they would have been respectful toward me as though I were their teacher.

But once we went to a play together and I met a few of them, though I have only a fleeting image of the inside of the theater, in fact only a corner of it near the front door, and a memory of shaking hands with a collection of people he knew.

I don't know if it was on that day that we went out to a café afterward or if there was one more visit to the theater together, after which we met a friend of his, went to a bar or café for beer, and talked about plays and movies. But I never particularly enjoyed talking about plays or movies. And I was never very interested in the theater. He wanted to write for the theater. Just before we lost touch completely, he told me he had been given a scholarship to go to drama school. It was a scholarship he had been hoping to get, yet he told me he had decided not to take it. If he took it, he said, his life would be too easy. The reasons he gave me could have been the real reasons, or they could have been reasons invented or exaggerated to impress me. If they were the real reasons, I was impressed by them, but at the same time I was aware that they might not be the real reasons.

I did not know if he wanted me to know his young friends. I knew he wished I would be more playful with him, and not so serious, because he would sometimes tell me explicitly: "I wish you would play with me more." And I knew he wished we would spend more time where he lived. But I was more comfortable surrounded by my own things, close to the things I could do and the things of mine that interested me.

For the same reason, I think, I almost never rode in his car. I told him I did not want to ride in it because the roar from the broken muffler was so loud, but now, of course, that does not seem to be a very good reason. I could have put up with the deafening roar, or even enjoyed it, if I hadn't been afraid of being consumed by his world, if I hadn't clung stubbornly to my own—my own car, my own house, my own town, and my own friends.

I have been trying to remember the inside of it. I see something red in it, but I don't know if this was his plaid jacket, or a blanket he kept in the car, or the seats. I am almost certain the air inside was heavy with the musty smell of a very old car, of the dried leather of the seats or the stuffing inside them, and that this smell was overlaid with a smell of fresh laundry, since his clothes were always fresh. And I am certain that the back seat of it and even the front seat were cluttered with clothes and books, notebooks, loose paper, pens, pencils, sports equipment, and other odds and ends. I know that after he lost his second apartment, when he was sleeping in his girlfriend's apartment but had no place to put his things, he carried all his clothes around with him in the car and probably other things besides, whatever would fit.

Yet after he left me I used to look for his car all the time, so constantly and for so many months that I never quite lost the habit afterward of noticing cars like his, and the car began to assume its own independent life, became a living creature, a kind of animal, a pet, a pet dog, friendly, loyal, or a strange dog, menacing, vicious.

•

It surprised me, over and over, to find that I was with such a young man. He was twenty-two when I met him. He turned twenty-three while I knew him, but by the time I turned thirty-five I did not know where he was anymore.

The idea that he was twelve years younger interested me. I did not know if I was moving back through those twelve years to be with him, or if he was moving up through them to be with me, if I was his future or he was my past. I sometimes thought I was repeating an experience I had had a long time before: once again I was with an idealistic, ambitious, talented young man, as I had been when I was that young myself, but now, because I was older, I had a confidence and an influence over him that I had not had with that other young man. But there was also a distance between us because of this that would not have been there otherwise.

I said to him that it made me feel younger than I was, to be with him, and he said it made him feel older to be with me. But of course the reverse must have been true at the same time: I felt even older than I actually was, by contrast with him, and he felt even younger. He must have been uncomfortable about how old I was, some of the time, because it made him so careful about what he said when he was talking about things I knew well, but at the same time this difference in age must have made him feel more sophisticated.

He told me he was afraid of saying something that would make him seem young in my eyes. I realize now what an effort it must have been for him, each time he spoke, to imagine, before he opened his mouth, what would seem young to me, and to avoid saying it.

I knew more than he did, at least about certain things, and now and then I corrected him when he said something wrong. I wasn't used to knowing more than another person. I wasn't used to feeling I knew much of anything at all. I knew more only because I had lived twelve years longer. More knowledge was in me, not because I went after it and held on to it the way he did, but because it had accumulated in me as though against my will.

He was embarrassed or uncomfortable that I knew more. But what I saw was that our minds were simply different, and his opened out over its own territory and mine over its own territory, and one was not richer than the other. But he wanted to be able to teach me things, he told me, he wanted to be able to help me, even find a job for me, though I had a job already. He wanted to find me a job, but he couldn't have found me a job, he couldn't even find a job for himself at that time. More than once, he said he

The End of the Story

wanted to take me away somewhere. I don't remember if he named any other place but Europe and the desert. But we never went to the desert, and he couldn't have taken me to Europe, he couldn't afford to take me anywhere.

A friend of mine once told me about a love affair he had had with a woman much older. He, too, had wanted to take her away to a place where nothing would distract her and she would belong entirely to him, a place so inaccessible it was almost imaginary. As he told me the story from beginning to end, with all its details, I saw other similarities, though I said nothing to him: their first night together also began with a moment at which shoes were taken off, though in his case, she asked him to take off her shoes, and he took them off in her bedroom. She was the one, in this case, who worked at a gas station, and after she ended their love affair, he was the one who would go find her at the gas station and argue with her—though I am sure that since he is a gentler person than I am, he was not as persistent.

My friend told me he could not stop writing down certain things about it. He could not speak to her because she would not listen to him, so he wrote things about it that other people would read, so that she might read it, too, and be not only affected by it but more affected because it was public. If she was not, he would at least have the satisfaction of telling it all out loud, and also of turning that love affair, which had not lasted as long as he had wanted it to, into something that would last longer.

It was as though I were taking part in the very beginning of his life, his life as an adult, and this was exciting to me. There was a simple strength in him that had to do with his youth, a pure vigor, and a sense of limitless possibilities, which was something that would change, I thought, in twelve years. In the beginning there was every possibility, I thought, and over the years some of those possibilities disappeared. I did not mind that, but I liked being with a person who hadn't gone through it yet.

But now and then I needed to talk to someone who had experienced those twelve years and arrived at the same sort of point with the same sorts of conclusions I had, and then I wanted to be with people my own age, and I would even go so far as to turn away from him, if we were at a table in a restaurant, and toward people my own age, and when I was in that mood, if he spoke to me I would turn to him to answer, but immediately turn away again, as though he were a contagion, or as though I were afraid of being pulled back into his youth, of losing my grip on my own age and my own generation, slipping back through those years to an innocence or freshness that also had a certain helplessness attached to it. I did not want that youth for myself. I only wanted it there with me, at arm's reach, in him.

Yet the fact of leaving him out so pointedly, at these times, also made me more intensely aware of him at my side either sitting silent, stunned by my rudeness, and listening to the conversation or thinking his own thoughts, or overlooking my rudeness and talking to the person on his other side, so that mingled with my uneasiness at what I was doing was an intensified pleasure in his proximity, as though the fact of leaving him out, having him next to me but behind me, only increased my sense of how close to me he was, a richness still intact. It was as though refusing, for a moment, the pleasure he and I took in each other only further concentrated it. But he must have been aware of this division in my feelings for him, and must have been hurt by it.

One evening I hadn't expected to see him, either because he was busy himself or for some other reason, and I had asked Mitchell to come have dinner with Madeleine and me. We had finished eating and were still sitting at the table in the arcade by the terrace, Mitchell talking about a recent trip, when he came through the gate and across the terrace to us. The sight of him provoked a sharp feeling of annoyance in me, because I did not want to see him just then, but he must not have suspected that I could feel anything like that. Quite comfortably, he sat down with us and listened while Mitchell finished telling us about his trip. After Mitchell went home, he took me down the hill to the bar at the bottom of my street, to meet a teacher of his whom he admired very much. Two other students were present also. My feeling of annoyance only continued, and increased, as I sat there vehemently disliking both this teacher and his students, who paid such close attention to him they barely seemed to see or hear anything else. But I don't know if my dislike of those three men fed my annoyance at him, so that it did not dissipate all evening, or if I disliked them so vehemently only because I was already annoyed.

Now that I have remembered this teacher, whom I had forgotten, I also remember that he lived farther up the hill and a little to the south of me in that same town, and that he used to hold his classes at his house, so that his students, in small seminars, would gather there.

And I recall that this was another place he might be in the evening, before he came to me at the end of the evening, whether he was actually a student in the class or he was only occasionally invited to join the others. And when I recall a specific place he might have been, then it is easier for me to hear him, again, telling me he would come by at the end of the evening from that specific place, and it is easier for me to remember how the knowledge of where he was and the plan we had, the prospect of his coming later, was as distinct, as perceptible, and as sweet as a piece of ripe fruit near me, within sight, and within reach, as I worked comfortably through the evening, beginning to listen, toward the end of it, for the sound of his car and then the sound of his footsteps by the gate.

•

When he was silent with me I found his silence difficult and uncomfortable. I am almost certain he was silent because he was afraid to speak, afraid that I would think what he said was wrong—inaccurate, or not very intelligent, or not very interesting. Even when I did not mean to be unkind to him, I was unkind, and made him afraid to speak.

His silence hid things, as his face hid things, what was in his mind and what he was feeling, and forced me to look at him more attentively, to try to search out what lay behind his silence. He never explained himself, unlike another man I had known who explained himself so fully that I never had to guess. I guessed at his reasons, I guessed at his thoughts, but when I asked him if I was right in my guesses, he did not answer me and I had to guess further, whether I had been right.

This kept my attention on him, but at times I became impatient. I knew I should not be impatient with his silence, or with his indirect way of doing things, or with his slower way of doing things, and yet I was. I wanted everything to be quick, most of the time, except when I chose it to be slow. I simply wanted everything to be the way I chose it to be, quick or slow.

If I look at how impatient I was with him, I have to wonder about the way I loved him. I think I was irresponsible in handling his love. I forgot it, ignored it, abused it. Only occasionally, and almost by chance, or on a whim, did I honor or protect it. Maybe I only wanted to be entrusted with his love: then I was willing to let him suffer, because I was safe in the trust of that love and did not suffer myself.

It was not easy for me to speak to him, either. I wanted to speak, and my voice spoke inside me, I thought of the words to say and said them, but what I said was dry and stiff, the words did not communicate anything of what I was feeling. It was easier for me to touch him and to write things down.

So there was sometimes this strange formality between us, a vacancy and difficulty, because of the awkwardness of what he said to me when he spoke, and the awkwardness of what I said to him, and the vast silences that fell between us. Maybe we did not have to talk, but when we were together we must have felt we should have something like a conversation. We tried over and over again to talk, and did it badly, there were so many barriers in the way.

Other things about him bothered me, and he must have known that. I was uneasy if he sat very silent in company with other people, or if he made a remark that showed he had not understood what was being talked about, his enunciation clearest when he was most nervous, his *t*'s noticeably crisp, or if he laughed in his self-conscious way, his voice tense and rising. Even his smile, broad as it was every time, seemed tense and self-conscious, as though he were offering himself to me then, standing behind his smile and behind his wide body, so straight and tense and quiet. I thought his body was unusually wide, his arms and legs unusually thick. I thought his skin was strangely white, the flesh of his limbs so wide and white it almost shone in the dark. It did shine in a dim light, in a darkened room with light coming in through the windows from the moon or a streetlamp. He was certainly nice-looking, his features were agreeable, but his nose was oddly pointed and up-turned in his wide face, the skin of his face was pale, pink, and freckled, even his lips were freckled. He often fell into one self-conscious pose or another, his head thrown back, smiling or wary, or his head bowed, when he was not smiling and seemed angry, or ready to fight, but was not angry, looking up at me from under his eyebrows, his lips tight shut. I could not say his eyes did not have a pretty color of blue in them, though even the blue was very pale, and the whites often a little bloodshot.

When we were no longer together, what had bothered me did not bother me anymore. It was harder for me to see anything wrong with him, because although the same things were there, they had shrunk, in my attention, to a point where they were barely visible.

∙

I have been counting things today. I have been counting quarrels and trips. I need to put more order into what I remember. The order is difficult. It has been the most difficult thing about this book. Actually, my doubt has been more difficult, but my doubt about the order has been the worst. I don't mind working hard, but I don't like not knowing what I am doing, or not knowing if what I am doing is the right thing to do.

I have tried to find a good order, but my thoughts are not orderly—one is interrupted by another, or one contradicts another, and in addition to that, my memories are quite often false, confused, abbreviated, or collapsed into one another.

I have trouble organizing things in my life anyway. I don't have the patience to try very hard. One reason this book has taken so long to write is that instead of thinking it through and organizing it beforehand, I have simply kept trying, blindly and impulsively, to write it in ways that weren't possible. Then I have had to go back and try to write it in a different way. I have made many mistakes, and couldn't see them until after I had made them.

I still find myself forgetting things I had intended to do, and doing things I had not planned to do. I find myself doing things sooner than I had planned to do them: Oh, I say to myself, so I'm already at *this* stage.

I complained to Ellie a few weeks ago that although the novel was intended to be short, it had been growing and growing and was clearly going to become quite long before I could cut it down to the size it should be. But she said this seemed like a perfectly reasonable way to proceed. She had done the same thing with her dissertation all those many years ago, she said. That reassured me for a while. But now I am worried all over again. If it grows any more, will I still have time to cut it back before I run out of money?

I can't stop translating altogether. Recently I tried to figure out how much money I spent each month, how much I had on hand at present, and how much I needed to earn

xt few months to supplement that. Pleased with
went downstairs and explained to Vincent that I
to spend about $2,300 per month, and had enough
for about a year if I translated just a little. But
Vincent reminded me that my calculations are often wrong.
I often forget what he calls hidden costs. And I forget that
I will have to pay taxes on what I earn.

I am not very good at managing my money. One problem
is that when I'm paid for my work, the payment always
comes in a single lump sum so large it seems limitless. I
begin spending it, and each thing I buy seems to be the
only thing I will buy, each small sum seems like the only
sum. I don't understand that one sum will be added to the
next until the original sum is all gone.

Now and then a day comes when I have almost nothing
left, and no prospect of work either. I am afraid. It is not
that Vincent would not try to make up the difference if I ran
out of money altogether, but if I don't pay a share of our
expenses we can't maintain what we have. At this point I
look at what money is left and at last, because I have no
choice, make a budget and try to live within it.

Sometimes, then, the phone rings and I hear the voice of
a cheerful person who wants to pay me to translate a book.
Because I speak to her in a calm, professional way, she has
no idea of the despair that had surrounded me until that
moment, there at the other end of the line.

I'm not tired of translating, though I probably should be.
Maybe I should also be embarrassed that I'm still translating after all these years. People seem surprised that a
woman my age is a translator, as though it is not wrong to
translate when you are still a student, or just out of school,
but you should have stopped by the time you are older. Or

it is fine to translate poetry but not prose. Or it is all right to translate prose if you do it as a pastime or a hobby. One person I know, for instance, does not have to translate anymore, and that is one of the many signs that he is now a successful writer. He will occasionally translate something small, like a poem, but only to oblige an old friend.

Part of it may be that translators are paid by the word, so the more carefully they work on a translation, the less they are paid for their time, which means that if they are very careful they may not earn much. And often, the more interesting or unusual the book, the more painstaking they have to be. For one or two difficult books, I took so long over each page that I earned less than a dollar an hour. But I'm not sure this explains why so many people do not respect translators or would simply prefer not to think about them.

If I am at a party and I say to a man that I'm a translator, he often loses interest immediately and prepares to move on and talk to someone else. But in fact I have done the same thing to other translators at parties, usually other women. At first I talk to the woman with enthusiasm, because there is so much I have wanted to say about translating to a person who understands the work, things I have thought about a great deal and have kept to myself because I don't often meet another translator. Then my enthusiasm slowly dies, because everything she says to me in reply is a complaint, and I see that she has no joy in translating—no interest in her own work and no interest in me or my work either.

One woman I remember even looked like me, or like what I think I look like until I go and look in the mirror again. She had very long, straight, light brown hair held back from her face by two small barrettes, she wore glasses, she was tall and thin, she had regular features that might have been pleasant if her expression had not been so dull, and she wore neat but drab clothes of no particular style, maybe a colorless sweater and a plain skirt. The main impression she made on me was one of dullness, narrowness, and dissatisfaction. Maybe this is how I appear to others. Maybe I seem too dull and full of complaints, though I think I am too enthusiastic, if anything. But maybe my enthusiasm is worse, because to them it is enthusiasm about dull things.

I complained to another friend about my confusion over this book. He had asked me a direct and clear question, like "How far along are you?" or "How much do you have left to do?," as though I should be able to answer that. He said he always knew exactly how much he had left to do on a book. He said he wrote about a page a day and always knew that he had, say, 100 pages left to write. Only one book of his, he said, was confusing, and for that book he had made elaborate diagrams. But I feel I would lose too much time if I stopped to do that, even though I should know I lose more time by not doing it.

Yesterday, for about an hour, I thought I understood what to do. I thought: Just take out the parts you don't like. That way, everything that is left will probably be good. But then another voice spoke up. It is a voice that often interrupts me to confuse me. It said I shouldn't be too quick to eliminate things. Maybe they only needed to be rewritten, it said. Or moved to a different spot. Moving a sentence to a different spot could change everything. And changing just a single word in a bad sentence could make it good. In fact, changing a punctuation mark could do that. So then

I thought I would have to keep moving each thing and rewriting it until I was sure it did not belong anywhere and could take it out.

Then again, maybe there is nothing that does not belong in, and this novel is like a puzzle with a difficult solution. If I were clever and patient enough, I could find it. When I do a difficult crossword, I never quite finish it, but I usually don't remember to look at the solution when it appears. I have been working on this puzzle so long by now that I catch myself thinking it is time to look at the solution, as though I will only have to dig through a pile of papers to find it. I have the same sort of frustration, at times, with a problem in a translation. I ask, Now, what *is* the answer?—as though it existed somewhere. Maybe the answer is what will occur to me later, when I look back.

Because of the kind of puzzle this is, though, no one else will ever know that a few more things belonged in the novel and were left out because I did not know where to put them.

This is not the only thing I'm afraid of. I'm afraid I may realize after the novel is finished that what actually made me want to write it was something different, and that it should have taken a different direction. But by then I will not be able to go back and change it, so the novel will remain what it is and the other novel, the one that should have been written, will never be written.

•

There were five quarrels, I think. The first was in the car after the reading. The second was just after we returned from a trip up the coast together. I can't remember what that one was about, only that we had not quite made it up when the piano tuner arrived to tune my piano, walking through the fine brown dirt of the driveway carrying his black satchel and whistling a song from a popular Broadway show.

There were two trips up the coast that I can remember, one to a large city where we bought books and one to visit that cousin of mine who took us sailing.

There were two trips out on boats together, one on my cousin's sailboat and one on a whale-watching boat with an older man who ignored me almost completely. I have not so far included the whale watching, the sailing, or the trip to the city, where we had dinner in a crowded restaurant with our bags of new books by our feet.

I went off on three trips by myself. One was for a weekend. The second was for three weeks in early winter, when my term of teaching was over. We wrote letters to each other and spoke on the phone once or twice. The last trip, and the longest, came at the end of winter. I called him a few times and wrote him one letter that never reached him. That was when I was staying in a borrowed apartment and he was living above the cactus nursery.

The third quarrel was more serious than the first or the second, and occurred five days after the quarrel that was interrupted by the piano tuner. I was about to go off on the first of my trips away from him, the shortest one. I think he was angry at me for going away, no matter how good my reasons were, and this was why, the evening before I went, he left a brief message with Madeleine, who passed it on to me indignantly. In this message he told me he couldn't see me despite a plan we had had. He did not explain.

He spent that evening with Kitty instead, first going to the movies with her and then talking to her in his room. He said she had a problem and needed to talk to him. I kept calling him until I reached him, then I quarreled with him on the phone, then I called him again, and at last, though it was so late, I got into my car and drove to where he lived. I wanted to be with him even if only for a short time.

Because of the lateness of the hour, or the absurdity of what I was doing, my lack of dignity, the fact that I had had to change out of my nightgown and back into my clothes to do this, or for some other reason, when I came to the long, wide curve of road around the racetrack parking lot, heading toward the trailer camp and within sight, in the distance, of the highway with its pairs of yellow lights moving down the coast and red lights moving up the coast, and I could see far up the train tracks a train coming south, with its single headlight and its two long tines of reflected light shining down the straight tracks at me, with nothing but darkness and emptiness on either side of me, layer upon layer of different shades of darkness and emptiness, only enough light just here to see the dark side of the hill beyond the barbed fence, beyond the dirt flat, beyond the channel of brown water, I felt I was no longer observing this landscape, but that, instead, it was now observing me: I was the only moving thing right here, by this empty lot, and I was suddenly turned back on myself, as though reflected by the landscape, and forced to see what I was doing at this moment.

But no matter how clearly I saw what I was doing, I would go on doing it, as though I simply allowed my shame to sit there alongside my need to do it, one separate from the other. I often chose to do the wrong thing and feel bad about it rather than to do the right thing, if the wrong thing was what I wanted.

I was traveling that mile up the coast with only one

purpose, to consume that mile and reach the other end of it. I found him, but he wouldn't let me into his room. We talked outside, and he apologized. I drove back home and went off on my trip the next morning without being sure what was true and what was not, about his story.

It was Thanksgiving Day. I was flying to a city north of us, the same city, in fact, where years later I spent most of one afternoon looking for his latest address, though of course in my memory there are two cities, quite different. Not long after I arrived, I was taken to a house I had never been to before, and then later that night I was taken, in the dark, through streets I didn't know, to another house I had never been to before. It was a cottage that stood by itself back from the street over the distance of a very large lawn, a full city lot, I think, unless the size of the lawn has grown in my memory over time. I did not know where I was in the city and I had not known I would be going there.

I was left there, and no one else was in the house but someone's teenage son sleeping upstairs, whom I never saw, either that night or the next morning, so that I seemed to be alone in the house. I felt not only the hours separating me from him but the succession of strange places, too, as though the more hours passed and the more strange places I went into, the farther I moved from him, and I would have to go back through that time and each of those places to find him again. Then, though it was late, the phone rang, and when I answered it, what I heard in the receiver was his voice. He could not know where I was, I thought, since even I did not know where I was. He could not have called me. But he had found me, simply because he wanted to find me.

The same sort of thing had happened a few weeks earlier, when I had wanted more than anything else to hold him in my arms, and thought he was somewhere else and with other people. I had opened a door to go out into a hall and he was there in front of me, waiting for me.

It was at times like these, and maybe only at times like these, when I was away from him and wanted to be with him, that there was no confusion in me and I didn't hold anything back from him.

I returned home two days later and found a small bunch of blue flowers on the piano and a note from him saying he was waiting for me down the hill, at the bar. All I had to do was choose the moment to go, wash my face and hands, walk down the hill, and find him in the crowded place, where he would be sitting on a stool, one of a row of backs, a close line of people shoulder to shoulder, his back, when he turned to look for me, pressing against the back of another man, as I made my way through the crowd to him. Then I would have him in my arms, where I wanted him.

But even so, I put off the moment a little, I looked through my mail and opened a few letters before I went down the hill. I held that moment a short distance away, maybe in order to enjoy it just where it was, in the near future. In fact, maybe I was happiest in exactly that situation, having him nearby, having the prospect of him there before me, feeling the desire to be so close to him that nothing separated us, and knowing I would be able to satisfy it at any moment I chose. It was a perfectly secure position, untouched by any trouble, any conflict or contradiction, and I had the time to savor it. Nothing could disturb it, except to try to stay in it too long.

And when I realize that, I go on to consider that maybe what I found so intolerable after he left me was not the obvious thing, that he and I were no longer together, that I was alone, but rather the less obvious, that I no longer had that wonderful possibility available to me, of going to find him wherever he was and being welcomed by him. I wanted to go find him but did not know where he was, and if I knew where he was, and found him, I was not welcomed by him.

.

When he had appeared suddenly, as though brought by the force of my wanting him there, in the hall outside the door, a party was going on in my house. It was a party he and I were giving together, although I can't remember if there was any particular reason for it. There were many people in the house. We were trying to roast pieces of chicken to feed these people, but we had not planned it right and were not fast enough. So many people crowded around and tried to eat or waited or asked to eat that we became almost frightened by their hunger. We were roasting the chicken outside on the terrace, on a grill built of stone, and over and over again we turned the soft flesh of the chicken with its gleam of fat in the dim light from inside the house, but the chicken would not cook. Some of the people ate, at last, and others never did, and as the hour moved on, the hunger of all these people was satisfied or not satisfied but forgotten. The next morning there was a pleasant smell of beer in the rooms, and piles of crumbs from crushed bread here and there on the tiles, and someone's felt hat left behind on a table.

.

Soon after I returned from my weekend trip, I went to see him in his garage. I had not gone there very often. I did not ask how he worked or when he worked. I would have asked, or maybe I had asked once, but there must have been something in the way he answered, maybe too briefly, that made me think he did not like me to ask.

I came away with a few books I had been wanting to read. I put these books on the shelf in the alcove above my bed alongside the other books I had recently acquired: the books given to me on my trip and the books I had bought with him a few days before.

I looked at their spines often. The colors of their spines, and the few words of their titles, naming other possible visions of the world, were always part of what I saw in the room, and I always liked to have these signs of other worlds near me, even if for months or years I did not open the books, even if there were many I never read but packed into boxes and unpacked again, over and over, taking them with me from one place to the next. Some, in fact, I still have on shelves here in this house, still unread.

When I visited him in his garage, he showed me more closely what he had in this place where he worked, and I was impressed by the books, not knowing, yet, that most of them were not his. The garage was larger than his room in the back of the building. Harsh yellow light shone over the concrete walls and the tall bookcases that stood strangely in rows in the middle of the space. He stepped lightly and easily around the bookcases, showing me how he had arranged the books. He never wasted his motions. He moved, and yet always seemed still. He paused before he moved, then moved economically and deliberately, whereas I often hurled myself at things, stumbled, and was awkward. He seemed to think economically, too, as though he also paused before he thought, as he also paused before he spoke. Of course even pausing and taking care, he sometimes said something wrong, or clumsy, and I thought of the way a cornered animal will pause and then, with its perfectly developed instincts, make a move that should be successful but is not, because there are elements in the situation the animal has not understood and could not have understood.

I did not visit him in his garage again after that, as far as I can remember. I did not help him move, when he moved a month or two later from that place to the rooms overlooking the concrete yard of a nursery full of potted cactuses. I can't remember just when that move was. I think I was away, I think I had gone back East. There was a dispute surrounding the move. Either he owed rent, or the landlord did not like him, or a friend came back and claimed the place, or that friend or a different friend was angry about the books, either that they had been left behind in the garage or that they had not been left, or that the landlord had kept them, or that they had been damaged, or that some were missing.

•

I noticed even then, before I was angry at him myself, long before Ellie told me the story of another woman who was deeply insulted by a proposition of his, something he offered to do for her in exchange for money, that many people seemed to get angry at him. Certainly in any sort of business arrangement, anything involving practical matters or money, sooner or later he did not do the right thing and caused disturbance in the person he was dealing with. In the beginning, he would make a good impression, as for instance on a landlord, since he was neat and clean, friendly and intelligent, and good-looking in an open, unassuming way, and the landlord would be pleased with the arrangement and well-disposed toward him. But then he would be late with a rent payment, or offer only a part of it and then miss one altogether, and the landlord would be first puzzled, then nervous, then angry, and then adamant in asking him to leave.

He had been quick to pay back the first loan I made him, the $100, but he did not pay back the $300 I lent him later, enough to have his muffler fixed, probably because by the time I returned he had left me, so the debt was not something that might come between us but something he would want to forget, just as he would want to forget me, too, as quickly as possible, put me behind him and move on.

I realized later that he went to a woman and became attached to her in somewhat the same way that he moved into an apartment and lived there a few months and then moved out again after some unpleasantness with the landlord, always defaulting on the rent and owing money. He needed to stay with her and become part of her, not lose himself completely, but not keep himself entirely separate either. Then, after a time, he left her and became attached to another woman.

A woman anchored him in the real world, connected him to something. Without her, he floated. He did not keep track of the passing hours or the passing days very well, anyway, he did not plan how to make money or spend it or save it, or if he did, his plans were not connected to anything very real, though he kept himself clean and neat, and began projects and worked at them hard, and was a hard worker, if he did not often finish them.

He did not always know what he was doing or how to plan what he had to do, and in the same way, he sometimes did not know what he was saying, or did not think about how it related to the last thing he had said, or to what he was doing, or to the true situation, so that there was often a lack of connection between one thing and another in his conversation and in his life. Many of the things he said to me were not true, and even more were not what he meant to say. He did not always know what he was saying because his mind was often on something else. Once he told me he made Portuguese fish soup very well, then corrected himself and said that he had never made it but believed he could make it very well. Sometimes he said something he thought was true but said it in such a strange way that it did not express what he meant to say. Sometimes he was simply confused or mistaken. Some things he said wrong out of nervousness and then either heard what he had said or did not hear. Some things he deliberately distorted or exaggerated. Sometimes he deliberately lied.

When I first knew him, I did not know that he could lie, so I believed everything he said. Later, when I looked back at what he had said, knowing he could lie, I had to wonder which thing was true and which was not. And each thing I doubted made me change what I thought I knew about him.

·

I think he wanted to forget me as well as the money he owed me, even though he did send me that French poem a year after I last saw him. Sending it could have been a momentary impulse. Maybe the memory of me broke through his cloud of forgetfulness briefly and was then swallowed up again, so that by the time he received my answer, if he ever received it, he was once again inclined to forget me and only read it quickly, suppressed anything he felt reading it, and put it away to be forgotten as soon as possible—not deliberately in a drawer or a box, and not in the wastebasket, but in a place on his table or desk where it would look like something he intended to answer, but would be buried by other papers, mislaid, and eventually forgotten.

When I received that poem from him I read it through once quickly, then several times more that day, until I understood most of it, and after that I could not take it out of its envelope again, as though it had too much power, as though the force of it was safe enough in the envelope, but not safe once it was out and unfolded.

Just now I have taken the poem out again and have been looking through different anthologies to see if I can find it and identify it. I found it once before, quite by accident, so I thought that when I next needed to, I would be able to find it easily. It is probably a well-known poem, or at least this was my impression after I found it by accident. It is probably one I should know, or one other people would think I should know because of my profession, but my knowledge of French literature is surprisingly poor, as is my knowledge of French history. Oddly enough, this doesn't usually affect the quality of my work. At worst I will miss only one or two references. But now and then it has embarrassed me.

The poem is a sonnet, and begins with the word *Nous*. I looked in the index of first lines of the book where I had been certain, all this time, that I would find it and saw only other first lines beginning with the word *Nous*, in the literal translations offered by the book: *We two have our hands to give. We have a clergy, some lime. We will not always live in these yellow lands.* I did not find the line I was looking for, which would be something like: *We have thought pure things.* I gave up, for the time being.

Then a peculiar thing happened. I watched, as though from a distance, while my two hands put his letter back in its envelope. I did not handle it carefully, almost reverently, as I had a short time before when I took it out, but hastily, and carelessly, because I was frustrated that I had not found out what the poem was. And because I am so used to seeing my hands do this every day to other letters, I believed, or some independent part of my brain believed, for an instant, that this was a letter I had just received, just brought home from the post office to open at my desk. Now his handwriting on the envelope suddenly had a sense of purpose and immediacy all over again—the letter seemed to be a real, active communication.

Then the instant passed, or the part of my brain that knew the truth caught up with the part that had believed something different for an instant. Once again, the letter had the faded permanence, the immutability, of a relic.

The letter is one of a small collection of things here in my room that seem to have some life of their own. Relics, they are heavier, or more magnetic, than the other objects in the house. Besides the poem he sent, and his story, the photograph of him, other letters, and a page he and I wrote together, on which his handwriting alternates with mine, there is a blanket he left in my house, a plaid shirt he gave me, a second plaid shirt whose sleeves are so frayed they have fallen into rags, and at least three books. One of the books is a novel by Faulkner that I read after he left me, a paperback so old that its pages are yellow and its outer margins brown, its glue so brittle that each page, after I had read it and turned it, fell quietly off the spine, and because I did not close the book whenever I put it aside, but left it lying open face up on the windowsill by my bed, not really a bound book any longer but two piles, one of bound pages and one of loose pages, the book did not close on the story, and the story remained present in the room while I was reading the book and for many days after, as if it were loose in the room, had floated up from the pages, and hung there under the raftered ceiling—the woman's sullen illness, the thrashing of the wild palms around the prison where the man sits, the high wind, the wide river the man can see out the cell window, the frail cigarette that he can't roll tightly because his hands tremble so badly.

•

I thought the feeling of emptiness and bleakness did not appear until February. I thought it was mild. The truth is, it appeared in December, before I went East for the first time. In fact, it had been present before then, even close to the beginning, but in the beginning it did not matter. Because I went away, in December, and came back again, I forgot my uneasiness. I missed him and then I had him back. But in February it reappeared, and was acute, and went on day after day.

There were two trips East, but I don't know if I will describe the first one first and the second one second, because today I am feeling that chronological order is not a good thing, even if it is easier, and that I should break it up. Is it that when these events are in chronological order they are not propelled forward by cause and effect, by need and satisfaction, they do not spring ahead with their own energy but are simply dragged forward by the passage of time?

Or is it only that I am irritable today? I have to be careful, because there are days when I am so irritable that not only do I want to disrupt the chronological order, I also want to delete a great deal of what I have written. Take this sentence out, I say to myself, with a kind of furious pleasure, and that paragraph, too—I never liked or respected it.

But if I give in to all these impulses when I am in a bad mood, I will have almost nothing left.

At such times, the irritation I feel toward the writing is just as personal as the irritation I feel when the old man gets stubborn and I come up against the blank wall of his refusal, or during an argument with Vincent when he will not listen to me but either rolls his eyes up at the ceiling or closes them or looks at the newspaper. As though I think this novel has a life and will of its own and is simply refusing to do what I want it to do.

I don't always trust myself, because I have never tried to write a novel before. At first I thought this novel should be like the sort of novel I admire. But then I realized that of course I admire more than one sort of novel. For a while, I thought it should be like the novel I was translating at the time he left me, not because that was what I was doing then, but because I admire that novel. But if I took that as my model, I would have to cut out most of what happens in this one. In that novel, the characters only walk in and out of rooms, look through doorways, arrive at apartments, go up and down stairs, look out windows from inside, look in windows from outside, and make brief remarks to each other that are hard to understand.

For a while after that, I wanted this to have the same high moral tone as the work of another writer I admire, but it won't, because I don't have the same strong moral principles he does.

My uneasiness in December was sometimes boredom, and sometimes, at its worst, a panic at being trapped in the

The End of the Story

empty space of our silence or the awkwardness of the way we tried to talk to each other.

Once, we were alone together in a restaurant and I was becoming exhausted by the effort of sitting there across from him trying to talk to him, trying to make him talk to me, and then trying to think about other things when I couldn't talk and couldn't make him talk. I was moving through the time of our evening together as though I were pulling a weight along with me from one minute to the next. It didn't seem to help that I was going to leave a few days later. I became so tired, then, feeling so little life between us, that out of the deepest boredom I proposed that we play a game: taking a piece of paper and passing it back and forth, we would make up a story together, each writing one sentence.

We did this, but the story was bad, or worse than bad: each sentence followed from the sentence before, but seemed arbitrary, clearly produced by boredom and anger, and this arbitrariness began to frighten me after a while, because it seemed to show how arbitrary other sentences were that followed from one another, and other stories, too. When we stopped trying to write it, there was even less life between us.

How strange it is to realize now that although I was frightened of the emptiness between us, that emptiness was not his fault but mine: I was waiting to see what he would give me, how he would entertain me. And yet I was incapable of being profoundly interested in him or, maybe, in anyone. Just the reverse of what I thought at the time, when it seemed so simple: he was too callow, or too cautious, or just too young, not complex enough yet, and so he did not entertain me, and it was his fault.

Another thing that bothered me more acutely now was the way I changed when I was with him, into a person I did not quite recognize, even though I told myself I did not have to be the same. I was only a little different with another woman, or with a man who was a friend, but with a man who was to me what he was to me, my constant companion, the one who shared my bed not just now and then but every night, the one I came back to when I was away, the one who came back to me, I would often play the part of a person I hardly recognized and usually did not like, and the more uncomfortable I was, the nastier this person became.

I wasn't even playing a part, really, since I did not do it deliberately. And I didn't really become a different person either. It was not a different person who appeared at these times but a side of myself that did not appear when I was alone or with other friends, one that was flippant, condescending, self-centered, sarcastic, and mean. To be all these things was quite natural to me, even though I did not like them.

During this time when I was often bored and restless, Madeleine was often angry, and I did not know why. It would begin early in the morning. Dawn would come with a band of milky white below a cloud. The sky would turn a cool, snowy blue. The first sounds would be a neighbor closing his gate, starting his car, and driving off. He awoke one bird who made a noise like a plucked wire and then went back to sleep for a while. I looked to see how much light was in the sky and the cat mewed once. Now the bird was awake again, and it made a noise like a cricket chirping.

Madeleine would begin banging around in the kitchen, and I would begin daydreaming. The palms would thrash. Later Madeleine would go outside and rake. I would lie on my bed indoors and hear the sound of the rake's teeth grating over the dirt of the driveway. She was raking up the pine needles. She would work her way around the hummock of rubbery sea fig by the road and the bags of red clay sitting in plastic under the cedar tree. She would rake the needles into little piles all over, and then burn them. She liked making fires of them.

Morning would be warm and clear. Then, after noon, the fog would move slowly up the hill from the ocean, cars coming up out of it with their headlights on while the air was still clear where I was. Then the air near my windows would turn white, the trees at a distance become faint, and the bushes close to the house very distinct, suddenly, against the white fog.

At this time of the year there were monarch butterflies all over the hillside, in fives and sixes. Because it was close to Christmas, special services were conducted in the church down the hill, and organ music and singing came up to me. Listening to it, I would look out the bathroom window and see, over car tops and rooftops, the Santa on the chimney of a brick building down the hill, turning by electricity slowly one way and then the other.

Madeleine raked, and she slammed doors. She would pick up the receiver of the phone, which was just outside the door to my room, dial a number, and then slam the receiver down. Or there would be a gentle rattle as she picked the phone itself up and carried it out of my earshot, down the hall or around the corner into the kitchen, where she would talk in a hushed, angry voice, often in Spanish or Italian, the kitten mewing again and again in the background. Once, I know, she was angry at a friend of hers, a wealthy Spanish woman who lived at the top of our hill. I was sure Madeleine's relationships with all her friends and lovers were complicated, but she never told me anything about them and I never asked.

She always preferred to eat with chopsticks, often a dish made with millet and garlic, and she drank many cups of tea during the day. The sink was often littered with chopsticks and teaspoons and separate scattered grains of millet and tea leaves, and in these days, because I knew how angry she was, even the chopsticks and the perforated, hinged metal spoons looked angry lying there in the pale green sink.

●

But despite my discouragement and impatience, I did not want to leave him when the time came for me to go East. It seemed true, just then, that he belonged to me and I belonged to him beyond any boredom, beyond any diminishing of feeling between us. At the same time, I did not know which to believe—that I had only a little feeling for him, as I seemed to have sometimes, or a great deal.

In the East, I was suddenly surrounded by so many difficulties and sorrows unrelated to him, unrelated even to me, that his importance shrank to something very small.

But when I thought my mind was altogether taken up with other things, as I stood on a railway station platform, waited by a car, entered or left a house, walked up or down a driveway, went out into the cold, went back in out of the cold, I would suddenly remember the sweet smell of his skin, and I would miss his open arms, how perfectly still he was when he opened his arms to me, as though all his attention was on me and on taking me into his arms, whereas with another man before him, and then another, there had been no room for me, they were all hard surface, they were always moving too quickly, rushing here and there, usually away from me, or past me, intent on their own business, only now and then straight toward me, when I, too, became their business. He paid attention, he watched, he listened, he thought about me when he was not with me, nothing was lost on him, nothing of me as he perceived me. Even in his sleep, he was attentive, and woke up enough to tell me he loved me, whereas other men, intent on the business of sleeping, would be disturbed and hiss at me: "Stop moving!"

I thought of combining the two visits East into one, in the novel, in order to be economical, since I don't know how much he was involved in those days, if I was so far away from him. But even at a distance my feelings about him changed from day to day, either because each thing that happened to me, though it had nothing to do with him, changed the way I felt about him, and what happened during the night, too, in a dream, or because my feelings simply aged and developed, day after day, like independent creatures, grew in intensity or weakened, deteriorated, sickened, healed.

And the two visits were not the same. During the first, I stayed in my mother's house, a difficult place for me to be, and he and I missed each other intensely and straightforwardly. He wrote at least four letters to me, and I wrote back to him, though I don't know how many times. I telephoned him at least twice. By the time I went East for the second time, my mother's sister had moved in with her and I stayed in a borrowed apartment in the city and felt that what he and I had together was almost over.

I see that I'm shifting the truth around a little, at certain points accidentally, but at others deliberately. I am rearranging what actually happened so that it is not only less confusing and more believable, but also more acceptable or palatable. If I now think I shouldn't have had a certain feeling so early in the relationship, I move it to a later point in time. If I think I shouldn't have had that feeling at all, I take it out. If he did something too dreadful to name, I either say nothing about it or describe it as dreadful without identifying it. If I did something too dreadful, I describe it in milder terms or do not mention it.

After all, there are things I like to remember and others I do not like to remember. I like to remember times when I behaved decently, also events that were exciting or interesting for another reason. I don't like to remember times when I behaved badly, or ugliness of a drab sort, though I don't mind a dramatic sort of ugliness. My boredom is unpleasant to remember, and so are certain events, like the visit he and I paid, after we were no longer together, to acquaintances of ours whom I did not like very much, in their ugly rented apartment, though for a long time I could not figure out why that particular visit was so unpleasant to remember.

One night, as I lay in bed in my mother's house, I stopped to think about the hero of the book I was reading, who was good, innocent, handsome, intelligent, illiterate, gifted in music, and of noble but mysterious birth. I was reminded of him, not because they had many qualities in common, but because of the position the hero occupied in the story, and the attitude of the other characters toward him.

Close to midnight, I left my bed to call him. I carried the telephone into the kitchen and shut both doors. My mother was a light sleeper, often wakeful, and she would not close her bedroom door at night because she did not like to feel shut up in a room, and also, probably, because she liked to know as much as possible about what went on in her house. She therefore heard every noise, often thought a noise was unusual, wondered what it was as she continued to lie in her bed, or got up out of bed to see what it was. But there were nights when she was not worried about anything, when she slept soundly and did not hear what was happening in her house, and I thought there was a good chance, by now, that she was too deeply asleep to hear me.

I was sure he would be surprised and happy to hear my voice, but he was quiet and rather cool, no more than mildly polite. After we had talked for a short time we hung up, and I stayed there in the kitchen sitting on a stool, trying to reason out why he was not more affectionate. I began to accept my disappointment. Then the phone rang. He was calling back, apologetic. Now he was everything he had not been before, ardent and talkative. He said he was sorry, and explained that he was trying to accept the fact that I was away, and had been managing pretty well, and that to hear my voice on the phone and to have to talk to me was difficult because it unsettled him, it undid the work he had done. He went on to say that he loved me and missed me very much, so much that it was painful.

At this point, over his voice, I heard my mother's footstep in the hall. The door from the hall opened, and my mother looked in. Her face in the full fluorescent light of the kitchen was swollen with sleep, disfigured, her eyes half shut against the light, her features disorganized. While I covered the mouthpiece of the receiver, as his tiny voice continued to talk on, unaware, away from my ear, she asked, "Is someone dead?"

By now, two letters had arrived from him. I read them over again and again, until the style in which they were written, impassioned and elegant at the same time, was so deeply impressed on me that when I myself wrote a letter to an old friend I found, as I wrote it, that I was writing in his style, and this felt like some sort of betrayal, though whether of him or my old friend I was not sure.

The distance made him seem even more silent, though in his two letters he might speak to me endlessly, as often as I read them and even when they only lay by my bed, unread but open.

A third letter arrived. I could tell it had been written a few days before, but it was dated a month earlier. He had these lapses, when his mind wandered, when he was not aware of the day and the hour or how the world outside worked, what schedule it worked to. At these times, he seemed to be looking away, and while he was looking away I could come closer to him than I could when he was fully conscious of the time and the place. And his lapses also seemed to be a proof of sincerity, because if he was not aware of the day of the week or the month, clearly he was not calculating all the moves he made, though he might be calculating some of them.

There are really only three things to include from that trip: my phone call to him, the letters he sent me, and my introduction to a certain man at a New Year's Eve party. I kept the phone number this stranger wrote down for me, and I called him two months later when I was in the East again. I think I kept it not because I was unhappy with what I had already but for quite the opposite reason, that coming together with one man in such perfect harmony, for a while anyway, had made me think that anywhere I went now, I might meet another man and come together with him in perfect harmony. The party was attended mainly by college teachers I did not know in a village a hundred miles from the city in the midst of a cold so bitter that the slightest breeze burned my face.

•

When I came back, my mind was more on my work than it was on him. It held my interest for longer periods of time without any thought of him distracting me.

There were other changes. Madeleine was always changing. She was always discovering something about herself, or entering a state or leaving a state, or entering a discipline or leaving a discipline, or consulting a specialist, or finding a new medium in which to work, or a new process, or a new place to work, and from time to time a new relationship, though whether it was more than a passionate and tumultuous friendship I could never be sure.

Now she had cut her hair very short. It gave her pale, lined face a look of frightening severity. She had been seeing an acupuncturist who told her everything in her body was reversed—the yin things were yang, he said. I did not understand very well what this meant, but with Madeleine I did not try to understand if I did not immediately grasp what she said. Now I would like to understand better, now I would ask what this meant.

He and I quarreled again. For two nights in a row, Madeleine had asked me for a potato and baked it, and this was all she had for supper. The third night I was cooking a steak and he had brought a bottle of wine to have with it, which was unusual. Madeleine asked me if she could eat with us. I thought I could not say no. She was generally spare in the way she lived and ate, she had very little money, and also seemed to prefer a way of life in which she needed and used very little. But now and then she would join me in a feast or another extravagance and partake with high spirits and wit, as though she were returning to an earlier way of life. This evening she ate a large piece of steak and drank several glasses of wine. I enjoyed her company, but he was angry that she was eating with us.

The next morning I became angry at him in turn, about something else, something he and Madeleine had done at dinner, and we quarreled. As for Madeleine, she complained to me that she had had trouble digesting the food, that so much meat and wine were not good for her. She spoke out angrily against all meat-eaters and went on for some time without appearing to expect an answer from me.

Only a few days later, he and I quarreled again. I had read aloud to him a story I had written in which he appeared and he was pleased, but then I took him out of it before I read it aloud to other people and he was angry. He thought I was ashamed of him. I denied it. As we quarreled, we became increasingly angry. I was angrier than he was, maybe realizing that what he said was true, in a certain sense, and why it was true, though I hadn't recognized it before. I wished it were not true, and I did not like him to point it out to me.

He left the house. I went to bed calm and angry and read

a book, and a few hours after, he returned. He admitted later that he knew that staying away would have no effect on me, since I was too angry to care whether or not he stayed away, so he returned. Months later I put him back in the story in the same place he had been before, because I was sorry for what had happened. But by then he did not care anymore.

At some point during these days, maybe because he felt things between us were coming apart a little, he said we should get married. But since he could be almost certain I would refuse, his proposal did not seem sincere. Because it was sudden and even a little desperate, it seemed to mean only that he was trying to capture me, to keep me.

I think I made fun of him for it. But after he left me, I was the one who said I would marry him, if he wanted me to, and when that had no effect, when he resisted me, I went further, I offered more. I realized later that it was perfectly safe to say anything then, since nothing was possible. He seemed either insulted or ashamed for my sake, and impatient with me, as though I had belittled what he had once felt, and my own feelings, too. Now that I was willing, or said I was willing, to give him everything I had not been willing to give him before, he didn't want anything from me. Or all he wanted was for me to leave him alone, and I couldn't do that.

•

I was walking along a path surrounded only by cliffs, rocks, and sand—there were no plants of any kind. A young man ran past me, then stopped and turned back, disoriented and anguished, and told me that his home kept changing, so much that he could not recognize it. I woke up a little and realized that this was a dream, and went on dreaming. He and I entered a wooden house together. It was evidently his home. Then, even as we stood in it, it became the set for a play, and it changed each time the act changed, though I don't remember what went on in this play, if anything went on.

We quarreled again, it must have been for the fifth time. That night he left me, angry, and then came back. He came back as though against his will, since he was still angry. The next night and for several days after that he did not come to me at all, and during that time I did not know where he was. I had told him something that shocked him. It did not shock me, because I was only saying to him what I had been thinking for some time, and it did not hurt me, because I was the one saying it. It only shocked me later, when I saw it differently, and saw how he would not have wanted to hear it. At the time I thought I could tell him anything I liked, quite openly, and he would be able to understand it and sympathize with it, as though he were not a separate person anymore but a part of me, so that he could feel what I felt along with me and not be more troubled by it than I was.

He was calm at first, after I said what I said that shocked him, but then he became angry and went away. He went away, and then came back later, still angry. He took sheets from the dryer and put them on the bed while I watched. He went to bed and fell asleep without saying anything.

He did not appear the next night and did not call me. I called his apartment, and there was no answer. I kept getting up out of bed to call him and then going back to bed and trying to read. I was surprised to find, however, that even though he had slept in my bed nearly every night since we had met, I felt I had immediately returned to what I had been before, alone at night, as though I had never met him.

Yet at the same time I was thinking of him so constantly, so much more constantly than I had when he was with me, and with such concentration, that he was extremely present in the room, coming between me and whatever else I tried to think about. I could see that I had betrayed him by feeling what I had felt and saying what I had said, but I could also think that such a betrayal produced a kind of faithfulness, because I had aroused such feelings of ardor and remorse in myself that I managed to achieve a passionate loyalty I had not achieved before. So there I lay, alone, as though I would always be alone, but also strangely in his presence.

I was afraid to turn off the light, though it was past one in the morning, and then two, and then three. As long as the light burned next to me and I held a book in front of me and read the page now and then, I was safe, I was distracted from certain thoughts. The worst thought was that he might have gone to someone else out of revenge, and I could not avoid that thought for long before it came back to me. And this turned out to be what he had done, I found out later.

I knew it was not fair to believe I could do what I liked and he could not, that I could have a certain feeling for another man and he could not go to another woman, but I never decided anything according to what was fair, or maybe never decided anything in the first place but allowed myself to be pulled in one direction or another by what I wanted just at that moment.

Early in the morning, after I had been asleep a short

time, I dreamed I heard his step on the terrace outside. In my dream the dog whined and he said to her gently: "Is she here?"

But he had not come by the time I woke up. Later in the day Madeleine and I went down the block to the corner café and sat at a table outside studying Italian together. We went through the lesson slowly because we were both distracted: I was watching out for him, and Madeleine was convinced that two people standing at a nearby corner were talking about her. She kept looking over her shoulder at them and mumbling, so that I, as I tried to take dictation from her, couldn't hear very well. After a while we stopped trying to work and just sat there in the sunlight.

Waiting for him again that night, when he would not come, created a dark space like a large room, a room that opened into the night from my room and filled it with dark draughts of air. Because I did not know where he was, the city seemed larger, and seemed to come right into my room: he was in some place, and that place, though unknown to me, was present in my mind and was a large dark thing inside me. And that place, that strange room where he was, where I imagined him to be, with another person, became part of him, too, as I imagined him, so that he was changed, he contained that strange room and I contained it, too, because I contained him in that room and that room in him.

Because he was so absent, and in doubt, having disappeared without a word, without the connection of a plan, a day or hour when we would see each other again, the only way I could keep him near me was by the strength of my will, summoning all of him to me and holding him there moment by moment, so that now all of him seemed present to me, whereas at other times only a part of him was present. And in the same way that the smell of him would hang in my nostrils when he was with me, now an essence of him filled me, a savor of him that was more than his smell or taste, a distillation of the whole of him permeated me or floated inside me.

He was doing this to me. I felt it very much coming from him against me. But the very strength of it, the very force of it, was also the force of how much he loved me, and I felt that, too, so that in the extreme force of the harm I felt from him, I felt his love, too. And the longer he stayed away from me, the more strongly I felt how much he loved me, and the more strongly I believed I loved him.

I couldn't stop listening to the sounds of cars, waiting to hear the sound of his. I paid attention to the sound of each car as though it were a voice.

After two days of this, his absence had gone on so long that I was falling into a trance with it and the tension was going out of it. I no longer had to hold it in my mind or sustain it; it had grown so large that it surrounded me and sustained me now, and I rested in it.

Out driving in my own car, I tried to decide what I could be sure of and what I didn't know. I said aloud to myself: I don't know where he is. But he is somewhere. He is alive. Either he is alone or he is with another person, a man or a woman. If he's with a woman, either he will stay with her or he won't. If he has spent a night with her, that is one thing. If he also stays on through the next morning, and stays on into the next night, that is another thing.

I reached this point in seeing what I knew and didn't know, and then went back to telling myself the least I knew, that he was alive somewhere, in his skin, sitting, lying down, standing, walking. I knew he had color, had warmth, moved ceaselessly, even if with small motions, and yet he was beyond the range of where I could see him. But I was thinking so hard about him I was sure I should be able to see him wherever he was.

The way it ended was not the way I thought it would. I did not hear the sound of his car grow louder and louder with an awful, frightening loudness until it drew up next to the house, and I did not call him until at last he picked up the phone. I can remember only two things about how he came back. One was that he parked his car at the bottom of my street, whether I heard it or not, and the other was that when we came face to face again, we were meeting in the bar down the hill, on the back terrace, and I had waited for him a long time, listening to a conversation about Australia that continued beyond any interest—whether the people all spoke English there, what they drank there, the population of Sydney.

I don't remember what we talked about on the terrace at the back of the bar, though I must have apologized, and we must have agreed on something and we must have decided something together, but I do remember lying awake later that night, with the light on, watching him sleep.

He had fallen asleep with his back to me, his broad white shoulder outside the sheet. I lay next to him, raised on one elbow, and looked at all of him that I could see, every detail, and especially his head, especially his pale forehead, the side of it that I could see, since it was turned away from me, and especially his hair, which was close to the light, right under the lamp. I looked at it, then I touched it, and he was not disturbed. His hair was straight and not long, thin over his forehead and thicker in back, a light reddish-brown with blond streaks in it. I looked hard at the color of it and touched it again. Although I knew it did not matter what color his hair was, that night everything about him seemed important to me. I thought I loved that hair and the color of it, and it seemed to me that everything about him had to be the way it was, and could not have been any other way.

Then, in his sleep, he murmured something. I leaned over and asked him what he had said, though I thought he would only go on sleeping. But he said the same thing again, a purely gentle and loving thing.

I got up, finally, at two in the morning and made some warm milk for myself, and sat smoking a cigarette in the kitchen. I thought about what I had just been thinking about his hair, that he was with me now, even more so because he was asleep and I was awake, but if he left me again, or if I left him, and we stayed apart, he would still have hair of a light reddish-brown color with a few blond streaks in it, and I would know exactly, closely, the particular way his hair looked, and would still have that, so that a part of him would still belong to me and there would be nothing he could do about it.

The fact that he came back to me after leaving me, that time, may have made me think that no matter what I said, no matter what I did, and no matter how long he stayed away from me, he would always come back to me, and that I did not have to love him very deeply, or considerately, for him to go on loving me.

The noise of traffic is becoming heavy, a constant din above the sound of the rain, the tires hissing on the wet road surface, and this tells me that four o'clock has come and maybe even gone and I will have to stop work soon.

The cars are right under my window. The road is one of the main routes for traffic going north and south along this side of the river. Many heavy trucks go by, shaking the ground. The heaviest even shake me up here in my chair. Now and then whole houses go by.

Vincent and I bought this place despite the road, because we liked the back yard so much, with its grapevines and raspberry patches, pear trees and lilacs, shagbark hickories and other trees and flowering shrubs. Then we began trying to block out the noise of the traffic. I would look down from my window and see Vincent standing in the front yard and I knew he was trying to figure out where the worst of the noise came in. I would join him and we would talk about the noise. We talked about the noise a great deal, how it was reflected off hard surfaces and how it was best absorbed. Vincent built a fence inside the hedge along the front of the property. Then we planted a line of arborvitae inside the fence. Some of the noise seemed to be coming in under the fence, so we moved dirt from other parts of the yard to pile up against the base of the fence. Then Vincent extended the fence around the sides of the property, and we planted some hemlocks inside the line of arborvitae. A neighbor offered us a young pine from his yard and though it is only a foot high we have put it in among the hemlocks. Now we are thinking that we can further shield the back yard if we build a room off the side of the house at an angle.

At times I am not just nervous about this work but frightened, and think I am going through a crisis, one that could be called existential. Then I realize the problem is much simpler—I have had no breakfast and too much coffee, and my nerves are raw, so tender that I am almost unbearably disturbed to look out the window and see a truck carrying one car on its back and pulling another behind it.

But at other times I am really confused and uncomfortable. For instance, I am trying to separate out a few pages to add to the novel and I want to put them together in one box, but I'm not sure how to label the box. I would like to write on it MATERIAL READY TO BE USED, but if I do that it may bring me bad luck, because the material may not really be "ready." I thought of adding parentheses and writing MATERIAL (READY) TO BE USED, but the word "ready" was still too strong despite the parentheses. I thought of throwing in a question mark so that it read MATERIAL (READY?) TO BE USED but the question mark immediately introduced more doubt than I could stand. The best possibility may be MATERIAL—TO BE USED, which does not go so far as to say that it is ready but only that in some form it will be used, though it does not have to be used, even if it is good enough to use.

Sometimes I think that if only I could go away for a while my mind would be clearer and I could work better. I spoke to a friend the other night who said he had gone away for two weeks to a colony in the mountains to work on his novel and had just come back. He wrote eighty pages in those two weeks. I have never written eighty pages in two weeks. He said that he worked all day long and after dinner, too. He said other people there would leave their rooms and go for walks, even two or three times a day. He said it was pretty quiet. A man down the hall from him played exercise tapes and did exercises, but this did not really bother him. He said the food was not very good. It was plain American food. At first it seemed good enough, but after a while it became hard to eat. For instance, they served ham in very thick pieces, almost an inch thick, and after a few bites he would feel sick. He learned to eat very little at dinner and more at the other meals, which were better. I asked him many questions about this place because I was thinking I should try to go away somewhere to work on my novel, even though I went away once and it didn't make any difference.

I was living alone in the city then. I was given a grant and I used part of the money to pay the overdraft on my bank account. I used more to rent a cottage for the summer. After stocking the cottage with food and repairing my car, I had almost nothing left of the grant, though I had received the money only two weeks before.

The cottage was one of a cluster of small summer bungalows built about sixty years earlier by a German woman named Mary and her husband. The doorways of the cottage were odd sizes, the ceilings and walls bulged, nail heads showed everywhere, the linoleum on the floors bent up at the edges, and mushrooms grew out of the bathroom floor next to the shower stall with its platform of wooden slats. Mary's husband had died and after a few years she had sold the property to one of the summer tenants, another woman named Mary, whose husband then died also. A bench was erected in his memory halfway down the path to the lake. It was unveiled just before I rented my cottage.

It was very peaceful there. Most of the other tenants were about thirty years older than I was, which made me feel young and energetic. When I went down to the weedy lake to swim in the middle of the day, I always seemed to meet old women I hadn't met before walking firmly but slowly up and down the steep path, or resting on the bench halfway down, or unfolding deck chairs on the warm, warped boards of the dock with its hovering wasps. Almost everyone I met seemed to be named Ruth, or if not Ruth, then Mary. Some were the sisters of other women named Ruth or Mary, or the sisters-in-law. Some had their husbands with them. I worked well there in my cottage, but did not do as much as I had thought I would.

A year later, after I met Vincent, I left the city often to visit him. Again, I thought that away from the city I would have the peace and quiet I needed to work on my novel. I even thought the bus would be a good place to work. On the way out of the city, in the early evening, the other passengers were often tired and cross, and when they were cross they were usually quiet. There would be conflicts at the beginning of the ride, when everyone was getting settled, a woman might put her wet umbrella on top of a man's luggage, but then they would quiet down. I would stuff kleenex in my ears and tie a kerchief around my head so that I could concentrate better. If I looked down at my page I did not have to think about anything but the work I was doing. If I looked up I could stop thinking about my work and watch the other passengers. But although I wrote a few short things on the bus, it was not a good place to write anything long.

•

When I wrote down what happened during the fifth quarrel he and I had, I left out what he said when I was watching him sleep. I said it was a gentle and loving thing, but I did not say what his actual words were. He said, "You're so beautiful." But now I don't think it was gentle and loving, after all. I think it was a cry of frustration. He knew he was more helpless than he wanted to be, that if he hadn't found me so beautiful he could have worked his way free of me, as he knew he should. In the end, he did get free of me, but it took longer, and I had to hurt him more often than if he had not been tied to me by what he saw as my beauty.

I also see, when I look at my notebook again, that I lost track of a few days, collapsing them into one. I say he came back to me and it was later the same night that I watched him while he slept, his reddish hair under the lamplight, and then went out to the kitchen and smoked a cigarette while I heated my milk. In fact, it was several nights later, and other things happened in the meantime.

After he came back, I asked him where he had been during the two days and one night that he had been away, and he told me. He told me he had gone to see Kitty in the afternoon and had made love to her to spite me. He went home in the evening, listened to the phone ring with my calls, and then went out again to a nightclub down on the beach, where he drank by himself. He spent all the next day with his friend the old man.

But even though I now knew where he had been, this did not change what I had imagined while he was gone, so that the two versions continued to exist side by side, and in fact, the version I had imagined was the stronger of the two, because it had developed in me so slowly and I had lived with it so much longer.

But this was not the end of it either, because he couldn't simply do what he had done and then forget it as though it had never happened. Kitty would remind him, and he would have to continue or end something with her.

Though we woke up together the next morning, we were apart all day, and when I called him at home that night, he was in bed and did not want to see me.

The End of the Story

He said he would come to lunch the next day, and I waited for him, but he was three hours late. As I waited for him I knew my nervousness would be out of all proportion to his explanation or apology, which would be very brief, as his apologies and his explanations always were when he was at fault in any way, brief and a little angry, as though he were angry at me first for putting him in a position to disappoint me and then for being disappointed in him.

We ate lunch, and then he left to go see Kitty again, and while he was with Kitty I walked down into the town with Madeleine. He returned late in the evening.

The next day he was cool to me, and told me he did not know whether to stay with me or go back to Kitty. It seemed to me it was all over between us. He left at three in the afternoon, then returned at four and said he wanted to stay with me. In fact, he wanted to move in with me, as though to make everything clearer. He thought he could move into the spare room. He said he would talk to Madeleine about it. I did nothing, but simply let him talk to Madeleine, as I let Madeleine do what she wanted in response to him. She did not want him living there and would not consider it. I had guessed that she would not want it, but I did not know whether I was relieved or not.

Although I did not really think she would agree to have him live there, I convinced myself briefly that she would want the money he could give toward the rent because she often had such trouble paying her share. But I was misjudging her yet again. Although she had so little money, money was never the most important consideration for her, and usually not a consideration at all. In fact, I think she was insulted that we were offering money in exchange for this disruption of her life.

The three of us went off in the car after talking about this, to a birthday party. As we drove, there was silence in the car. Madeleine sat in the back seat feeling insulted by us, while we sat in front feeling angry at her that she refused us what we asked from her, and wondering what we would do next about the two of us, although I don't think my anger was very sincere. I had the luxury of being angry at her while at the same time I was not entirely unhappy that she had made this decision for me.

The next evening, despite the fact that he had been on the point of leaving me and had not left me, I went out to dinner with another man. I had already made that plan and I did not change it. He was not happy about it. While I was out, he stayed alone in my room reading and then took a walk, and when I returned he said very little to me and kept turning away from me, and because he kept turning away from me, I was frightened and couldn't sleep after he fell asleep. It was then that I stared at him under the lamplight for a while before getting up to smoke and read in the kitchen, watching a mouse that came out of the stove to walk over the burners hunting for food. It was when I went back to bed that he said, as though in his sleep, "You're so beautiful."

In the morning, after he said what he said to me in his sleep, he sat on the same stool where I had sat the night before and held the young cat in his lap, rubbing the crown of her head. I stood behind him and held him around the shoulders. I put my cheek down against his soft hair. Now that he was with me again, after frightening me, I wanted to do something for him, to give him something, though I did not know what. But that impulse grew weaker after a few days and then passed.

The End of the Story

The entire quarrel, starting with his leaving the house so angrily and ending with my staring at his white shoulder late at night, had lasted a week.

I think I did not at first write down the actual words he spoke because I was afraid this would seem vain, even though the novel claims to be fiction and not a story about me, and even though it was only his opinion, not necessarily the truth. In fact, I had to believe he saw something I could not see, because when I looked in the mirror or at a photograph, the face I saw, tense and motionless, or frozen in a strange position, only rarely seemed even pretty to me, and more often either plain or unpleasant, with features that floated or spun when I was tired, one cheek spotted with four dark moles in a pattern like a constellation, hair flat, of a dull brown, on a large squarish head, neck so thin as to seem scrawny, eyes startled or apprehensive, of a blue so pale as to be almost white staring out from behind the lenses of my glasses, though if I took my glasses off, as I occasionally did, I tended to frighten people, as I was told quite frankly by at least one friend.

What I also left out of this version was that when Madeleine and I were studying Italian together on the café terrace and then gave it up because we were so distracted, what finally stopped us was that a small green dropping landed on a page of the Italian grammar book. It had come from a sparrow in the tree above us. I did not put this in my account of that day because it did not fit in with the mood of what I was writing.

•

Not much time has gone by since I last worked, but when I sat down at my desk I was immediately confused by my new system. I have four boxes with pieces of paper in them. They are labeled MATERIAL TO BE USED, MATERIAL NOT YET USED, MATERIAL USED OR NOT TO BE USED and MATERIAL. Most of what is in the last, "Material," has nothing to do with this novel. "Material Used or Not to Be Used" means what it says: material I have already used or don't intend to use. What puzzled me today was the fact that there didn't seem to be any difference between "Material Not Yet Used" and "Material to Be Used." Then I remembered that the "Material to Be Used" was in finished form, ready to be incorporated, and the "Material Not Yet Used" was in rougher form. It was the word "ready" that would have clarified things, if I hadn't been afraid to write it on the box.

I've just spoken to another friend who is about to go away to work on his novel. He is going to a hotel in Mexico. A surprising number of friends are writing novels, I realize, now that I stop to count them. One woman leaves her apartment every morning to write in a local coffee shop. She says she can write for only about two hours at a time, but if she moves on to another coffee shop she can extend the morning's work a little. A man I know writes in an old shed behind his house while his children are at school. Another goes away to an artists' colony to write, then returns home for a while to work as a carpenter so that he can earn enough money to go back to the colony. Another writes at night while his roommate is out driving a taxi. He has written 700 pages so far, and he says he is trying to make the novel funny, but that it is hard to be funny for so many pages.

•

I don't know exactly why things were going wrong just when they were, but a day came that later seemed to be the beginning of everything going so wrong that we couldn't get it right again. He had told me on the phone that he was at home working. Madeleine and I went out for a walk through town and stopped in at an art gallery. There he was, among the few people gazing soberly at the paintings, his army bag hanging from his shoulder. He seemed unpleasantly surprised to see us. He said he would come by later that night. I went out for the evening with two friends, leaving him a note, but when I returned he wasn't there and hadn't come.

I called him, letting the telephone ring fifteen times. I hung up and then drove over to his apartment. His car was there outside the building but his lights were off, and I was sure he was not alone. I went up to his apartment and knocked at the door. He opened it for me in the dark and went back to bed. He lay completely still and did not respond when I got into the bed and tried to talk to him. I got out of the bed. I said I was leaving, and he said nothing, unless it was "Goodbye" or "Whatever you like."

At home I lay down on my bed and ate a slice of bread and cheese. I got up and brought another slice of bread and cheese back to bed, and then another. While I ate, I read a book of poems by a friend, a book that had come recently in the mail, so that while I was filling my mouth with food, I was also filling my eyes with the printed pages and filling my ears with the sound of my friend's voice, and all this filling, all this feeding into different channels, did at last change my condition, whether it really filled something or simply calmed something.

•

Three nights later, I went to his room again, this time with him. But our companionship was not very strong now.

It did not go much beyond the appearance of companionship. There was this appearance, and there was also a certain familiarity, though even the most complete familiarity would not have removed all the awkwardness between us. On the way there, we stopped to buy a pack of playing cards, a few bottles of beer, and a bag of corn chips. I can see now, and I sensed then, though I tried to ignore it, that I was bored, and that without the cards, the beer, and the chips I would not have known what to do with him, that these things were a distraction from the emptiness that would have been there in the room between us, they were a distraction I had to have in order to want to stay there with him at all and not prefer to be at home alone eating and reading and more fully engrossed in that than I could be in him.

I was probably there in the room with him then only because there had been something different earlier. If he was still there, with me, the same person, and I was still there, and there had once been something between us, certainly something ecstatic from time to time, it was hard to believe that that ecstasy was not still within our reach. But what we made together, now, was the form of a thing not alive anymore—a thing left behind that showed what the living thing had been like.

Now the very thought of those things we bought and took to his apartment fills me with a queasiness that tastes of tepid beer and stale chips and slides around like a playing card with warm grease on it. How miserable that attempt was. What weakness of character it showed, that I could not simply admit there was nothing I very much wanted to do with him, nothing left to do, that the only thing left was to say goodbye with all the friendliness I really felt for him.

The End of the Story

But instead I went to a store with him, one of those large, brightly lit stores, so vast they are disheartening, and bought with him things other people bought to have a good time together, as though by doing that we would have a good time, whereas I had no illusion that I would enjoy myself, or maybe I did think I could achieve something that would feel, at least for a little while, like a good time simply by going through the motions of it, that if I just carried on like that, my mood would suddenly change, and what had not been enjoyable would become enjoyable.

Now I would like to be in that room again, on that night. I am curious to see what he would say and what I would answer, because I have forgotten so much of the way he talked and the things he might think of saying to me. Now I would bring so much interest to the meeting with him that it would be full of a kind of life it did not have then.

There was no table where we could play cards, so we sat on the carpet by his bed. We drank the beer, ate the chips, and played gin rummy. The game was not interesting. I might have known, if I had been willing to think about it, that I could not hope for anything from the game itself, because if there was boredom between us, there would be no tension in the game either.

We played on and on, as though trying to force some interest from it. We drank more beer than we wanted, or at least it was more than I wanted, and were not affected by it either. The alcohol seemed to have no more power to intoxicate me than the game had power to interest me, and the situation was not changed by it, as I had hoped it would be, knowing that alcohol could usually change a situation at least a little. We ate the chips and maybe other things as well before the chips, or maybe we had had something odd or excessive earlier, for dinner, because when we finally went to bed, I began to feel sick, and I lay awake feeling sick, and then my sickness became so bad that I kept going into the bathroom and sitting on the floor next to the toilet, my arms on the toilet seat and my head on my arms, and then on the toilet, and then down on the floor again next to the toilet, for most of the night. He woke up slightly, once, but did not seem to notice that I was going back and forth so often or was awake for so much of the night.

The next day was his birthday. We went to a movie. After the movie, we went home to my house, ate thick sweet cake and ice cream, and sat on the foot of my bed while across the room, so large and empty that the bed at one end, and the piano, the card table, and the ugly metal chairs at the other seemed small on the expanse of dark tile floor, Madeleine, sitting on one of the hard chairs, read aloud to us in the light from one of the bare bulbs attached to the white plaster wall long, complex horoscopes from a magazine. Again I was uneasy, and sensed that without the food and Madeleine's company, there would have been emptiness between him and me, and boredom, that the presence of Madeleine, in fact, who was so separate from us, drew us together a little, at the same time that what she was reading was so entertaining, and beyond that, her own reactions to it were so sharp. I ate too much, and I laughed too much. But the food held most of my interest and attention as long as it lasted and I was restless as soon as it was gone.

What did boredom mean then? That nothing more would happen with him. It wasn't that he was boring, it was that I no longer had any expectations for this companionship with him. There had been expectations, and they had died.

And why did that boredom make me so uncomfortable? Because of the emptiness of it, the empty spaces opening up between him and me, around us. I was imprisoned with this person and this feeling. Emptiness, but also disappointment: what had once been so complete was now so incomplete.

The evening before I left on my last trip contains another memory that is difficult, not so much because of my bad feelings about him, I think, as because of a combination of other things: the awkward spaces and ugly concrete walls of the barnlike building where the reception was held, the sickening sweetness of the cheap white wine, the rain afterward, the bare lawn outside, with no plantings on it at all, and the word "reception," which I don't like.

I was moving from one person to another, with a glass of that sweet wine in my hand, looking through the crowd from time to time, when suddenly I saw him standing there with a few of his young friends. I did not expect to see him, though now I can't think why I wouldn't have talked to him about the reception. This is the sort of question that bothers me the most, because I will never have an answer for it—what our relations were at that point, if I was planning to do something without him and without even mentioning it to him. Maybe that was not unusual for us, but it seems especially strange to me in this case, since I was leaving the next morning.

I can't remember which friends he was with, or if I even noticed who they were, since I didn't care, and I can't remember if I went over to him as soon as I saw him or, remaining a few yards away, caught his attention and waved to him and continued to talk to other people, or didn't try to catch his attention but simply watched him and kept track of where he was in the room. The last seems the most likely to me, maybe because this is what I have believed all these years. But it was also something I would be likely to do, given the reaction I had when I saw him, a reaction I do remember unmistakably. It was a feeling of absolute displeasure to see him there, as though he were a hostile element in that place, a thing that intruded where it didn't belong, so that as I watched him among the moving figures, over the shoulders of the other people in the crowded place, those same features of his that had held such a positive attraction for me not long before, and that would exert such a fascinating force again not long after, were just then repugnant to me, blunt and deadly, primitive and vicious, without intelligence, without humanity, the color of clay.

Rain was coming down hard and a few people gathered by the open door, preparing to run to their cars. Although I don't know how I came to stand by the door with him, I did go with him to my car, the two of us running across the sodden lawn under my umbrella or my raincoat, and I drove him the short distance to his own car. I certainly remember the spongy grass under my feet better than I remember what I said to him, or what he said to me. I was on my way out to dinner, and he was going off to some place where his friends were giving him a birthday party. He said he would come to my house late in the evening.

By the time he came, I had been at work several hours on a job I had to do before I left in the morning, and although it was already late by then, I was not finished. He went to bed at the other end of the room and fell asleep. I worked on, impatient to be done with what had turned out to be much more tedious than I had thought it would be. I was checking a friend's translation, and I was doing it as a favor. The friend never really thanked me later, or not in any way proportionate to the amount of work I had done or the awkward moment when I had had to do it, though of course it wouldn't be fair to expect her to know how awkward that moment was, especially since even I did not know it was the last night I would spend with him.

I finished and went to bed. He woke up, and then we talked to each other for close to an hour, unusually companionable and relaxed, as we might have been all along, as though we were taking our last chance for it.

The next morning we got into his car and he drove me to the airport. I did not see him again until I came back more than four weeks later, when he met me at the same airport and we got back into the same car. He waited until we were on our way up the highway to begin telling me that everything had changed. The distance in him was enough to let me know something had happened, though he had said nothing about it in the corridors of the airport or by the revolving tables of luggage. The distance was there because he had already begun a different way of being with me, whereas I was still in the old way of being with him.

I lost most of another day of work yesterday, because Vincent and I took his father to the county fair. We put a cap on him because it was a blistering hot day, and as we wheeled him around he peered out at everything attentively from under his visor. We took him to see the sheds of cattle, sheep, rabbits, and poultry, and the rubber tires of his chair rolled pleasantly over the fresh sawdust. A goose put its beak to the wire grille of its cage and honked at him and he kissed his hand back to the goose. I don't know what he was thinking.

I suppose we were trying to entertain him with a spectacle more unusual than his television shows and what he sees from the back porch, where he sits so much of the time—the trees moving in the wind, the branches bobbing suddenly and rustling these days as the squirrels run back and forth, the green hickory nuts thumping down onto the lawn. It is true that as we left the animals and moved toward the exhibition halls and racetrack and Ferris wheel the intense heat, the brilliant sun, the constant motion of the crowd, the sweet smells of cotton candy and fudge washing up against him did seem to awaken a response: little spots of color appeared on his cheeks, his eyes brightened, and his gaze from under the visor was as intent, almost angry, as the gaze of one of those roosters in the poultry shed. Among the crowd were other speechless men and women like him, old and middle-aged, even young, being wheeled about or guided by the elbow or hand, making a visible effort to absorb what was around them, and they, too, seemed to have been brought out in order to be shocked into some kind of accelerated motion by the assault of this rowdy scene. So there we were, just another small group, another parcel of the seething mass, two middle-aged, our shirts damp with sweat, pushing a third, who was old, tiny, with an egg-like head under his cap, his body barely perceptible in his loose clothes.

Today he is cranky and a little sunburned on his freckled forearms and the backs of his bony hands. The nurse remarked, after being with him only a few minutes, that he was acting strange. I assured her he was only tired.

The End of the Story

I had a dream last night in which I was looking for a good photograph of him and at last found one. The strange thing is that this photograph was a sharper and more complete picture than any waking memory I had of his face, and when I woke up I could still see him clearly, though by now the image has faded. So somewhere in my brain there must be a clear memory of his face that is hidden most of the time and was uncovered once, like a photograph, in the dream.

I am working more systematically now, and I feel more in control. But then I find things that disconcert me because I have no memory of them at all, such as an early plan for the novel which I jotted down in pencil in a spot where I wasn't likely to find it again except by accident. It may not be a plan for the whole novel, though, since I see that large parts of the story are missing.

When I find something like this, I don't know what I may find next. Then I become annoyed with myself, as though someone else had made these careless notes and left them lying around for me to figure out without a clue as to what they are for or what they mean.

I am trying to sort out the different phone calls I made to him while I was away in the East for the second time, staying in an apartment borrowed from an old friend who was in the West. There was one call late at night, after the stranger left me. There was one during which I could hear the sound of typing in the background. There was one in which I learned he was seeing another woman, one of his friends, the one who had given him a birthday cake the night before I left, and the one, in fact, that he later married. And there was a phone call in which he assured me that this was not important, that she did not mean as much to him as I did, and it did not change anything. But I don't know if these were all different phone calls.

I seem to have written two accounts of one of these phone calls and the days surrounding it. I have just rediscovered the earlier one, and it seems less accurate and more sentimental. For instance, I say that after he told me he was seeing another woman, I was in pain because I still held him in a little corner of my heart. Now the idea of my heart having a corner bothers me, and other things about the sentence bother me, too. I also said I remembered how happy it made me to hear him laugh and see him smile, which was certainly not true.

The earlier account includes things I later left out because although they had to do with my life at the time they had nothing to do with the story: how I attended a university lecture, and a dinner beforehand, with very pale university professors; how I did not understand their questions after the lecture; the lofty conference room overlooking the lights, far below, of a poor and dangerous part of the city; the wide hallways of the empty building; the bags of trash around every bend and crowding the elevator as we were leaving. How I had dreams about certain men and there was far more anger in the dreams than I ever felt when I was awake. How the apartment in which I was staying was in a part of the city where many old people lived, and the sidewalks were full of canes and walkers, the old people swaying among them. How I knew I was trying to find the answers to certain questions, answers that would probably come only with time, by trial and error.

I didn't seem able to understand much, after all. I didn't understand what my attachment to him meant, or what it meant to love and honor a man, or even what he had said on the phone. As I strained after answers, I was more confident about the correctness of certain kinds of thoughts than others. Those others seemed weak and tentative, or the muscles with which I was thinking them seemed weak—yet they were the very thoughts that should have been correct, that could have helped me if they had been correct. There would be a question, and next to it an answer, obviously wrong, and I couldn't seem to find any other answer. The question of what it meant to love a man was one that would take a lot of time and thought to answer, but an easier one, which I felt I should have been able to answer, and couldn't, was why it had embarrassed me to hear him play the drums.

Neither account includes a literary party I went to, where a writer said to me: "What anybody will buy, that's what I am."

I recently found the phone bill from that time, and it shows five phone calls to his number within twelve days. One conversation lasted thirty-seven minutes, and it may have been that night that they were making bread, though it may equally well have been an earlier night, when I spoke to him for only fourteen minutes.

I wrote a letter to him and watched it lying there on the desk before I sent it, and wondered what kind of communication it was if it was written but couldn't be sent because of the lateness of the hour, or if it was written and could be sent but wasn't sent. Would it be any kind of communication as long as he had not read it?

In the earlier account, I seem to be sure the letter I'm studying is the same one that was later returned to me by the post office, and in the later account I only guess that this may be so. I can't decide why I was sure one day and less sure another.

The letter that never reached him was sent back to me unopened by the post office, though it was correctly addressed to the place where he was living at the time and was still living when I returned. Since it was sent back, I still have it and can read it now, and I have just done that again. I don't know if my impression of it is the same or nearly the same as the one he would have had. It seems cheerful, uncomplaining, and very young—young because it is so open, so frank, without guile, wariness, innuendo, or insinuation. In the letter I tell him how I telephoned a man I had met at a New Year's Eve party and invited him up to my apartment. I don't know why I told him about this, since the encounter with this stranger had not worked out very well and certainly did not reflect well on me.

I had been out to dinner with an old friend who left early because he had to go home and walk his dog, he said. I was alone in my apartment, and restless. Although I didn't recall this stranger very clearly, I telephoned him and invited him to come up. I had an idea that only later seemed odd to me. I thought I had learned to do something I hadn't known how to do before, and it would always be enjoyable, never again dry, colorless, strained, hasty, or awkward, so that all I had to do was to invite a man I found attractive to come to me, and it would be enjoyable.

But when this man appeared, climbing the last steep flight of stairs, and looked up at me, as I looked down into the stairwell at him, his face was not what I had remembered. Inside the apartment, he talked about his religion, and he went on talking about his religion. He had changed

The End of the Story

distinctly between the first meeting and the second. He had been attractive and spirited in the midst of the party and now, some weeks later on the top floor of a narrow brownstone, was not so attractive, as though every part of his face had in the meantime shifted slightly, or thickened, at the same time that his mind had slowed down considerably and become fixed on one idea. I sat there and let the time pass and pass, because I thought that although it was too late to change anything, at least I could be as tired as possible and a little drunk when it happened.

In bed with me he continued to talk about his religion. Then, after he was finished, because I lay with my back turned to him and only grunted when he spoke to me, he must have seen that I wanted him to leave, and he did leave, at last, and after he was well out the door I got up and went into the living room in my bathrobe. I was trembling violently, in large quakes and shudders. I went to the phone.

It was three hours earlier there. He was with a friend, he said, and they were making bread. He asked me a question about the bread and I told him not to let it rise too long. I thought if he was making bread with this woman there must be something between them and it was probably all over for him and me, considering how badly things had been going before I left. I said some of this to him, and he answered with sudden irritation that there was nothing to worry about. His irritation convinced me he was telling the truth. I said I missed him. I didn't tell him about the man who was then riding home on the subway, who had left a present of three books of his for me to find after he was gone, three books I looked at but did not read or keep or even give away. I considered taking them to the bookstore down the street, but instead threw them in the wastebasket. I had never done that before, to a book.

Since the letter I wrote to him about the stranger's visit is dated, I can now figure out the date on which I saw the stranger and then telephoned with my pathetic question, and I see I was right: that was the conversation that lasted thirty-seven minutes. But what I also learn from the letter is that he had told me in an earlier conversation that he was now seeing this woman, and once I knew this I became more passionate, or more frantic.

I knew she was living there with him by then, spending nights with him. I knew she was more than just a friend from school. What worried me, what I wanted to know from him, and what he did not tell me honestly, was whether this thing that was going on between them was going to be permanent or was going to end when I returned home. I did not want him to see another woman, though I could see another man. I could see another man because that did not hurt me, and I avoided what would hurt me and went after what would give me pleasure.

But not wanting him to see another woman was more than jealousy. If he was with someone else, he was suddenly very far away from me. His attention was turned on her and not on me, as it had been before, even from such a distance. The light of his attention was off me.

It doesn't matter to me that we talked for exactly thirty-seven minutes, but it did matter to the telephone company, and while I was brooding about the conversation in the privacy of my borrowed apartment, and later, far away from there, not knowing just how long it had lasted, this large company, the phone company, was recording on this document, the phone bill, exactly how long the conversation

The End of the Story

had lasted, along with the other long-distance conversations I had on that phone, and it then sent out that information, though it didn't care what use was made of it as long as the bill was paid.

I don't know why I need to reconstruct all this—whether it is important for a reason I haven't discovered yet, or whether I simply like to answer a question once I see how to answer it.

The night I came home, he met me at the airport in his car, as he had promised he would, but he was not very friendly and told me on the way up the coast that he had some bad news.

I knew what the bad news was, but I didn't want him to tell me until we were sitting in the bar and I had a glass of beer in my hand. Then he told me everything had changed. He said it was all over for him, it hadn't been working out and he didn't want to go on with it. We had both ordered large meals. After he told me this, I couldn't eat anything, so he finished his meal and then ate most of mine. Because he had no money with him, I paid for the food. I didn't get angry or cry. I tried to be friendly, because as long as I was sitting there with him, it didn't seem to be over. After he was finished eating, a little more relaxed because of the beer, or touched by my protests, he kissed me and said he would have to come to see me again because he had nowhere to live.

He later denied saying this. It didn't make sense even to me, because he had a place to live. He was still living in his apartment. He was living with a woman his own age—a small, dark, athletic woman, Madeleine told me. She had seen them together in the supermarket. She was angry. She said he had left me while I was away, after I had helped him out of so many difficulties.

Later that evening, when I was alone, I was sorry I had been pleasant. In the days and weeks after that, I occasionally cried or got angry on the phone talking to him. But whenever I was with him again, I felt there was still a chance, so I was pleasant again.

I had trouble sleeping that night. I fell asleep at two, and dreamed about him, then woke at six, toward dawn, and lay awake. I had a grim vision that seemed true just because it formed so quickly and so distinctly: I saw myself turning forty within a few years, leading what I called an "empty" life, doing dull work and doing it badly, and not loving any man, or at least no man who also loved me.

Only some of this happened the way I had predicted it would. When I turned forty, my life was not empty. Some of the work I did was dull, and I did some of it badly, which embarrassed me, but I did more of it well, and most of it was interesting. I did love two men who did not love me, or not at the same time that I loved them, but I also loved one man who loved me, too, and at the same time, which seemed to me a rare piece of good fortune.

Although I was with other men after him, some who mattered only a little to me and others who mattered more, my feelings for him did not change as quickly as I would have thought. Where did I keep them during those years? Did they sit intact in a group in my brain somewhere? Did I have only to open the door to that small area of my brain to experience them again?

•

The next day, the hours passed slowly, as though much more time were passing, as though whole days were passing. Yet I could not get used to the new situation. I felt I had just heard this news a moment before.

There were other, smaller changes. The dryer was broken. Madeleine had been wearing my clothes, and she had burnt one of my shirts drying it in the oven. She told me she had allowed a friend of hers, a policeman, to sleep in my room while I was away, and he had left such a smell she had had to air the place out. There was something wrong with my car. It wouldn't start at first, and when it did start, it roared. He had had his car fixed but had not paid me back my money. Now his car was quiet and mine roared. Maybe he had been getting his car fixed with my money on the same day I had called that man I barely knew.

Because the dryer was broken, I hung my damp clothes from the rafter of the spare room, so that it was full of white garments swaying in the breeze that came in through the window.

I did what I had to do, though it was hard because I kept thinking about him. I was afraid of what would happen when the evening and the night came. A band of tightness around my throat now made it hard for me to swallow, and I kept pulling at the neck of my sweater. It was not my sweater choking me but something inside me.

I could hardly eat, though I wanted to get a little food into my body. I felt sick to my stomach at the smell of food and then at the first bite. I could only take a little fruit, dry bread, certain vegetables, water, and juice.

I seemed to float, as though anchored to nothing. Nothing was quite real, or it was hard to tell what was real and what was not. Real things in the room looked thin and transparent, part of a flat surface of colors and patterns lining the sides of the room.

When at last I went to bed that night, I couldn't stop coughing and lay in the dark trying to keep very still. Although I wouldn't be able to hear the sound of his car, now that it was fixed, I still listened for it because my ears were used to doing that, and I heard cars that had nearly the same sound his car had once had.

As I lay there, coughing, not sleeping, I became more and more angry. Though it was late, I got up and telephoned him. There was no answer. Now I was angrier, because if he was in another place, he was not alone, and if he was not alone, he was not even thinking of me. This was what disturbed me most, that he was almost surely not thinking of me. If he had forgotten me, where was I, and who was I? I could tell myself I was still there, and still myself, but I didn't feel it.

I went back to bed, tried to read, couldn't read, turned off the light, became angry at myself, too, and then at everyone I knew. I started to fall asleep, was woken by my own surprise at falling asleep, and began coughing again. Later I fell asleep again, and woke up coughing again. This happened over and over, until at last I put two pillows on top of a bolster and slept the rest of the night leaning up against them with a piece of wet kleenex on my forehead.

In the morning, Madeleine called a friend of hers, a mechanic who did independent work, and he came over to look at my car, first outside the house in the rain and then, after he got it started, down in the garage. The phone rang while I was watching the mechanic out the window.

At this point in the story there is another difficult memory. He had called to say we were invited to the house of a man and woman who did not know we were not still together. I think I should include the visit just because it took place, but it irritates me. The four of us sat in a small living room and I kept looking across the carpet at him and feeling sick, pinching myself on the neck so that I wouldn't faint, looking away from him out the plate-glass window or at the man and woman who had invited us here. The man was the one who had gone out on a boat with us to watch whales and ignored me so completely. After an hour or so, we left and he drove me home.

I don't know why that visit bothers me so much. What I was looking at, through the picture window of their rented apartment, was a square patch of lawn and beyond it the tall grasses or reeds that bordered a narrow stream. This was the same stream, though at a different point in its course, that I had seen from the other side, and much farther away, when he and I walked out on the coast road to buy beer at the small grocery many months before.

Was it that I didn't know these two people very well and didn't like them very much? Or that their rented, furnished apartment was so small and so ugly, with its brown furniture, brown walls, and metallic, yellowish drapes? Or that he and I had to pretend, in this place and with these people, that nothing had changed? The man and the woman were coming to the end of their stay here, and this was part of their preparation to leave—one last, awkward social visit with us and then a few days later they would call him and ask him if he could drive them to the airport.

·

After he told me so abruptly that it was over, I lost interest in everything else. What he was doing to me now, the fact that he was not with me but with someone else, had become a substance that seeped through my brain, that ebbed, rose again, was present and then gone, like a smell or taste. It would fade away for a while, and I would be aware that it was not in me. Then suddenly, for no reason, it would rise again and its bitterness would spread and penetrate everywhere.

I couldn't help thinking he might still come back to me because he had loved me so much before, and because I had never known him any other way but loving me. For the first few days, I did not give up trying to persuade him to talk to me. I did not care that he was with another woman. I used the telephone. He had to answer it, since it might be someone else. Then he had to talk to me at least briefly, to be polite.

I couldn't argue with him if he said he didn't want to go on with it, but I also couldn't help trying to make him talk to me about it. He wouldn't talk to me in any way that satisfied me. I thought he should tell me he had once loved me deeply, and that he was still the same person, but that his feelings had changed for certain reasons that he could explain. He should then explain what his feelings had been and why they had changed. He should also admit that he had left me without warning, and that when he had told me on the telephone, long distance, that things were still all right, he was lying.

If I couldn't be with him and he wouldn't talk to me, I at least wanted to know where he was. Sometimes I found him, though more often I did not. Even if I did not, I still preferred looking for him to sitting at home.

One evening, I drove several towns north to have dinner with Mitchell. I could hardly talk to him and only felt sick, again, at the sight of the ham rolled up into little bundles and the butter on the table. Mitchell always took great care

The End of the Story

over his meals, so there must have been good bread, maybe special pickles and special mustard. He was concentrating on his plan for the meal and on serving it, while I was trying to stay in control of what I was feeling. At last he mentioned something too difficult for me to hear just then and I could not go on eating.

Soon after dinner I left and drove down the coast road toward home. It was raining hard, but because the road passed through the town where he lived, within a block of his apartment, I could not drive on through it but had to turn and drive a block toward the ocean, through a small square with a fountain. I turned right again, out of the square, and stopped the car by the curb where I could look over a rooftop to his balcony and his lighted windows. There were no curtains over the windows, but I couldn't see anything inside the apartment very clearly because it was far away and high up, and because of the heavy rain.

I rolled down my window. I saw a form moving back and forth across his kitchen window. It seemed to be moving more quickly than he would move, and the hair on its head was darker than his hair. I decided to go up to the balcony and see exactly who it was. I started the car again, and drove into the parking lot behind his building. The rain was drumming on the concrete balcony, covering the sound of my footsteps as I climbed softly up the stairs. Below me, as I walked along the balcony, was the roof of the cactus nursery, and around it, in the nursery yard, the indistinct shapes of the massed cactus plants. I was wearing a dark slicker and boots. It was dark outside, where I was, and light inside, in his rooms.

I looked in quickly through a window and saw a woman with short brown hair lying on his bed reading. Her legs were crossed at the ankles. From this distance, across the wide room, and through the wet window, her face looked smug and unpleasant. I looked to the right and saw him moving around silently in his little kitchen. I turned away to look again at the woman on his bed, and he appeared suddenly in the doorway to the room, unexpectedly close to me, though on the other side of the glass, and he was speaking to her, though I could not hear what he said but could only see his mouth moving. I stepped back from the window.

I left the balcony, went down to the car, and drove away. My cheeks were hot. I turned the radio on. I realized later that the rain had made it easier for me to do what I did, because it separated me not only from what I saw outside the car but even from myself, and the sound of the rain separated me from what I might have thought.

As soon as I took my slicker and boots off, at home, I went to work putting the hooks back in the curtains I had washed earlier and began hanging them up on their iron rods. I was moving fast in order to avoid what I might start thinking. Then, knowing for once just where he was, I left the pile of curtains and called him. He was not unfriendly, and he agreed to come see me the next day. I finished hanging the curtains and got undressed for bed, but then, though it was late, sat down to work at my table.

My eyes were wide open as though stuck. I did not feel tired. I had gone out to dinner, and come home in the rain, and the brandy I had had with Mitchell did not make me too sleepy to go on working at my table with my brain moving fast. I was not hungry, though I could feel that my stomach was empty. I had looked at what I might eat. I couldn't swallow any of it.

I worked hard and the work seemed to go well. As I

worked, I seemed to be waiting for something, though I did not know what. Then I realized I was waiting until I could be sure he and she had stopped making love and had gone to sleep. Once they were asleep I could go to sleep myself.

The next morning I sat at my table translating again. He had said he would come at a certain hour of the morning and he did not come, and he did not call. I kept looking up from my work, out the window. Each time I looked up I saw the same things: the fence across the street, the top of the house set back behind it, and a few trees. Now and then something came between me and what I saw, and then I watched it, whatever it was, until it was gone.

The young girl came home to the house across the street with her tennis racket in her hand and a sweater over her arm.

An old man passed, moving slowly down the hill with many small steps. He was the one I often saw kneeling among the flowers in his front yard next door to the church.

Before a small breeze, a red blossom tumbled, end over end, in the soft dust.

Two dogs came up close to the window. The larger dog sniffed at a bush, its nose and neck outstretched. The smaller dog stood behind the large dog and stretched its nose and neck up to sniff under the tail of the large dog.

Several times I went down the hall to the bathroom, looked at myself in the mirror, brushed my hair, rinsed my mouth out, and then returned to the table. Finally I went out to the store, came back, and called him. There was no answer. I called him a second time, and then a third. The third time he answered and said he had called me, but I knew he hadn't, because Madeleine had been in the house while I was out. He asked me what good it would do to talk.

•

On another day I persuaded him to meet me after work. Passing the time until the evening, I went downtown to a music store and from there to Ellie's apartment, where Evelyn and her children were sitting on the floor and the sofa. We walked out into the rain and down half a block to the seawall to look at the high gray waves, then drove up in Evelyn's car to a restaurant for supper. The car was steaming from the dampness of our clothes, with so many of us crowded in together.

I made sure to be home in time, but he did not come. He called instead and said he could not come because he had to get up early the next morning. Then he asked to borrow my car. He had to drive that older couple to the airport. He must have thought my car was more suitable than his. I told him I kept it in the garage now, and that I would leave the keys in it.

Later in the morning, after he had gone to the airport and brought my car back to the garage, we met for breakfast at a restaurant up the coast. I was afraid that if I was clumsy and let food fall from my mouth or dropped my fork, everything would be ruined, though I knew this could not be true.

We sat side by side on a wooden bench with hanging plants over our heads. He leaned his shoulder against the back of the bench, facing me. He talked a great deal, mostly about himself and his plans, and I listened. I was not eating more than a little toast from the heavily filled plate in front of me. I wanted to smoke. After we paid and walked out, we stood on the sunny terrace and he hugged me for a long time.

When I was alone in my car again driving south, I thought only about the different things he had said, trying

The End of the Story

first to make sure I understood them and then to see if they meant what I thought they meant.

The memory of that meal is another one that bothers me. Is it because meeting him did not make any difference, it was only hours wasted, as I was pulled weakly here and there by my thin string of hope? But the scene itself and every aspect of it seem to become an enemy—the uninteresting landscape of brown dirt outside the window, the earth-moving machines and brand-new wooden constructions standing nearby, the bland sunlight inside, the foolish hanging plants, his smiling with a cruel friendliness, his talking with a cruel openness, the poisonous blond wood paneling on the walls, and the load of breakfast food.

Later that day Ellie told me a friend of ours was giving a party. I thought I would call him and see if he wanted to go to it with me. But when I tried, there was no answer. I drove up to the gas station and to his house. Then I drove up and down the streets of my town. I had heard that friends of his lived near the water, though I did not know exactly where. All the streets below the coast road were near the water, so I drove through all those streets looking for his car. By now I wasn't planning to speak to him, since that would have meant ringing a stranger's doorbell. But once I started looking for him I had to do everything I could to find him. This time I couldn't find him. At last I reached him by telephone late in the evening. He asked me abruptly what I wanted. He said he did not think he could go to the party. He yielded only a little in the conversation after that, enough to laugh once, though maybe he was merely being polite. I did not understand how he could be so affectionate in the morning and so cool to me now.

I sat down at my table to work, but every time I looked up, his face appeared in front of me.

I must have known there was not much hope. But still, for four days after I returned, I told myself there was some hope that he would come back to me, though he did almost nothing to encourage me: he hugged me once, he kissed me once, and two or three times he mentioned things in his life that might include me.

Late in the afternoon of the fifth day, on my way home from the party he had not wanted to go to, I stopped by the gas station, a little drunk. I asked him lightheartedly if he had changed his mind yet.

Across the road from us where we stood awkwardly near the gas pumps, as though waiting for something, a freight train rolled by slowly. Beyond it, at some distance, rose another hill with a straight line of palm trees along the top of it. Behind us, hidden by low buildings, the sun hung above the ocean, and its warm orange light lay over the palms on the hill and the palms closer by, lower and thicker, that stood around the fountain in the middle of the town. The sense of the ocean so far below us made the level asphalt of the station seem to be a high plateau. A cool spring evening was beginning, but the air was soft and fragrant. A camper stopped by the pumps and a thin, wide-hipped woman climbed out and asked timidly where she might buy some butane or propane. Before I left, he said, also lightheartedly, that he had not made up his mind yet, and he thanked me for stopping by.

While I was standing there with him, I could tolerate what was happening, but once I was alone again I could not. I had nothing to distract me, and Madeleine was not there to stop me, so I called him at the gas station. We talked for half an hour. He kept leaving the phone to wait on a customer. Each time he left, I planned what I would say to him next, as though I could say the right thing and he would come back to me. Each time he returned to the phone I said what I had planned to say. I finally told him I wanted to see him, and he said I must not drive up to the gas station. But he would not come down to see me after work either. We hung up, and then I got back in my car and drove to the gas station.

From the road I could see him sitting in the office that was so fluorescent in the darkness it was like a showcase where he was behind glass, flooded with light. He sat at the desk reading. When I walked in he stood up and came around the desk, his broad shoulders braced as though against the sight of me and stronger than they needed to be.

He talked to me about what he was reading, because he clearly did not want to talk about the two of us. Sitting at the desk, he had been reading a novel by Faulkner. He was reading all of Faulkner now, just as months before he had been reading all of Yeats. He wanted to talk about Faulkner, but I did not, and now our talk went nowhere, because I could not bear the situation as it was and he would not do what I wanted him to do.

I began to cry and he put his hands on my shoulders and said, "Go home." He said he had to close the station. He walked me out to my car. He walked away toward the office. I got into my car and went on crying with my head on the wheel. He came back out, said my name, was silent a moment, and then said that if I did this I made it all impossible. I did not understand what I could be making impossible. He left to serve a customer, then came back angry, an oily rag in his hand. He said he had to go and clean the toilets, it was nearly nine o'clock, now he would not get out of here until nine-thirty, and he would not be paid for any work he did after nine o'clock. All his anger at this small job was in his voice. Then I became angry, too, that he valued his four dollars an hour more than he valued me, and at last I drove away. His anger felt better than his kindness. I couldn't have left if he hadn't become angry and made me angry. Then I was back in my own hands, and I could act again.

•

After those five days, I gave up, or at least I stopped trying so hard to go after him, and a different kind of bleakness closed down around me. I was so angry I wanted to hurt someone. I told myself how careless he was, how vain, shallow, and vulgar he was, how nasty, unfeeling, irresponsible, and deceitful. I said he had no conscience, betrayed friends, insulted women, and abandoned lovers. I said he was so deeply selfish that even his good friends became irritations to him, and when they tried to help him, he saw this as just another irritation.

Now I passed in and out of several different states of mind every few minutes, first anger, then relief, then hope, then tenderness, then despair, then anger again, and I had to struggle to keep track of where I was.

My mind kept filling with the thought of him, and it was painful every time. I knew that part of the reason it had ended was my own dissatisfaction. While I was still in it, I had been restless. But out of it now, I was still attached to it. I had had to ruin it to get out of it, but once I was out of it I had to remain attached to it, as though what I needed was to be on the edge of it.

The End of the Story

I had not understood how to love him. I had been lazy with him and did not do anything that was not easy to do. I had not been willing to give up anything for him. If I could not have everything I wanted, I still wanted it and did not stop trying to have it.

I felt more tenderness and concern for him now that he had left me, even though I knew that if he came back my feelings would weaken. Now I would have done anything to have him back, but only because I knew I could not have him back. Before, I was difficult, and sometimes harsh toward him. Now I was only easy, and soft, though he rarely felt my softness, since I was mainly alone with it in my room. Before, I would tell him what I found wrong with him, without sparing his feelings. Now it would have hurt me to do this, though maybe not as much as it had hurt him. Before, I liked to listen to myself talk and was less interested in what he said. Now, when it was too late and he did not particularly want to talk to me, I wanted to listen to him.

After thinking of these things, I became inspired to start all over again with him. Excited, I thought I could do it very differently this time, if only he would agree. But this resolution was just as empty as my hope that he would come back to me. It could not mean anything as long as I knew he did not want to share it with me.

In the first few days, I had been impatient, as though things were resisting me. Now I was angry, not only at him, but also at myself, at certain other people, and at things in my room. I was angry at my books, because they did not hold my interest enough to stop me from thinking about him—they were not alive now, they were not ideas but only paper. I was angry at my bed, and did not want to go to bed. The pillows and sheets were unfriendly, they looked off in another direction. I was angry at my clothes, because when I looked at them I saw my body, and I was angry at my body. But I was not angry at my typewriter, because if I went to use it, it worked with me and helped me not to think of him. I was not angry at my dictionaries. I was not angry at my piano. I practiced the piano very hard now, several hours a day, starting with scales and five-finger exercises and ending with two pieces which improved steadily.

There was a lot of hatred in me. It was a feeling of wanting to get rid of the thing that was bothering me. The hills that had been brown in September were now green. But now I hated this landscape. I needed to see things that were ugly and sad. Anything beautiful seemed to be a thing I could not belong to. I wanted the edges of everything to darken, turn brown, I wanted spots to appear on every surface, or a sort of thin film, so that it would be harder to see, the colors not as bright or distinct. I wanted the flowers to wilt just a little, I wanted rot to appear in the creases of the red and violet flowers. I wanted the fat, water-filled blades of the sea figs to lose their water, dry up into sharp, rattling spears, I wanted the smell to go out of the eucalyptus trees at the bottom of the hill, and the smell to go out of the ocean, too. I wanted the waves to become feeble, the sound of them to be muffled.

I hated every place I had been with him, and by then that was almost every place I went. If I saw a woman ten years younger than I was, I hated her. I hated every young woman I did not know. And there were a great many young women walking through the streets of the town where I lived, though most of them were tall, with fluffy blond hair

The End of the Story

and sweet smiles, while she was short, dark-haired, and rather sour, from what I had seen.

I did not want to say his name anymore. It brought him too much into the room. I let Madeleine say his name, and I answered with *he*.

•

At times, during the weeks that followed, the days seemed like an endless succession of difficult mornings, afternoons, evenings, and nights. It was often hard to leave my bed in the morning. I lay there and thought I heard footsteps in the dirt outside my window, but it was my own pulse, beating like sand in my ears. I was afraid of what was ahead. For as long as an hour, with my eyes closed, I dreamed, then began to worry, then began to plan. I often perceived things most clearly then, though what I perceived usually appeared in its worst possible guise. When I had planned enough to stop worrying so much, I would try to open my eyes. If I could keep them open, I would look around the room. I would think about him, and try to think about something else. But I could not think about anything else, and it seemed as though my body itself were preventing me, as though my flesh were steeped in some essence of him, because this essence would rise into my brain and fill every cell, and it was so strong that my attention would be drawn back to the thought of him, in spite of myself. Then at last I would get up. I would work in my nightgown and bathrobe for another few hours, and then finally dress, but in soft, loose clothing that was not unlike pajamas.

I could usually work till the morning was over. But the afternoon would be long and slow, so slow it just stopped and died where it stood. I liked to have daylight outside, and darkness hours away ahead of me and behind me. But

I did not often want to go out into that light, and I kept the curtains closed. I liked to see the light at the cracks of the curtains, I liked to know it was out there. Then, when evening came and there was darkness outside, I kept the lights burning inside.

I did what I could to distract myself. I kept moving, cleaning something in the house, or walking outside, or I talked to friends and listened to them talk, or I tried to read a book that kept my mind busy, or do a kind of work at my table that did not allow my mind to wander. Sometimes the table in front of me seemed to be the only level place, and everything else fell away from it or rose steeply from it.

A good kind of work to do was translation, and I had a short novel I was supposed to be translating. So I sat at the card table on a metal chair and worked. I usually translated in the morning, but I also went back to it at other times, even late in the evening. It was a kind of work I could almost always do, in fact I worked better when I was unhappy, because when I was happy or excited, my mind would wander almost immediately. The more unhappy I was, the harder I concentrated on those foreign words there on the page in a strange construction, a problem to solve, just hard enough to keep me busy, and if I could solve the problem, my mind was captivated, though if the problem was very difficult and I couldn't solve it, as sometimes happened, my mind would knock up against it over and over, until at last it just floated free and drifted away.

It wasn't a long book, but it was difficult, and because I was distracted, I did not do a very good job of translating it, even though I was working so hard and felt my mind was so sharp. What I put down in English was strange, as I saw later.

As long as I was reading the sentence to be translated, or writing down the translation of it, or reading an entry in the dictionary, I was absorbed in the words of these other people, not the voices of the characters in the novel, since they seldom spoke, but the voice of the author of the novel, and the dry, precise voices of the editors of the dictionary offering definitions of the words I looked up, and the livelier voices of the different writers quoted in the dictionary. But during the brief interval when I stopped typing and picked up the dictionary, an interval that could not have lasted more than five seconds, when I was not staring at any words but looking out the window, and these voices died away, his image would swim up between me and the work and cause a fresh pain just because I had forgotten him for a few minutes, or pushed him to the back of my mind with these words I was studying so closely.

I also had letters to write. I wrote one to the man whose book I was translating, and as I wrote, I looked at myself and said: Look at her, writing to this man, and at the same time she can't stop thinking about that gas station attendant up the road. And yet the man I was writing to would have understood, because this was the sort of thing he wrote about in his novels.

I would work at my table, then I would often wash something, myself or something in the house, my clothes or something in the kitchen. I took one shower after another, scrubbing myself as if I could erase my body, rub out not only the dirt but my skin and my flesh, too, right down to my bones. I worked on the windows in my room. I cleaned both sides of every pane of glass until I could see through it as though it weren't there, see the plants outside and the red terrace and the white underside of the arcade roof, which turned pink in wet weather, reflecting the wet red terrace.

It rained a great deal that month. The darkness would gather around, the clouds massing up, and the rain would fall, coming straight down, heavily, and then stop after a short time. The sun would come out and shine from a clear sky. Reflections from the puddles outside the house would move like snakes up the dark wooden cabinets in the kitchen. The sun heated the wet roof so quickly that steam rose from the black shingles all over and the wind blew it down off the eaves in clouds like smoke. After the sun had shone for a little while, the dark would come again suddenly, and I would look down the length of the room at my bed and see the dark spreading, as though from that corner, from the dark blankets on the bed.

I could not always do what I had to do. For instance, I could not always do even a small cleaning job, and I stepped in my own messes. Once it was a wide smear of tomato pulp I had left on the kitchen floor. I was walking around in my socks talking out loud to him. I stepped in the tomato pulp, and instead of changing my sock I lay down on the bed and read a story, a quiet, well-written, but dull story about deer hunting, while my damp foot, hanging off the edge of the bed, grew colder and colder.

I had to think clearly, make good decisions, make plans, and could not. I was in the wrong place to understand, either too far inside each thing or too far outside it. I would believe a thing was the right thing to do, and then wonder if I would soon believe the opposite. Sometimes I would know what I ought to do but have no will to act; at other times, I would have the will to act but not take action. And because I came up against myself this way, I had to wonder how I could change what I was, so that I would not always be this person I had to contend with, this person who defeated me.

Then I would stop questioning everything and become stubborn. I would withdraw into myself, keep my head down, and not care what anyone did to me or what I did to anyone.

On other days I could hardly stop moving, and my brain would not stop working. Everything I turned to seemed to have an idea in it. The concentration of solitude around me, so thick, seemed to make the ideas press in on me and feed me without interruption. Only if there was a leak in that balloon of solitude, some of what I might have thought would seep away. And every idea had to be written down, on any piece of paper at all, on a shopping list, in a checkbook, in the margins and blank pages of a book I was reading. It had to be written down so that I would not forget it, even though I knew that later some of these ideas wouldn't seem worth remembering. And I was not always quick enough to write the thought down on paper and knew I had lost it and couldn't recover it, and was as aware of that thought as though it were a blank space on a page. I would have been even sorrier if I hadn't known that each thought was accidental anyway.

At these times, I talked fast on the telephone, I was impatient with everything that held me up, I did not want to bother eating, I did not eat until I was too distracted by hunger to go on thinking, and then I walked back and forth on the floor of my room while I ate. It was hard to eat anyway. There was already so much inside me, working so hard, that I had almost no room for food. I watched, as though I were outside myself, how my stomach turned when I tried to eat a bit of toast, biting and chewing slowly, swallowing a little at a time, the same with an apple. Sometimes I could swallow a little soup, or a bit of raw vegetable. It was bad one day, better the next.

I worked my body hard, walking, running, moving fast, and I began going to Ellie's health club now and then, not for health, but because I thought that if I hardened my body I would beat out those quivering, jellylike emotions that were so uncomfortable. I grew thinner, my muscles became as hard as my bones, my arms and legs felt like pieces of jointed metal. My pants hung loose, and the ring on my middle finger slipped off easily.

I smoked more and more cigarettes, one every few minutes, smoked in bed, smoked in the car, and smoked walking out to the shops. My lungs were congested and I coughed dryly all day long. I had not stopped coughing since I returned home. At times the coughing kept me awake for hours and I would get up and eat a spoonful of honey or drink some water and then try to sleep again, swallowing over and over.

The nights were always the worst. I thought that at least I should be able to read a great deal, but it was hard to concentrate. It was hard to rest. I could not go to bed early. It was hard to get into bed and stop moving, and hardest of all to turn off the light and lie still. I could have covered my eyes and put earplugs in my ears, but that would not have helped. Sometimes I wanted to plug up my nostrils, too, and my throat, and my vagina. Bad thoughts came into bed and crowded up against me, bad feelings came in and sat on my chest so that I couldn't breathe. I would lie on my right side, my bony knees pressing together until they were bruised, the right on top of the left and then, when I turned over, the left on top of the right. I would turn onto my back, then onto

The End of the Story

my stomach, first with my head on the pillow and then pushing the pillow aside and lying flat, then turning onto my right side again, holding the pillow between my knees and arms, then turning onto my back again and putting three pillows under my head, beginning to fall asleep and waking suddenly, startled by the fact that I was falling asleep.

I wondered, as though I were far away from all this, what would happen now, if I would eat less and grow thinner, if I would become still more occupied by the thought of him and go to further extremes in trying to make him talk to me and in searching for him.

I called an Englishman named Tim, and his voice was soft and high in my ear. I asked him if he wanted to have lunch with me. But when I hung up the phone, I did not feel encouraged. Now, I thought, I was left behind, he had left me behind, in a world that contained only gentle, delicate Englishmen.

I had planned that we should go to the corner café down the hill from my house and that we should sit at an outside table by the coast road. I had planned that I should sit facing the road where I could watch the traffic. Everything was arranged as I had planned it. Tim was an intelligent man, and he should have been good company, but nothing really interested me about this lunch except the cars that might go by on the road.

I sat over lunch for a long time, watching the traffic at the same time that I talked to Tim. Then at last, just as the light turned red, better than I could have planned it, his car came level with us, and he stopped, looked over at me, and kept his face turned toward me almost as long as the light was red. I could see this much out of the corner of my eye. I might have felt uncomfortable making such use of a decent man like Tim for my own purposes, to arrange to be seen eating lunch with another man, but feeling uncomfortable would not be enough to stop me.

Later that afternoon, Madeleine had to persuade me not to go up to see him at work. I should not make a scene where he worked, she said. She told me I was older than he was and should be able to handle this better. She sat with me and talked to me. Although I could have given myself the same reasons she gave me, I could not have stopped myself. If she had gone out just then, I would have called him. She offered to go to the movies with me again, or play cards. Then she cooked dinner. She said, "At least we've eaten dinner. That's something."

Madeleine kept telling me not to go to the gas station when he wouldn't talk to me on the phone. She thought I should have more pride. She would have had more pride. But unless she was actually there to stop me, I would go. Sometimes I had excuses. I knew they were transparent, but they still served a purpose.

For instance, I invited him to parties at least three times. I knew these were parties he would want to go to and that probably no one else would invite him. He did not go to any of them, though each time he hesitated before refusing. The first time he waited a few minutes, the second time half a day, and the third time a week.

The second time, I found him playing basketball in the parking lot above the beach near his apartment. Seagulls wheeled around overhead, crying above the pines. I sat in my car watching him. My car filled with smoke from the cigarettes I kept lighting. I was watching him over the roofs of several cars and he was playing at the far end of the court, but I was close enough to study him carefully—his short, scanty trace of reddish beard, his reddish hair, straight on top with a little curl at the back of his neck, his white skin, his flushed face, his skin turning pink in the sun in a V shape down his chest, the exuberance of his body, how quickly he moved, how he sprang up suddenly, turned suddenly, always braced, always balanced. He was playing very well.

I was content, because for once I had him there in front of me, I knew where he was and what he was doing, and I could watch him as long as I liked, and from a safe distance: he couldn't do anything to hurt me and I didn't have to worry about how I looked or what I did or said.

When he and I were still together I either knew where he was or did not mind not knowing, because we would not be separated long, and did not want to be separated. Now that he was away from me almost all the time, I knew he was away by choice and might not reappear unless I fought to get him where I could see him and keep him there. Worse, he might disappear completely, I might never be able to find him again.

A part of me had grown into him at the same time that a part of him had grown into me. That part of me was still in him now. I looked at him and saw not only him but myself as well, and saw that that part of myself was lost. Not only that, but I saw that I myself in his eyes, as he regarded me, as he loved me, was lost, too. I did not know what to do with the part of him that had grown into me. There were two wounds—the wound of him being still inside me and the wound of the part of myself in him torn out of me.

For an hour or so I watched and smoked. Was I also

bored? Did I, just for a moment anyway, see him as nothing more than a boy in the distance, a college boy playing basketball? Or did it give me pleasure to reduce him to that, since it appeared to make him harmless? Or is it only now that I think I should have been bored, and my need was so strong just to know where he was that to satisfy it was enough and there was no question of being bored?

Then he walked away from the court toward my car, which I had parked in a spot he would have to pass on his way back to his apartment. He came close enough so that I could lean over to the open passenger window and call out to him. He looked around, surprised, at my second call, came over, laughed to see me there, and got into the car beside me. The heat from his body gradually covered the windows with mist. He smiled at me and put his hand on the back of my neck. While I talked to him and drove the few hundred yards to his building, I wondered exactly why he had his hand on my neck. Then he took his hand off my neck. I went up to his apartment with him. I sat on the edge of the bed and he sat on the floor, leaning against the wall. He seemed to consider going to the party with me. He was damp all over and still flushed. His sweat was drying on him, probably chilling him. I thought he was waiting for me to leave so that he could take a shower, and after a short time I left.

⋅

Vincent sits there in a flowered armchair in our living room and winces at the thought that I might put anything sentimental or romantic in the novel. He says that if the novel is about what I say it's about, there shouldn't be any intimate scenes in it. This makes sense to me. I don't like the intimate scenes that I have in it so far, though I'm not sure why. I should probably try to see why before I take them out, but I think that, instead, I will take them out first and try to understand why later. For instance, I have never liked describing my visit to his apartment after the basketball game, and I have made it shorter and shorter. I have not minded describing the thoughts I had while I sat smoking in the car.

Vincent happens to be reading a novel that includes the same sorts of things he hopes I will leave out. He doesn't think they belong in that novel either—he describes to me how the woman lusts for the man until she can hardly bear it, and how he consents to satisfy her, though he deserts her again after only a few hours. I don't think Vincent likes the book enough to go on with it.

But I suspect he thinks I should also leave out my feelings, or most of them. Although he values feelings in themselves and has many strong feelings of different kinds, they do not particularly interest him as things to be discussed at any length, and he certainly does not think they should be offered as justifications for bad actions. I'm not writing the book to please him, of course, but I respect his ideas, though they are often rather uncompromising. His standards are very high.

It occurs to me that although I used to go to a lot of parties, I describe only two in the novel and, in the case of the second, only what was missing from it. Now even the word "party" seems to belong to another time, to the life of a younger woman.

It is not that I don't go to parties. But I don't go often enough so that I think of myself as a person who goes to parties. Only a few nights ago, though, Vincent and I went to a reception. It was at a nearby college, for the incoming head of a department. It did not sound exciting even on the formal invitation, but for some reason which he would not explain, Vincent thought we should go. He said we should send back the formal acceptance card and ask the nurse to stay late.

When the night came, it was raining, as Vincent pointed out several times. He said it was supposed to turn colder and asked what we would do, for instance, if we came out of the reception and found that the road was a sheet of ice. He said we probably wouldn't know anyone there, but then he named two people who might be there. He said we would have to change our clothes, but since he clearly still felt we should go, we changed our clothes. I put on a woolen suit and he put on a clean shirt and a tie and an old sports jacket, and we started off through the rain. We were very late.

But the reception was at its height. There was a dense crowd of older men in dark suits, sober-looking younger men, and women in cocktail outfits. There was space only around the jazz trio. Vincent didn't seem to know anyone there, and if I drifted away from him to look at the selection of drinks or the platter of cheese and grapes on a table by itself in a corner, I would glance up to find he had followed me, agreeable and open to conversation, a plastic cup of mulled cider in his hand. We lingered here for a while, then went to look at the fire burning in the lobby fireplace, and then at a reading room in the back of the building. When we returned to the main room, the din of chattering voices was the same, and we still didn't see anyone we knew, so we found our coats in the hall and headed for the door. As we were leaving, a friendly young woman with a name tag pinned to her dress talked to us for a minute or two and thanked us for coming.

I had not drunk anything, and had eaten only a couple

of grapes. On the way home, Vincent said that in fact he had recognized one man and spoken to him, but the man did not seem to remember him. Then he added that it was quite possible some people we knew had been there earlier and had left.

But the strange thing is that because the rooms in the old college building were so spacious and handsome, because food and drink and music were offered, because the young woman with the name tag said good night to us so pleasantly, and most of all because so many people were smiling and talking, even if not to us, a feeling of welcome and festivity still lingers today, despite the fact that Vincent and I arrived there and left almost unnoticed.

•

Madeleine often sensed, through the walls, from her part of the house, that I was about to do something I shouldn't. Then she came and kept me company, talked to me, told me stories, or took a walk with me. At least twice we went to the movies.

She told me how she met the man she later lived with in Italy. She was with another man at the time, a sailor. She was washing the side of a boat which her lover was about to take to Tahiti, when the end of her broom fell off into the water. The Italian, who happened to be nearby, paddled up, fished it out of the water, and handed it back to her. A few days later, she sat crying on the dock. Her lover had hit her in the mouth. The Italian saw her again and felt sorry for her. They lived in Cuba together and then in Italy with his family, where she had servants who did everything for her, who ironed her clothes for her. She said that made her uncomfortable.

I have been assuming that the port in which the boats

were docked was in the city near where we lived, the same port where he would later be packing sea urchins, but this may not be true.

Other friends told me stories, too. Ellie told me about her life with her husband. After she agreed to marry him, she did not like him anymore, though she had liked him before. They went off to a resort town on the Atlantic coast, and there he seemed very short to her, shorter than he had ever been before. Once they were married, they argued. She was very loud and angry, and he was silent and anxious to end the argument, and this made her even angrier. She told me that there might be an argument before friends came to their house for dinner, and the argument would stop when the friends arrived. She and he would pretend there was nothing wrong, even though she had been throwing cheese and crackers around the room. By the time the friends left, her husband would think the argument was over, but the moment they were out of the house, she would start in again.

It is not easy to live with another person, at least it is not easy for me. It makes me realize how selfish I am. It has not been easy for me to love another person either, though I am getting better at it. I can be gentle for as long as a month at a time now, before I become selfish again. I used to try to study what it meant to love someone. I would write down quotations from the works of famous writers, writers who did not interest me otherwise, like Hippolyte Taine or Alfred de Musset. For instance, Taine said that to love is to make one's goal the happiness of another person. I would try to apply this to my own situation. But if loving a person meant putting him before myself, how could I do that? There seemed to be three choices: to give up trying to love anyone, to stop being selfish, or to learn how to love a person while continuing to be selfish. I did not think I could manage the first two, but I thought I could learn how to be just unselfish enough to love someone at least part of the time.

•

I have opened the envelope Ellie sent me and looked at the pictures. I won't look at them again very soon because I did not like the shock of seeing them. I did not know those faces, I did not recognize them. I did not know those prominent cheekbones. I did not know the man who belonged to them. And I could not make myself look at them long enough to get used to them.

Looking at the pictures made me think that I don't really know what sort of person he was, either, because I never saw him from the outside. I knew him for only half a day before I was too close to see him from the outside, and by then it was too late ever again to see him from the outside. I would like to know what I would think of him now.

I have images of him in my memory, fragments of things he said, and impressions, some of which are contradictory, either because he was inconsistent or because of my own mood now: if I am angry, he will seem shallow, cruel, and conceited; and if I am soft and tender, he will seem faithful, honest, and sensitive. The center is missing, the original is gone, all that I try to form around it may not resemble the original very much. I am thinking of some example from the natural world in which the living thing dies and then leaves a husk, sheath, carapace, shell, or fragment of rock casing imprinted with its form that falls away from it and outlasts it. Not knowing him now, I may be imagining his motives and feelings to be quite different from what they were, or since I am so constantly with Vincent, I may be borrowing motives from Vincent. I try to identify a motive, and identify one that could only belong to Vincent.

.

The first time Madeleine and I went to the movies, we drove several towns north to a small theater, a friendly place, warmly lit in the midst of the blackness around it. We saw a movie that frightened us both, about a dangerous political situation.

The next time we tried to go to the movies, it was in the same small movie theater. We were too early and had to sit through the end of the previous movie, then through a dreary short with fuzzy, underexposed still photographs of the town we were in, accompanied by inappropriate music. When the movie began, we were both so disturbed by the opening scenes in a Roman bath, involving white-faced figures in togas, that we left.

I had forgotten him while I was inside the movie theater, but as we drove back down the coast, we passed through his town, and then, at home, pictures of him kept floating between me and the pages of the book I was trying to read.

I had told myself to read books that would make me forget everything else. But I know the book I was reading that night was by Henry James. I can't understand why I would choose to read Henry James at such a time. Maybe I was simply more ambitious in those days. Now I will read almost anything, if it has a good story in it—the trials of a nurse in a large city hospital, the account of an English missionary leading Chinese children over the mountains to the Yellow River, the tale of a woman who cured herself of cancer in a Mexican clinic, the autobiography of a teacher of Maori children in New Zealand, the life of the Trapp family singers, etc. If I am trying to take my mind off something painful, this is the sort of book I will choose now. But then I did not choose books that really distracted me, only books that left part of my mind still free to wander away from what I was reading and search around restlessly for the same old bone to gnaw on.

The book was open in front of me, but I could not understand what it was saying, or if I concentrated hard on the sentences, whose many parts all had to be kept in mind at once, and understood it, I forgot almost immediately what I had read. My mind wandered from it constantly, I constantly pulled my mind back to it, and finally I was exhausted by this struggle, and still didn't remember anything from the few pages I had read.

I stopped to think about other things, people in other places who had injured me. For instance, he was not the only person who owed me money. There was the owner of a small city newspaper who had given me bad checks for my typesetting work, and also a couple from Yuma, Arizona, who had backed their van into my car in a state park. I couldn't forget these sums of money, though I knew other people might feel that a debt could gradually be forgotten as time went by, until it no longer had to be honored.

There was also a landlady of mine, a ruthless, heartless woman who owned many properties in the part of the city where I lived and who had charged me rent for several days during which I no longer lived in her apartment. I thought about the shabby apartment I had rented from her, its large, empty rooms, how the streetlights shone in through the curtainless windows, how the traffic lights at the corner clicked as they changed in the silence of the early morning, how during the day the heavy trucks and vans rattled over the dents in the street under my windows, how she would not spend the money needed to maintain the place, and how she was later murdered in her garage. I thought about the streets I walked through in those days on my way to work, early in the morning, how I unlocked the empty newspaper building with my own key, how I sat alone typesetting ads and news items in a small windowless room on the ground floor.

The checks with which I was paid for this work kept bouncing, I kept putting them back into my account, and a few never cleared. But still I had more of a regular income and more to live on at this time than I would later. Twice later, that I can remember, I spent what money I had until I had nothing left and no other money available anywhere, except for, once, the thirteen dollars that a friend owed me. She paid me back and I don't know what I did then, unless it was just at that time that I had an opportunity to earn some money giving private language lessons to two women. They offered to come to my apartment, but I did not want them to see the place where I lived, so for the first lesson we agreed to meet at a restaurant some distance away. I had a strange lapse that day, figuring that in order to meet them at one o'clock I would have to leave home at one o'clock. By the time I arrived they had given up on me and were in the middle of their sandwiches, with mayonnaise on their fingers. They couldn't handle papers or pencils, or even talk very well.

Instead of making up a plausible excuse, I told them the truth, which only mystified them. There was no time for a lesson after they were finished with lunch, but they politely offered to pay me anyway. I took their money, though I was ashamed. It was just the opposite of what I wanted to do, but I had no other money. One of them stopped the lessons soon after that, but the other, who was wealthier, went on for a few months.

I picked up the book again and forced my eyes onto the page and read. Though the weight was on me, the darkness pressing in on me, I wouldn't look at it, I wouldn't think about it, I held it off a few feet away from me. Line by line I forced my eyes across the page, and with great attention at last began to see the story for myself, though it took all the strength and attention I had to shape this thickness of words.

Little by little, as though the pages I had turned were forming a shield between me and my pain, or as though the four edges of each page became the four walls of a safe room, a resting place for me within the story, I began to stay inside it with less effort, until the story became more real to me than my pain. Now I read on, still stiff and heavy with pain, but having a balance between my unhappiness and the pleasure of the story. When the balance seemed secure, I turned off the light and fell asleep easily.

Then, before dawn, I woke a little. I was still asleep, really, but I opened my eyes and thought I was awake. I was lying on my side. Directly in front of me across the width of the bed, across the sheet, I saw his face, over near the wall. I reached out my right arm as far as it would go and put up my hand to touch his face. His face vanished, and there was nothing there but the wall. Then the pain I had been holding away from me by force rushed into me with an unexpected violence, and tears sprang into my eyes so suddenly they seemed to have nothing to do with the pain or even with me. They filled my eyes, spilled over, and rolled down like glass beads before I could blink, and then, as I lay perfectly still, too surprised to move, collected in the hollows of my face.

During these weeks, each day had the same center—the question of whether I would see him or not, or his car. I drove into the college parking lot one morning just in front of him, and he saw me and pulled in next to me. We got out of our cars and talked to each other. I saw him put money into the parking meter and then I remembered to do the same. Our conversation had a jerky, fitful rhythm to it. He would make a remark and I would respond without thinking, so distracted that what he said registered only on a superficial level. A moment later I would respond a second time, more thoughtfully. He was reacting the same way. Together we walked away from the parking lot toward the college buildings.

A few hours later, returning to my car, I was sure his would not be there anymore, and it wasn't. A strange car was there instead, one I had never seen before, one that was profoundly uninteresting to me, that I found ugly because it was so small, dark, and new, instead of large, white, and old, even somehow nasty because it had nothing to do with me and belonged to another life that must be small and neat like the car.

He had driven away without leaving a word, a note. He had been with me, our cars had stood side by side for an hour or more, and now he was gone again and I did not know where he was. All I had now, though it was a piece of information I valued, was the fact that he came to the campus every Wednesday morning.

The End of the Story

If I did not actually meet him, I might catch a glimpse of him from a distance. He might be standing outside the gas station or walking away from it, his car in the shadows by the building, or he might be turning a corner in his car, sitting very straight, alone or with his girlfriend. Or I might see what I thought was his car and follow it through town or around the campus, and it might be his and it might not. Once I saw an old white car of the same model in front of the supermarket, but the license plate was different. I said the number over to myself as I shopped, trying to remember it: I thought I might try to learn the numbers of all the old white cars of that model in town. But when I came out, the car was gone. All I knew was that there were three others like his in town, one license starting with a C, one with an E, and one with a T.

That night, on my way out to dinner with friends, I caught sight of him from a distance. He was walking through a thin rain to the office of the gas station wearing a blue denim jacket. As soon as we arrived at the Chinese restaurant, I went into a phone booth by the restrooms and called the gas station. A man with a cheerful voice answered the phone and told me that he had finished work and left not five minutes before. I stayed by the phone for a while. The booth, a small, private place within a larger, public place, was closer to him at that moment than any other spot in the restaurant, because I sometimes could, if I was lucky, even though I was in a public place and far away from him, bring him so close to me that his voice was in my ear, his thin voice coming through a wire into my ear like a face inside my head.

On my way home later, I drove past the gas station and it was closed, the lanes of pumps dark under their roof, the empty office and the rubbish in the large wastebasket brightly lit in their fluorescent bath. I drove through a few streets of his town and then headed down the coast to my own. Although I had told myself I wouldn't go looking for him again, when I entered my town I turned right instead of left and drove down by the railway station and went along through the streets very slowly. I had seen an old white car like his there the day before at a time when I could not stop, and the car was there again in the same spot. I drove a little past it on the other side of the street, made a U-turn, and inched back alongside it. I thought the license number was not his, but just to make sure, as though I might look harder and discover that it was his after all, I turned around again, in a driveway, and drove straight at it on the wrong side of the street, my headlights on the front of it. It was not the same car.

When I couldn't find him after circling the town, I grew discouraged, then listless, looking in the windows of one house after another as I passed them, seeing in almost every one the white-dotted blue flicker of a television screen.

Back at home the tough branches of the jade plants poked out over the brick path, bumping me as I pushed by, their thick rubbery leaves full of water, so thick and aggressive they were like animals, there in the dark. A white moon hung in the black sky, three bright stars near it, and a shred of white cloud, and the moonlight filled the terrace where I stood still for a while just looking at it, the shadows very black under the eaves of the arcade.

Inside, Madeleine asked me to guess what had happened a little while ago. I waited. She said he had come by the house. The dog was barking and she went out and

The End of the Story

found him there. He had walked up the hill. He had talked for five minutes with her. Later she saw his car parked in front of the convenience store nearby. She thought his car had broken down and he wanted my help. "He probably wanted to borrow your car," she said.

I had imagined a visit like this many times, including the dog barking. Now it had happened. But as it was happening, I was down near the railway station nosing my car back and forth around a different old white car.

·

It occurred to me that if he did not want to be with me anymore, then when I went to find him, just because I wanted to see him, smell him, and hear his voice, regardless of what he wanted, I was turning him into something less than another human being, as though he were as passive as anything else I wanted, any other object that I wanted to consume—food, drink, or a book.

Yet when I went in search of him I was passive myself, more passive, really, than if I had done nothing, because I was trying to put myself in his hands again, to be a thing he should do something about. Doing nothing about him in the first place would have been the most active thing to do, and yet I couldn't do that.

I felt that my eyes themselves had a place in them for the image of his body, the muscles of my eyes were used to tightening just the right way to take in his form, and now they suffered from not having it before them.

·

The day I invited Laurie to dinner, telling her to bring her flute, I tried to call him, but there was no answer. It was growing dark and beginning to rain. I went out in the rain and walked down the main street of the town looking at cars, turned back toward home, and then saw his car, I thought, go by with two people in it. I looked at it: it was gone in a moment. I could not be sure it was his. I walked past my own house to see if Laurie was there yet, but she was not, so I went on toward the supermarket. If his car was there in the lot, I would not do anything more to find him. I only wanted to know where he was. I was walking down the middle of the road. When I had nearly reached the end, a van turned suddenly into it in front of me and caught me in its headlights. I stumbled into a shallow ditch to one side and stopped there while the van drove on past. Then I climbed out of the ditch. I stood still in my rubber boots and slicker and looked at myself, at what I was doing, a woman my age—something drifting around in the night and in the rain, not so much a person as something else, like a dog.

I walked on into the middle of another road, a broad road that ran steeply down from the crest of the hill far above to the park by the ocean, and stopped there again, disoriented, turning my head this way and that. I looked down at the supermarket parking lot, the last place I would look for his car. It was not there.

I knew he sometimes shopped in that supermarket. A few weeks back, Madeleine had seen him there. He did not look as happy as he used to, she said, but rather troubled. She had thought he would stop to talk to her, but he had headed on to the meat section. He was with his girlfriend. Madeleine had said, "She looks very young—seventeen. Very young. Nice. Yes, quite pretty." I had not seen her yet, then.

I saw her only twice, I think, once across the room through that wet pane of glass and once when Ellie and I were coming away from a movie. We were in a bleak part of town with many empty spaces, driving out of what seems to me now a vast parking lot outside a vast movie theater, passing a long line of small black figures waiting for the next showing of the movie, when Ellie, gazing out the window to her right as I drove looking straight ahead, spotted him and pointed him out to me, standing there in line with his girlfriend and another woman, a fellow student so much taller that he and his girlfriend were both bending their necks back to look up at her, all three of them ridiculously tiny and dark in that sprawling white landscape.

They could not actually have been as small as I remember them—they have become smaller and smaller in that memory, and everything else larger and larger, as time has passed.

Why did I ask Madeleine if she was pretty? How much did that matter? Was it some kind of witchcraft, to be pretty?

But I myself wanted to be as pretty as I could be, in case he should see me, as though it did matter, even though he had always accepted me just the way I was, looking tired, with a few wrinkles. But I was not as pretty as I could be. I had cut my hair too short, my face looked older, more worn, and my clothes were loose on me. Because I was so often indoors during the day, my skin was white, like other things that stay out of the light. Or, when I looked at my face in the mirror in the morning, as though I were looking at the sky or the newspaper, I would see that today my skin was not white but yellow and orange, or sometimes a mottled pink, and my eyes were smaller.

I did not have time to check everywhere again, walking

through the town and back. I sometimes did this. I sometimes went to one end of the town and imagined he was at the other end, and then went back to the other end and imagined he was at the end I had just come from. Since time kept passing as I did this, it was always possible that he might have come to one place while I was at the other.

Back at home, I heard a car stop outside and then the gate latch click. It was Laurie. She did not know that she had so little to do with what was going on here, with me. She must have thought she was at the beginning of a pleasant evening in which she would eat a good dinner and have some good conversation and play some music, and she probably thought I was also looking forward to our evening together. She smiled and started talking right away. But there was a sort of fog over my eyes and I had trouble hearing her. Other things already filled my brain, pressing on the walls of it, so that there was barely any room for anything she said to me and even less room for me to make any kind of answer. And as I tried to listen to her and think what to answer, I was cooking our dinner at the same time.

I could have told Ellie I felt sick, but I could not tell Laurie—she was hungry for gossip, and she was always pleased by other people's misfortunes, because they made her feel fortunate. She was pleased to see others overweight or plain, because they made her feel slim and pretty, though she was slim and pretty enough without that. She was pleased to see others lonely, because then she felt safe from being lonely.

The rain had stopped, so we put the card table out on the terrace and ate there, though it was dark. A little light came from candles on the table and the electric lights under the arcade, but it was still hard to see the food. I had

The End of the Story

not made any bad mistakes with the main part of our dinner, but I had put so much salt on the salad it was almost impossible to eat. Laurie said it was fine.

Laurie had brought a box of pastries for dessert. Madeleine came out of her wing of the house to say hello, and I invited her to have one. She took one, and stood there a little back from us eating it in the shadows of the large shrubs that grew against the glass wall of the arcade. She said a few things to Laurie that had an edge to them I don't think Laurie heard, mainly because Laurie did not think Madeleine was a person who needed to be listened to carefully, and then returned to her part of the house. I knew that later she would make fun of Laurie, for this was the sort of woman whose behavior, whose very nature, Madeleine despised—the glib sort of intelligence, the compulsive flirtations, the prurient curiosity, the lack of compassion. Laurie had other, better qualities, but they would not be likely to appear in Madeleine's presence.

I also knew that while Madeleine would now be sitting in her room brooding with disapproval about Laurie, her face no longer tender and kind, as it sometimes was, but sly and sarcastic, Laurie would also be contemplating Madeleine, and feeling comfortably fortunate compared to Madeleine with her solitude, her strange ways, her severity, her faded and musty Indian clothes, her smell of stale linen and garlic, her poverty.

By the time Laurie was gone, several hours had passed since I had walked around in the rain, and those hours now stood stoutly, as a good protection, between me and what I had been feeling and thinking before.

I spent the next morning working on a long letter to him. Then I stopped, not at the end of it, but because I had become more and more hopeless the longer I worked on it, and at last my hopelessness was too heavy to drag any farther: how weak those cramped black letters seemed, lying there on the page, page after page of them, babbling on to themselves, explaining, reasoning, complaining, pointing out logical inconsistencies, describing, persuading, etc.

I realize now that Laurie must also be the "L.H." I was having lunch with when the skunk appeared among the students and faculty.

•

Late at night, when things were quiet, I heard not only the waves pounding on the beach but often, too, voices rising all around me, first the cat yowling with cries that were almost articulate, then the dog roused from its sleep, sleepy and gruff, and then, if I was reading, I would also hear the words I was reading, and if I was angry, they would be thin, mean, or querulous, traveling in lines across the page.

Trying to sleep, I lay on my side with my knees together and my hands, palms together, between my thighs. Or I lay on my back with my hands crossed over my chest and my feet crossed at the arches. I needed to touch my limbs together in a symmetrical arrangement, I needed to connect everything as much as possible, to feel tied together, and tied down to the mattress. If I lay still long enough, my body would seem to melt into the mattress so that there was nothing left there but a head on the pillow, eyes blinking, a brain in the head.

At times I could sleep only if I sat almost straight up against the bolster and two pillows. I coughed less in this position, and could fight off the disturbances that came to

The End of the Story

settle on my chest. I was less in the position of a person sleeping, and if I had the light on, too, I was closer to a person in a waking state, which was an easier state because it was more in my own control.

I was learning to wake myself up as soon as I began to fall asleep, and to correct myself when I began to dream: This is a dream, my mind would say, and I would wake up in order to start over again correctly. Sometimes my mind would not stop working in the first place.

Or sleep would descend suddenly on every part of my body at once, and my mind would notice this with surprise and wake me up. Or an odd noise would wake me up and first my heart would pound, then I would be filled with anger, and then my mind would begin working again, and go faster and faster.

In the middle of the night the cat, outside, would mew over a kill, then jump onto the screen, climbing and tangling her claws in the web with a harsh racket. Or a car with a loud motor would stop at the corner and my eyes would fly open. Either I lay still and listened or I kneeled on the bed and looked out the window. The car would drive on, and I would lie down again. Though my eyelids were closed, behind them my eyes were still open, staring into the darkness.

If I turned on the light, though it was so painfully bright, and wrote down what I was thinking, that might be enough. Or I read, or I got up and made warm milk or tea and went back to bed to drink it. It was not the drink that helped, probably, but the fact that I had done something to take care of myself, like a mother or a nurse.

And occasionally my mind would stop overseeing and correcting, my thoughts would become unreasonable, as they began to turn into dreams, and I had the sense, then, that my mind was actually eager to change everything from what it was into something else, that, in fact, it was just sitting there waiting for me to let go of my tight control.

As I was falling asleep, he would walk into a scene and wake me up, or images of him would become confused with other images and go on to become part of a dream. In one dream he said to me, "I've never had another lover like you," but then he went away, to work in a café, he said. I followed him into the café, because, as always, I had more to say. But inside, he was in the driver's seat of a small dark car filled with other people, including a very pretty woman in the back seat. I felt betrayed again, that he had lied to me, and that he was with other people. He left the car and went into the men's room. I could not follow him there, so I went into a phone booth. But I did not call him.

Asleep, I was even more helpless against him. Yet sometimes it was a comfort to be with him that way in the night, even if it was only in a dream. Once, he came to where I was, in the dining hall of a public institution. He had changed: his face was lined and thinner and very sober. What mattered to me was that he had come back. There was a finality to it that ended many things besides my daydreaming. It was so final that we did not even discuss it, I simply knew we would be getting married now. I told my mother, and she was surprised, not because I had been on the point of marrying another man, as I had been, but because, as I told her about him, she confused him with a certain black man in show business. In the morning I stayed in bed as though to stay inside the long dream that still lay over the sheets.

All I remembered from another dream was that his vulgarity had not bothered me, though I did not know what that vulgarity had been. In yet another, my mother, old and not well, though still independent and cheerful, needed a companion. She told me, embarrassed, that he had agreed to go to Norway with her if the university would pay him a certain grant twice over.

On another night I was reading a book by Freud, and applying what I read directly to him as I read it. He had lent me three books that I had not given back. He had also brought over, one chilly night, a green plaid blanket that I had not given back. Now I lay under the blanket with two of his books next to me, reading the third. What I was reading was about forgetfulness. I read that for the person who forgot, forgetting was an adequate excuse, but for no one else. Everyone else correctly said, "He didn't *want* to do it! The matter did not interest him!" Freud called it "counter-will." I said to myself that he forgot everything that did not touch him at the moment. But that was not entirely true or fair. If he wished to, however, he could forget everything else, particularly everything he found unpleasant, such as old creditors, old lovers, and other angry people in his life.

After turning off the light, I lay in the dark, relaxed and peaceful, and conjured up his image for the pleasure of looking at him, and for company, though I was too tired to imagine anything more—only his image standing in a well-lit place, against the wall of a room. I had him there, though he looked irritated, but as I began to fall asleep, of his own accord he turned and walked away, out of my sight, as though off a stage and into the wings, and I was startled. I woke up to think about what had happened: I had brought him there, but I had been too weak to hold on to his image and had lost control of it. Even though he was only an image, he had his own feelings, and he was there under protest, and as soon as I grew too weak to hold him, he walked away out of my sight.

•

I still have trouble sleeping. I am always a little short of sleep. If I slept more, the color might come back into my face and I wouldn't have such trouble holding on to a thought, or two at once, and I wouldn't keep getting sick. But it's complicated: if I get too much sleep one night I'm not tired enough to sleep well the next—either I can't fall asleep in the first place or I wake up in the middle of the night and start worrying. So I'm afraid of getting too much sleep and would rather get not quite enough so that I will sleep soundly.

Now and then I am too excited to sleep, because I have a plan to reform something: if not what we eat, which should be the diet of the hunter-gatherers, then what we have in our house, which should include as little plastic as possible and as much wood, clay, stone, cotton, and wool; or the habits of the people in our town, who should not cut down trees in their yards or burn leaves or rubbish; or the administration of our town, which should create more parks and lay down a sidewalk by the side of every road to encourage people to walk, etc. I wonder what I can do to help save local farms. Then I think we should keep a pig here to eat our table scraps, and that the Senior Citizens Center should keep a pig, too, because so much food is thrown out when the old people don't eat it, as I used to see when I went to pick up Vincent's father at lunchtime. The pig could be fattened on these scraps until the holiday season, and then provide the senior citizens with a holiday meal. A new baby pig could be bought in the spring and amuse the senior citizens with its antics.

Nowadays my nights are broken anyway, by Vincent's father, who has taken to rising at all hours. He wanders the hallways, creeping softly because he is so slow, and each time, when I hear the creak of a floorboard and get up, it is unnerving to find him out there barely moving, dimly lit by the streetlamp and the headlights of passing cars, his nightshirt white, his skin pale, his crooked hands outstretched for balance, his stale smell floating around him, a rather kindly smile on his face.

And then the next day, because I am so tired or maybe because of a state of mind induced by something else, as I sit here working I will see, out of the corner of my eye, mice running across my floor, but when I turn my head and look, they are only knotholes in the floorboards.

Tired, I try to make out a word I've written. I can't be sure of it. At the same time, I hear a voice in my head. It is my own voice speaking the word, strangely insistent, though my eyes still do not know what the word is.

On other days, my hand will keep typing a period after a word, trying to end a sentence before I'm ready to end it, as if my hand is trying to stop me from saying what I want to say.

The old man is up during the night, but he sleeps more and more during the day. Even when he is awake he sits quietly in one place, staring into the distance. His company is peaceful, like the company of a cow. In fact, like a cow, he often chews his cud as he stares into the distance. But it was not so long ago that he would grow excited if a visitor came to the house, and stand up, leaning on his walker. If he was asked a question about his health, he would begin to talk about Communism.

I have had trouble sleeping lately because I have been worrying about time and money again. I thought I could finish this in a year even if I stopped now and then to work on a translation. I did stop once to translate a very difficult story by an eighteenth-century writer I had never heard of. It was a silly story about a tryst in a summer house. But I was glad of the change, because in that work, the most important decisions had already been made by another person. I stopped again to translate another story from the eighteenth century, and then a third. Then I realized this was not a very good idea after all, because the year was passing quickly and I had no time to work on the novel. I had to think of something else. So I signed a contract for another, more extensive project, took a large advance for it, and then did not start working on it but instead continued working on the novel. Soon, whether I like it or not, I will have to begin translating again.

Because of all this worry, I began having problems with my stomach. I fussed over it, but I also abused it. I had to have my three or four cups of coffee in the morning even though I knew they were bad for me. I also ate no fruits or vegetables, only white bread and crackers. My health began to suffer.

Maybe I am trying to sabotage this as I come within sight of the end so that if I can't finish it I will have good excuses: a cold over the holidays that grew worse, turning into a mild case of pneumonia; two cracked ribs from coughing so hard; then what seemed like acute food poisoning but turned out to be a stomach flu. The flu lingered and became a general squeamishness about food, but when

The End of the Story

I realized my stomach problems were by then self-induced, they got better and I came down with another bad cold, this time affecting my sinuses.

A silly thought occurred to me the other day as I stopped work, went into the bathroom, and glanced at myself in the mirror. When I started trying to write this novel, years ago, I thought I looked pretty much like a translator but not at all like a novelist. Now on certain days I think I am beginning to look like a novelist. Glancing in the mirror, I said to myself, Maybe as long as I do not look like a person who has written a novel, I will have to go on working on this, and when at last I look like a person who could have written a novel, I will be able to finish it.

If I finish it, I will be surprised. It has been unfinished for so long now that I am used to having it with me this way, unfinished—and maybe I will always find ways to procrastinate. Or maybe I will become too exhausted to go on. But if I do go on, I know I will reach a point where for one of several reasons I won't be able to change it anymore even if it should be changed.

For a long time I told myself I had to write it even if it wasn't going to be quite what I wanted, and I would put everything into it that I could. Now, if I finish it, I don't know if I will be satisfied. I know I will be relieved, but I don't know if I will be relieved that I have told the story or simply that the work is over.

It isn't turning out the way I thought it would. I don't know how much control I ever really had over it. At first I thought I had a choice about every part of it, and this worried me, because there seemed to be too many choices, but then when I tried certain options, they didn't work, and I had only one option after all: many parts of the story either refused to be told or demanded to be told in only one way.

For instance, I used to wonder if I had to use the vocabulary I was using or if I could use a different one or a larger one, if only I tried harder. I thought I should read the thesaurus just to remind myself of words I might have forgotten. Of course there are some words I would never use. A woman once told me with sudden passion that she wished more people would use the word "vex." Only English people seemed to use it, she said. I wanted to agree with her, but I don't really like the word as much as she does, though I might use it in a translation.

But now I suspect that I did not really have much choice about my vocabulary either, or anything else, and in fact the novel had to be just this long, leave out this much, include this much, change the facts this much, have this much description, be precise here but vague there, literal here but metaphorical there, use complete sentences here but incomplete there, an ellipsis here but none there, contracted verbs here but not there, etc.

Two poets visiting the university from England came to stay with us for a few days, and Madeleine and I conferred about the arrangements like two spinster sisters unused to having men in the house.

One was young, the other older, with a little pot belly and a white beard. They slept on the twin beds in the spare room. In the afternoon they practiced their performance out on the terrace.

Considerate guests, they left new arrangements in the house, clean coffee mugs bottom up on the clean counter. They were polite, smiled often, and gave a high giggle now and then—the younger one heavy-lidded, slower, sitting on a stool in the kitchen, and the older one, more energetic, standing there holding his round belly before him, cup in hand or empty-handed. When they left, I found short silver hairs pasted on the edge of the bathroom sink which then stuck to my black pants.

The English poets performed in a room with a glass wall behind them. Through it I could see a small, dimly lit courtyard bounded by a brick wall on which was painted a portrait of a bearded political leader. Behind the wall, showing over the top of it, was the darkness of the eucalyptus wood that covered the campus. In the first piece, the poets read together, and what they read were sounds that had no meaning: they were making a kind of music with broken words, single syllables. And because these sounds had no meaning, they did not stop my mind from going out through the wall of glass, searching the darkness for him, flying beyond the faint light of the courtyard out to wherever he was. Because I did not know where he was, I located him in all of the large darkness, filling it, as though I had to make him large enough to fill the darkness and the night.

The younger poet sat down and the older one went on by himself with a new poem in which words were used. A word was spoken that had meaning, and soon after came another. These words were used in the same way as the syllables that had no meaning, and maybe they were intended to lose their meaning. But they did not lose it for me, and with each name of a thing came a picture, and each picture could be a place for me to be, other than where I was. If the poet spoke, in his English accent, through his narrow yellow teeth, above his white beard, the word "hedge" quickly followed by the word "wall," I was in England, it was summer, I was by a hedge and a wall, and the hedge was fragrant, with an untidy grace to it, and the wall was of irregular large stones, and warm from the sun. I wanted more words, but the poet didn't use any more words for a long time, he spoke only syllables without meaning.

Later, at home, in bed, when I turned off the light, I went on calling up for myself images from the book I had been reading. I wanted to see if I could keep putting things between me and what I might think about. From the book I was reading I took a scrubbed oak table, a pantry, a dimly lit buttery, gray buckwheat pancakes, black sour gravy, a porch, raindrops in lines on the eaves of the porch, and spears of purple desert flowers. The very innocence of these things, of the food, the parts of the house, the light in the house, helped me to fight against him. I lay there with my arm hanging down out of the bed into the current of cold air that ran across the tiles of the floor and I thought of other things, things near me, roads running down to the sea, slopes and levels, a plain between the desert and the sea, flats at low tide, small figures walking to and fro seen from the cliff above. I listened to the tick of the clock, the thrashing sound of the cars going by fast on the road below, and the dim roar of the ocean. But the sound of the ocean was an uncomfortable sound. So was the sound of a train coming through, which was like the sound of the ocean but heavier, steadier, and longer, with a beginning and an end to it. All the sounds of the night, in fact, were uncomfortable, carrying the same associations. Now I had come to a bad place, and when I tried to go back to something safer, when I tried to imagine things in England again, the large sound of the ocean was by then so heavy, so dark, that the hedge and the wall became thinner and flatter, until I couldn't hold on to them any longer and they faded away.

Sometimes, at night, when I had done everything else I had to do, when Madeleine had gone into her rooms, and when the activity close around me, and for miles around me, began to subside, when the silence grew and grew, down through the town, when the darkness seemed to open out into wider and wider areas, giving me all the room I needed, I would sit at my card table on my metal chair or up against several pillows in my bed and write about him. I wrote down everything that had anything to do with him, including catching sight of him on the street or looking for him but not finding him. I wrote down not only whatever happened and didn't happen, but also anything I thought about him. It was possible to relate everything to him. Even when there was no relation, his absence from a situation forced him into it even more strongly. I wrote down everything I remembered about him, even though I could not always remember everything in the right order, or would realize I was mistaken about a certain thing, or hadn't understood it, and would go over it again. Even after I fell asleep, sometimes, I would continue to write in a dream, I would write even the smallest thing, in my dream nothing happened without my writing it.

Since he wouldn't do what I wanted him to do, then I would do something I could do without him. I had written things about him when he was still with me, whatever surprised me. Now I still wrote out of surprise, but what I wrote about him did not go along with other things. I didn't know if writing so much about him meant I had already moved away from the pain, or that I was only trying to. I didn't know how much I was writing out of anger and how much out of love, or whether the anger was actually much greater than the love, and there was a strong passion in me but love was only a small part of it.

First there was anger, then greater and greater distress, and then I would see how a part of it could be written down. And if I wrote it down very precisely, the thought or the memory, then I would often have a feeling of peace. It had to be written carefully, because only if I wrote it carefully could I deliver over my pain into it. I wrote with fury and patience at the same time. I had a feeling of power as I wrote: bending over the paragraphs, one paragraph after another, I was convinced they were important. But when I stopped working and sat back, the feeling of power went away, and what I had written did not seem important.

There were days when I wrote about him so much that he was no longer quite real, so that if I came face to face with him suddenly on the street, he was changed. I had managed to drain him of his substance, I thought, and fill my notebook with it, which would mean that in some sense I had killed him. But then, once I was back at home, the substance seemed to be in him again, wherever he was, because what was now empty and lifeless was what I had written about him.

Maybe I should have been more resigned. If this was the only way to possess him now, then I was doing all I could. And for a brief time, it did satisfy me, as though all the pain was not for nothing, as though I was forcing him to give me something after all, as though I had some power over him now, or was saving something that would be lost otherwise. In fact, I was not forcing him to give me something but taking it myself. I didn't have him, but I had this writing, and he could not take it away from me.

I tried to imagine that what was happening now was actually happening in the past. Since the present would soon be the past, I could imagine I was looking back at it from the future at the same time that I was in the midst of it. In this way I removed it a little from myself and was more comfortable with it.

Certain things I wrote down in the first person, and others, the most painful things, I think, or the most embarrassing, I wrote down in the third person. Then a day came when I had used *she* for *I* so long that even the third person was too close to me and I needed another person, even farther away than the third person. But there was no other person.

So I went on in the third person, and after a time it became bland, and harmless. Then it became too bland, and too harmless—all those women who were not I but Ann or Anna or Hannah or Susan, weak characters or no characters, only names.

So that after it had been in the third person a long time, it had settled into that person so firmly that I could be convinced it had happened to someone else, and take it back into the first, claiming, as though falsely, that it had happened to me.

I don't know why I didn't stop writing about him after a while. I suppose I had written so much by then, and the idea of writing about him had been with me so long, and the frustration had continued so long, that I didn't want to stop before I had finished something.

Maybe another reason I couldn't let go of it later was that

I did not have good answers for my questions. I could always find a few answers for each question, but I wasn't satisfied with them: though they seemed to answer the question, the question did not go away. Why had he claimed on the telephone, when I called him long distance, that we were still together and there was nothing to worry about? Was he ever truly tempted to come back to me after I returned? Why did he send me that French poem a year later? Did he ever receive my answer? If he did, why didn't he answer it? Where was he living when I went to look for him at that address? If he wrote to me once, why did I never hear from him again?

I began to wonder how the things I was writing could be formed into a story, and I began to look for a beginning and an end. One reason I was willing, later, to have him move into my garage was that it would give me an end to the story. But if he asked to live there and Madeleine refused to consider it, it would not make a very good ending, especially since I was not even the one who did the refusing. That was what happened, so I had to look for another ending. I could have invented one, but I did not want to do that. I was not willing to invent much, though I'm not sure why: I could leave things out and I could rearrange things, I could let one character do something that had actually been done by another, I could let a thing be done earlier or later than it was done, but I could use only the elements of the actual story.

•

I have just been staring at a note I wrote to myself some time ago. It is typical of the unhelpful notes I have now and then made. It has two blanks in it that must have seemed to me at the time too obvious to need supplying. It reads:

"Strangely enough, once she had written down x—— it seemed ——. But then that feeling disappeared."

I have come back to this note again and again, trying to get through to the thought that must be behind it. It must have something to do with reversals, things seeming true until they are written down, or true at one time and then untrue later. In fact it seems to refer to two reversals, one that occurs just after writing a thing down and one later, when the first reaction weakens. Of course, I may have written this thought down in another, clearer form somewhere else and incorporated it already without recognizing it.

In ink of a different color, on this same card, I instruct myself, with a certain officiousness, to include this thought with my other thoughts about writing about him. But if I don't understand what the thought is, I can't include it.

I never like losing a thought, but I regret losing this one more keenly than most because it seems so familiar I can almost recognize it. But I know I lose thoughts all the time. One day is always disappearing behind the next, carrying things off with it. I work hard to record a few things as accurately as I can, and even so I get a great deal wrong, but there is much more that slips away.

I take another note out of the box and try to read the top line, but the handwriting is upside down. I turn it around, but the handwriting is still upside down. Whichever way I turn it, the top line still seems to be upside down. At first I think I must be imagining things, or that my handwriting has gotten very bad. But then I see that the bottom line is always right side up: I ran out of room on the card and wrote around the edges of it.

On another card, there is another note full of reversals:

by writing about him, I thought, I was taking him away from himself and doing him harm, even though he might never know it. This troubled me, not because I was doing him harm, but because I did not mind doing it. Yet as soon as I said this to myself I was more troubled, even frightened, and I wanted to ask him to forgive me. But at the same time I could see that this would not stop me from doing what I was doing. These feelings merely passed through me one after another.

I am sometimes afraid he will appear now, or call me on the phone suddenly, without warning. If I am thinking about him so much, won't he feel it, wherever he is? I am having a hard enough time writing this: I don't know what would happen if he interfered.

It is quite possible, though, that if only he had spent just a little time talking carefully to me as it was happening, and listening to me, he might have saved an immense amount of trouble, all this work. The novel might not have had to be written. Because I see that I really can't bear it, and never could, when someone refuses to listen to me for as long as I want to talk. I think I could talk endlessly if only someone was interested. I could probably stand outside the post office here in this town and just talk about some current issue.

I have many strong opinions about current issues. Vincent won't listen beyond a certain point. First he tells me to calm down and then he changes the subject. When we go out with friends I have to stop myself, because I become so interested in what I am saying. This is the opposite of what used to happen, when I was too shy to speak easily and waited so long that the room would fall silent when I finally spoke. Then what I said was not interesting, because it was always the safest thing to say. Now I'm afraid that when I have to stop talking, at what should be the end of the novel, I will not want to stop.

Occasionally a friend like Ellie has been generous enough to listen to me for a very long time, even though I could see her face grow more and more exhausted. For many years after I returned East, Ellie lived near enough so that I could call her cheaply and go visit her, even after I moved out of the city. Now she is gone and I miss her. But the strange thing is that when she told me she was leaving, it did not bother me. Maybe it seemed so right for her at that point in her life that I could not be disturbed by it, or maybe I thought I would see her almost as often. Then again, maybe I thought she had to leave so that I could finish the novel on my own. It is not that what she decides to do in her life depends on what I may happen to be doing, or that she has been helping me with the novel, except in the beginning, when I gave her the first pages to read. But the feeling persists anyway: I had reached a certain point with it, and had to continue on my own, so Ellie moved away and left me to it.

Certain friends, the ones with the strongest moral principles, were now keeping me company even when they were absent. Their voices had become voices in my head, because I had been listening to them so hard. I now let them decide things I couldn't decide for myself, and stop me from doing things I shouldn't do. "Stop!" the voices would say, shocked. "You can't do *that!*"

I said to myself that I would be alone now, and this thought was a secure place. Something in me seemed dead, or numbed, and I was glad to feel nothing, or very little, just as, at other times, I had been glad to feel something, even if it was pain.

I did not see myself particularly as a woman. I did not feel that I had any particular gender. But in a restaurant one day, where I sat with my foot in its sandal up on the edge of a chair, a stranger came over to talk to me and went back to his seat and then later, on his way out, passed me and leaned down to touch my bare toes. In my surprise, I was forced out of one way of being and into another. When I returned to the first way of being, I was not quite the same.

I was forced to remember there was something in me besides this mind working so hard and so monotonously, and that this body could appear to be not just for the use of this mind, to be alone with it for long periods of time, that this body and this mind could be social things.

In Ellie's health club, one afternoon, I sat on a tiled step in a bath of warm water and looked at all the different bodies of women around me, of different shapes and proportions. Some had small, flat breasts, and some heavy breasts that hung down toward their bellies. Some had round, sloping shoulders, and some had straight, bony shoulders. Some had plump, curved backs and square, dimpled buttocks, and some had narrow, straight backs and round buttocks. What surprised me most, about some women, was that the areoles of their nipples were so large and so dark, or so small and so pale as to be nearly invisible, and then, about others, that their pubic hair grew so far up their bellies, or was not dark but blond, or red.

In fact, all these other bodies were surprising to me if they were not like my own, as they came in an unending succession around one corner or another, out of the shower stalls, out of the steam room, down the tiled steps into the water, up the steps out of the water. And all these others seemed more fully sexual to me than my own, simply because I was accustomed to my own and because I used it for so many things that were not sexual. Though my breasts were always there under my shirt, most of the time they merely accompanied me as I walked through the town, or shopped, or drove the car, or stood holding a drink or a plate of food at a party. If I sat at my table working, my body merely supported me, my buttocks pressed into the chair seat, my legs and feet bracing me on either side of the chair, or stretched out in front of me, or crossed under me, my breasts resting on the tabletop as I grew tired and leaned on my elbow, my rib cage against the table edge. When my body stopped being merely useful and became what was supposed to be a sexual thing, this change sometimes appeared odd to me, and arbitrary.

After an evening spent in my room in the company of a few people, a man stayed behind when the others left, and then stayed on. He was a kind and gentle man, I thought, and I thought it would be a comforting thing for me to be with him and also a pleasure, but it was not either pleasant or unpleasant, in the end, just something to watch and wait out. This was not the man I was used to, and when I touched this body I had not known before, each part of him was a shock to my hand, which had known a different shape for each part: his buttocks were smaller and flatter, his thighs bonier, and on and on—wherever my hand reached for something, it was not familiar.

This man gave me instructions, though gently, and I lay there thinking that it was beginning to seem like a distant, mechanical operation. There was so much glass in the way, I thought, as though I had my glasses on, there in bed, and were looking at it all too clearly, or as though I had a microscope and were looking at it all too closely, in too much detail, with too much science in it, or as though I were watching him come together with me behind the plate glass of a shop window, with fluorescent light on it all, or as though there were sheets of glass between us, between all the parts of our two bodies, between our two skins as they met, so that while I saw it all so clearly I could not feel anything at all, or if anything, only something smooth and cold.

There was no confusion of our bodies. I knew which arm was his and which mine, and which leg, and which shoulder. I did not lose track and kiss my own arm, or whatever came near my mouth. The smallest motion did not immediately lead to another motion. It was not endless, I did not go more and more deeply into my body and his body as though to go as far as possible from my mind, and his mind, so conscious, so unrelenting. It did not end while it was still in the middle.

He woke up early in the morning, and when I only wanted to go on sleeping, he lit a cigarette and lay there smoking while I lay there waiting for him to be done smoking. Then he put out the cigarette and went back to sleep, while I lay there awake.

Later in the morning, when I got up and he got up, I did not feel comfortable, I did not feel easy, walking back and forth through the room, talking to him, moving around him in the kitchen, passing him in the hallway. Every movement of mine was too deliberate, every remark too planned, while every response of his was also too deliberate, I thought, and I thought, missing what I had had, how it had been so much easier, but then thought again, and remembered that it had not really been very different walking around and trying to talk to him, there was the same feeling, often, of shining a bright light on each word because he was so silent and looked at me so intently. He smiled more often than he spoke, he laughed quickly and readily, most of the time, when he wasn't angry at me, and he was almost never angry at first, though he was often hurt, probably, and he would now and then tell me he wished I would be silly with him. I was not silly, and I was not gentle.

I thought I had been missing him a long time, even though it had not been long since he left me. But at about the same time that my friends stopped asking me how I was, I, too, did not want to talk about it any longer. I woke up one morning to the same grief and felt I had simply had enough of it. It had run its course, I thought, it had been born, lived, and died. I no longer had part of my mind on him all the time, several hours would pass in which I did not have him in my imagination, for company, but only myself. I was pleased, as though at a piece of good news, something that should be celebrated.

But then I said to myself that since I seemed to be cured of my grief, he and I could enter into a new kind of relationship, and in the joy of that feeling I went looking for him yet again. I fooled myself every time, because at such moments part of me became clever and the other part stupid, just as much as was necessary.

This time I found him and he said he would have dinner with me, and this time he did not cancel the date. He came to the house after work, he took a shower, he sang in the bathroom while he dressed as though to keep me at a distance. He reappeared in clean clothes, with wet hair. We went down the hill to the corner café, and after dinner he came back to my house. He did not leave until late in the evening, but not because he wanted to stay with me, only because he had to stay somewhere. He could not go home until everyone in the place where he lived had gone to bed. He did not tell me why. He told me he usually spent the evenings in the library.

We talked about the library, and we talked about the desert, which was in bloom, and we talked about many other things. On the way out to his car, he had his arm around me. He said my house was very nice, and when I did not understand why he said that just then, he said he missed being there. Then I asked him if he would like to go to a party with me. This was the third party I invited him to. He said maybe he would, and he would call me in a week to let me know. After he was gone, I was sure the evening had been the beginning of something different. I was sure I would have more evenings with him. But I was wrong, so being sure meant nothing.

I thought he might turn around and come back that same night, but I was wrong about that, too, and I was wrong to think he would want to call me sooner, before a week had passed.

•

I was in the orchestra of a theater, walking toward a crowd at the door, telling everyone to leave, and around the corner I found him standing still, looking defiant. I woke and slept again, and I was sitting in the back of a taxicab, in darkness, when he appeared suddenly next to me, took my hand in his, and said "It's all right." Trying to fall asleep again, I imagined wrapping my eyes in images of whiteness, white sheets floating around my eyes, and as I fell asleep these sheets became a dialogue in which nothing was said—blank, blank—until there was one last remark at the end of the exchange of silences.

I woke up in the morning to a heavy storm, the sea booming, the earth trembling under my feet, something just outside the house shaking and rattling, the wind wailing and the trees swaying into each other and rustling.

When I told Madeleine about my broken night, she remembered that she, too, had had a bad hour during the night. Her face became serious, almost angry. "I had a chill at three in the morning," she said. "I wasn't really cold, but I had a chill. It was psychological." I imagined, as though looking down at the two of us from above, how I in one part of the house had been lying awake while she in another part was having a chill.

The storm passed and the day became very hot. Across the street, three or four men were cutting down trees on my neighbor's property. I walked past their dented, rusty blue car on my way home from buying groceries, and looked in at the front seat, where a black dog lay on its back, its legs splayed, its eyes open, its long chain looping down out the window and in again.

Inside my house, sitting at my table trying to work, I saw the blue car from a different angle directly in front of me across the street. The sun beat down, baking something outside so that its fragrance floated in on the breeze in gusts. It was the lemony perfume of the jade bush by the fence, entering through the open window. It reminded me of the perfume of his skin, and came between me and my work, and then me and my reading. I wondered again why this had to go on so long.

He was still so much a part of me, inside me, that his body in all its sweetness, succulence, fragrance seemed to lie full-length inside mine. Now, after an evening in which he had been with me and had held almost nothing back, he had withdrawn into his silence again. His terrible silence put him at such a distance from me that he was in another country. I tried to guess what was in his mind and couldn't imagine it. His vast silence seemed as heavy as a cloud pressing down on a landscape that shrinks beneath its bulk, every living thing bending to the ground, continuing to wait in the airless presence of that awful cloud.

During this week, as I waited for his answer, I had lunch with three different men in three days. The first was a classics professor at the university. The second was so quiet and self-effacing I forgot him almost immediately, even though, having no other place to stay, he slept in our spare room that night and the next. I remembered him only months later, when I found among my things a modest note he had left the second night he was there: "Have gone to bed. Not feeling too good." The third was Tim again. When it occurred to me that all three of them were English, I wondered if I could now tolerate only the gentle manners of Englishmen, or if it took three Englishmen to fill his place, or if he had somehow split into three Englishmen.

In this same week, my mother and her sister arrived to stay with us for a while, and the house seemed suddenly full of people, because the two of them talked so much more, and so much more loudly, than Madeleine and I did, and made so many complicated plans, and left their things, their sweaters and purses, newspapers, magazines, pens, and glasses, in little heaps in whatever room they entered. Madeleine felt crowded and went up the hill to stay with a friend.

It was while they were here that I had the worst dream of all, though a very simple one: I was fondling the body of some sort of wild animal, probably a warthog.

.

At last, on the afternoon of the party, he called to say that he did want to go, but added quickly that he intended to take his girlfriend with him. I became angry and told him he could not do that. Now he became angry. I became even angrier, that he had dared to be angry at me.

Over and over again, after I hung up, I imagined him walking into the party with this woman. I saw them standing together in the front doorway, even though the front doorway would have been too narrow. I imagined being violent in some way toward him. But as I sat there in my room, and then stood and walked around, being violent in my imagination, he could not feel this violence, wherever he was. At the time, it seemed to me it would not be wrong to be violent.

Since I spent most of that evening within sight of the front door, waiting for him at the same time that I was talking to other people and drinking, the party seemed empty, though it was crowded. Part of my mind was always outside, on the wide, dark highway floating or gliding down the coast between high gasoline signs, in the car with him and his girlfriend as they sat together looking ahead at the road, the lights of the oncoming cars shining on their faces, and then in the small streets in the neighborhood of the party, where the stores were all closed, the low clouds in the sky pink from the downtown city lights nearby, the tall and short palms dark against them, and the old, single-storied, stucco houses set back from the road on uneven, weedy lawns behind shabby stone walls and rusty iron railings.

I returned from the party in the early hours of the morning. As I waited, nearly home, for the light to change at a deserted intersection, as I kept my eyes on the red light and the green light, surrounded by silence after the babble of voices I had been hearing for so many hours, music came suddenly from somewhere very loud in the stillness and then stopped just as suddenly, and I felt two or three things coming together to reveal something to me. Then there was no revelation, after all, only a blank space.

In the afternoon, I sat outside on the terrace in the sun. Little lavender flowers were appearing in the beds of rubbery sea fig out by the road, and because I hadn't expected this, it was like a sudden gift. Nearby there were larger cups of yellow on another plant, and then on the heavy jade bush that leaned over the fence, those tiny white blossoms with their thick, sweet lemon smell that so often blew in the window or hit me in a wave as I walked in under the trees from the road.

For several hours I sat on the terrace, my head in the shade of a tree, now and then thinking of my mother and her sister at the animal park, waiting for them to come back. It was a long wait. His anger floated over the pages of my book. He had told me it wasn't good that I still cared for him. Really, I thought, he was angry because he had wanted to go to the party. His anger was a childish anger that excluded everything but himself. Then there had been his sudden violence when he said, "No!" to some question of mine.

The mourning doves in the cedar tree flapped and cooed. Laughter nearby echoed off a wall. Either a kite or a bird floated up against the clouds in the far distance.

I missed him all over again now that my mother and her sister were here, as though I had to miss him all over again in every new situation. That evening, I left them in their room and went into my own room, though I did not close my door. I sat down to work at my card table, but only stared at the window. Although it was early in the evening, I was too tired to work and too tired even to go to bed. I moved my work aside and started putting together a jigsaw puzzle instead. An hour went by. The evening was warm, and through the open windows floated the smells of the flowers again and of the cedar tree. Along with the smells came the sounds of a party across the street: bursts of loud laughter, music on a piano, and car doors slamming. My mother and her sister started talking in low voices in the hallway, worried about me, I was sure. Then my mother, wearing a soft robe, came in with the air of an emissary, evasive, hesitant, touching the edge of my table, wanting to communicate something. I did not want to communicate anything or hear anything, and as I barely spoke to her, at last she left.

Now I was too embarrassed by their attention to continue with the puzzle. I took a step out the door and walked away from the house. My errand was to buy some cat food. The road was dark and quiet. The cat was very pregnant and we were waiting for her to have her kittens any day now. We were worried because she was so young. I walked to the store smoking a cigarette and bought the cat food and a pack of cigarettes and lit another cigarette before leaving the store. I walked down the street slowly. I walked to the supermarket parking lot. By now I had done it so often that it was not much more than a habit. The road was the most likely place I would find him, if I was going to find him, or his car. And a dark road at night always reminded me of other dark roads, so that there seemed to be more room to breathe and to think, and more possibilities. Even away from the house, a strong smell of flowers continued to hang on the air, from other gardens. Old people were walking in one direction and another. I saw many cars in the parking lot, but not his. I had never seen it there, all the many times I had looked for it.

I walked back up the steep hill. In the darkest shadows under some trees, away from the lights of the supermarket, a bowed old man stood still, hugging a large brown bag of groceries. When I came up to him, he asked me with formal politeness what was happening: there were so many cars in the parking lots of the church and the supermarket. It took me a minute to connect one thing with another, and when I did, I told him the teenagers one street over were having a large party. He merely said, "Thank you," and turned away up the hill while I entered my own road, darker and narrower. Returning to myself after going out to the old man, I found that most of my difficult mood was gone, as though he had taken it away up the hill with him. His dignity, and the simplicity of his question and my answer, had changed something.

Later that night, after the party quieted down, I heard cicadas trilling rhythmically, steadily, and in the distance a mockingbird singing a song that kept changing in the dark and went on and on, for hours. In the shower, I watched a soaked little moth climb the inside of the shower curtain. The wallpaper peeled up from the gray plaster with its black mildew stains. When I got into bed there were drifts of dark gray sand in my sheets.

I saw him only two or three more times after that, as though the spring, growing hotter day by day, were drying him, a damp spot, out of my life.

He came to the house one evening. He must have realized from the way I stood or talked to him that I was not trying to go after him anymore, because he said a few things, and made a gesture or two, that seemed to invite me back to him again.

Out on the street, looking around at the house and the neighborhood, he said suddenly, as though he had just thought of it, that maybe he could live in my garage. I walked down to it with him and we stood inside it in the dark. There was enough light to see the oil stains in the concrete. He asked me if he was crazy to think of it. It was dry inside and smelled clean. Yes, I thought, he could live there, in my garage, we would fix the electric light, I would make sure he was all right, I would have him there where I could watch him, where I could see him come and go, and he would have to be friendly to me, because he would be living in my garage. I did not know whether or not he meant to bring his girlfriend with him.

But Madeleine did not want this. She said she would not be able to stand it, and no, it wouldn't help him, no, it wouldn't help us either, and no, in this sort of neighborhood you certainly couldn't have people living in a garage.

After this, I thought he wouldn't communicate with me again. Why would he bother?

I was again trying to plan how I would write the story of it, though it was still going on. I thought I would start it in the sun and end it in the sun. I thought I would start it in his garage and end it in a different garage, my garage. Though he hadn't moved into my garage, I would say that he had. There would be a great deal of rain in the middle of the story.

But I was wrong. After a few days, he did call. It was evening. In the background was a violent clatter of laughing voices. It was too bad about the garage, he said. He said he didn't actually need a place to sleep, just a place to work. And he really had in mind the garage, not the spare room. Well, it didn't matter, he said.

Two weeks later he called again, this time to say that he needed a place to store his things. He asked me if he could keep them in my garage. I was just then putting my mother and her sister and their luggage into my car. I must have said I would call him back. I drove them down to the airport. I don't know if it was then that I saw so many soldiers and sailors in the airport, as though the country were mobilizing for a war. They were strolling about in pairs, their heads closely sheared, or sitting silently between their parents, their elbows on their knees, staring at the carpet. I do remember that the music in the background had nothing to do with the mood of any of us, my family or the soldiers, and that outside the window was a black figure, spread-eagled, cleaning the plate glass. Instead of talking, we let our eyes follow the motions of this figure as we waited for their plane to be announced.

He did store his things in my garage, but I don't remember just when he moved them in. I walked down to see it while he did it, he and another man. They unloaded a small truck, I suppose it was a pickup truck.

He put his things in my garage, and Madeleine lent him and his girlfriend a pup tent, because now they had nowhere to live. They slept in the pup tent in the thick eucalyptus woods on the campus, continuing to go to their classes during the day. There was hardly any sign of him through May, or through June.

I saw him once in that time. I was walking past the cafeteria on campus, and he called after me, but I could not stop to talk and he seemed sorry. It was still hard for me to see him. But I don't know if the pain still came directly from the separation or if by then I associated a certain familiar pain with the sight of him and always would, so that even now, all these years later, I would feel the same pain if I saw him, though it would be strangely unconnected to anything else in my life.

In June a fair came to town. By the coast road the lights of the fairgrounds at night were reflected in the water of the inlet, the colors turning on the Ferris wheel and the other rides. From a distance the sound of the Ferris wheel was like a steady wind in the trees, blowing on and on. It was a little colder at night now. The smell of woodsmoke hung in the air over the streets, and around the house a smell like honeysuckle. The spare room, empty and chilly, filled with the pungent smell of eucalyptus.

Classes were over, people went away, and there were long periods of time, that summer, when the town was quiet and I was alone so much that I sank into a peculiar listlessness in which everything became exaggerated, what

I perceived and how I reacted. I was acutely aware of the smallest sounds in the room, in the silent house. Sometimes the sound came from a living creature, usually an insect, and these creatures felt like companions because they had chosen, as far as they could choose anything, to be in the room with me. Any encounter I had with them, even watching them, became a personal encounter.

A beetle with a hard carapace ticked along the top edge of the room, locating itself in its flight. A tawny moth clung to the white wall like a chip of wood. A gray moth flew straight at me out of a closet and landed on my glasses. I walked into the kitchen, saw a cockroach on the floor, and took care to step over it. As I lay reading in bed, a large black moth blundered into my cup of water and thrashed around in circles there on its back. I went on reading. The moth stopped moving and floated, then began thrashing again. At last I lifted it out with a piece of kleenex, and after it had rested, it began diving through my light again, slapping into my book, my glasses, and my cheek. I had saved it so that it could continue annoying me. But for all its persistence and energy it would not live much longer anyway.

The dog kept coming in, so silent that I never noticed at first. I would hear a wet smacking sound and look up to see her lying on the cool tiles in the far corner, gnashing at fleas, her face anxious, her hair stiff and yellow as straw.

Inanimate things became animate, and then they, too, became companions: a cigarette ash glimpsed out of the corner of my eye as it sped across the desk in a stray breeze became a spider running and stopping, running and stopping. A single inked letter in a white margin became a kind of a mite walking up the page. Or a lock of hair shifting on my head was some other small creature making its way in toward my scalp.

Because I was alone so much, I would think about how I could do things in a more logical way, as though it weren't enough just to do what had to be done one way or another. I would make a system of rewards for myself: no smoking until evening, for instance. Or I set aside different hours of the day for different activities. I said I would write one letter every day after the mail came. But I did not do that for long. I did not answer most of the letters that came to me. I would plan to walk south in the early part of the afternoon, so as to get a little sun on my face. But I did not do that for long. Although I liked the idea of a rigid order, and seemed to believe that a thing would have more value if it was part of an order, I quickly became tired of the order.

There were many things I had to do that were necessary, and a few that were not necessary but good, and then others that were not necessary and not especially good, like lying on my bed eating and reading. But even these things seemed to have a purpose, if only to give me some relief from the good or necessary activities.

The solitude itself seemed to pull me down, as though by gravity, into a dull kind of depression. When I tried to think, I could not think. I felt that the constant state of my mind was ignorance. My mind seemed to contain almost nothing. I felt that the constant state of my mind and body both was paralysis: each alternative I considered was so strong I could not act, or each act I considered was countered by an unspoken criticism.

Falling asleep one night, I began to dream, and in my dream I asked what I should do with these two nouns "ignorance" and "paralysis," and then watched as they turned into two different cheeses, one of which I chose not to eat because it was less savory than the other. I dreamed again, that in a dangerous situation I was about to cross the desert on a horse, but heard the rattling of bones or something like bones on the high mast of a ship. I dreamed again, that the beam of a flashlight was following a tiny mouse as it ran in panic back and forth in front of the doorsill.

Sometimes, if I was among other people, I was asked a question and couldn't answer. An essential part of me seemed to be frozen. My brain still functioned, and observed, in a detached sort of way, how I could not speak— could not formulate an answer, could not take a breath deep enough, and could not move my tongue and lips.

Sometimes I could not even understand the words: I could only see them hanging there, as though surrounded by ice crystals, and hear them ringing in the air.

At this time, a friend wrote me a letter. He addressed me with the word "Dearest." But however often I looked at the word "Dearest" and my name, I could not keep the two words together, because they did not seem related. He closed the letter by telling me to "have courage," and I found, to my surprise, that if I simply looked at the words "have courage" there on the page, I had courage that I had not had a moment before.

I kept the letter in its envelope by my bed. Each time I looked at it, my name and address in my friend's handwriting became loud and declarative, because his hand was speaking my name, repeating who I was and where I lived, and in that way locating me more securely.

I dreamed, a few days after receiving this letter, that I

asked my friend to help me. But he was not big enough, in my dream, to help me, he was just as big as he was, he did not extend beyond the outline of his body.

•

A man came to the gate to ask a question, and I answered him over the top of it. He was courteous, gentle, and attractive but for his odd glasses. I met another man in a supermarket aisle. Younger, sportier than the first, he was attractive, too, but for his odd hairstyle.

I saw how recovery worked. I saw how, as time passed, other things came in between, as though a wall were being built. Events occurred and then receded in time. New habits formed. Situations in my life changed.

As long as everything stayed the same, it seemed possible for him to come back. As long as everything was the way he had left it, his place was open for him. But if things changed beyond a certain point, his place in my life began to close, he could not reenter it, or if he did, he would have to enter in a new way.

•

It was at some point now, in the middle of summer, that I saw him for the last time, when he came to remove his things from the garage, though I am remembering it a little differently today. He came through the gate onto the terrace, he was sweating, and he stopped to chat for a moment, asking if he could get himself a glass of water. But I'm not sure, after all, that he was relaxed and friendly. He may have been uneasy in the presence of the other woman, or in my presence, or because these two women were looking at him together. He may have had difficulty smiling, and spoken awkwardly. I remember now that he moved his things from my garage into the garage of a friend, and I heard later that he left them there much longer than the friend had expected.

At first I was sorry he had seen me this way, as one of two older women, especially when I realized it was the last time he saw me. But then I remembered how he loved women of all kinds, older women as well as younger women. He did not love only tight, smooth skin, or narrow hips, or perfectly round, plump breasts, he also loved wide hips, heavy breasts, small flat breasts, fleshy arms, a thick calf, a broad thigh, a sharp kneecap, loose skin under the chin and cheeks, a fold at the neck, lines around the eyes, a tired face in the morning. Each part of a woman, so particular to her, became precious to him if he loved her, more precious than it was to her.

As the summer wore on, people came to the house, stayed for a few days or a week, and then left again. I think Madeleine only said to me, each time, that we would be having a guest for a few days. But the silence was not disturbed. Whether Madeleine told them we did not like noise or they were quiet by nature, these people crept from room to room, handled pot lids gently, and spoke in whispers. Quietest of all was a plump woman in long robes, some sort of Buddhist, who was slow to move, slow to speak, and slow to respond when spoken to. She washed rice in the sink and carried it outside to dry in the sun. When I asked her why she did this, she said she did not know, but she had been told to do it.

With these other people coming and going, Madeleine was angry more often now, though I did not know if some particular thing made her angry. In the heat of midday she would turn on the oven and bake a sweet potato, so that for an hour or two the kitchen was hot and the house filled with the sweet smell. Or she would hide her pot, her pan, and her bowls where no one would find them and stay in her room, coming out only when the others were gone.

·

Months went by in which I had no news of him. I still looked at the gas station each time I passed it. Though I knew he didn't work there anymore, I still expected to see him or his car. Then I learned that the pup tent and everything in it had been stolen and that he and his girlfriend had gone to stay with friends, and that after some time these friends had asked them to leave. I heard they were now living downtown, in the city, and he was working the night shift at the docks, packing sea urchins.

I imagined driving there in the middle of the night looking for him at the docks, by the water. He would be sweating hard, packing and lifting crates, the water would be black behind him, the warehouses dark around him, floodlights shining on the boards of the piers and on a moored fishing boat, and a few isolated patches of light floating on the black water. There would be a strong smell of the sea, of dead fish, and of oil.

The other men working with him would stop for a moment to watch as he came over to speak to me. He would be tired and preoccupied, annoyed at being interrupted because now the night would seem all the longer, or embarrassed that I should see him doing this work, or embarrassed before the other men to be hav a visit from a woman, or else happy to have a break in the monotony of the work, to have unexpected company at his job in the middle of the night, and pleased in front of the other men.

Since I now knew he lived somewhere in the city, I tried to find out what his telephone number was, but he didn't seem to have a phone. He probably owed the phone company some money, because it was during this time that a woman from the company, surprisingly courteous and understanding each time, called me occasionally to ask me where he could be reached. He must have given my name as a reference. I was courteous, too, but I did not know where he was. I heard later that he had not paid his last phone bills and that when he and his girlfriend started another phone service in her name, they couldn't pay those bills either.

I heard something about the merchant navy and then something about a job washing dishes. I heard that he had started a magazine and then that he had moved north and was looking for work again. I seized upon each new, discrete piece of information and added it to what I already knew. Sometimes it was neutral and came to me fairly directly, and sometimes it was distressing and came to me by a circuitous route, first conveyed by a woman he had insulted, who passed it on to another who hated him, who conveyed it to another who was puzzled and disappointed in him, who passed it on to me. I was always curious to learn the next piece of information in the story of his life, and I imagined his end. When I heard distressing news I imagined a bad end. Would I visit him in prison?

I heard all this news before I moved back East. Ellie had not moved back East yet either, though she would go before I did, and she was the one who told me he was married now. She told me it had happened in Las Vegas. The brother of the woman he married worked near her in the library and he had told her. On the afternoon that she gave me this news, I sat in my coat at a long table in front of a wall of books waiting for her to finish work. This was in the Rare Books section behind a locked metal gate. Ellie sat across from me in front of another wall of books. To one side of us, a curtain was drawn across a plate-glass window, hiding the view I knew was out there, of a small canyon behind the library.

After she told me this news, Ellie looked at me across her piles of books and asked me if I was upset. I couldn't say exactly, though as I tried to explain it to her I began to understand: in one sense, it didn't matter what became of him, since he no longer had anything to do with me, but each piece of news was painful when I heard it because it reminded me that now he was only someone I heard news of, from other people, and that there were many things I didn't know about him now, whereas I wanted to believe I knew all there was to know, that what I didn't know didn't exist—that he himself didn't exist, in fact, except as I knew him.

As we talked, the woman's brother, who was now his brother-in-law, worked near us beyond the locked gate, shelving books. He walked back and forth, disappeared among the bookcases, and came out again carrying small stacks of books or wheeling a cart, and sometimes stopped to talk to a friend or answer the question of a stranger. Whenever he appeared, I stared at him, in his dark pants and white shirt.

Later, walking with Ellie toward the elevators, I passed him where he leaned over a desk speaking on the telephone. I stared again at what I could see of him, his body and the side of his face, as though it were important to notice whatever I could about him. I was acutely aware of the way in which he and I were related, but if he had looked around at me now, he would have seen only a woman he did not know.

But this marriage didn't actually change anything for me in the way I went on thinking of him, watching for him, searching for him, with a part of my mind anyway, while another part had moved on, away from him. I don't know whether it was because searching for him had become such a habit by now, or because I thought he might marry a woman as easily as he might ask me if he could live in my garage, for the sake of convenience.

When spring came around again, he sent me that poem in French, and for once I could be sure that although I did not know it, he had been thinking of me.

•

Things did change, and as more time went by, more things changed. The young cat had her kittens. Madeleine kept them on the floor of her closet. They were anemic from flea bites, and although Madeleine cared for them tenderly, either she did not know the right thing to do or she was not willing to do it, and most of them died while they were still tiny. We buried them, one by one, in the red earth of the yard under a large pine tree at the side of the house. When Madeleine moved away, the cat stayed behind, but lived outdoors on her own, fed by neighbors.

We had to leave the house because the owner was planning to remodel it and move back in with her family of stepchildren. I left before Madeleine, and went to an apartment complex for married students rather like a military compound. The smells were different, the sounds were different. There was open country and a canyon nearby, with sage on the slopes, crows overhead, a yellow bulldozer at the bottom of it, and I would come indoors from the canyon with my skin smelling of sage and yellow dust on my clothes and under my fingernails. Yellow dust covered the inside of the apartment, which smelled of straw from the mats on the floor. I heard the crows cawing in the canyon and tennis players calling out on the courts across the street as their balls pocked over and over. I heard the voices and thumps of families on the other sides of the walls, snatches of opera like mosquitoes whining, water running, and something like applause, almost constant, and then in the bathroom, something like a whisper or a moan, and, during a rainstorm, water blowing across the flat roof and pebbles rustling as they rolled in the water. I stayed in this place for a few months.

After Madeleine moved out, she lived in one house or cottage after another. She seemed to be housesitting or caretaking. Then, for a while, after I went back East, she sent me letters in which she said she was not living anywhere, though I did not know what she meant. I always wrote to her at the same post office box number. I visited her only once, when she was in another spacious and handsome house at the top of the hill above our town. That was where the dog, who was very old by then, finally died. Madeleine wrote to me about the death and said that the spirit of the dog was always near her.

After Madeleine left, the house was enlarged. She repeated to me angrily in several different letters that the handsome jade bushes had been cut down. One letter I had from her enclosed a photograph of a necklace she had made. She was wearing the necklace in the picture, I could see her shoulders, but she had cut her face out of it. She told me in the letter that she was living with the cat again, but that she did not like the cat, or any cat. When I wrote back asking for a picture of her that included her face, she sent me three in which she was holding the cat out in front of her at arm's length toward the camera. The cat, who looked angry, was very large by now.

During the time when the telephone company used to call me, a new, wide bridge was built beside the old narrow one I used to cross toward the racetrack and the fairgrounds. After it was finished and in use, the old one was closed off, then dismantled and removed. I realized that in a few years no one would know it had been there. And if houses were built on the mud flats, as I was sure they would be, everyone would forget that the flats had been bare and brown and that during the fair every year people had parked there, bumping over the ruts.

The friends who gave the last party I invited him to moved away not long after, so that what I have been imagining, the living room where the party was held, and the front door through which I kept thinking he would come with his girlfriend, as vivid and present to me as if I were still standing there, have changed in a way I can't imagine, in the hands of other tenants. In fact, not only these friends but almost all the other friends I had in that place have also moved by now, either away from that city and those neighboring towns or out of whatever house they were living in when I knew them there, and some of them I have not visited since, so that I have to imagine those familiar faces within the walls of houses I have never seen.

The living room in which the party took place while I waited all evening for him to appear belongs to the same house in whose back yard the other party took place months earlier, after his reading, in the shade of a lime tree with airplanes flying overhead. But because these two parties were so far apart in time and so different in mood, for me, I find it difficult to bring them close enough together to be located on the same plot of land. He and I entered that back yard party through a gate at the side of the house, without going into the house itself. When we went indoors to get another beer from the refrigerator, we went up a short flight of wooden steps through the back door into the kitchen. Most of the kitchen, though, is not part of my memory of that afternoon but of other visits to the house in which I went to the refrigerator for another beer or looked for a paper towel and didn't find one or washed some lettuce in a sink that was already full of pots and dishes. That day we did not go on into the dining room, which belongs to other memories, of one evening, or maybe two, spent playing a word game at the large dining table, and of a birthday party at which one of the table legs gave way suddenly and the birthday cake either threatened to slide off and fall onto the floor or actually did.

These memories are sometimes correct, I know, but sometimes confused, a table in the wrong room, though I keep moving it back where it belongs, a bookcase gone and another in its place, a light shining where it never shone, a sink shifting a foot from where it was, even, in one memory, an entire wall absent in order to make the room twice as large. But there is always the same food in the cupboards and on the counters, the same din of voices, and the same shadowy figures of people moving just out of my direct sight.

He might say it was not true that I invited him to that party. He might say he was invited by the people giving the party. I was presuming too much to say he should not come with his girlfriend. He was thinking of my feelings, in the end, when he stayed away.

He could be right. What I remember may be wrong. I have been trying to tell the story as accurately as I can, but I may be mistaken about some of it, and I know I have left things out and added things, both deliberately and accidentally. In fact, he may think that many parts of this story are wrong, not only the facts, but also my interpretations. But there was only what I saw, what he saw, and what other people saw, if they gave it any attention. A handful of them, still, must remember some of this, and if I mentioned it to them they would almost certainly make a remark about it that would show it in an entirely different light or remind me of a horrifying or absurd thing I had forgotten, something that would force me to change everything I have said, if only slightly, if it were not too late.

There are some inconsistencies. I say he was open to me, and I say he was closed to me. I say he was silent with me, and that he was talkative. That he was modest, and arrogant. That I knew him well, and that I did not understand him. I say I needed to see friends, and that I was alone a great deal. That I needed to move very fast, and that I often lay in bed unwilling to move at all. Either all these things were true at different times or I remember them differently depending on my mood now.

•

I will want to show the novel to someone before I say it is finished. I may show it to Ellie, even though she knows most of the story already. I will show it to Vincent, but not until I have shown it to someone else who says it is finished. I can't show it to anyone until I think it is finished

The End of the Story

myself. And before I show it, I will have to guess what its weak points may be, so that I won't be taken by surprise.

When Vincent asked me who I was planning to show it to, I mentioned a few names, and he said, "Aren't you going to show it to any men?" I added another name to the list, because I had not intended to exclude men.

•

The last piece of news I heard of him a few months ago, from Ellie, was that he turned up unexpectedly, well dressed or at least formally dressed, in the office of a mutual friend of ours in the city. I don't remember why he appeared there. I don't know if Ellie knew and told me or if Ellie did not know. I think it had to do with an odd request, either for a favor or for information. He was working at a hotel at the time.

Now that Ellie is living in the Southwest, she will be less in touch with mutual friends and I will be less likely to hear anything more about him.

•

The sun is sitting on top of a hill that I can see beyond the back yard out my bedroom window. If he is on this coast, he may be ending a day's work just now, since many kinds of work end at five o'clock, or he may be ending something else, like an afternoon of reading in his room. He may be preparing to go out and take a walk in city streets older than the streets on that other coast.

He could just as well be on the other coast, but the very fact that it is two o'clock there, a time of day I don't like, makes that seem less likely.

•

I have not moved the cup of bitter tea from the beginning, so it may make no sense to say that the end of the story is the cup of bitter tea brought to me in the bookstore as I sat in a chair too tired to move after searching so long for his last address. Yet I still feel it is the end, and I think I know why now.

But first I have to ask myself a question that has been nagging at me: Have I gotten even that particular incident right? Did I look at the expression on the face of the man in the bookstore and sense that the man saw me as a vagrant, and did I later articulate to myself what that impression had been? Or was it only later that I searched for that man's face in my memory and looked at it and then at the position of his body, motionless or nearly motionless and slightly stooped behind the counter as his face conveyed puzzlement; that I either took the face out of my memory or returned in my memory to stand in front of that man's face and study it? I know that I must have read more on that face later than I did immediately, because later I had more information—for instance, that he had felt enough compassion to bring me a cup of tea, and that therefore behind his expression of puzzlement he was feeling compassion or was about to feel compassion.

I think one reason the cup of tea in the bookstore seems like the end of the story even though the story went on afterward is that I did stop searching for him at that point. Although I still thought, from time to time, that I might see him around the next corner, and although I went on receiving news of him, I never again tried to get in touch with him by phone or by mail.

Another reason, maybe even more important, is that this cup of tea, prepared for me by a stranger to give me some relief from my exhaustion, was not only a gesture of kindness, from a person who could not know what my trouble

was, but also a ceremonial act, as though the offer of a cup
of tea became a ceremonial act as soon as there was a
reason for ceremony, even if the tea was cheap and bitter,
with a paper tab hanging over the side of the mug. And
since all along there had been too many ends to the story,
and since they did not end anything, but only continued
something, something not formed into any story, I needed
an act of ceremony to end the story.

E
D

DeCesare, Angelo.

Anthony, the perfect monster

$13.14

DATE DUE	BORROWER'S NAME	ROOM NO.
10-18-99	Danny	AM K
11-24	Gina	1
12-13	Megan	PM K
	Jack D	PM K

E
D

DeCesare, Angelo.

Anthony, the perfect monster

Notre Dame School

55 NORFOLK AVE.
CLARENDON HILLS, ILLINOIS 60514

848968 01314 01839C 01884F   001

But always perfectly...himself!

So that's how
Anthony stopped trying
to be the most perfect kid.
He became, instead, a kid
who was sometimes angry,

sometimes sad,

sometimes happy.

Anthony's mother
was waiting for him after school.
"Do you still love me?" he asked.
"Even though I'm not perfect?"
His mother smiled.
"Of course I do!" she said.
And she gave him a great big hug.

"A monster?
You sound like
a normal kid to me!"
said Anthony's teacher.
"Nobody can be perfect,
no matter
how hard he tries.
It's a lot easier
to be yourself...
and a lot more fun!"

"But how can you all like me?"
Anthony asked.
"I said no to my mother.
I ran wild and played rough.
I cried and growled.
I acted just like a monster!"

Anthony's teacher smiled
and led him into the hall.
All his classmates were there—
cheering!

A while later, his teacher opened the closet door. "Maybe I can help," she said kindly. "I tried so hard to be perfect," he said. "But nobody likes me!"

Anthony hid in the hall closet.
Inside, he cried
as only a monster could.
A very sad monster.

Anthony's feelings were so hurt
that he ran out the door.

All the kids laughed.
They laughed
and laughed
and laughed.

Finally, the teacher asked,
"Anthony, do you know
the Spanish word for 'yes'?"
"Growr-rowr!" Anthony yelled.

In school,
Anthony crouched on his seat.
Not once did he raise his paw
to be a helper
or give an answer.

"Sure!" said the boys.

They charged at him.

Anthony let out a growl!

He charged back.

Down they went with

a monster bump.

"Wow!" said the boys.

Anthony raced down the street.

He saw the two Super Splurter boys.

They were playing Crasher Smashers.

"I want to play too!" roared Anthony.

He let out a long, loud growl.
It sounded a lot like
"I don't want to wear it!"
Anthony ran past his mother.

And it happened!

"If I were a monster," said Anthony,
"I could do whatever I wanted to do!"
Anthony got madder. And madder.
"I wish I were a monster!" he said.
"I wish, I wish, I..."
Anthony hiccuped.

Then his mother said,
"Anthony, put on
your raincoat.
It's going to rain!"
But Anthony knew
it was a sunny day.
He didn't want
to wear his raincoat.
Anthony got mad.

The next morning,
Anthony woke up tired and cranky.
He didn't comb his hair
or brush his teeth.
He didn't even button
all his buttons.

Anthony went back to be
And thought about
Horrible Harry Hiccup.

Horrible Harry ran wild.
He growled and he howled.

OWOOOOOO

He jumped
on the bed
without taking off
his shoes.
Horrible Harry was not
perfect at all.

It was about a man named Harry.
Harry turned into
a horrible monster
whenever he hiccuped.
He was called Horrible Harry Hiccup.

Anthony's baby-sitter
was watching a movie.
It was the kind of movie
Anthony never watched.

That night,
Anthony's parents went out.
Anthony went to bed early.
But he couldn't sleep.

Anthony walked home.

He had tried so hard to be perfect.

But no one seemed to like him.

No one even seemed to care.

But the boys didn't listen.

That day after school,
Anthony saw some boys
with Super Splurters.
Anthony stood between the boys.
"Let's play a nice game
like Tippy-Toe Tag," he said.

He raised his hand
when the teacher
asked for a helper.
And he raised his hand
each time the teacher
asked a question.
"Please give the others
a chance, Anthony,"
said his teacher.

Some even pointed and whispered.

It made him feel shy.

But he tried to be perfect anyway.

But when Anthony got to school,
the other kids stared at him.

Then his mother
decided it was chilly outside.
So Anthony bundled up.
"Now everyone will see
how perfect I am!" he said.

On the first day of school,
Anthony combed his hair

and brushed
his teeth

and buttoned
all his buttons.

But even perfect boys
have to go to school.
"I know you'll be perfect,"
his mother said.
"Yes, Mother," said Anthony.

He was perfect when his father said,
"Eat your spinach."
Even though Anthony hated spinach.

He was perfect
when his baby-sitter said,
"Play quietly."
Even though Anthony
wanted to be loud.

Anthony was perfect
when his mother said,
"Wear your raincoat."
Even though it was sunny outside.

But being perfect was hard.
Every day Anthony had to
comb his hair
and brush his teeth
and button all his buttons.
Then he had to be
nice and quiet and polite.
All the time.

"Perfect," said his mother.

"Perfect," said his father.

"Perfect," said his baby-sitter.

"Purr-fect," said his cat.

Everyone said
Anthony was perfect.

ANTHONY
the Perfect
MONSTER

by Angelo DeCesare

BEGINNER BOOKS   A Division of Random House, Inc.

For Maria with love
—A. D.

Copyright © 1996 by Angelo DeCesare. All rights reserved under International and Pan-American Copyright Conventions. Published in the United States by Random House, Inc., New York, and simultaneously in Canada by Random House of Canada Limited, Toronto.

Library of Congress Cataloging-in-Publication Data:

DeCesare, Angelo. Anthony the perfect monster / by Angelo DeCesare.
  p. cm.—(Beginner books)
SUMMARY: Anthony has always been perfect, but starting school makes him feel like a perfect monster instead.
ISBN 0-679-86845-3 (trade) — ISBN 0-679-96845-8 (lib. bdg.)
[1. Perfection—Fiction. 2. Monsters—Fiction. 3. Schools—Fiction.] I. Title. II. Series.
PZ7.D3553An 1996 [E]—dc20 94-26105

Printed in the United States of America 10 9 8 7 6 5 4 3

Table of Contents

Foreword

Every once in awhile, I meet someone who holds an exceptionally bright light within their soul, and Cal Garrison is one of those beings.

Her work with astrology, to me, is amazing. I have known many brilliant astrological authors in my life, but Cal somehow holds an intuitive understanding of the heavens that is a gift to anyone who is fortunate enough to have her give a reading for them.

Because of her natural talent, I felt that if Cal were to write a book on the 2012 (End of Time), it would be of great assistance to humanity during the transition period we are all living in now.

Her view, while moving through and along the traditional understanding for this transitional period around 2012, is unique because of her inner way of perceiving the reality.

There is no doubt, the Mayan Council has accepted the date of Oct 24, 2007 as the date the planet entered the End of Time, which ends in about seven or eight years. If you are serious about your life and how to find your way through the confusion and destruction of the old cycle, and wish to enter into the new cycle of great human awakening, then hopefully this book will help you prepare.

Love is always the answer to every question, and within these pages you will find the female love holding a lantern up for all to see.

May God bless our new journey into higher consciousness.

Drunvalo Melchizedek, Fall 2008

Introduction

I fell in love with astrology when I was sixteen years old—and it wasn't too long after that before I became preoccupied with the End Times. If you study astrology from an astronomical perspective you soon find out that all of the smaller solar and planetary cycles are part of what is known as the Grand Cycle, or the movement of the entire solar system through time and space. If the perfection of this universal mechanism impressed me at sixteen, what impressed me even more was the fact that the world happened to be at the tail end of a 26,000 year process that was due to reach its climax during my lifetime.

This realization pretty much leveled the playing field as far as I was concerned. The way I saw it, if we were barreling toward the End of Time I wasn't going to waste mine focusing on outer things—and before I was old enough to think about having a life, I was thinking more about what I needed to do to prepare myself for the next one and wondering what the Great Shift of the Ages might involve.

This obsession kept my thoughts focused on finding answers to things that weren't taught in school and that nobody in Sixties suburbia was talking about. With no other means to call upon, my curiosity drove me to read—and what I read led me deeper into the mystery. Over time, the volume of material written on both astrology and the End Times filled me with ideas that were so far over the top that for years I played the role of the resident nutcase and/or the witchy astrologer who lived upstairs.

Many times I've wondered if I should have listened to my mother, who could never figure out what I was up to, and whose well-meant advice always ran along the lines of, "Why don't you drop all this nonsense and go get a job at the post office?" But even her words weren't enough to convince me that getting to the bottom of things was a waste of time. I kept it up—and I am glad I did—because if I'd listened to Mom, I wouldn't be talking to you now.

Like so many other things in my life, this book came out of nowhere—and it seems to be the end result of a desire that never knew it had a purpose. When I was asked to write it, I wasn't sure if Weiser had picked the right gal. But if everything happens for a reason, I figured that there had to be a reason why I wound up being in the right place at the right time once again, and why I felt compelled to say "Yes" to the proposal, instead of "No."

I knew enough about astrology to feel confident about the project, and I knew enough about the End Times to know that I could talk about them as intelligently as the next person. The one thing that I wasn't too sure about was how the Indigenous prophesies—the Original Teachings of Indigenous Peoples—meshed with what I already knew. My exposure to that body of wisdom was not only relatively recent, it was shrouded in Spiritual traditions that were totally unfamiliar to me.

As I began to explore the prophesies, I discovered that most of the people who claim to be experts on the subject have never had access to the Original Teachings or any of the oral traditions that are kept by the Elders. This piece of news helped me to see that being well-informed about these prophesies doesn't necessarily mean that what you know has any truth to it. If I had gone into this book thinking that I knew anything about the how the Indigenous teachings filtered in to the astrology of the End Times, it would have limited my ability to examine the connections objectively. Aside from that, it would have been both presumptuous and premature, because what the Indigenous People have to teach us has yet to be fully revealed.

You are about to read the chronicle of a discovery process that unfolded one aspect at a time. Even though I've spent over four decades studying the map, when I got into the territory everything changed. Any preconceived notions fell by the wayside as I went along. Between the planets and the Prophesies what came together left me with a clearer sense of what we are about to go through—and my hope is that what gave me more clarity will do the same for you.

Most of the astrological references in this book include the asteroids. Blown away by Martha Lang-Wescott's research, I began using asteroids in all of my horoscopes back in 1995. The devil is in the details, and it's safe to say that the asteroids cover them better than the planets do. The generalizations you can make by looking at the big planetary configurations can be made more specific if you take the asteroids into consideration. I have come to rely upon them heavily in the last fourteen years, because they reveal details and give more insight into side issues that have so much to do with how events play out.

Speaking of how things play out, as you read this book keep in mind that everything that's written here is my opinion, or my interpretation, of what the stars have to say about the next few years. Any other astrologer could do the same work and see it differently—so take what you can from an earnest effort and keep in mind that it's just one way to look at a state of affairs that concerns all of us.

If you take anything from these words I hope that they serve to remind you of what a privilege it is to be alive at this time. May the light in your heart awaken you to your purpose for being here, and may all of us lift our eyes to the vision of a new and better world.

Cal Garrison
Sedona, Arizona
October 15, 2008

CHAPTER 1

Wheels within Wheels

We all look out on the world through our own private windows of experience. Under the illusion that this is all there is, we live out our lives consumed by the events that unfold and the laws of karma that bind us to a particular set of circumstances. If we pay attention, over time it becomes clear that we are locked into patterns that we don't fully understand. As we age, those patterns recur in cycles. Because we all learn through repetition, these recurrences teach us, not just about the pattern, but about the idea that our fulfillment depends upon evolving out of it.

Caught up in our personal matrix, rarely do we think about anything beyond our selves. Life becomes so routine that our trials and tribulations supersede any thought of outgrowing them. Only in moments of great joy or great sorrow are we prompted to wonder if there is a point to it all. When we go far enough into the question, we wake up to the idea that what we do has an impact on the greater whole and that there must be a purpose to the time we spend here on Earth.

Once it becomes clear that we are connected to something greater than ourselves, we begin to see that the microcosm and the macrocosm are identical—that, like us, the entire universe is evolving toward the fulfillment of some larger purpose. We can only assume that it has a greater intelligence and some awareness of the master plan - but whether it does or it doesn't, the universe is governed by the same laws that keep all of its smaller components operational. It, too, is locked into rhythmic patterns and predictable, recurring cycles.

As this immense mechanism turns on its axis, it appears as if we etch the same pattern over and over again. But the idea that we are repeating ourselves is an illusion, because the universe is in constant motion, spiraling toward a central point at the heart of creation. Stretched through time all this circling forms a helix, a gigantic "Slinky" of sorts—and while each new cycle seems to replicate the ones that preceded it, we evolve as we go, making quantum leaps with every turn.

Because time and space are spherical rather than linear, approximately every 26,000 years, the big cosmic "Slinky" meets up with its tail end and forms an enormous, energetic donut. Within this huge magnetic field, so too do myriads of successively smaller cycles come full circle at exactly the same time. This simultaneous return to Zero Point manifests as a giant step forward in the evolution of consciousness.

Commonly referred to as the Apocalypse, Armageddon, 2012, The End of Time, Doomsday, Judgment Day, and other portentous nicknames, this part of the Grand Cycle is formally known as "The Great Shift of the Ages." From an Earthly perspective it marks the dawn of a new era, or the pivot point where darkness becomes light, separation becomes oneness, and everything in Creation returns to Unity Consciousness—and as most of you know, we are at that point *now*.

.

Coming Full Circle

When people talk about the Great Shift, rarely do they reference anything but its apocalyptic aspect. Isolating one point in a cycle and trying to understand its significance without relating it to the bigger picture is like looking at one frame of a very long film and using that to decide how the movie will end. The truth is, we don't know what will happen—but our uncertainty would be less so if we stopped focusing on the Doomsday element and tried to see this as just one part of a much larger evolutionary process that has been going on since the beginning of time.

What most of us don't know is that the Great Shift of the Ages has happened many times before—and since it's quite obvious that we are still whirling through space, one wonders how we managed to ride it out on every previous occasion. Popular wisdom suggests that, on December 21, 2012, life on this planet will be over and done with. But given what's happened in the past, that fear may not be justified. To fully understand what is required of us now, we need to place the Great Shift within the context of the Grand Cycle as a whole and be open to the idea that the Apocalypse may have less to do with the end of the world than it does with birthing a new one.

By nature, anything cyclical is polarized. For that matter, everything has a dark and a light, or a positive and negative side to it—at least from our perspective. The Grand Cycle is not immune to this law. During one half of it, we are bathed in light; during the other half, we circle around in total darkness, or what many refer to as the Galactic Night. This process of moving in and out of the light has been going on forever.

About 13,000 years ago, we entered the dark part of the Grand Cycle. Gradually spinning farther and farther away from the great Central Sun, as the light diminished, we lost our connection to Spirit and fell into separation. Over time the fundamental truths about the nature of reality got replaced with new thought forms—thought forms that evolved gradually into core beliefs that were too far removed from the light to contain any truth. These distortions were transmitted down through the generations and implanted themselves in the collective mind, forming our reference point for everything.

At the time of the Fall, as the Galactic Night swept over the planet, the Original Truths were handed down to those who were chosen to preserve them. That information had to be protected; without it, we would have no way of knowing how to return to the light when the time came for us to leave the dark part of the Grand Cycle. Too important to commit to paper, that knowledge was entrusted to the Indigenous Wisdom Keepers, who guarded it faithfully, passing it along through their ceremonial practices and their oral traditions for thirteen millennia.

The Three Outer Planets

In the latter days of the dark half of the Cycle, the Universal Intelligence knew it was time for us to wake up. Faced with the task of rousing humanity from its sleep and clear that a full awakening would take time, it sounded the initial alarm by turning on the switch that lit up the three outer planets.

The astrological take on the discovery of any new planet suggests that a planet is "discovered" when the forces that it rules are ready to be seeded in the collective unconscious. Prior to the late 18th century, Saturn was the outermost planet. As the archetype of restriction, male dominance, and death, Saturn held the solar system and our consciousness within its rings—but Saturn was impeached when Uranus, Neptune, and Pluto made their debut. History shows us how much has changed in the last 200-odd years, and it doesn't take much to see that the three outer planets opened doors of perception that were locked prior to their discovery.

First sighted in 1781, Uranus ignited the revolutionary impulse that inspires the soul to break away from everything that restricts it. Its discovery gave us the power to alter our core beliefs, bust through every thought form that keeps us asleep, and awaken to a greater vision of the truth. The great revolutions and the events that restored power to the people coincided with the triggering of the Uranian impulse. The higher mind woke up at that point, too. As the higher octave of Mercury, Uranus awakened portions of the brain that were inaccessible to us under Saturn's rulership.

When Neptune appeared sixty-five years later, it opened the portal to the Spiritual realms. Neptune released us from the belief that we exist apart from all that is, and installed the chip that made it possible for us to see that everything coexists in an ocean of unity and unconditional love. After eons of separation and restriction, this breath of fresh air expanded our concept of divinity to include *all* of life in the equation.

If you want to verify this, take a quick peek at the social movements that began to flower in the mid 1800s. All of them were predicated on principles of oneness and compassion. Séances and table-tapping became popular diversions during this period as well. Intrigued by the idea that the invisible realms were now as accessible as our physical reality, the Spiritualists pierced the veil and in the process dissolved belief patterns that separated one world from another.

In 1930, one Uranus cycle after Neptune's first sighting, Pluto was discovered. Not coincidentally, it showed up arm in arm with Adolph Hitler, Sigmund Freud, The Great Depression, and the atom bomb. Ruling over the forces of life, death, and the secret corners of the mind, Pluto brought us to the gates of hell and unleashed our dark side in the process. Hard lessons in the use and abuse of power showed us what happens when that aspect of our consciousness is left to run wild, unenlightened by any reverence for Spirit. Pluto almost killed us—but what he gave us in return was a deeper understanding of the life force.

In addition to the arousal of these new planetary impulses, the Universal Intelligence used other, more direct measures to support our awakening. Back in the 19th century, the world was blessed with a wave of souls whose purpose for incarnating involved reinstating our connection to Spirit. The Transcendentalists, Madame Blavatsky, the Rosicrucians, Alan Kardec, MacGregor Mathers, A. E. Waite, Rudolf Steiner, Annie Besant, Krishna Murti, Georges Gurdjieff, and even Aleister Crowley are just a few of those who came to pry open the collective mind and resurrect the memories that were buried so long ago.

As the 20th century unfolded, many more great lights showed up to help us shift out of the darkness. If we have even a cursory awareness of the changes we are about to go through, we owe it to the plethora of metaphysical systems that flourished in the 1800s, and to the teachers who later carried that wisdom forward. Our New Age tenets wouldn't have a leg to stand on were it not for those who laid the groundwork for them, long before our time.

Speaking of the New Age Movement, we can't ignore the fact that its emergence coincided with the discovery of Chiron. Another one of those planets that showed up precisely when the energies it governs were ready to take root in the collective mind, it's no wonder that the zodiacal hippie, also known as the Wounded Healer, appeared in 1977. Chiron legitimized the maverick archetype and gave us the ability to go up against the system and burst through almost 13,000 years of programming. Its frequencies gave us the power to change what wasn't working—and because it has so much to do with transcending our primary wounds, Chiron also reminded us that nothing will change "out there" until we rise above them.

In a way, Chiron put the capstone on the work that was done by Uranus, Neptune, and Pluto. While they were the ones who broke down the old paradigm, Chiron gave us the power to dream up a new one. Fond of new, 100 percent natural approaches to everything,

Chiron spearheaded the environmental movement, the holistic healing movement, the free energy movement, and all of the self-help systems that emerged in the late Seventies. Chiron even dared to suggest that the church was all wrong about God. According to him, the power we attribute to God is alive and well, inside each one of us.

Opening our minds to the thought that we are our own personal saviors, Chiron made it more than clear that no Messiah can do that for us. The long-awaited Second Coming of Christ is, in fact, the awakening of the Christ Consciousness within—and the extent to which we can activate and embody that principle has everything to do with how the End Times unfold. Because we're all at Zero Point—it isn't just the universe that's evolving here—each and every one of us is going through The Great Shift of the Ages, looking out upon the events that are about to unfold through our own private window of experience.

Who knows how many lifetimes have brought us to this place? And why is it our turn to be the ones to wake up from a 13,000-year nap looking down the barrel of a loaded gun? Here we are, charged with dismantling the biggest time bomb in history, with no instruction manual and thirteen millennia of false beliefs making the whole process even more confusing. Where is James Bond when we need him?

Perhaps the only thing in which we can take comfort is the fact that we're all in the same boat. And now that we're clear about our position, the next question is: "What if the gun isn't really loaded?" Either way, just three years shy of 2012, it behooves us to examine the Great Shift from as many perspectives as we can, and to inform ourselves about what it may involve.

CHAPTER 2

Searching for the Truth

Where do we begin? The last Shift happened 13,000 years ago. If we have memories of it, they are either gone for good, or they are stored in the part of the brain that we can't access. With no frame of reference for our current dilemma, it appears as if we're expected to ad lib our way through an experience that would seem to require a script, and maybe a rehearsal or two. If we assume that we aren't supposed to know what the plan is, we can only imagine the worst, or hope for the best, neither of which lends any clarity to the situation.

I am pretty sure God didn't place everything else in perfect order without loaning the same order to the biggest turning point in the universal time line. Hello?! If we think we've been left to improvise and fumble our way through the Greatest Show on Earth, it doesn't say much for the man upstairs. Could he really be that careless? Would he take the time to design everything so perfectly and, just for kicks, leave out the instructions for the last act? It just does not make sense. The script for the End Times has to be hiding around here somewhere.

Our belief patterns make solving this puzzle even more complicated. Assuming that the puzzle can be solved, we have to consider that we have been living in darkness for 13,000 years. Our core beliefs were formed in ignorance; they deny the truth to such an extent that it is difficult for most people to even see it. If you wonder about this, try talking to a history professor about the Great Shift and see what kind of response you get! Bring it up with anyone and they'll write you off as a nut-case.

Most people can't wrap their minds around Grand Cycles, planetary influences, equinoctial precession, or the Great Shift of the Ages because these things have not been part of the vernacular for such a long time—we have no frame of reference for them. When they are discussed, their full implications are obscured by belief patterns that make it difficult for the average person to even understand what they mean.

And the idea that the Indigenous People might be better informed regarding what lies ahead than we are—Are you kidding? The notion that an Indian or a shaman from a Third World jungle may know more about these things than civilized, educated white folks poses a challenge to too many mental constructs, too many prejudices, and too many hallowed theories to be credible.

Coming out of our sleep, suddenly confronted with the demand to reverse our perspective on everything, the prospect of supplanting 13,000 years of programming would seem futile—were it not for our old friend, the hundredth monkey. The hundredth monkey theory comes from a scientific study done in the 1950s. Observing the habits of monkeys on a Japanese island, researchers noticed that one of the primates discovered that his sweet potatoes tasted better when he washed them in a nearby stream. Other monkeys observed this behavior and quickly followed suit. Increasing numbers of monkeys picked up on the idea, until monkeys all over the world started washing their sweet potatoes without having to be shown.

The little critter who triggered this phenomenon became known as the hundredth monkey. His behavior gave rise to the theory that as individuals begin to tune in to some new awareness or belief pattern, a critical mass or tipping point is ultimately reached. When that magical moment occurs, another form of energy takes over, transmitting the awareness or belief to huge numbers of individuals simultaneously, creating a natural, effortless, virtually invisible transformation.

That a monkey would be the one to open our eyes to the full extent of our connectedness is both ironic and amusing—but regardless of how the information came through, when he rinsed off his sweet potato he became humanity's Great White Hope. Now considered to be axiomatic in the scientific community, the hundredth monkey theory suggests that as soon as the collective mind reaches a tipping point, 13,000 years of false programming could be reversed instantaneously.

We have our own private epiphanies in cycles. A collective epiphany seems entirely possible. What if one of us is the hundredth monkey? What if one day, something we do inside ourselves allows the rest of humanity to wake up? With that glimmer of hope, the futility factor ceases to be one. This leaves room for the idea that if there is an answer, searching for it would seem to make a whole lot of sense at this point.

The textbooks don't talk about this stuff. Neither do the history books. Trust me; a trip to the library won't get you too far. Embarking on this quest requires an open mind and a willingness to leave the mainstream behind. When you step outside the box, you find yourself in the weird, wild, and wonderful world of prophets, visions, and arcane secrets—before you even know it.

Prophecy 101

Since the Bible is reputed to be the last word on everything, it's our custom to look to it, before we search elsewhere, whenever we need serious guidance. Lo and behold, there's plenty of End Times coverage there! According to the Book of Revelation, the Earth will shake and the sky will fall, but once everything settles down, the sinners will be weeded out and the Jesus freaks will find themselves in paradise.

Having gone beyond our black and white Bible pictures, the Book of Revelation has too much fear and damnation in it to even be plausible, let alone useful. At one time there might have been something to it—but we know what happened to the Bible—and what's left of it is so butchered up, only God knows what he was trying to tell us in the Book of Revelation. Once the Bible ceases to be a trustworthy resource, the next stop on the prophecy train is usually Nostradamus. His quatrains are cryptic and open to interpretation. The fact that they were translated from French into English makes one wonder how much truth got lost in the process. The other issue is that Nostradamus was a physician/astrologer/alchemist who happened to be plying his trade during the Inquisition. The story goes that if he hadn't been so good at curing the Black Plague, he would have been burned at the stake.

While there may be some truth to that tale, what seems more likely is that Nostradamus made a bargain with the political forces that were active at the time, trading his genius in exchange for his life. His affiliation with the Priory of Sion makes one wonder if he doctored his prophesies just enough to keep the Inquisitors from sending him to the fire. If that is the case, it seems foolish to rely on him.

Even if he wasn't an Illuminati pawn, what Nostradamus tells us about the End Times is only accurate up to a point—and since his quatrains do nothing but rattle off a series of events, there isn't much we can take from them; nothing in the way of advice, no tips on how to conduct a fire drill, no concrete information that might tell us what we need to do as we enter this critical time.

Edgar Cayce is usually the next prophet in line for those seeking illumination. Cayce did more to open our minds to the reality of the Great Shift than anyone. By the time he started trancing out, the public was ready to hear about these things. While he gifted us with a Spiritual perspective on ourselves and on our purpose and role in this event, the wheels fell off his predictions back in the 1970s. Like Nostradamus, Cayce offers very little in the way of instruction, and no advice on what to do if you're driving down the freeway and the poles shift. He gives no words of caution that might save us time and trouble.

Deeper Water

If you get beyond the ABCs of End Times research, you'll probably find yourself poring over Madame Blavatsky's Secret Doctrine. First published in two volumes in the late 1800s, "The Secret Doctrine" and "Isis Unveiled" outline the nature of the universe and the evolutionary process in formidable detail. Blavatsky's writings are impressive and the information they contain appears to be credible. Many are of the opinion, however, that the famous occultist was under the thumb of the Dark Forces and that her work is nothing more than a brilliant pile of disinformation. Others suggest that, because the dear Madame was a pot-head and all of her books were written under the influence, nothing they contain warrants serious consideration.

Even if you can get around Blavatsky's supposed Illuminati connections and her Rastafarian habits, you are still left hanging, because her Secret Doctrine takes a lifetime to read and requires a genius IQ to even get what the old lady is talking about. Blavatsky may very well have had all the answers, but only a solitary genius with all the time in the world can figure out what they are—which leaves 99 percent of us out of the loop.

Works like *The Urantia Book* and Gurdjieff's *All and Everything* are filled with truth about the nature of reality and about the terror of our current situation. But the same problem arises that came up with Madame Blavatsky's work; all of these books are so weighty and intimidating that even smart people feel stupid when they sit down to read them. Great information doesn't do much good if it's inaccessible.

Beyond the heavier duty occult texts you'll find that there are endless old and new books on the subject. Most of them hijack their information from the Theosophists; some are based purely on what's left of the Atlantis story. The Bock Saga* has the truest ring to it, but you have to be descended directly from the Aser Kings to get the inside scoop on that body of information. I am pretty sure every member of the Bock lineage knows exactly what we are up against and exactly what to do about it. Too bad they're under strict orders to keep it to themselves.

If you research this stuff, after a while it becomes clear that everyone has his or her own spin on the subject. What we're left with is a crazy quilt of perspectives that agree on some points and differ on others. Like the blind men who set about to describe the elephant, as yet no one has come up with anything that fully explains what we are about to go through. When all is said and done, we end up with a pile of interesting remnants that don't match. With too many loose ends to consider, trying to stitch it all together is enough to make one want to give up on the idea that there's any way to solve this mystery.

* For more information on the Bock Saga, see my article in the February 2007 issue of *The Spirit of Ma'at*. (*www.Spiritofmaat.com*. Click on "Archives," then click on "Feb. 07." Or go to *www.bocksaga.com.*)

So Much for Books

Once you put the Bible back on the shelf, the prophets in their place, the occultists on the back burner, and the catastrophobics in the "open to question" file, there's virtually nowhere left to look. Could it be that we're missing something? It looks like it's time to venture further out of the box—because sometimes the truth is hidden where we least expect to find it.

By the time most of us get to junior high school, we have learned that Julius Caesar burned down the library at Alexandria about 2000 years ago. When you find out that all of the records that were written prior to 48 B.C. were destroyed by the Romans, it makes you wonder how much knowledge disappeared in the blaze and raises doubts about the permanence of the written word.

We have come to rely so heavily on reading and writing that we've forgotten that, long before books and alphabets, there were other ways to convey information. At one time, we communicated telepathically; words and language weren't even necessary. Alphabets evolved when we lost the ability to transmit and receive thoughts in a formless state. And the written word came into being as a natural extension of this. When we remind ourselves that books are a relatively recent development, it opens up the playing field considerably.

While we know very little about the older, telepathic methods of communication, we do know that the mystery schools that thrived before the common era transmitted their secrets orally, from one initiate to another. Down through the generations, those who were chosen to pass the word along understood that the future of the human race depended upon their ability to preserve the purity and integrity of those traditions.

The Druids are by no means the only example of this, but they are perhaps better known for it than anyone else. Having survived the Atlantis cataclysm, they knew better than to trust that anything they committed to paper would be preserved in the event of a similar disaster. It could very well be that their teachings were transmitted orally prior to the flood, but who knows? When the Druids landed on the shores of the British Isles, they either preserved that method, or their experience shook them up enough for them to realize that oral traditions outlive fires, floods, and other people's attempts to destroy the information.

If you read enough books, it soon becomes clear that the Druids weren't the only ones to survive the fall of Atlantis. The Egyptians, the Tibetans, the Mayans, the North American Indians, and the Maoris all came from Atlantis. Studying the correlations between these ancient cultures, what they share in common are their stone megaliths, their understanding of astronomy, and the custom of passing their teachings on by word of mouth.

It has been said that all of the people who lived through the Atlantis disaster knew that after the floods and the fires and the volcanic eruptions, it would be 13,000 years before humanity returned to the light. Charged with preserving the original wisdom during the dark time to come, they kept those memories alive in their hearts, in their minds, in their crystals, in their ceremonies, and later encoded them in the stone megaliths that were built after the Earth stopped quaking. If there is any truth to be found, it appears as if it lies hidden in the stones and in the oral traditions of the wisdom keepers who have guarded those secrets for countless generations.

What has been well protected was kept intact for very good reasons—but every generation of Elders has always known that one day they would be instructed to come forward and share their secrets with the rest of the world. Apparently, that time is now, because the Elders are beginning to speak out—and they all seem to agree on what's about to happen. Even though their prophesies and all of the Original Teachings have yet to be fully revealed, the prevailing wisdom is that all of them remember not only what happened when Atlantis fell, they have memories of what the world was like before the fall. As that information comes to light, it could erase our Doomsday fears and move us to see the End Times from a completely different perspective.

Those of you who are of a more skeptical mindset may doubt everything I've just said. If that is the case, I understand. I would have plenty of doubt myself if I hadn't figured out some of this on my own, through direct observation, *before* I knew anything about the prophesies or the true importance of the indigenous traditions. I was led to connect the dots by something that I can't explain; suffice it to say, it just happened. In order to help you understand what pulled me down this rabbit hole, I want to share a little bit of my own experience, if only to show you that the answer to the End Times mystery has been hidden in plain sight since the beginning of time.

CHAPTER 3

Four Corners Revelations

My interest in Spiritual things got turned on over forty years ago. Caught up in the world of occultism and convinced that the secrets of the universe could be found in some dusty old book, I developed a form of tunnel vision that made it hard to see that they might be hidden elsewhere. After four decades and a head full of information, I thought I knew everything—until 2001, when fate took me on a pilgrimage to Anasazi land.

Plopped down in the middle of the Four Corners region of the United States, surrounded by ancient ruins that held more secrets than all of the books on my shelf, I discovered that the American Indians were the keepers of a body of Spiritual wisdom that I knew absolutely nothing about. How could I have lived so long and missed all of this? For the first few days of the journey that question kept repeating itself—until my mind got blown by forces that defied all logic and by the power vibrating in the land.

The Great Mother is omniscient in this place; you'd have to be deaf, dumb, and blind to miss it. Between the rocks and the sky, her heartbeat resonates in everything, touching some lost chord that is reactivated in her presence. That timeless, unchanging force lives in the hearts of the people who have inhabited this place from the beginning—which may be why, in the face of every attempt to wipe them off the face of the Earth, the North American Indians have preserved themselves and their traditions through all of it.

The scenery in the Four Corners region is so awe-inspiring that you're more aware of the natural beauty than you are of the fact that you're in reservation territory. When you take your eyes off the postcard, another picture presents itself. Corrugated tin shacks, mangy old dogs, emaciated horses, beat-up trucks, and broken-down trailers attest to levels of want and scarcity that make you wonder about the virtues of living in a free country. Reservation territory is as depressing as every other deeply impoverished area—except for one strange twist. Adjacent to every hovel is a six-sided outbuilding, or kiva, that is used exclusively for prayer and ceremony.

My pictures of poverty did not include this—standing out like beacons of light, one kiva after another bore testimony to the strength of the Native American Spirit. At the time, I had no idea what these sacred spaces were for, but the thought that people who lived in such abject poverty could still, after centuries of abuse, remain deeply connected to the holiness of life made me wonder what it was about their traditions that defied every attempt to annihilate them. Whatever they were doing, it didn't take much to see that the Indians were connected to something that had everlasting roots.

My journey to the Anasazi lands introduced me to the Mexican people for the first time as well. The south west territories were once shared by the Indians and the Mexicans. The two cultures thrived in this area for God knows how long, until the Conquistadors and the Catholics came along with their own agendas and manifest destiny gave the United States government permission to seize their lands. It's quite obvious as you travel through the Southwest that the Mexican people and Pueblo tribes were raped right along with the American Indians. The Indians survived the ordeal by holding fast to their beliefs; the Mexicans survived it by giving them up to the Catholics and wound up losing more in the process.

As if my Indian epiphany wasn't enough, thoughts about what might be going on with the Mexicans lit up the screen for months—needless to say, I didn't know anything about them either. Embarrassed by my own ignorance of this part of our national history, I went on a search to find out as much as I could about these people and their ways. Once I got past the layer of Spanish Catholicism that obscures their more ancient traditions, I discovered that underneath it all, the Mexican people are directly descended from the Mayans.

Moving Right Along

Knowing that the Mayan calendar is the centerpiece of Meso-American Spirituality, I went down that road for about six months, thinking that it might shed some light on the original Mexican traditions. Without realizing that my curiosity would lead me to answers that I didn't expect to find, it soon became clear that the Mayan experts didn't agree on anything. Faced with a bundle of conflicting information, I wondered if I would ever be able to make any sense of it. It didn't necessarily answer my questions about the Mexicans, but what it *did* do was reveal how well the Mayans understood the Grand Cycle and the precession of the equinox.

We often set out looking for one thing and end up finding another. As an astrologer, I was so intrigued by the astrological element in my Mayan studies that my original line of inquiry got lost in the shuffle. I could tell from the way the Mayans set up their calendar that they understood exactly where they were in relation to Galactic Center at any point in time. Having studied the precession of the equinox, the thought that these supposedly uncivilized people knew more about it than I did reminded me that they had a complete understanding of astronomy long before Galileo had even figured out that the Earth revolved around the Sun. By itself, this wasn't something any book on the subject couldn't tell me—but I'd been cross referencing and putting two and two together long enough to have the astronomy piece bring me to yet another realization.

During my stay in the Anasazi lands, I discovered that the Indians who occupied that region also had a clear understanding of the Grand Cycle. They used horizon astronomy to ascertain where they were in the scheme of things. Stone slabs at Chaco Canyon's Fajada Butte funnel light onto carved petroglyphs that measure both the solar and the lunar cycles. The entire butte was once an observatory where the Pueblo Wisdom Keepers kept track of the stars. Evidently, the North American Indians understood their place in the universe as well as the Mayans did, because similar rock calendars, observatories, and ceremonial enclaves are scattered all over the Southwest.

It seemed pretty obvious to me that the Native American and Mayan cultures had been connected at some point in the far distant past. If the Mexicans were originally descended from the Mayans, it didn't seem too farfetched to think that all three cultures were once one civilization. Archeological and anthropological evidence supports this idea. These peoples shared the same territory centuries before the White Man even knew that they were here. They engaged in commerce and moved back and forth between South America, Mexico, and the southwestern United States. They had a full understanding of the Grand Cycle and the precession of the equinox. Were they once the same people? Did they share the same Spiritual roots, and perhaps the same origins?

Mine wasn't what you'd call a scholarly review, but, with half an ounce of common sense, anyone would draw the same conclusion. Even though there was plenty of support for it written in stone, there were no written records to support my hypothesis. While this lack of written information created problems, it formed yet another link between the Indians and the Mayans—because all of their wisdom was transmitted orally. This shared custom seemed to indicate that these ancient cultures were privy to a body of knowledge that was older than time and most likely too precious to transmit in any other way.

If these secrets were held within an inner circle of chosen ones, no one outside of that circle would have access to them. This calls all the theories that have been constructed around their traditions into question. The Indian and the Mayan experts couldn't possibly know what's going on with either culture, because the true knowledge has always been kept by the Indigenous Elders. If that information was ever meant to be revealed, it could only be revealed by them.

The idea that this wisdom was reserved for a chosen few was hard for me to accept. I had hoped that their knowledge of the Grand Cycle would answer my own End Times questions. From what I could gather, the indigenous tribes' people understood the precession of the Equinox better than anyone else—and if they understood it from an astronomical and mathematical perspective, it could be presumed that they had a full understanding of how those calculations might translate into real-time events.

It would be a few more years before I found out that all of my observations were accurate.

In retrospect, I see that I picked up a thread of inquiry that unraveled a body of information that fascinated me simply because I knew nothing about it. My addiction to knowledge served as a catalyst, but what ended up pulling me along was the idea that the astronomical knowledge could help me decipher secrets that I couldn't access directly.

I was convinced that all of the oral traditions were out of reach, and that the indigenous prophesies might never be fully revealed. Yet it occurred to me that my knowledge of the stars was the one thing I shared in common with the ancient ones. If I could dive in and do the research, maybe I could use that information to figure out for myself what the End Times were all about.

That idea got sidelined by life and personal changes that distracted me, until it became clear that even those distractions were meant to bring me closer to the truth. A serendipitous move from Vermont to Arizona put me right in the middle of everything. Being a die-hard observer living in the Four Corners made it impossible not to see what had been hiding in plain sight since the beginning of time. Within two years, much to my surprise, the Elders from all of the indigenous tribes came together and started downloading their secrets one at a time—and because I happened to be working for Drunvalo Melchizedek, the man who is the liaison between the Elders and the outside world, I was hearing about these things as soon as they were spoken.

On the day this book was conceived, it was originally meant to be about something else. That plan was changed spontaneously by an unexpected visit from Drunvalo, who stopped by for tea late that afternoon. Just off the phone with my publisher, I was so excited about the idea of writing another book I told Drunvalo about it. At the time, the subject matter for the new book was up in the air. In the midst of my outlining several possible topics, Drunvalo said, "I know what you need to write this book about. Somebody needs to write a book about the astrology of the End Times."

When I heard him say this, I lit up at first, and then withdrew a little, wondering if I was up to the task. After thinking about it, I said to myself, "Well, this wouldn't be happening if I wasn't up to it." So here we are. What follows is an attempt to frame the current prophesies against the backdrop of astrological and astronomical patterns that have come into play since the fall of 2007, and those that will show up between now (summer 2009) and the year 2012.

Hopefully, this book will give all who read it an intelligent frame of reference for the future. Because we are in the middle of something that is bigger than all of us. If it is true that "we are the ones we have been waiting for," it's up to us to heed the signs and pay close attention to what the Indigenous People have known all along. As the Elders continue to come forward with these truths, it seems reasonable to think that what was foretold so long ago may be more easily understood if we drape their prophesies against the backdrop of planetary alignments that are no secret to anyone who understands how the stars interact. If the astrological component has as much to it as I think it does, that information may enlighten us as to how the Great Shift will affect us and our future here on planet Earth.

CHAPTER 4

Indigenous Prophesies

I've learned a lot about indigenous prophecy, but I'd be lying if I said I was an expert on the subject. Too much of that wisdom is still under wraps for anyone to lay claim to having it all figured out. Even though every tribe has its own prophesies, what's been revealed so far comes from the Hopi Nation. At this point, the Indigenous Elders from all over the world are talking among themselves and to those they trust, but none of their prophecy keepers have gone public with their stories—not yet anyway—but within a year it's rumored that there will be full disclosure.

For those of you who haven't had a chance to read the Hopi prophesies, I have included several passages throughout the book. These transcripts have been widely circulated and all of them say essentially the same thing. As you review each one, keep in mind that the whole story is yet to be revealed.

For now, what I would like to do is share a few excerpts, just to give you a sense of how deep the prophesies go, and to show you how these ancient predictions came true, thousands of years after they were made. What follows may be enough to prove that what the Hopi have kept to themselves is so pertinent to our current situation, that we'd be wise to listen more closely to what comes out of their mouths from here on out. Let's start with their description of how it all began.

At the beginning of this cycle of time (13,000 years ago), the Great Spirit came down and He made an appearance and He gathered the peoples of the Earth together, they say on an island which is now beneath the water, and He said to the human beings, "I'm going to send you to the Four Directions and over time I'm going to change you to four colors, but I'm going to give you some teachings and you will call these The Original Teachings—and when you come back together with each other you will share these so that you can live and have peace on Earth, and a great civilization will come about." (Excerpted from the Hopi Prophesies)

Long before their numbers were reduced from 60 million to 800,000, the Indians knew that the Great Shift would come, that "they would see America come and go," and that we would ultimately reach a point of trial and purification, followed by renewal. If you study their petroglyphs, the whole story is right there in front of you. These ancient rock drawings not only trace the path of our evolution, they establish the Hopi as the guardians of the American continent.

One of the many instructions given to the Hopis by the Creator at this time was that they should migrate all over this continent and, while doing so, they should leave their picture writing and clan symbols upon the rocks near their ruins as a sign that the Hopis were the first and were rightfully holding this entire continent in trust for the Creator. In regard to this, they were told by the Creator that a time would come when another race would come upon this land and claim it all, but that these Hopi writings upon the rocks would justly retain and hold the ownership of this land by the Hopi in trust for the Creator. (Grandfather Martin Gashweseoma, Hopi Elder)

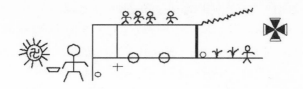

One of the stones on which the Hopi left their mark can be found in Oraibi, Arizona. The petroglyphs at Prophecy Rock tell the story of our origins and depict our journey from the beginning of this time cycle to our present position. Now, it appears that a choice must be made about whether to return to the Original Teachings, or follow the crooked path we are traveling toward destruction. How things unfold is entirely up to us, but it is obvious from the imagery that we are at a crossroad of great problems. What the Native People have always known is that "One day, they would rise out of nowhere, to lead a Spiritual revolution, so all people on this continent would become attuned to the Great Spirit."

If there was a formal "beginning" to the Spiritual revolution referred to by Thomas Banyacya, the prophesies indicate that it began between 1969 and 1976.

They said (and I know there are many tribes that also have this prophecy), "You're going to see a time when the eagle will fly its highest in the night and it will land upon the moon." Some tribes say the eagle will circle the moon. Some tribes say the eagle will fly its highest in the night. "And at that time," they say, "Many of the Native people will be sleeping," which symbolically means they have lost their teachings. There are some tribes that say it will be as if they are frozen: they've been through the long winter. But they say, "When the eagle flies its highest in the night that will be the first light of a new day. That will be the first thawing of spring." Of course, at the first light of a new day, if you've stayed up all night, you notice it's really dark. And the first light, you want to see it, but you can't. It sneaks up on you. You want to see it change but it's dark and then pretty soon it's getting light before you know it.

We're at that time now. The Eagle has landed on the moon, 1969. When that spaceship landed they sent back the message, "The Eagle has landed." Traditionally, Native people from clear up in the Inuit region, they have shared with us this prophecy, clear down to the Quechuas in South America. They shared with us that they have this prophecy. When they heard those first words, "The Eagle has landed," they knew that was the start of a new time and a new power for Native people. There was absolutely nothing strong before us now. We may do anything we wish.

In 1776, when the United States Government printed the dollar, in one claw [of the eagle], if you've ever noticed, there is an olive branch in this claw. They said that it represented peace. The Indian Elders shared with me in South Dakota that to them that represents the enslavement of black people . . . In the other claw are 13 arrows. The founding fathers of the United States said that it represents the 13 States. But the Elders say that it represents the enslavement of the Native people.

When the Eagle landed on the moon, they decided to print a special silver dollar to commemorate that. I don't know how many of you noticed it. The original design showed the spaceship landing on the moon but at the last minute it was changed to an actual eagle. And in the eagle's claws is the olive branch, but the arrows are gone. The Elders said, "That's our prophecy, we have been released." (Grandfather Martin Gashweseoma)

The bicentennial silver dollar was issued in 1976. Within seven days, the Native American Freedom of Religion Act was introduced in Congress. Within a few months, the planet Chiron was discovered.

That the indigenous prophesies coincided with the debut of the planet that holds rulership over the revolutionary impulse is no accident. These things are all connected. If it is true that a planet shows up when the energies it rules are ready to be seeded in the collective mind, Chiron's discovery was a sure sign that the people of the Earth were about to rise up and conquer all forms of suppression and systematic abuse. Anyone who can recall what was going on in the late

1970s will agree that it was an era when the old paradigm began fading away.

All of us were involved in this transformation, but it can be said that the Native American people were the standard bearers for it. Their wounds are deeper, and the wisdom trapped in those wounds has its own destiny. If the Original Teachings are about to be reinstated, and a Spiritual revolution is part of that process, it will be the Native American Indians who will lead the way.

It boggles the mind to think that all of this was not only foretold so long ago, but that the legends remained intact for all that time. Equally amazing is the idea that our collective fate hinges on the wisdom of a people who, after being put down, tortured, and dehumanized, have no Earthly reason to favor us with anything, let alone the keys to our survival. I'm not much of a Bible buff, but if the first shall be last and the last shall be first, whoever came up with that line sure got it right.

Unlike the predictions of the esoteric prophets and the trance mediums, all of the Hopi prophesies have come true. One could chalk this up to the idea that the Indians are more deeply attuned to the invisible realms, or that the Original Teachings, delivered by the Creator at the beginning of this time cycle, were permanently encoded in their DNA. Those things would be enough to explain why these prophets were so clear about when certain signs would appear. But then we remember that the Native American people know more about the stars than most of our current-day astronomers. Can it be that their ability to forecast certain celestial patterns and planetary alignments are part of an equation that guarantees that their prophesies will be 100 percent accurate all the way down the line?

Every time I reread the Hopi prophesies, I am amazed at how clearly their symbolism translates into real-time events. Their descriptions of what has happened since the White Man arrived in North America trace the path of materialism and destruction that has brought us to the impasse that we are confronted with now. As you read the list of signs that follow, keep in mind that all of them were foretold at the time of the fall of Atlantis. This particular excerpt comes from a conversation that took place in the summer of 1958 between a young minister named David Young, and White Feather, a Hopi Elder who happened to be hitchhiking on a desert highway. After riding in silence for several minutes, White Feather began to speak—and this is what he said:

I am White Feather, a Hopi of the ancient Bear Clan. In my long life I have traveled through this land, seeking out my brothers, and learning from them many things full of wisdom. I have followed the sacred paths of my people, who inhabit the forests and many lakes in the east, the land of ice and long nights in the north, and the places of holy altars of stone built many years ago by my brothers' fathers in the south. From all these I have heard the stories of the past, and the prophesies of the future. Today, many of the prophesies have turned to stories, and few are left—the past grows longer, and the future grows shorter.

And now White Feather is dying. His sons have all joined his ancestors, and soon he too shall be with them. But there is no one left, no one to recite and pass on the ancient wisdom. My people have tired of the old ways—the great ceremonies that tell of our origins, of our emergence into the Fourth World, are almost all abandoned, forgotten, yet even this has been foretold. The time grows short.

My people await Pahana, the lost White Brother [from the stars], as do all our brothers in the land. He will not be like the white men we know now, who are cruel and greedy. We were told of their coming long ago. But still we await Pahana.

He will bring with him the symbols, and the missing piece of that sacred tablet now kept by the Elders, given to him when he left, that shall identify him as our True White Brother.

The Fourth World shall end soon, and the Fifth World will begin. This the Elders everywhere know. The Signs over many years have been fulfilled, and so few are left.

- This is the First Sign: We are told of the coming of the white-skinned men, like Pahana, but not living like Pahana—men who took the land that was not theirs. And men who struck their enemies with thunder.

- This is the Second Sign: Our lands will see the coming of spinning wheels filled with voices. In his youth, my father saw this prophecy come true with his eyes—the white men bringing their families in wagons across the prairies.

- This is the Third Sign: A strange beast like a buffalo but with great long horns, will overrun the land in large numbers. These, White Feather saw with his eyes—the coming of the white men's cattle.

- This is the Fourth Sign: The land will be crossed by snakes of iron.

- This is the Fifth Sign: The land shall be criss-crossed by a giant spider's web.

- This is the Sixth Sign: The land shall be criss-crossed with rivers of stone that make pictures in the sun.

- This is the Seventh Sign: You will hear of the sea turning black, and many living things dying because of it.

- This is the Eighth Sign: You will see many youth, who wear their hair long like my people, come and join the tribal nations, to learn their ways and wisdom.

- And this is the Ninth and Last Sign: You will hear of a dwelling place in the heavens, above the Earth, that shall fall with a great crash. It will appear as a blue star. Very soon after this, the ceremonies of my people will cease.

These are the signs that great destruction is coming. The world shall rock to and fro. The white man will battle against other people in other lands—with those who possessed the first light of wisdom. There will be many columns of smoke and fire such as White Feather has seen the white man make in the deserts not far from here. Only those that come will cause disease and a great dying.

Many of my people, understanding the prophesies, shall be safe. Those who stay and live in the places of my people also shall be safe. Then there will be much to rebuild. And soon—very soon afterward—Pahana will return. He shall bring with him the dawn of the Fifth World. He shall plant the seeds of his wisdom in their hearts. Even now the seeds are being planted. These shall smooth the way to the Emergence into the Fifth World.[1]

For the American Indians, the First World War wasn't a 20th-century thing. According to them, it began when the White Man arrived in America and took by force what didn't belong to them. The thunder that White Feather refers to in the first sign is the sound of the guns that the white men used to overpower the Native People.

The spinning wheels in the second sign tell of the westward expansion, and the decimation of the buffalo herds is alluded to in the third sign. Wiping out the buffalo herds was a systematic attempt to bring the Indian tribes to their knees. When the United States government sanctioned the slaughter, they killed off the creatures that provided the Native People with everything they needed. On a Spiritual level, this outrageous act cut even deeper, because the buffalo embodied something so sacred to the Indians that killing it was tantamount to killing their Spirit.

The fourth, fifth, and sixth signs describe the building of the railroads, the installation of telegraph and telephone wires, and the construction of concrete highways, which, at least in their territory, form mirages in the heat that they describe as pictures in the sun. These three signs span a few decades and can be seen to include the Internet and the cell phone matrix that has us trapped in a web of frequencies that are totally destructive to life.

That the sea would turn black needs no explanation because our oceans started dying when greed overruled our reverence for nature and we began polluting the waters with no thought given to the idea that we were tainting the blood of the planet—destroying the connective fluid that keeps us alive. It's no secret. Talk to any fisherman; our oceans are now dead.

The long-haired youths and their affinity for Indian ways are, of course, the hippies, who, back in the Sixties and Seventies, turned their minds toward nature and became adamant about living close to the land. Out of all the ones who aligned themselves with the hippie precepts, many sold out along the way; the ones who didn't are still in touch with that ideology, which at this point seems to have a lot more to it than we ever dreamed.

White Feather's ninth sign can be interpreted in many different ways. Some think that the dwelling place that fell from the heavens with a great crash refers to the U.S. Space Station Skylab, which fell to Earth in 1979. While I don't discount this, I have to confess that I am not so sure about it. In my opinion, what they're talking about here has something to do with UFOs.

Many are aware that UFOs explode and fall to earth pretty regularly. Because the powers that be have an investment in hiding the truth about our extraterrestrial brothers, they go out of their way to suppress any information regarding events like this. UFO crashes never make the headlines because our governments want us to think there's no one out there. Who knows how many UFOs have crashed? Who knows how big they were or what was inside them? If the crashing of the dwelling place refers to a flying saucer incident, there's no way anyone who didn't have access to classified information would ever know about it. When and if there is full disclosure regarding all the UFO activity that has gone on since the late 40s, the ninth and final sign might be less of a mystery.

Part of the ninth prediction relates the crashing of the dwelling place to the Blue Star. When I read this for the first time, it gave me chills, because the Blue Star appeared in the northern skies in late October 2007. Since I don't read the papers or watch the news, I didn't hear about it when it happened. A few months later, however, Drunvalo enlightened me on the subject. When I went back to review the headlines, sure enough, there it was.

Dubbed Comet Holmes by astronomers, this anomalous celestial body showed up at the end of their telescopes on October 26, 2007. None of them could figure out what it was, because it didn't conform to their definition of a comet. Blue in color, Comet Holmes wasn't a ball of rock like most comets; it appeared to be made up of gases. What confounded the scientific community even more was that it expanded, day by day, until it was even bigger than the Sun. On clear nights, it is still visible to the naked eye.

According to the Hopi, "When the Saquahuh (Blue Star) kachina dances in the plaza and removes his mask, the time of the great trial will be here." Even though I caught up with this prediction a few months after it came to pass, I was moved, not only by the fact that I had lived to see it, but because it heralded the beginning of the End Times. Without knowing exactly what it meant, my first assumption was that it had to be an evil omen. Tracing the patterns in my own life since the Blue Star started beaming out of the heavens, I could see that a lot of good things kicked off for me in late October 2007. My sense of purpose lit up like a flame and this coincided with synchronicities that made me feel like everything that kept me from knowing what I was here for was being washed away. I also noticed that my thoughts began to manifest instantaneously. If the Blue Star was a bad thing, its effect on me wasn't bad at all.

Caught between my preconceived notions and the reality of my experience, I 86'd the former and decided that, while the comet was purported to herald a time of great trial, for me it seemed to be a vehicle for awakening. I reread the prediction, which refers to the "Blue Star kachina." For Native Americans, a kachina is a Spiritual presence, one that is not of this world. Kachinas have no evil intent, so even though the Blue Star may have marked the beginning of the

End Times, it was not destined to wreak havoc. I was later told by someone who knows that Comet Holmes holds Spiritual energies that are totally benign—that it is actually there to give us a vibrational boost, to fortify us spiritually and strengthen our hearts for what is to come.

So what is to come? The next sign is supposed to show up in the form of a Red Star. It's been said that the Red Star will fulfill every one of our worst Doomsday pictures—fires, floods, earthquakes, famine, pestilence, disease, death, destruction—the whole nine yards. Without further ado, I'd like to look at what is to come from an astrological perspective and see what the stars have to say about how things will unfold. As I said before, my sense is that, if we know more about what we're facing and examine potential time frames, we can use that information to guide us outwardly, keeping in mind that no amount of preparation will help us if we remain blind to the ways of Spirit.

The Hopi and others who were saved from the Great Flood made a sacred covenant with the Great Spirit never to turn away from him . . . in spite of all the pressures against them, the Hopi were told they must hold to their ancient religion and their land, though always without violence. If they succeeded, they were promised that their people and their land would be a center from which the True Spirit would be reawakened.

The Emergence to the future Fifth World has begun. It is being made by the humble people of little nations, tribes, and racial minorities.

Those who are at peace in their hearts already are in the great shelter of life. There is no shelter for evil. Those who take no part in the making of world division by ideology are ready to resume life in another world, be they Black, White, Red, or Yellow race. They are all one, brothers.

CHAPTER 5

The Age of Light

We've all heard about the dawning of the Age of Aquarius. In the last forty years, that catch phrase and everything we associate with it has become part of the vernacular to such an extent that it is now a worn-out cliché. Trivialized in countless ways by the media, its true significance got buried underneath a pile of claptrap. And because we tend to believe anything the spin doctors tell us, we consume what we're fed and assume that's all there is to know about it.

Unfortunately, most of our thoughts on this particular subject came from the Broadway musical *Hair*. As entertaining as it was, the play turned the Age of Aquarius into a joke. While we may give the producers credit for inspiring us to let the Sun shine in, I'm here to tell you that the Aquarian Age has nothing to do with the Moon being in the Seventh House, and even less to do with Jupiter aligning with Mars.

Otherwise known as the Age of Light, the Age of Aquarius is one part of the Grand Cycle. It takes approximately 26,000 years for our entire solar system to complete its journey through each of the twelve constellations. Every 2000 years or so, we move from one Age to another, in a cyclical pattern that is ultimately meant to bring us closer to the light. Because of the way the Earth spins, from our point of view, this process takes us *backward* through the Zodiac.

Because these big balls of rock aren't digitally mastered, the boundaries between a sign and its respective Age aren't calculated down to the minute. So there's a lot of debate as to exactly when we made our formal entrance into the Aquarian Age. Some say that it happened in 1972. Others believe it was 1987. The idea that it will occur in 2012 is thought to be true by many. In my opinion, we entered the Age of Aquarius between 1998 and 2001, when our Sun finally made its way into a region of space known as the "photon band."

There's as much debate about the photon band as there is about the timing of each Age. Scientists aren't too keen on this subject—and I've heard that the CIA invented the concept just to test the gullibility of the New Age mind. For those who ascribe to the theory that it does in fact exist, the photon band is directly connected to the Source, and it is filled with higher light frequencies that stream out from Galactic Center. These frequencies enlighten anything that falls in their path, expanding consciousness on every level.

Any shift implies a movement into a different gear, and the Great Shift is referred to as such because, whenever we enter this phase of the Grand Cycle, the light pouring out of the center of the galaxy literally beams us up out of the darkness into a state of enlightenment and oneness that lasts for 2000 years. From any perspective, this is cause to rejoice. From the Native American perspective:

The True White Brother and his helpers will show the people of the Earth a great new life plan that will lead to everlasting life. The Earth will become new and beautiful again, with an abundance of life and food. Those who are saved will share everything equally. All races will intermarry and speak one tongue and be a family.

Looking at this from an astrological/astronomical perspective, our entrance into the Age of Aquarius brought us to the thirtieth degree of that sign.* The study of degrees and their meaning is something that astrologers placed a lot of emphasis on at one time. For the most part, those of us who still make use of this interpretive tool lean on the research of Marc Edmund Jones.

Known as the dean of American astrologers, Marc Edmund Jones lifted astrology out of the realm of charlatanry at the beginning of the 20th century. The man was a genius and it was through his work that the science gained the respect that it has today. Back in 1925, Mr. Jones downloaded a series of 360 symbols through medium Elsie Wheeler—one for each degree of the Zodiac. This transmission came in the form of images that appeared, one by one, on the screen of Ms. Wheeler's inner vision. These are known as the Sabian symbols.

I have used the Sabian symbols in my own astrological practice for many years. They are a great tool for getting to the heart of any matter. Figuring that what has served my interpretive work so well in the past would serve me in a slightly different situation, I decided to use them to check out the imagery associated with the thirtieth degree of Aquarius. My sense was that the symbol would capture the essence of where we stand as we cross the threshold into the Age of Light. What follows is a direct quote from my Sabian Symbol book:

> Phase 330 (Aquarius 30 degrees): Deeply rooted in the past of a very ancient culture, a Spiritual brotherhood in which many individual minds are merged into the glowing light of a unanimous consciousness is revealed to one who has emerged successfully from his metamorphosis.
>
> **Keynote:** The ability for the person with an open mind and a deep feeling for self-transcendence to come in contact with higher forms of existence.

---

* There are 360 degrees in the Zodiac, each of the twelve signs being made up of thirty degrees.

The originally recorded Sabian symbol stated: "The field of Ardath in bloom," which referred to a scene in an occult novel by Marie Corelli centering upon ancient Babylon. The reference may well have been a "blind" inasmuch as Marc Jones has stressed his inner contact with a Brotherhood with Babylonian (or "Sabian") roots. [Author's note: Mr. Jones claimed that these symbols were transmitted by a collective soul, or brotherhood of souls whose origins he traced back to Babylon.] A Spiritual Brotherhood constitutes a state of "multi-unity"—i.e. a multiplicity of individuals, if one thinks of the paths they trod to reach their final metamorphosis, but a unity of consciousness and "soul"—thus unanimity ("anima" meaning soul). In this Spiritual Whole each unit is a recognizable "form" or entity if one looks at it with the eyes of personality; but when seen through a unified Spiritual vision or from a distance, the Whole appears to be one single area of radiant light. Similarly, when studied by the modern physicist, light can be apprehended either as a stream of identifiable particles (photons) or as one continuous wave. Whether it is seen as one or the other depends on the point of view.

This is the last and culminating symbol of Scene Twenty-two of the cyclic ritual. This is indeed a fitting symbol, as the number 22 symbolizes all forms of mastery. At any level, it is a symbol of Spiritual group fulfillment—of CONSCIOUS TOTALITY OF BEING." [2]

Need I say more? The symbol goes above and beyond the call of duty so I won't patronize you by analyzing it. But something powerful is confirmed here, and we can hold that thought as we move from the general to the specific and dig into the astrology of what is to come. Let's start with what happened right after the Blue Star appeared.

Pluto

Planets move from one sign to another at different rates. The Moon changes signs every two and a half days. The Earth changes signs every thirty days. Mars takes about a month and a half to move through a sign, and Jupiter spends a year doing the same thing. The further out we go in the solar system, the slower the planets move, with Pluto taking approximately twenty years to get from one sign of the Zodiac to another.

Because Pluto filters its influence through the same constellation for two decades, it is referred to as a generational planet. At the experiential level, this means that everyone living within that time frame is encoded with frequency sets that will ultimately move the gears of consciousness from one level to another. The big social and cultural changes that cause one generation to see things differently from the previous generation are all engineered by Pluto.

To verify this for yourself, all you have to do is look at the mindset that prevailed in the 1940s and compare it to how we perceived things by the time the 1960s rolled around. Pluto entered Leo in 1940. Twenty years later, it was fully ensconced in the sign Virgo. In two decades, we went from God, Mom, and apple pie to a whole new set of thought forms that basically denied all three of those things. If any specific planet can be held responsible for that shift in consciousness, most astrologers would agree that it was Pluto.

For reasons that I can't explain, the outer planets have begun to move faster in the last forty years. Pluto's twenty year cycle is now twelve years long and it has held steady at that rate since 1971. If this planet governs the expansion of consciousness, it's safe to say that things have accelerated to the point where it seems as if it's taking less time for us to get the picture.

On January 26, 2008, exactly three months after the Blue Star appeared, Pluto crossed the celestial boundary that separates Sagittarius from Capricorn. Its ingress into a new sign marked the onset of changes that will take sixteen years to complete. To help you get a sense of what this may involve, consider what I said in an article I wrote in December 2007 on the subject of Pluto's entrance into Capricorn:

This transit is about to inform us with markedly different frequencies—and if we are receptive to those vibrations, our primary coding will be infused with new thought forms that will alter our perceptions of who we are in the world. To better understand what this could mean for us, it might help to look at what happened the last time Pluto entered the sign, Capricorn.

With an orbital cycle of approximately 275 years, Pluto hasn't been in this region of space since 1733. The history books tell us that the seeds of the American Revolution were planted around that time. It was then that our country declared its independence from the British crown and established what everyone thought would be a democracy. Playing its usual trick, over time the Law of Polarity managed to turn one thing into its opposite. Two hundred and seventy-five years later we are faced with the fact that what evolved out of the desire for life, liberty, and the pursuit of happiness became a tightly controlled, fascist dictatorship.

It's safe to assume that the revolutionary Spirit that followed Pluto into its last journey through Capricorn will be part of this next go-round. These new frequency sets will move us to re-examine our relationship to authority in all its ramifications. Astrological sources bear this out. Every good astrology book will tell you that whenever Pluto enters Capricorn, what we are charged with is transforming our relationship to, and our beliefs about, the whole concept of "who's in charge here?"

Examining that question from a long-term perspective, one could say that for the past 13,000 years, the Male frequency has been in charge of everything. It was the Masculine force that held everything steady during our passage through the dark half of the universal cycle. At the tail end of that cycle it is clear that the Male force has reached extremes of expression that make it seem as if our authority exists outside of us. Over time, the strength and protective energy that is intrinsic to this polarity went so far beyond the pale it morphed into total dominance. Like a father who is so overly protective of his children he decides to maintain control of his fears by forcing them to abide by strict rules, our Spirits have been locked up by the Illuminati, the governments, the "system," and by religious and educational constructs that deny the Higher Self and promote the idea that God exists "out there" somewhere, separate from us.

The ultimate side effects of placing our authority outside of ourselves have rendered us impotent against forces that have taken their power to the extreme—or so it seems. My hunch is that when Pluto begins its passage through Capricorn, (a transit that will be active till 2024) new frequency sets will open the space for us to see that our real power and true authority lies within.

It will be interesting to see how all of this comes down. Pluto isn't one to suffer fools. When it's in Capricorn, the fools that it refuses to suffer are the ones with all the power. Anyone who holds power and isn't using it to serve the greater good will be brought to their knees by this transit. Anyone who clings to the beliefs that the power possessors have systematically programmed us with will be charged with reconnecting with their own truth and have to relearn how to abide by it, instead of conforming to artificial law. The lies that have held us in bondage will all be exposed and when that happens all the books will have to be rewritten and so will our history—because we have been living in darkness since the fall of Atlantis and everything we have been led to believe is false.

Try to imagine what will erupt when these new frequency sets demand that the leaders of the world become accountable for their actions. What will happen when every man, woman, and child wakes up and realizes that they have been at the mercy of systematic agendas and false belief systems that have done nothing but hold them in bondage? The ones who don't go into a state of cognitive dissonance will be extremely angry. And what will happen when the ancient truths reveal themselves to have absolutely nothing to do with what we've been told about our origins, our history, and our purpose for living? Think about that for a minute and see what you come up with.

It would be naïve to assume that this process will be a gentle one. Anyone who thinks it will be easy isn't being realistic. Like I said, Pluto does not mess around—and Capricorn? Forget about it. He's a tough old dude who will most likely raise the bar and call us to live up to a much higher set of standards—real standards—ones that are born out of truth. Our entire world is about to be rocked. The initial tremors have already started. If Mother Earth is a barometer for what's going on in the collective mind, the rising tide of quaking and shaking is a clear sign that our rebirth will be attended with some difficulty.[3]

This is just the beginning, but much can be learned from taking note of what happens at the onset of any process. Astrologers differ when it comes to the question of planetary ingress, but in my opinion the point of entry into a new sign sets the tone for the entire cycle. If that is the case, a little common sense would tell us to check out the

Sabian Symbol for the first degree of Capricorn, just to see if it offers any insight into what this new evolutionary cycle is all about.

Phase 271 (Capricorn 1 degree): An Indian chief claims power from the assembled tribe.

Keynote: The power and responsibility implied in any claim for leadership.

The religious ideal implied in the preceding symbol (Phase 270—Sagittarius 30 degrees—the Pope blessing the faithful) has now materialized or crystallized into sheer power—the power to lead the community and to ensure its welfare or even its physical survival. The energies released through group cooperation (Libra) deepened and emotionally experienced as forces of great potency (Scorpio), and given meaning and conscious purpose (Sagittarius) are now stabilized and hierarchized. The power of the group is turned into a measurable and carefully managed "capital." The words "chief" and "capital" come from the same Latin word, caput, meaning "head." A time comes in many lives when the individual finds himself placed in a situation that allows him to assume power over his comrades, however limited this power may be. Is he ready to do this effectively and responsibly? This is the supreme test of man in society . . . This represents the first stage in a five-fold process—the fifty-fifth sequence of five symbols. It refers to the capacity latent in every individual to claim and assume authority in a vital group situation.[4]

Considering the image of a Spiritual brotherhood rising from the roots of a very ancient culture, and an Indian chief claiming power from the assembled tribe, you have to wonder if Marc Edmund Jones and Elsie Wheeler had read the Hopi prophesies or had any idea how prophetic these images would turn out to be.

As hallmarks for the times we're in, the above symbol and the previous one suggest that, after a long time, the ones who held fast to the Original Teachings will come together as a unity of souls in order to fulfill a collective purpose. The Indian chief claiming power from the assembled tribe implies that all authority, at this point, will be granted only to those who use it effectively and responsibly. Taken literally, both symbols come right out and say that the resurgence of Unity Consciousness and a new understanding of what constitutes true authority will come from the Indigenous People.

If all of the above exists as potential, where do we stand with it right now? Between the war in the Middle East, the poverty epidemic, the economic situation, governmental corruption, the environmental crisis, natural disasters, and no solid evidence that those in authority have the slightest clue, it's hard to believe that we'll be able to transmute any of this into light—that is, until you look around and consider not just the big things, but the small things.

During a break in my writing today I drove to my local gas station and noticed that gas prices are up to $5 a gallon. Supposedly, there's an oil crisis (Pluto rules oil)—but many are aware that the IMF and the World Bank are using it as an excuse to line their pockets. As I write this, the water-fuel car is ready to roll on more than one front, giving rise to the thought that at this point, it really doesn't matter what the big shots do with their oil.

When I went in to pay for my gas, the gal running the cash register was giving a Reiki treatment to a worn out tourist with a bad back. Since when did stuff like this become available over the counter? Waiting for my turn, I noticed that Hilary Clinton, the Illuminati Queen, is all over the newspapers. She just got 86'd as the Democratic presidential candidate. A black man with a lot of integrity took her spot—which makes me think that maybe people are starting to wake up. That may be more than my wishful thinking, because three bumper stickers caught my eye on the way home. One said,

"BUSH BELONGS BEHIND BARS." The second one said, "THE ONLY BUSH I TRUST IS MY OWN," and the third joyfully proclaimed, "THE GODDESS IS ALIVE AND MAGIC IS AFOOT!" Real change begins on the subtle level. As galactic forces rain down on the world of form, they touch the grass-roots first. Over time, whatever these forces were meant to install in the collective mind rises up and becomes evident on every level of experience.

By definition, Pluto is a "subterranean" influence. He makes his way through the lower realms and slowly works his way up, one cell at a time. Any impulse he sends out is absorbed first by the masses. We may not know the whole truth about what's going on upstairs, but the truth about what's going on out there in the everyday world indicates that minds are opening, one by one.

In the early stages of any process, the direction things will ultimately take is revealed by whatever's going on at the grass-roots level. Pluto's been in Capricorn for only five months. He has just opened the door to a whole new level of being. With fifteen and a half years to go, traces of his presence will be virtually unnoticeable unless you're paying attention. So look for signs of change in commonplace things and keep in mind what the Hopi say:

The Emergence to the future Fifth World has begun. It is being made by the humble people of little nations, tribes, and racial minorities.

If "we are the ones we have been waiting for," this includes all of us. Now that we're on the subject of "all of us," let's move on to the next chapter and talk about what the masses have to do with the Aries Point.

CHAPTER 6

Pluto and Saturn Meet the Cross of Matter

The last thing I want to do is turn this into an astrology lesson, and I definitely don't want to bore you with a lot of technical details, but we can't have this conversation if you don't understand a few things.

When you study astrology, you learn very quickly that there are two Great Circles that form our connection to what is above and what is below. The hoop that connects us to Spirit is the ecliptic, or the circle that is defined by the path our Sun follows as it moves through space. The second Great Circle, the one that grounds us to the Earthly sphere, is defined by the equator.

If we shrink down the circumference of the ecliptic and wrap it around the Earth, that circle intersects the equatorial circle at two points. When you draw a line between those points of intersection, and then a second line perpendicular to the first through its midpoint, you draw the Cross of Matter. The Cross of Matter, otherwise known as the Four Directions, is the loom that our reality is suspended upon. It is the warp and woof of this invisible loom that grounds us here in the space-time continuum.

Within this matrix, Mother Earth supports every living thing. But she herself is alive and, like all living things, her connection to the stars is axiomatic. The Cross of Matter sustains that connection and defines the framework, or the main angles, of the Earth's horoscope. Those four points contain Mother Earth's experience and help anyone who works with astrology to beam in on what that experience might be, at any given time.

Because the Sun is the source of all life on this Earth, and because it is in its most potent position at the summer solstice,* many astrologers seat the sign Cancer at the top of Earth's horoscope, right at the apex of the Cross of Matter. The fact that the Great Mother is a feminine entity has a lot to do with this too; Cancer is the sign of the Universal Mother, after all. In any horoscope, its zenith represents what we are known for, or how we are perceived by the outside world. As her children, from our perspective she is a maternal entity, and because she lives for us, it makes sense that the sign of the 'Mother' would sit on the point that governs her role in the community.

With zero degrees Cancer positioned at the pinnacle of the vertical axis, move counterclockwise around to the three arms of the cross that remain. Zero degrees Libra sits on the left arm. Zero degrees Capricorn shows up opposite the apex, at the base point. Zero degrees Aries sits at the right arm of the cross. The point governed by Libra is Mother Earth's rising sign, or Ascendant. With zero degrees Aries occupying the opposite end of the Libra axis, the Aries Point becomes the ruler of her Descendant.

In any horoscope, the descending sign represents "other,"—the world out there, or who we are in relationships. For an individual, the Descendant always sheds light on the who, what, when, where, how,

---

* The summer solstice takes place on or around June 20, at the point in the yearly cycle when the Sun begins its run through the sign Cancer.

and why of relationship patterns. In the Earth's horoscope, because the Great Mother exists in relationship to the humans that were put here to serve her, the Descendant rules all of humanity. It is for this reason that astrologers look to the Aries Point whenever they want to figure out what's going on with the masses. Any transits or aspects to that point will show up in our reality as changes that impact large segments of the population.

Right now, Pluto aspects the Aries Point from a very difficult angle. In the early minutes and degrees of Capricorn, it will maintain an exact square to that point on and off until the fall of 2009.* By itself, this gives us plenty to think about. To make things more intense, Pluto will also conjunct the base of the Cross of Matter for the same length of time. When the Lord of Hell stations himself right on the point that not only anchors humanity into the Earth but rules "the end of all things," it is bound to affect each and every one of us. And the square to the Aries Point compounds the issue.

As I mentioned earlier, Pluto works on the subtle levels. Before anyone even senses it, he uses his power over the life force to undermine and weaken the atomic bonds that hold everything together. If this seems insidious, we need to remind ourselves that disintegration and decay have their place in the hologram too. Nothing is intrinsically bad, and neither is Pluto. Like anything else, his power can be used to create or destroy. In the current state of affairs, the direction things take isn't so much about what Pluto will do; it's more about what we will do with energies that are potentially volatile.

When we first met this planet, he introduced us to one atrocity after another. Between Nazi death camps and nuclear bombs, Pluto blindsided us with things we were totally unprepared for. But the nightmarish forces that ushered him in don't necessarily define who

---

* A square is a 90-degree aspect that is considered "conflictual" by most astrologers.

he is—and if everything has a purpose, it seems as if Pluto's lessons involve learning how to take every form of madness and evolve to the point where we know enough to stop replicating it.

Current Events

In order to see if we've learned anything from this character, let's take a quick peek at some of the events that have occurred since Pluto began hitting the Aries Point. This may give us some indication, not just of what's on his mind these days, but of how our relationship with him has grown in the last 78 years.

More has come down in the outside world since January 26, 2008 than time would allow me to elaborate on—but two things stand out above all the others as perfect illustrations of what happens when we continue to blindly give all our power and authority away to the wrong people.

On May 12, 2008, when Pluto stood at the base of the World Tree, ninety degrees away from the Aries Point, a huge earthquake ripped open the Sichuan Province of China, killing 90,000 people. Within a month, the entire midsection of the United States was besieged by devastating floods. Both catastrophes would seem to be acts of God, and totally unrelated, until you look under the covers and find out that neither one was a "natural" disaster. The following report from the alternative press makes this clear:

> China Orders Strike Against The U.S. For Catastrophic Earthquake—By Sorcha Faal—May 30, 2008
>
> Russian Foreign Ministry reports are stating today that Prime Minister Putin's "sudden" diplomatic trip to France was made at the behest of China's President Hu in order to "warn" the European Union not to become involved with the U.S., following what is widely expected to be a "retaliatory

strike" against the United States who the Chinese military has blamed for the catastrophic May 12th earthquake that has killed nearly 90,000 human beings.

Chinese and Russian Military scientists, these reports say, are concurring with Canadian researcher, and former Asia-Pacific Bureau Chief of Forbes magazine, Benjamin Fulford, who in a very disturbing video released from his Japanese offices to the American public, details how the United States attacked China by the firing of a Billion Million Volt Shockwave from the Americans' High Frequency Active Auroral Research Program (HAARP) facilities in Alaska.

So powerful was this shockwave, Britain's Times Online News Service is reporting that the entire atmosphere over the Chinese earthquake zone became mysteriously changed 30 minutes prior to the 8.0 magnitude trembler . . .

Russian military analysts note that though China's military has ordered its vast submarine fleet to "disperse" throughout the Pacific Ocean, the Chinese "attack" against the United States would, most likely, take the form of economic warfare instead of an actual clashing of forces.

As the United States and China battle for their very survival in a world becoming increasingly volatile due to the rapidly growing shortages of both food and fuel, one does indeed wonder if the End Times are now upon us all."[5]

Rumor has it that the floods in the United States were engineered by the Chinese government with the same technology we used on them, as a retaliatory measure, in an attempt to decimate our food supply. As of June 20, 2008 the entire Bread Belt was underwater at the peak of the growing season. If the Chinese government wanted to hit us where it hurts, they did a fantastic job—and you can be sure that the masses will bear the brunt of it.

How things got to be this way is a long story, one that many of you are already familiar with. For those of you who haven't heard it, suffice it to say that the use of scalar technology to manipulate elemental forces came into vogue a long time ago. An outgrowth of the atomic energy research that began in the 1930s, for the mad scientists and the warmongers, this weapon of mass destruction proved to be just what the doctor ordered. With the right frequencies and the proper amount of voltage earthquakes, floods, tsunamis, tornadoes, hurricanes, mass hysteria, mind control, and pandemics, *anything* became possible. They found out how to engineer all kinds of madness without ever having to be accountable for it—because to anyone who didn't know better, it would always seem as if Mother Nature did the dirty work. Have we learned anything from Pluto? It's quite clear that seventy-eight years in his course of study have taught us very little.

The same aspect that gave us the Sichuan earthquake and the flooding in the United States will recur several times between now and the fall of 2009. My hunch is that we will see many varieties of warfare before Pluto ends this battle with the Aries Point. Let's see if the Hopi prophesies have anything to say about it:

Hopi prophecy states that World War III will be started by the people who first received the light—China, Palestine, India, and Africa. When the war comes, the United States will be destroyed by "gourds of ashes" which will fall to the ground, boiling the rivers and burning the earth, where no grass will grow for many years, and causing a disease that no medicine can cure. This can only mean nuclear or atomic bombs; no other weapon causes such effects." (Author's note: this was written before frequency wars and chemical warfare became fashionable—both are now part of the picture.)

The Hopi also have prophesied that "Turtle Island" (The United States) could turn over two or three times and the oceans could join hands and meet the sky. This seems to be a prophecy of a "pole shift"—a flipping of the planet on its axis. The Hopi call this imminent condition—and that of society today— "Koyaanisqatsi," which means "world out of balance . . . a state of life that calls for another way."

That the Third World War will be started by the ones who first received the light is already obvious. We have known for some time that, if war comes, it will come from the Far East. When I looked at the planetary positions for May 12, 2008, Pluto stood halfway between the asteroids Siva and Klotho. Siva translates as all things Asian. It is also a wrathful, vengeful influence, one that is obsessed with destruction. Klotho has to do with how things begin. With Pluto at the midpoint, the picture presents us with something that suggests surges of wrath and a desire for revenge mark the onset of power struggles with an Asian country; this would include the idea that "the Chinese started it."

The reference to "gourds of ashes" could mean anything. Our governments have so many secret weapons—for all we know they could have gourds of ashes and gourds of plutonium, too. I am not sure what this refers to, but I am clear that if boiling the rivers and burning the Earth were on their 'to do' list, someone upstairs would be able to handle it. Right now, the depleted uranium blowing in on the air currents that flow in from the Middle East might be a suspect as far as that goes. Its long-term environmental effects have yet to be fully determined, but if it does to the Earth what it does to the human body, God help us.

We've heard before about the possibility of a pole shift. These things happen in cycles and I am pretty sure that the ones who received the Original Teachings understood that the Great Shift would be accompanied by a shift in the poles. At this moment, based on the Pluto-Aries Point configuration, it is a possibility. I say this because the main axis of the Cross of Matter is the etheric blueprint for the Earth's axis. With Pluto loitering at its root forming a hard square to the Aries Point, the picture created is one of a very dark and powerful force shaking the axis of the world in a way that serves to uproot all of humanity.

This seems like a recipe for a pole shift, but in my opinion, one aspect isn't enough to set off an event of this magnitude. I don't want to take anything away from Pluto, but I am not sure that, all by himself, he has enough muscle to turn the world upside down.

Aside from that, we need to remind ourselves that Pluto does have his good points. When he's at his best, Pluto has the power to generate major shifts in consciousness. The question that's been popping up among those who take an interest in these things is whether the predicted pole shift will take the form of a shift in consciousness this time around. Between the seeds of awareness that are spreading among the grass-roots and the hundredth monkey factor, there is much to suggest that it may.

The dates when Pluto will re-form an exact square to the Aries Point are between November 27, 2008 and December 25, 2008, and between August 5, 2009 and October 18, 2009. Use the 2008 dates to reflect on what happened in the world during that period of time. Hindsight is always useful. As for the 2009 window, the potential for more of what we've seen so far should be active at those times. World events and natural forces will be the indicators. Pay attention to the weather reports; don't assume that any catastrophe is Mother Nature's handiwork.

Disturbances are bound to show up in the public sector as well. The public response to food and fuel shortages will be angry and perhaps violent enough to cause riots. Authority figures will be questioned and conflict over abuses of power seems inevitable. Much will come to the surface and, if the people in charge are found out, everything will change. Consider that a good sign, because if they are able to maintain their claim to power, they will take the upper hand by imposing tighter restrictions on our freedom.

It would make sense to expect all of our financial systems to collapse. Pluto's movements are exerting remote effects on points in the Earth's horoscope that govern her resources and the way those resources are distributed among her children. Gold, oil, precious metals and minerals, forests full of trees and wildlife, water, air, and sunlight have all been misused. In exploiting them for money and power, we have placed Mother Earth in a life-threatening position— one that will force her to teach us that those things were never meant to be bought and sold. What better way to do that than to collapse the systems that exploit them?

Saturn Enters Libra

Pluto leaves zero degrees Capricorn on October 12, 2009. Within eighteen days, Saturn will enter Libra, and move back and forth over the Earth's Ascendant until July 22, 2010 (see page 200). It's as if both planets have a date with the Cross of Matter, and the Lord of Hell has to sneak down the back stairs just as the Grim Reaper rings the doorbell. Saturn's about as "date worthy" as Pluto, and since he's rarely up for a good time, Mother Earth is looking at yet another piece of work.

The archetypal cop, Saturn enjoys restricting our behavior. If anything is out of order when he makes a hard transit, there's no way to hide it from him. You have to face things honestly, whether you want to or not. The truth becomes very important whenever Saturn's around, as does integrity. If either of those virtues aren't what they should be, Saturn creates a script that refines them, or leaves us to live with the consequences.

He is also the granddaddy of the old paradigm. As such, he has a huge investment in maintaining it. All the outworn structures and belief patterns in which we've lost faith are his offspring. Saturn's sense of authority over those things is probably as strong as it ever was, but at this point he's like a retired army general who once commanded thousands of troops, and is now sitting down at the Legion Hall with nothing to do. He can't bring back the good old days; he doesn't feel the least bit comfortable in this new paradigm, and all of his skills appear to be useless right now. What's a planet to do?

Pluto doesn't have a problem with change, but Saturn is geared more toward keeping things the way they are. He likes his institutions, he loves structure, and he needs both to survive. In spite of his old-fashioned tendencies, however, Saturn isn't stupid. He's enough of a realist to see that everything he's held in place for so long is in dire need of renovation. As all of that appears to be going down the tubes, he has to find a way to invent new institutions and new structures, or he will lose his place in the scheme of things.

His ingress into Libra will position him on the left arm of the Cross of Matter. At zero degrees of that sign, he'll transit the Earth's Ascendant for about ten months. In any horoscope, the Ascendant represents the physical body. It is the point at which the soul enfolds itself in a form that will allow it to manifest its purpose. Any transits to the Ascendant will have an impact, not just on the body, but on the way the physical entity experiences changes in its environment, because that axis is also "the horizon line," or the plane that circumscribes and defines the conditions each of us encounters in the world around us.

The form that things take where the soul meets its purpose is defined by the sign that rules the Ascendant. Anyone with Libra rising is learning what it means to maintain conscious and equal relationships with others. For the Earth, this implies that our Mother is looking for a way to create that kind of relationship with us, one where both parties share a common purpose and are willing to respect the others' individual needs as they join hands and pursue that purpose.

With the Aries Point at the opposite pole of the point of ascension, it appears as if Mom has a tendency to form relationships with people who are self-centered, war-like, and not the least bit interested in anyone but themselves. This happens because the Aries stereotype is inherently selfish, has a huge ego, and doesn't understand the whole idea of peaceful cooperation. So the Earth has to struggle to get her needs met and her rights respected in a partnership where the "other" has a hard time even acknowledging that she has a life, let alone needs and rights of her own.

Under Saturn's influence, our Mother will draw the line as she begins to redefine her relationship to a population that has selfishly exploited all of her resources. Like a battered woman who just woke up and decided to do something about her predicament, standing up for her rights will require her to make it clear to us that she is fed up with all the abuse—and if we want to keep this whole thing alive we have to change our ways, or she will be gone for good.

Fortunately for us, the reaper isn't as grim when he's in the sign of the scales. Ordinarily, he's prone to just cutting things down and being done with them, but Libra leaves him open to appeal. This means that there will be a moratorium on matters that pertain to our debts to Mother Earth, and she will give us one last chance to redeem ourselves before she decides to end this whole affair.

Underneath all the metaphor, we are looking at a prolonged period of redefinition that may lead to renewal if our awareness increases. As worn-out structures, institutions, and belief patterns dissolve, the keepers of the old paradigm will try to defend them with all their might. At the same time, we will see evidence of new leadership and new alternatives gathering strength, and their interests will clash with those of the old order.

With the Aries Point sitting on the receiving end of all of this, in direct opposition* to Saturn, the masses will bear the weight of the conflict.

---

* An opposing aspect is one that creates problems that appear to come from others. Oppositions can be difficult unless we understand that what comes at us is a projection of something we don't wish to deal with internally.

I would imagine that that weight will be increased by environmental problems and earth changes. In the wake of those things, everything we have come to value and loan significance to will go through a reconstruction phase. As the rubble piles up all around us, those who are overly invested in either the beliefs that uphold the old structures or the structures themselves will have to find meaning elsewhere.

Aspects that show up on the day that Saturn moves over the Earth's Ascendant for the first time reveal several themes and scenarios that will become more evident as this ten-month window opens up. Pluto forms a close opposition to the asteroid Nemesis in that horoscope. The textbook interpretation of that aspect tells us that "the reach for power, the need to control, and the inability to forgive is at the core of every situation that doesn't work."⁶ Pluto also opposes Ophelia on that day, an aspect that suggests the powers that be have gone mad—and because everything gets reduced to the lowest common denominator, levels of collective insanity are bound to increase.

Another planetary picture involving the asteroids Hekate and Prosperina and the planet Uranus implies that much of the nightmare will be caused by large numbers of people displaced by unexpected occurrences, electrical outages, explosions, frequency warfare, unpredictable weather patterns, and widespread upheaval. With the asteroids Siwa and Psyche positioned at the midpoint of that picture, we could predict that most of the damage will either be felt, or perpetrated by, a Far Eastern country. This may include China, Japan, India, or a Middle Eastern state.

A conjunction between Toro and Siva indicates that bullying and intimidation tactics will be used to enforce the idea that "might makes right." This aspect involves themes of brutality and destruction generated by those who wish to retain their power. Displays of force will be used to disguise the weakness of a worn-out system and it looks as if the old guard will do whatever it takes to hold on to that over which they no longer have any control.

As all of the above unfolds, it will be exacerbated by the fact that Saturn and Pluto will be within orb of an exact square during the entire ten-month period. Critical points show up between October 30 and December 2, 2009, and between January 21 and February 9, 2010. Any level of tension between these two planets signals hard times. With no other celestial body to act as a buffer, Saturn and Pluto will probably do what they always do when they're left alone in the room. Using just a few of their more recent tête-à-têtes as examples will give you some idea of what happens when they disagree:

- 1931 saw the rise of Hitler and the Great Depression.

- 1940 saw the start of World War II.

- 1947 saw the bombing of Hiroshima and Nagasaki.

- 1965 saw the beginning of the war in Vietnam.

See what I mean? I wish I could tell you that something will come along to take the edge off all of this, but I don't see any buffers. There appears to be nothing but trouble. Part of that trouble will be generated by a secondary conversation between Saturn and Uranus. Why they decided to resolve their differences at a time like this is beyond me, but if bad things happen in threes, it looks like we're getting a package deal.

Saturn and Uranus are in opposition to each other on and off from January 30, 2009 until early August 2010. Under normal circumstances, that alone would give us plenty to think about. But the situation is far from normal this time, because the two planets will eventually wind up arguing back and forth, with Saturn sitting on the Earth's Ascendant and Uranus conjunct the Aries Point. If we thought we had a problem with these two birds perched on the main axis of the Cross of Matter, it won't be any less of a hassle—unless Uranus does what I hope he will do.

But before we talk about what that might involve, let's look at what we need to be asking ourselves, individually and collectively, before Saturn enters his reconstruction phase:

- ❋ Where are we with our truth?

- ❋ Where are we with our integrity?

- ❋ What needs to change in order for us to move through this period of transition?

- ❋ What do we need to let go?

- ❋ Is there anything we can keep—anything of value—from the old paradigm?

- ❋ If it isn't too late, what do we need to do to make it up to Mother Earth?

- ❋ How close are we to her, in our hearts and in our lives?

- ❋ Knowing what we know, is there anything we can be doing right now to make things easier?

CHAPTER 7

Uranus Meets the Aries Point

In order to get a sense of what Uranus might do when he meets the Aries Point, we need to talk about how this planet behaves, and try to gauge what kind of an effect that will have on the collective mind. In Chapter One, Uranus was referred to as the force that inspires the soul to break free from everything that restricts it. This is always his ultimate purpose; but in accomplishing that purpose he'll go to any extreme, and his methods are always radical.

If Saturn is the one who keeps everything as it is, Uranus governs the principle that knows enough to change it, whenever things get stale. The lord of lightening, thunder, and electricity, Uranus doesn't play games when it's time to move on. He strikes suddenly, shocks us without warning, and makes it absolutely clear that certain things are over with. While his reputation for upheaval is legendary, it needs to be understood that anything he decides to uproot or tear apart has outlived its usefulness.

Often referred to as the Great Awakener, Uranus is as good at changing our minds as he is at changing the scenery. The flashes of insight that precede every stroke of genius, every new invention, and every major epiphany are all his doing. When the mind rises up to a new way of seeing things, Uranus is there installing a wider vision of the truth. If he didn't come along and blow our minds every now and then, we'd probably all still believe in the tooth fairy.

Uranus has one big problem; he is erratic and totally unpredictable. Because he functions in this way, and because most of us get uncomfortable when faced with the unexpected, we have come to regard him as a negative influence. In truth, there's nothing inherently wrong with anything this planet decides to do; what makes Uranus difficult is the human tendency to resist change. And the more we resist change, the more likely it is that Uranus will go right ahead and do it for us by blasting to bits whatever we're trying to hold on to.

Predicting the Unpredictable

From an astrological perspective, Uranus' arrival at the Aries Point is an evolutionary milestone—one that has been widely speculated upon. Because astrologers can never claim to know exactly what Uranus will do, however, all of their predictions go limp in the face of his eccentricity. Keep that in mind as you read this chapter. I am familiar enough with the Uranian impulse to know that, even with the best of my abilities brought to the table, everything I have to say could be dead wrong.

The point that rules the masses will be lit up by this impulse from May 28, 2010 to January 8, 2012 (see page 201). If one and one make two, what do you suppose will happen when the Che Guevara of the Zodiac installs himself on the point that governs all humanity? I don't know about you, but it smells like a revolution to me. And because the Aries Point also happens to be Zero Point, or the moment in time when the alpha and omega meet and everything dies and is simultaneously reborn, the imagery suggests that this revolution will bring an end to the old paradigm and mark the beginning of a new one.

On the surface, this formula looks pretty simple. But, aside from the fact that we don't know how Uranus will behave, his long-time rival, Saturn, will move in to oppose him as of January 2009 and that aspect will hold into the summer of 2010. This complicates things considerably.

Oppositions between Saturn and Uranus signal a time when the past and the future collide. Their conversations always center around how to bring about change without destroying everything in the process. Uranus has no use for the past; he just wants to be done with it. Saturn doesn't see it quite the same way; he's too identified with the past to let it go. So the two of them go back and forth, with Uranus always pushing the envelope and Saturn playing the role of the cop who comes along to arrest that impulse, saying: "Hey, wait a minute! You have no jurisdiction here and you're nuts if you think you can just waltz in and break all of my rules."

In a perfect world, these two forces might be able to resolve their differences amicably. But the "As above, so below" factor goes both ways, and things are so out of balance here that when Saturn and Uranus begin to face off, they will serve as a conduit for the differences that have been festering in us since the beginning of time. Lancing the boil will ultimately heal those problems but in the meantime they will surface as a contest between the keepers of the old paradigm and the proponents of the new one. From an astrological perspective, how things work out can only be gauged by looking at which planet has the most power in this situation.

Saturn is strong in Libra, but, even so, he's a "lame duck" planet at this point; his power has run its course and what's left of it needs to make so many adjustments it only weakens him further. Uranus, on the other hand, has nothing to block him. As the ruler of the sign Aquarius, he could be considered the King of the Age and the guiding force for the Great Shift. From that perspective alone, Uranus has an edge over Saturn. But Uranus has a few other things going for him. For starters, he just so happens to feel right at home in the sign of the Ram. The two principles have so much in common, the Arian urge that says, "We're pioneers. Let's go for it. It's time to start something new," will be in complete accord with anything Uranus decides to do.

All this would seem to give better odds to Uranus, but we can't discount Saturn. He's overseen the Earthly realm for such a long time that we'd be naïve to expect him to hand everything over without a fight—especially to an upstart like Uranus. At the same time, the history between these two planets reads like a mythic soap opera and, when we study their connection from that perspective, it becomes clear that Saturn has so much to account for as far as his eccentric brother is concerned that he may have no power in this situation whatsoever. Let's see if mythology can shed any light on the matter.

Story Time

According to the Greeks, Gaia, the deep-breasted Earth, was the first to emerge out of Chaos. It was she who presided over the darkness until Eros came out of the void to turn on the love frequency. In installing the chip that opened her heart, Eros gave Mother Earth the power to birth everything in Creation, and she took it from there:

> On her part Gaia first bore Uranus, the sky crowned with stars, "whom she made her equal in grandeur, so that he entirely covered her" . . . The universe had been formed. It remained to be peopled. Gaia united with her son and produced the first race—the Titans.[7]

Now that we know that Uranus and Gaia were once known as "the Immortal Couple," Uranus would appear to be the original Father Sky. Think about that for a minute and hear me out, because the plot thickens.

When Mother Earth and Father Sky gave birth to the twelve Titans, one of them was Kronos, who later became known as Saturn. The story goes that, after Gaia birthed the Titans, she and Uranus gave birth to six hideous monsters. For Uranus, this was more than just a reflection on his manhood; he couldn't cope with imperfection or the idea that his seed could produce anything so horrible. Repulsed by their deformities and without consulting his wife, he took it upon himself to hide these disgusting creatures underground, deep in the bowels of the Earth.

Enraged at the thought that her husband would do such a thing, Gaia gathered the twelve Titans together and beseeched them to reap vengeance on their father. Not one of them volunteered, for obvious reasons—until Saturn, who was either looking to score a few brownie points with his mother or plotting to replace his father (or both), stepped forward and took on the job. In the dead of night, while Uranus was asleep, Saturn stole into the immortal bedchamber and castrated his father with a steel sickle that had been given to him by Gaia.

What Goes Around, Comes Around

The myth suggests that Uranus and Saturn have a lot of old business to straighten out. And I can't help but think that the two of them facing off on the axis that represents Mother Earth's body and soul will bring up karmic issues that have never been settled. Saturn's position may very well be strengthened with Libra on his side, but that's about all he's got going for him. Whether that will be enough is questionable, because it's quite clear that he has more than one thing to own up to.

The whole castration thing is more complicated than it looks. Saturn didn't just castrate anyone; he had the audacity to castrate the Immortal Father! And then he went even further and *impersonated* him. Since that time, our perceptions of the male principle have been distorted by an imposter who defined that principle without having any real claim to it. This would imply that the pretender to the throne—who, as we already know, has to redefine every structure he has created since he usurped Uranus—now has to account, on top of everything else, for the fact that *he isn't our real father.*

Things are looking pretty grim for the "reaper." The true father is about to reappear. Armed with justifiable wrath, he's got the ultimate bone to pick with his son. In vying with Saturn over issues that have to do with "who's in charge here," Mother Earth will become a battleground, and the tension between these two planets will play itself out in her body, in her environment, and in the heart and soul of every living thing.

Look for signs of this now, and expect them to become more than signs as we approach January 2009. After that date, be prepared for anything, because this conflict between the old and the new will escalate, and God knows where it will go. I say this because what the Hopi call *Koyaanisqatsi*—a world out of balance, a state of life that calls for another way—has gone so far over the top, the tension between Saturn and Uranus, combined with everything we've said about the Aries Point, Pluto, and the stress on the Cross of Matter, could push everything right over the edge. As I look at all the possible outcomes, it is clear to me that the only thing that can keep this from turning into our worst nightmare is *us*—you, me, all of us—*We* are the ones who have to find another way.

Mother Earth has already woken up inside. As Drunvalo Melchizedek tells us in *The Serpent of Light,* her core has shifted and the Christ Consciousness grid is now aligned to hold space for the rise of what Drunvalo calls the Female Light. When one thing changes, everything has to change. Uranus' arrival at the Aries Point is a sign that, in adjusting to the transformation that has taken place within the female, the original male principle will reinstate itself and reunite with her on new and different terms—not as a strict, controlling father figure, but as her conscious and equal partner. By law, this process cannot take place without us, because the divine exists as a trinity. The reunion of the immortal couple will not be complete until the "child" aspect of God awakens to the role it plays in the process.

Since we happen to be the child aspect in this equation, it's clear that each one of us is changing as much as Mother Earth and Father Sky. When the Hopi say, "We are the ones we have been waiting for," it means that all of us are here now to serve as the neutralizing force, or the balance point between the male and the female polarities. The revolution that I spoke of at the beginning of this chapter is really about all of us becoming aware that we aren't separate from the divine; we are part of it.

When Uranus meets the Aries Point, we will find out that we have spent 13,000 years under the influence of many false illusions. Not only don't we know who our real father is; we have no idea who *we* are. This transit will inevitably open our eyes to the truth about our origins. That information is critical right now, because it's what we never knew about ourselves that got us into this mess. And when we find out where we really came from and who we really are, humanity will understand that Mommy and Daddy can only do so much. In the end, we are the ones who have been called to play midwife at the birth of the new paradigm.

So when I say, "Thousands of years ago, there were Native people that spoke of these things," that's exactly what I mean. They told their children and thousands of years ago, their children grew up and told their children, and then their children grew up and told their children. And they spoke about the people that will live in this time.[8]

And now it is us. We are the ones they spoke of long ago. They say to be alive, to come into creation and to live upon the earth at this time is a great honor. In the cycle of time, from the beginning to the end, this time we are in now will change the purification of all things. They say this is the hardest time to live, but it is also the greatest honor to be alive to live and see this.

CHAPTER 8

Mapping the Aspects

What the planets are about to go through reminds me of what it's like to be at a cocktail party with a lot of very important but difficult people who aren't on the best of terms with each other. And while it's not too hard to figure out how each of them will behave individually, knowing what these characters will do when they meet face to face is a huge question mark, because anything they say or do might trigger a confrontation that could ruin the whole affair. Mother Earth is the hostess and she's too busy playing her role to handle their idiosyncrasies. So she has asked us to do that for her—so it's now our job to keep an eye on the Lord of Hell, the Grim Reaper, and Che Guevara, just to make sure the three of them don't go ballistic and trash the place.

In order to get a sense of what this will involve, let's begin by looking at the lineup of major planets and aspects that will come into play between now and 2012:

1. Saturn opposite Uranus

2. Saturn on the Earth's Ascendant, opposite the Aries Point

3. Uranus at the Aries Point, conjunct the Earth's Descendant

4. Jupiter conjunct the Aries Point (We'll discuss this in a separate chapter.)

5. Jupiter conjunct Uranus (We'll discuss this in a separate chapter.)

6. Pluto at the base of the World Tree, loosely squaring Uranus, Saturn, Jupiter, the Aries Point, and the Earth's Ascendant—*for the duration*

7. Neptune entering Pisces (We'll discuss this in a separate chapter.)

In my opinion, this is the astrological version of "The Perfect Storm." Like the colossal weather fronts that generated the fatal hurricane depicted in the movie of that name, the dynamics are just as volatile and they need to be handled with care. As the planets move in and out of aspect, two or three (and sometimes four) of them will be active at the same time. It is at those points that we can expect periods of extreme difficulty.

What follows is a chronological breakdown of the transits we've discussed so far. Pay close attention to the dates for each one, but keep in mind that we will be under the influence of all of these aspects to a greater or lesser degree for the next three years. With the understanding that each and every one of us is here now to serve as a neutralizing force or referee in this "clash of the Titans," we can prepare for the worst and hope for the best by knowing when there will be more than one difficult conversation going on.

Pluto Conjunct the Root of the Cross of Matter

The inner planets move so quickly that their transits are only exact for a day or two. Like flies buzzing around our heads, if they light on our nose momentarily, it leaves no lasting impression. Halfway between the inner and the outer planets, Jupiter leaves his mark a little bit longer, but unless he gets involved in a retrograde pattern, his aspects don't linger for more than a week.

The big outer planets are a whole different story. Their rate of motion is so slow, they can grind over a point for a year, and sometimes two years or more at a time. Instead of flies buzzing in and out of the picture, they feel more like elephants who circle slowly, filling up our peripheral vision almost as much as they do when they are right in our face.

Waxing toward or waning away from exact aspect, when a slow-moving planet occupies the space on either side of that point, it is said to be "within orb" and its effects are considered to be operative. Astrologers differ when it comes to what constitutes being "within orb." In my experience, Pluto makes his influence felt five degrees before and five degrees after the point of exactitude. He often does most of his work when he is in these buffer zones.

For the next three years, Pluto will be positioned close enough to the base of the Cross of Matter to be within orb of an exact conjunction (see page 199). As he continues to rock that point, other aspects will form, and his behavior will be heavily influenced by the way we choose to translate the energies coming from Saturn, Uranus, and the Aries Point. Whenever the auxiliary aspects are tense or not handled properly, Pluto will undoubtedly rumble and shake at the root of all things just to keep us aware of what's really at stake. For better or worse, you must take everything we've said about Pluto into consideration as you read what follows. His shadow will be there in the background, overseeing it all.

Saturn Opposite Uranus

Beginning in January 2009, the game will start, with Saturn opposite Uranus (see page 200). What we are already witnessing in the outside world will escalate, and this is when the old guard will show signs of total resistance to any changes Uranus wants to install. At that time, Uranus will not be touching the point that rules the masses. This implies that humanity will still be half asleep and vulnerable—not just to the fear and pressure coming from Saturn's need to keep everything as it is, but from its inability to disengage from its old belief patterns.

I would expect to see various forms of law and order, doing whatever it takes to stave off change, pushing against a rising tide of dissent. During this time Saturn will appear to be more powerful than he really is. Overcompensating for what he can't handle, he will clamp down, imposing tighter security, more laws, and more restrictions. Our outer reality will look dark and feel oppressive. What we need to remember is that, throughout 2009, *what is apparent is an illusion* because Saturn is no longer in charge on the etheric level. At this point, he's virtually impotent. And in the face of a Uranian coup, any effort to hold his position will prove futile.

How do I know? Because, aside from being the King of the Age, Uranus never takes no for an answer. As John Townley tells us:

> "More importantly, though, when Uranus in its pure form
> of total truth meets resistance, it cannot compromise or
> blend. It must totally destroy its resistance or be destroyed
> itself."[9]

Everything depends on how the keepers of the old paradigm behave. Judging from where they're at now, the winds of change don't appear to be affecting them at all. As of July 2008, the banking systems had already started to fold. People are losing their homes, their jobs, and their minds. The media is whitewashing the truth and the powers-that-be continue to lie. Unable to connect the dots, the masses are oblivious. Every sign calls us to slow down and get back to what's essential, but we're so wound up and dumbed down that we don't even know what that means anymore. The Hopi saw this coming ages ago:

So he said at this time you're going to see that things will speed up, that people on the earth will move faster and faster. Grandchildren will not have time for grandparents. Parents will not have time for children. It will seem like time is going faster and faster. The Elders advised us that as things speed up, you yourself should slow down. The faster things go, the slower you go. Because there's going to come a time when the earth is going to be shaken a third time. The Great Spirit has been shaking the earth two times: the First and Second World Wars to remind us that we are a human family, to remind us that we should have greeted each other as brothers and sisters. We had a chance after each shaking to come together in a circle that would have brought peace on earth, but we missed that.[10]

If we refuse to face the truth, we can expect Uranus to haul out his heavy artillery and blast us with as much systematic turmoil and as many cataclysms as it takes for him to get his message across. A brief check on the earthquake and hurricane reports will show you that Uranus has been trying to wake us up for quite some time. He went into overdrive on the cataclysmic level close to twenty years ago. In a speech delivered at the United Nations back in 1992, the Hopi Elders made an attempt to draw our attention to the import of his messages. This is what Thomas Banyacya had to say when he begged the general assembly to open their eyes:

It should be the mission of your nations and this assembly to use your power and rules to examine and work to cure the damage people have done to this Earth and to each other. Hopi Elders know that was your mission and they wait to see whether you will act on it now. Nature, the First People and the Spirit of our ancestors are giving you loud warnings.

Today, December 10, 1992, you see increasing floods, more damaging hurricanes, hail storms, climate changes and earthquakes as our prophesies said would come. Even animals and birds are warning us with strange changes in their behavior, such as the beaching of whales. Why do animals act like they know about the Earth's problems and most humans act like they know nothing?[11]

The dates for the Saturn-Uranus opposition are:

❀ January 30, 2009 to February 12, 2009

❀ September 9, 2009 to September 17, 2009

❀ April 23, 2010 to May 1, 2010

❀ July 22, 2010 to August 2, 2010

During this entire period, what each one of us will be called to do in our private realities is look at what needs to change *in us*. The questions we should be asking ourselves are:

❀ How dependent are we on the system?

❀ What is our relationship to money?

❀ How hooked are we on technology?

❀ What do we have that we don't need?

❀ Are we being truthful in our relationships?

❀ How much do our fears and our security issues affect our choices?

❀ Are we living according to standards that are our own, or are we still beholden to what we've been programmed to believe is true for us?

❀ Do we know what our truth is?

❀ If we know what it is, do we have the courage to live it?

❀ If everything were to fall apart tomorrow, would we still be able to take care of ourselves and our loved ones?

❀ How would we do that?

❀ Do we have a solid connection to Spirit?

❀ How connected are we to Mother Earth?

- ❀ What are our real resources, internal and external?

- ❀ Do we really believe in our hearts that we can change the world?

You see, Saturn's issues with Uranus live inside us all. The only way we can do our part to defuse the tension between them is to eradicate everything that has outlived its purpose in our own lives. It makes about as much sense to run around like chicken little as it does to play ostrich and go into denial at a time like this. Even though the situation seems to warrant either response, we can do more by acting out the highest expression of this transit in our own private realities. And we can start right now, by accepting the need for change (Uranus), eliminating everything that stands in its way, and using whatever's worth keeping from the past (Saturn) as the foundation for this new life we're being called to create. The more we awaken to the idea of change and the more we are willing to let go of what is no longer meaningful or necessary for our survival, the easier it will be for everyone.

Saturn Conjunct the Earth's Ascendant

The forces of the past will continue to press their case until early August 2010. Their influence will appear to strengthen when Saturn conjuncts the Earth's Ascendant. His scythe will cast a shadow over Mother Earth, and the old guard will be confronted with the need to use their power, not for their own personal gain, but for the greater good of all.

In the process of redefining his role here, Saturn will learn that structure and form are only useful when the belief patterns that uphold them support the continuation of life.

Cutting down every irrelevant structure, system, and belief will serve all of us in the long run. As these things fall to the ground, chaos will reign, until we find a way to apply Saturn's gift for holding things in place to the new structures, systems, and belief patterns that Uranus is about to install.

During this time, the keepers of the old paradigm will pitch back and forth on the existing power base, feigning strength and using every means at their disposal to create the impression that their assets outweigh their liabilities. Resistance and denial invoke nothing but conflict, so this will only make things worse for everyone. Cataclysm and upheaval will increase or decrease in direct proportion to our ability to ride the horse in the direction it is going.

Aside from that, there is no doubt in my mind that the patriarchy will be affected directly by this aspect as well. Saturn may be the God of authority, but he's such a thorough, dutiful guy he will demand as much from them as he does from everything else. It's his job to keep us in line, after all. And the patriarchal forces are so out of line that it doesn't take much to see that, in some awful moment of truth, Saturn could very well cut them off at the knees.

Poring over the prophesies, I came across one very disturbing prediction that seems to support this idea:

This prophecy is related to the Biblical version of that which may yet come to pass. It goes on to say that common people will become concerned and frustrated because of their hectic world. They will be particularly against the bloodthirsty policies and deceitfulness of the world leaders. The common people the world over will band together to fight for world peace. They will realize their leaders have failed. People in high places will be hunted down like animals, perhaps through terrorism. In turn, leaders will retaliate and begin hunting each other. This condition will gather strength and spread far and wide. It will get out of control the world over. Revolution could erupt on our land.[12]

The dates for that conjunction are:

❀ October 30, 2009 to November 8, 2009

❀ March 26, 2010 to April 7, 2010

❀ July 22, 2010 to August 2, 2010

Uranus Conjunct the Aries Point

In the midst of working out his differences with Saturn, Uranus will move to the Aries Point on May 28, 2010 (see page 201). As soon as he hits that point, his strength will increase and Saturn's power will diminish. This is when we can expect to see a change on the part of the masses. It is entirely possible that humanity will awaken at that point; the potential is there—but because Uranus will move on and off the Aries Point for the next two years, my sense is that the matter of us waking up and supporting his cause is one of those things that will take time. Unfortunately, this includes the idea that he may have to shake us down a few times before we get it.

Those of us who got involved with alternative methods, technologies, and belief patterns back in the Sixties and Seventies will find nothing to interfere with the further development of our visions. The Uranian impulse will open the way for this in a much more powerful way than it did in our youth. What we had to fight against to make our dreams real back in those days isn't there anymore—and since Uranus is the consummate free-thinker, radical non-conformist, rogue genius, and King of the Age, all things alternative will finally be universally accepted and understood. As the seeds for every imaginable vision spread through the grass roots, I see infinite possibilities opening up in the realm of free energy, healing, education, agriculture, communal relations, and in our leadership as well.

Uranus' conjunction with the Aries Point will also be a time when the collective consciousness coalesces into a state of universal brotherhood. The Great Awakener, combined with the qualities that are intrinsic to the sign Aquarius and the Age they both rule, will enlighten all of us about the reality of our interconnectedness, including our connection to our Star Brothers. Don't forget; Uranus was once "the sky crowned with stars." He is not of this Earth. And when those energies reawaken in our consciousness, we will discover that the limitations we have placed on what it means to be human have very little to do with who we really are.

In my opinion our knowledge of those things will be completely clear in the collective mind *before* Uranus hits the Aries Point. I say this because he is a visionary and as such he is always way ahead of himself. In my experience, Uranus sets the stage for change and does most of his work at the energetic level a year before his transits are exact. At the point of exactitude events manifest outwardly in ways that only appear to be sudden to those who don't pay attention to the signs. The signs are already everywhere and they are bound to increase between the spring of 2009 and the end of May 2010.

The points at which Uranus will conjunct the Aries Point are:

⊛ May 28, 2010 to August 14, 2010

⊛ March 12, 2011 to March 29, 2011

⊛ November 10, 2011 to January 8, 2012

During and between all three of these windows, everything that transpires here on Earth, tumultuous or otherwise, will reflect Uranus' ultimate purpose—to usher in the Age of Light. Even though the last vestiges of the old order will offer plenty of resistance, their energies will only be active during the first window. As of August 2, 2010, when Saturn moves off the Earth's Ascendant, he and the powers-that-be won't be in a position to do much but unite with Uranus or be destroyed.

The most powerful point of conflict will occur between July 22, 2010 and August 2, 2010, when Saturn and Uranus line up in direct opposition on the horizontal axis of the Cross of Matter. That axis is *Mother Earth's body*. The level of tension between the two planets leading up to that window will determine how much of it translates into cataclysm.

During that nineteen-day period, Pluto will be retrograde at three degrees Capricorn—close enough to the base of the World Tree to create an extremely tense set of variables. With three of the most powerful planetary forces shaking the axis of the world, bringing all their might to bear upon it, the imagery alone gives fair warning. It is an understatement to say that this will be a precarious time.

If Saturn refuses to step down and mankind wakes up on the wrong side of the bed, Uranus will inevitably haul out his ultimate weapons and Pluto will respond accordingly. If a pole shift is meant to be part of our experience, it could very well happen between July 22 and August 2, 2010, or within the month of August that year. The Hopi refer to this possibility metaphorically in their prophesies:

There are two water serpents, one at each pole, with a warrior sitting on his head and tail. These command nature to warn us by her activities that time is getting short, and we must correct ourselves. If we refuse to heed these warnings, the warriors will let go of the serpents; they will rise up and all will perish.[13]

The Hopi have also prophesied that "Turtle Island" (North America) could turn over two or three times and the oceans could join hands and meet the sky. [14]

Yes, I can visualize everything blowing to bits. And yes, I can see that the way things are and have always been is about to be uprooted in ways that are impossible to predict with so many variables impacting the outcome. From an astrological perspective, the transits and angles that will be activated during the July-August 2010 window would prompt anyone in my field to pick those dates as "a definite maybe" for a pole shift. But that particular set of aspects should be considered only from the standpoint of what it embodies as potential, because there are several time frames that hold that possibility. We'll discuss these as we go along.

Based on his hair-trigger traits and the alpha-omega quality of the Aries Point, I am of the mind that the poles could shift on any of the dates on which Uranus moves over that degree of the Zodiac. But we're at a point in the precession cycle where wondering about aspects and dates comes down to "pick a day—any day;" the Earth's magnetic field has collapsed, her axis is way off kilter, and the prophets of doom aren't alone in their perceptions. Even the people at NASA see a shifting of the poles as imminent. It might be best if we lived as if the poles could shift at any moment, while holding the thought that such an occurrence may still be contingent upon a consciousness shift on the part of the masses.

The old adage, "There's many a slip between the cup and the lip," is another way of saying that it's difficult to be 100 percent sure that any set of variables will reach their logical conclusion. As much as Uranus is the master of disaster, he is also the ruler of all the unpredictable synchronicities that pop up between the cup and the lip.

With more than one method of operation, last-minute surprises fall under his jurisdiction as well. Completely empowered by sign and degree, Uranus could conjure up all kinds of miracles just as easily as he could do us in. It feels better to me to envision him taking the high road—and since the Spiritual element is such a big factor in this equation, if we do the same, without downplaying the pole shift issue, the End Times will unfold in ways that surprise even those who presume to have it all figured out.

Here are some thoughts from "Wisdom from the Elders of the Hopi Nation" as we cross the threshold into a cycle of our journey of awakening.

You have been telling the people that this is the Eleventh Hour. Now you must go back and tell the people that this is the Hour. And there are things to be considered:

- ✸ Where are you living?

- ✸ What are you doing?

- ✸ What are your relationships?

- ✸ Are you in right relation?

- ✸ Where is your water?

- ✸ Know your garden.

❀ It is time to speak your truth.

❀ Create your community.

❀ Be good to each other.

❀ And do not look outside yourself for the leader.

❀ This could be a good time!

❀ There is a river flowing now very fast.

❀ It is so great and swift that there are those who will be afraid.

❀ They will try to hold on to the shore.

❀ They will feel they are being torn apart, and they will suffer greatly.

❀ Know the river has its destination.

❀ The Elders say we must let go of the shore, push off into the middle of the river, keep our eyes open, and our heads above the water.

❀ See who is in there with you and celebrate.

❀ At this time in history, we are to take nothing personally. Least of all, ourselves. For the moment that we do, our Spiritual growth and journey comes to a halt. The time of the lone wolf is over. Gather yourselves!

❀ Banish the word struggle from your attitude and your vocabulary.

❀ All that we do now must be done in a sacred manner and in celebration.

❀ We are the ones we've been waiting for.[15]

CHAPTER 9

Jupiter Conjuncts Uranus at the Aries Point

Whenever a horoscope looks like it could go one way or another, Jupiter's influence on the situation becomes important. Often referred to as the "Greater Benefic," this planet is a harbinger of hope and good fortune. His movement over the Aries Point in conjunction with Uranus between the late spring of 2010 and January 2011 is one of those blessings that couldn't come at a better time.

A positive influence on an auspicious angle, his power is reinforced by other factors. Perfectly happy in Aries, Jupiter gets along with Uranus better than any other planet. Not only do they bring out each other's best qualities, they can perform miracles when they're together. Jupiter likes to expand things; Uranus mixes well in any situation that involves stepping outside the box, and both of them are great to have around when it's time to move on. In the middle of a paradigm shift, who could ask for better company?

Jupiter is also the one who raises our hearts to Spiritual things. The impulse to connect with what lies beyond the boundaries of time and space, and the faith that whatever that is, actually exists, belong to him. Any time we wonder about causal principles or think about God, Jupiter is behind the thought—and it's all the same to him how we choose to define those things for ourselves, because he has the capacity to embrace every belief.

That the planet that rules every possible blessing will shine down on the Aries Point for close to a year loans hope to an extremely tense set of circumstances. At a time when so many things could go awry, the Jupiter transit is a saving grace—one that, among other things, will have a powerful effect on the collective mind.

I say this because Jupiter's attunement to matters of Spirit will filter through the point that governs both the masses and the collective consciousness for close to a year (see page 202). Keep in mind that, during that period, Uranus will be actively involved in this process as well. Layer Jupiter's expansive traits over Uranus' rulership over portions of the brain that we don't have access to; then consider that the Aries Point is also involved in the aspect pattern. The three elements together could easily translate as a collective awakening on the part of the masses.

When that possibility became clear to me, my first thought was that I was reading too much into it—was there any justification for it? Shortly thereafter, I came across an excerpt from a book by Dr. Richard Boylan which, among other things, refers to extraterrestrial "Thunder Beings" sent to enlighten us, coinciding with our entrance into the Fifth World. Here's what he says:

> Native American tradition honors the existence of Thunder Beings. These Thunder Beings are understood by Native Americans to be messengers from the powers on high, the Star People (extraterrestrial visitors). The Thunder Beings are a force for both dissolution and re-creation. In

the Plains Indian tradition, a person who has a visit by a Thunder Being, in person, in vision or in dream, becomes a heyoka, a "contrary." This heyoka then customarily starts behaving in a way opposite to the conventions of the dominant culture. The heyoka does so, precisely in order to wake up society to see that there are other and fresher ways of doing things. Thus, the heyoka is the human counterpart of the Thunder Beings, who repeatedly dissolve the existing order and fashion a new arrangement from the pieces.

As we transition from the Fourth into the Fifth World, it occurs to me that not all heyokas are Plains Indians. Some have yellow skin, others black, others white. These heyokas of every color are experiencers, and have been changed by their experience of extraterrestrial contact by messengers from the sky (Thunder Beings). As modern-day heyokas, experiencers are charged to live as active witnesses against the ignorance and corruption of the Fourth World, and to live as witnesses of the Fifth World which is emerging. In doing so, modern heyokas honor the Thunder Beings, the extraterrestrials, who have come as cosmic midwives to help us birth the Fifth World.[16]

All of this suggests that we're about to get a little help from our friends. Due to the lateness of the hour, we can assume they are already here, working through the *heyokas*. The idea of help (Jupiter) coming from those who are not of this Earth (Uranus) awakening society (the Aries Point) to the point where we are able to live in harmony with the rest of creation is, in my estimation, the highest expression of the Jupiter/Uranus/Aries Point conjunction.

If I were to choose a time when any effort to wake us up might succeed, it would have to be during Jupiter's travels over the Aries Point. And if we take into consideration that, according to myth, both

Jupiter and Uranus are Thunder Gods, it adds weight to the prediction. My tendency to overanalyze things notwithstanding, between prophecy, the astrology, and the mythology, there's too much to confirm the idea that Jupiter's tour of duty at the Aries Point will involve a consciousness shift.

I have no way to prove it, but I have a feeling that the Native American prophecy keepers understood the stars well enough to foresee that the Thunder Beings would return when their planetary counterparts arrived at the alpha-omega degree of the Zodiac. And I am willing to bet that this three-way conjunction will mark a time when the collective mind opens to an influx of new and unusual energies. As those forces permeate our consciousness and that level of support becomes a universally agreed-upon fact, there is every reason to suspect that what is as yet beyond our comprehension will come out of nowhere to help us shift into the Fifth World.

Jupiter will conjunct the Aries Point on the following dates:

⊕ June 6 to June 14, 2010 (Uranus will be there too)

⊕ August 31 to September 10, 2010

⊕ January 22 to January 28, 2010

Ordinarily, Jupiter takes one year to move through a sign. Looking at the planetary movements for 2010, he enters Pisces on January 18 and moves into Aries on June 6. Pedaling twice as fast, Jupiter's rush to get to the Aries Point makes it seem as if he knows the hour is late and he's on a mission that takes precedence over his regular routine.

What is also worthy of note that Jupiter is exalted in Pisces; his best qualities emerge under that influence. Forgiveness, compassion, unconditional love, and a deep sense of connection to all that is, along with a desire to resonate fully with spiritual values, come out of the woodwork whenever these two archetypes overlap—and those things will be stirring at the etheric level prior to Jupiter's arrival at the Aries Point. I am sure that, through the process that in horary astrology is known as "the collection of light," all of that will be collected, carried with him, and brought to the table when he and Uranus have their first encounter in June 2010.

As far as timing goes, Jupiter aspects normally last no more than a week. It's interesting to me that his journey over the Aries Point involves a retrograde pattern that lengthens his trip considerably. There are many ways to explain the retrograde phenomenon. I like to humanize it by comparing it to what we do when we reiterate ourselves in conversation. We do this to emphasize or drive home a point. When a planet goes retrograde, it does the same thing, loaning importance to whatever the issue at hand is.

It seems as if Jupiter has more on his mind this time—either that or what he has to say is so important he wants to make sure we get it. He's certainly giving us plenty of time to download the message. In between his exact conjunction with the Aries Point, his influence upon it will still be active, so what would normally require seven days will broadcast for over seven months. Jupiter's such a benevolent guy that my sense is he's giving humanity a huge break, patiently tweaking our consciousness with three doses of enlightenment and more than half a year to assimilate what has to be a very powerful transmission.

Out of the three sets of dates, I see the June 2010 window as the most mind-blowing point of contact. On June 8 and 9, Jupiter and Uranus will form an exact conjunction at the Aries Point. In an earlier chapter I brought up the possibility that by itself, Uranus's movement over that degree of the Zodiac could generate a collective awakening; with Jupiter adding his support to the possibility, and the prophesies substantiating the idea, any number of surprises could materialize during that window, or during and between all them.

If I am being overly optimistic on that score, at the very least, the June 2010 window will fortify Uranus for his final showdown with Saturn. This preliminary meeting with Jupiter, his closest ally and wisest counselor, will help him get clear on what tack to take with the Reaper. My guess is that that conversation will inspire Uranus to approach the most powerful point of conflict (July 22 to August 2, 2010) from a place of goodwill.

If we consider that Saturn's place in the solar system occupies the space between Jupiter and Uranus, it's worth considering that he will be surrounded by energies that are totally in accord and mutually empowered until the end of January 2011. With two very powerful, positive characters presenting a unified front, and the masses there with them calling for change, peer pressure alone will make it easier for Saturn to consider merging with whatever those forces represent. If water always seeks its own level, it's hard to picture him or the keepers of the old paradigm, seeing any point in holding on to the past. Like the rest of us, they too will have to step up and figure out how to resonate at a higher frequency.

Is There a Downside to This?

On a bad day, Jupiter can be accused of self-righteousness; he can also be arrogant. In a similar vein, Uranus can get fanatic and adopt a "my way or the highway" attitude when he loses touch with himself. If there's a down side to this, it could translate into the tendency to get too righteous about our respective positions.

One problem I see with the two planets coming together is that self-righteous fanaticism could overtake the masses, causing us to exhibit intolerance toward any faction that doesn't share the same view. As we move toward Unity Consciousness, our habit of seeing everything as right or wrong will probably still be active enough for many of us to ignore the fact that everyone has their own truths. During this Jupiter transit, we'd be wise to keep an eye on the self-righteous fanatic switch and avoid any system or belief structure that uses that button as a control mechanism.

Lack of discernment is another issue. Jupiter is often so willing to give everyone the benefit of the doubt that he becomes gullible. At times, when he teams up with Uranus, he can go off the deep end with all kinds of crazy ideas. There will be many purveying their version of the truth in the days ahead; not all of them will do so with integrity. With that in mind, it would be good to connect with whether something feels right to us or not before we choose to align ourselves with it.

The other thing is that situations that require a saving grace are inherently messy. By the time Jupiter shows up, all kinds of difficulties will be in need of repair, so don't expect this transit to be a walk in the park. While there's a lot to suggest that he's got everything going for him, what he confronts when he gets here would cause Rambo or Superman to think twice about taking it on. Every facet of that mess will have to be exposed and cleaned up before we begin to sense that it's all part of the growth and renewal process.

I mentioned earlier that in my view, the point of ingress is the blueprint for everything that unfolds during any specific transit. When I erected the chart for Jupiter's arrival at the Aries Point (see page 202), the first aspect that caught my eye was an opposition between Kronos and Pluto. Kronos represents people in high places—he is running the show—and his opinions count, not because they reflect the truth, but because he happens to be in charge.

The following quote comes from Martha Lang-Wescott's book, *The Orders of Light*. The asteroid guru offers a detailed description of what happens when Pluto and Kronos meet up:

> Evaluation (of knowledge, competency, autonomy, or expertise) manipulation, destruction of or strange motives in the system; events that show differences of opinion, legalities, rules, or attempts to set procedures are actually power struggles, or arise from resentments and a need to push others to their limits; events wherein one's competency or

expertise is perceived as a threat (with ensuing dominance struggles); to see testing of laws, compliance with regulations or leaders (including leaders of governments and business, but also other "experts" or people of some—even fleeting prominence) mastery of or experts in psychology, efficiency, finance, or "personal evaluation"—and on their opinions or competency: attention to the finances of important people and regulations concerning debt, inheritances, mortgages, investments, grants, alimony, support payments, or interest rates and payments; manipulation through or defiance of laws, regulations, or opinion; to be aware that prominent persons (including leaders in government) are under substantial pressure; to push for leadership or control; to be aware of the power (and motives) of "people in charge"—and to see abuses of power through misuse of office, position, laws and procedures; attempts to manipulate or dominate through the tactic of questioning competency and testing the limits of rules, regulations, opinions, or autonomy.[17]

Making things right always involves exposing what's wrong. The Kronos-Pluto opposition indicates that the powers-that-be will be pushing the same old agenda without much luck. Defying credulity once too often, prominent people will be called to explain abuses of power; questions will arise as to their competency. Given Jupiter's association with the truth, it doesn't surprise me that the powers-that-be will be called to task for things that have been hidden for far too long.

This should be seen as a positive process, but the fallout will be big enough to make it seem otherwise. Jupiter's ability to repair every worst-case scenario will reveal the extent to which the powers-that-be have manipulated us. The financial systems and the banks form the keystone for those manipulations, and they will be out of commission by June 2010 or before. Once they go down, the secrets and lies that held them together will unravel one by one and the public will be furious when they find out what their leaders have been up to all these years. What goes around comes around, and the unpopular prophecy quoted in chapter 8 that alludes to people in charge being hunted down could become a reality during this time.

Hekate and Persephone will still be conjunct when Jupiter hits the Aries Point. The same aspect showed up in the chart for Pluto's ingress into Capricorn (see page 199). What began to surface in 2008 will be going full bore by 2010. If Hekate rules holocausts and things that happen in the dark and Persephone is the motherless child, lost and alone, the nightmare of homelessness and the chaos that erupts when large segments of the population are without food or shelter will continue as a theme that becomes more apparent over time. Knowing this now might give us pause to think about how well we are set up to handle vast numbers of hungry, homeless human beings. In keeping with the above aspect, a square from Ceres to Uranus, Jupiter, and the Aries Point suggests that food riots and/or disruptions created around the care of large numbers of children will be problematic. The truth about the "missing children" and the secrets surrounding "Project Monarch" and the "MK-Ultra Project" could very well come to light at this time. If there is full disclosure on those abominations, public outrage will be off the charts.

With all this and much more to indicate that Jupiter's influence will be more than necessary, one wonders how he will manage to come up with a solution for it. Fortunately, there are supporting aspects that buttress his position and reinforce the possibility of a last-minute miracle. Pandora in opposition to Hybris hints at the idea that what seems doomed or fated to happen will be diverted by an unexpected series of surprises. Pandora is the "anything can happen, let me see if I can pop out a miracle" asteroid, and Hybris holds rulership over what our conditioning allows us to expect.

The textbook interpretation of this aspect reads as expect the unexpected. Flipped over, it holds themes of wanting to know what to expect so as not to be caught off guard. Both translations are worth keeping in mind. Praying to Allah and tying our respective camels, we can hold the thought that the Thunder Beings or some last minute miracle may clean up this mess instantaneously, and prepare for whatever comes with plans A, B, and C, just in case Jupiter and his cohorts don't pull through.

To clarify things, it might help to beam in on what the Sabian symbols have to say about the Aries Point. Too many planets will sit on that angle, or form aspects to it, for us to ignore what always seems to get to the heart of the matter—and as far as Jupiter goes, any wisdom we take from the imagery will clarify the extent to which we can count on his support between the spring of 2010 and the end of January 2011. Here's what the Sabian symbols have to say about the Aries Point:

Phase I (Aries one degree): A woman just risen from the sea. A seal is embracing her.

Keynote: Emergence of new forms and of the potentiality of consciousness.

This is the first of the 360 phases of a universal and multi-level cyclic process which aims at the actualization of a particular set of potentialities. These potentialities, in the Sabian symbols, refer to the development of man's individualized consciousness—the consciousness of being an individual person with a place and function (a "destiny") in the planetary organism of the Earth, and in a particular type of human society and culture.

To be individually conscious means to emerge out of the sea of generic and collective consciousness—which to the emerged mind appears to be unconsciousness. Such an emergence is the primary event. It is the result of some basic action: a leaving behind, an emerging from a womb or matrix, here symbolized by the sea.

Such an action is not to be considered a powerful, positive statement of individual being. In the beginning is the act; but it is often an imperceptible, insecure act. The small tender germ out of the seed does not loudly proclaim its existence. It has to pierce through the crust of the soil still covered with the remains of the past. It is all potentiality and a minimum of actual presence.

In the symbol, therefore, the emergent entity is a woman; symbolically speaking, a form of existence still close to the unconscious depths of generic biological nature, filled with the desire to be rather than self-assertion. The woman is seen embraced by the seal because the seal is a mammal which once had experienced a biological, evolutionary but relatively unconscious emergence, yet which retraced its steps and "returned to the womb" of the sea. The seal, therefore, represents a regressive step. It embraces the Woman who has emerged, because every emergent process is susceptible to failure. This process is indeed surrounded by the memory, the ghosts of past failures during previous cycles. The impulse upward is held back by regressive fear or insecurity: the issue of the conflict depends on the relative strength of the future-ward and the past-ward forces.

The possibility of success and that of failure is implied throughout the entire process of actualization. Every release of potentiality contains this two-fold possibility. It inevitably opens up two paths: one leads to "perfection" in consciousness, the other to "disintegration"—the return to the undifferentiated state (the state of humus, manure, cosmic dust—i.e. to the symbolic "great Waters of space," to chaos).

This symbol characterizes the first of five stages which are repeated at three levels. This stage represents the initial statement, or theme, of the five-fold series which refers to the first level: Impulse to be.[18]

The symbol makes it clear that we are emerging onto a whole new level of consciousness. In the act of leaving the sea to explore a different aspect of herself, the woman (the Goddess, the Female Light, the Divine Feminine) makes a bold but insecure statement of her desire to grow beyond the boundaries of the known. Her emergence is threatened by the extent to which the evolutionary impulse competes with the fear that the attempt is doomed to failure, or that some force from the past may convince her to give up on the idea.

If this is a metaphor for where we are, we might as well be looking at the petroglyphs at Prophecy Rock. They too make it clear that we stand at an evolutionary crossroad and that, ultimately, it is our choice whether to take the high or the low road. There is no reference to divine intervention in either the symbol or the rock drawing, but there is enough evidence for that coming from other sources for me to think that there will be plenty of it.

If we are to take anything from this symbol, it might be this: Even though we are on our own in this actualization process, as we feel our way through the dark, if the "impulse to be" outweighs every other impulse, our emergence into the Fifth World, our entrance into the Age of Light, and the whole matter of our passage through the Great Shift will reflect the intensity of that desire and the extent to which we can embrace the infinite potentiality held in the flood of energy coming from the Aries Point.

CHAPTER 10

Chiron

Thinking about Thunder Beings, messengers from on high, and the implications of outside help might prompt us to wonder if we could make this transition without that kind of support. I'm as sure that the extraterrestrial presence will make itself known as I am that Jupiter and Uranus will install a whole new way of seeing things. But there's another piece to this and it has to do with our part in it.

We've talked about how important it is for all of us to change at the nuts and bolts level, as much as we've talked about the need to step up to a higher frequency. But we haven't talked about what it is in us that gives us the capacity to do either one. Getting a little help from our friends is all well and good, but something in us has to be able to respond to that support or match it, and our part in this has to do with cultivating the ability to do both.

I am also clear that not everyone reading this book buys into the idea of extraterrestrial beings, or planetary rescue missions, or miracles. And I am sure that many of you aren't the least bit impressed or reassured by predictions of some last-minute reprieve. For the skeptics, and those of you who aren't totally convinced that all of the above is a sure thing, you'll be happy to know that there are other signs that suggest we're fully capable of making this Great Shift on our own.

Chiron is the planet that actualizes Spirit here on the physical level and mediates all of the issues that crop up between Saturn and Uranus. He stands between the two planets, much like a half-note in a musical scale. If we've made no mention of him it's only because, up until April 2010, he isn't doing anything spectacular. No big aspects to speak of. No serious interaction with other planets or angles. Chiron is just taking his time moving through the later degrees of Aquarius. On April 20, 2010, however, he will enter the sign Pisces, and many things will be set in motion when he crosses that border (see page 203). Before we can talk about what that will entail, it might be good to give you a little history on this profound and unusual planet.

The Chiron Myth

Grandson of Uranus and Gaia, Chiron was Saturn's love child. Married to Rhea at the time, the story goes that Saturn was so taken by a sea nymph named Phylria that he strayed from the path and broke his marriage vows. That such an upstanding God would even dream of jumping the fence seems totally out of character, but apparently that's how it went; in a moment of passion Saturn disguised himself as a horse, seduced Phylria, and it was out of that escapade that the Centaur Chiron was born.

While the rest of his breed were overly fond of bacchanalian pursuits and too dissolute to do much of anything but abuse the life force, Chiron was known for his ability to tap into that force and focus it creatively for the good of humanity. What made him different may have had something to do with his immortal blood, but instead of turning him into the odd man out, the Centaurs had so much respect for Chiron that they made him their leader. High Priest to a pack of lustful, bloodthirsty, hybrid creatures, out of all of them he was the only one who knew how to channel his animal instincts toward a higher purpose.

The interesting thing about Chiron is that he was every bit a Centaur, but he was born with the understanding that his connection to nature was sacred, and he sought to learn as much about it as he could. In doing so, he became adept at healing, herbalism, gymnastics, hunting, martial arts, divination, chiromancy, alchemy, astrology, astronomy, and all of the natural sciences. Unlike so many of the gods, Chiron's wisdom came to him through practice and direct experience; none of it was bestowed magically. And while his desire for knowledge may have been god-given, he acquired every bit of it the hard way.

This hands-on approach applied to everything he did. When it came to matters of Spirit, Chiron knew that the only way to know God is through direct experience. It was he who informed the human race that the God force could be accessed directly, here in the physical realm, through the practical application of sacred knowledge. His own practices elevated him, and it was through them that Chiron attained unsurpassed levels of mastery.

Famous for all of his remarkable abilities, he became a mentor of the highest order. The likes of Achilles, Hercules, and Jason sat at his feet prior to embarking on their respective quests. All the great heroes of mythology were initiated by Chiron, and I suspect that it was his wisdom that gave them the ability to confront every test and reign victorious over impossible odds.

That we know more about these heroes than we do about the strange creature who taught them seems a bit odd, until we realize that, in Chiron's world, the quest matters more than any fame or recognition that might come from it. As the consummate Spiritual warrior, Chiron shows up as the unsung hero in many of the Greek myths. Out of all of them, the story of Prometheus is probably the most well known.

Story Time

Unwilling to bow to the unchallengeable might of the Olympians, Prometheus took it upon himself to steal fire from the gods and bring it down to Earth so that mankind could be warmed and enlightened by its flame. Unfortunately, his idea didn't go over too well with Zeus. When the king of the gods heard about the theft, he flew into a rage and sentenced Prometheus to be chained to a rock for all eternity. Just for good measure, Zeus called down a vulture to peck away at his guts and liver day in and day out, till the end of time.

Meanwhile, back on Mount Pelion, Chiron happened to be suffering a similar fate. Accidentally shot in the foot by a poison arrow from Hercules' quiver (an arrow that Chiron had not only taught the great hero to make and shoot, but whose poison was his own private recipe), the king of the Centaurs crawled back to his cave to nurse a wound for which there was no cure, knowing full well that his immortality would cause him to live with the pain forever.

Upon hearing about Prometheus' trials, Chiron decided to strike a bargain with Zeus. He would give up his immortality if Zeus would agree to unchain Prometheus and release the fire element to man. Zeus went along with the plan, Prometheus was freed, and Chiron descended into Hell, sacrificing his immortality so that mankind could understand fire and learn how to use its power in the right way.

Back to the Future

In an earlier chapter, we talked about how a planet's discovery coincides with the collective consciousness awakening to the principles it rules. When Chiron appeared in 1977, our relationship to everything, including God, changed. And it seems as if his original sacrifice and what he gave up to enlighten us finally came to its fullest realization—because it was at that point that we began to move away from beliefs that instructed us to, "Fear God and keep his commandments: for this is the whole duty of man" (Eccles, 12:13) to constructs that were more along the lines of, love God, abide by our own truth, and know that the purpose for living is to actualize the God within.

On the outer levels, the Chironic force called humanity to wake up to a million other lies and misconceptions. That he arrived arm in arm with the environmental movement, the holistic healing movement, the free energy movement, and what became known as the New Age Spiritual movement is no coincidence. All of those things bear Chiron's imprint, and each one of them brought our attention to the question of power and its use and abuse. Looking back now, it's almost as if, up until that time we were under some sort of spell that made it OK to rape the environment, give all of our power away to the establishment, remain blind to the fact that the ether is overflowing with free energy, and as oblivious to the idea that matters of Spirit are well within our reach and do not necessitate the presence of an intermediary.

Thirty years later, it's quite clear that Chiron totally blew the collective mind. His appearance in the heavens not only rearranged our perspective on everything, it opened up the channel to the Higher Self. His natural wisdom and his reverence for Mother Earth reminded us that everything is intimately connected in a way that makes it impossible to separate ourselves from one another, or from nature, or from God. If everything coexists in a state of unity and oneness, guess what? We're all God. And, like Chiron, our purpose for living involves developing a relationship to that aspect of our being so that we can actualize that principle and embody it fully here in the physical realm.

All of this presupposes that there is a way to do that, and fortunately, Chiron understands that there are many ways. As the archetypal mentor, or way-shower, he made it clear that the path to Spirit is unique to each individual. At the same time, Chiron knew that no one gets where they're going without a little effort, and our Spiritual development, along with the practices we engage in, require work.

The nature and purpose of that work is described in the following quote from Rudolf Steiner:

> Throughout antiquity, people believed that to acquire knowledge of supersensible truths one first had to develop supersensible organs. Everyone understood that Spiritual forces lie sleeping in all human beings. They knew that such Spiritual forces are not developed in the average person, but can be awakened and unfolded by prolonged exercises.
>
> Adherents of the Mysteries in fact described these stages of development as very difficult. It was generally felt that a person who had developed such forces and was able to research the truth in this way was related to the ordinary person as a seeing person is related to one who is born blind. This is the kind of "vision" those within the holy Mysteries aimed at . . . ancient peoples understood that, for a person whose inner senses are awakened, a new world appears, one that ordinary seeing cannot perceive. Those consecrated in the Mysteries sought to create from ordinary human beings a human being who had evolved to a higher stage of evolution. Such a person they called an "initiate." Only the initiate was thought to be in a position to discover anything about supersensible truths by direct vision, by Spiritual intuition.[19]

"Mr. Hands On," Chiron initiated himself by finding ways to awaken his inner senses without any outside help and he became an adept because he intuitively understood that the God force, or the life force, operates as much in the third dimension as it does on every other level of existence. Nature was his laboratory as well as his temple. By living in accordance with its laws, Chiron became the embodiment of and the archetype for the enlightened human being.

His example shows us that anyone living in 3-D has the same potential. And when Chiron finally appeared in the sky, he didn't just tell us we're all God and leave it at that; he came with the keys for the realization of that potential. The self-help systems and the healing modalities that emerged in the late Seventies attest to this. Those things popped the lid off the idea that, buried underneath our limitations, lies something quite precious and God-like.

Over time, the Chiron effect flowed so far into the mainstream that the media cashed in on it and started pumping all kinds of free, therapeutic advice directly into our living rooms. Oprah Winfrey, Dr. Phil, Dr. Ruth, Montel Williams, Maury Povich, and even the notorious Jerry Springer, all place their emphasis on helping us solve our problems, heal our wounds, and clear our issues. What was once restricted to initiates and later got passed on to the New Age Spiritual crowd is now in the hands of the masses.

We can joke about the fix-me-up craze, but we can't deny the fact that it brought our attention to the truth—that all of us are deeply wounded in some way, and that our wounds are what stand between us and the God within. Those blocks aren't what they appear to be, nor do they provide us with an excuse to remain unconscious. We came here to work those things out. The key to getting beyond them requires us to understand that, ultimately, what's in the way is the way. Regardless of who you are, the path to Spirit opens up the moment you recognize that your wounds hold the key to your unfoldment.

Chiron knew this better than anyone. Born to a race of profligate, barbaric creatures, his karma never became his excuse—he took what he was given and transmuted it into something else altogether. If the wound is the remedy, the Promethean tale takes that message one step further. Suffering from a self inflicted, incurable wound, rather than live with the pain forever, Chiron sacrificed his immortal Soul to heal it—and in healing himself, the God who later became known as The Wounded Healer knew that he gave up his life for a much higher purpose—one that involved helping mankind access the inner fire of their own divinity and the possibility of enlightenment.

Where Are We?

Thank you for your patience. You're probably wondering what all this has to do with the End Times. The Earth, along with each and every one of us, is about to go through changes the likes of which none of us have ever seen—not in this life, anyway. With the understanding that our part in this is of major importance, Chiron would seem to be a touchstone for all of us. His presence in the heavens alone is proof that even without the ET's, or some other out of the blue, last minute saving grace, the chip that allows us to transcend our limitations was reinstalled back in 1977. Chiron reminded the human race that we were born with the ability to enlighten ourselves and use our creative power for the greater good—activating that ability is where it's at right now.

If you've got wounds, issues, recurring patterns, old sob stories, anything that blocks your ability to connect with your full self-realization, it's time to leave all that stuff at the door; if it stands in the way of your unfoldment, you don't need it anymore. Whatever it takes to clear it out is your business, but it's time to do that work—no matter how far along the path you think you are. This is of premier importance, because, the clearer we get and the closer we get to what we really came here to do, the gentler this process will be for us all, and for Mother Earth as well.

Up to this point, I was convinced that Uranus is the "Man of the Hour." Now I am of the mind that the real hero here is Chiron. And I am happy to inform you that he is about to make some wonderful changes—changes that will make it easier for humanity to take full responsibility for our part in this.

Who Is Chiron and What Is He Doing Here?

We've only known about Chiron since 1977. With a fifty-year cycle, Chiron hasn't been around long enough for any astrologer to really understand the full import of his message or the full range of his expression. Judging from what he's done so far, it feels to me like the next twenty years could bring us to a place where wisdom and integrity reign over instinct and Spiritual power is valued far more than material things. If the one who reverses our perspective on everything, continues his work, I see us getting more and more tuned in to the ways of nature, more knowledgeable about how it works, and more enlightened about who we are in relationship to it.

As I say this, I am reminded of the Sabian symbol that came up in the Pluto chapter; the one that talks about the Indian chief claiming power from the assembled tribe. And I am also thinking of the Native American prophecy that pointed to 1977 as the year when the Indians would be free to go forward and lead a Spiritual revolution. That prediction coincided with Chiron's appearance in the sky.

It wasn't until I really got into writing this chapter that I began to see that Chiron and the Indigenous People are tied together in more ways than one, the most obvious being that they share the same values. And there's too much of the shaman and the medicine man in him for anyone *not* to see him as the embodiment of indigenous wisdom.

After close to forty years as a practicing astrologer, it amazes me that it took me that long to see this. My take on Chiron has always been limited by the Puritanical belief that what is instinctive in us, or what we call our lower urges, need to be reined in and controlled by the mind.

While that's one way to look at Chiron, the half-horse, half-man imagery flows in two directions—and the man, or the mind, or the Higher Self receives just as much instruction from the horse or the beast, or the natural, more instinctive wisdom that comes from the part of us that is inextricably rooted to the Earth.

This two-way trail tells me that we can meditate and transcend till the cows come home, but if we ignore the visceral truths that are only taught in nature's mystery school, nothing will change. Unfortunately, we have civilized ourselves to the point where the Original Teachings have been long forgotten by the White Man—and what we have lost our connection to can only be restored by the ones who have kept it.

If I am right about Chiron being the astrological standard bearer for all the indigenous tribes, his upcoming transit patterns will probably coincide with events that highlight their return to a position of honor, power, and respect. They will also coincide with the recovery of what we have lost. If we can restore that connection and integrate the Original Teachings with our inner wish to heal ourselves and serve Mother Earth, I have no doubt that our part in the Great Shift will make all the difference.

CHAPTER 11

Chiron Enters Pisces

When I say Chiron was "discovered" in 1977, I don't mean that the planet somehow magically came out of nowhere on that date. Astrologers have always known about Chiron—but what astrologers know has never carried enough weight with the scientific community to qualify as fact or truth. And while astronomers understood Bode's Law well enough to postulate that there had to be a missing link between Saturn and Uranus, for some reason they couldn't officially discover Chiron until they found a way to make his presence in the solar system fit into their definition of the universe.

That being said, the last time Chiron entered Pisces was in 1962. Reflecting back on that period in history, we see the 50s mindset had run its course and new thought forms were beginning to take root in the collective mind. Between the Vietnam War and the hippie movement, we didn't know if we were coming or going; by 1968, when Chiron left Pisces, we'd rolled enough joints to blow all of our 50s illusions, including Doris Day and Rock Hudson, right up in smoke.

After 48 years, Chiron's return to the sign of the Fishes would seem to indicate that we're about to get our minds blown once again.

If Chiron is a complex planet, the sign Pisces is equally complex. Ruled by Neptune, a planet that has too much to do with what is Spiritual in us for anyone to process its message clearly, Pisces is where we either ascend beyond the boundaries of time and space or become victimized by our inability to go there. The last of the twelve Zodiacal symbols, it is the end of the line. The two fish swimming in opposite directions tell us that, at the place where all things meet their final resolution, the consequences of our actions take us either one way or another.

The idea that Pisces is where everything terminates is only partially true. We do come to a moment of truth in this sign. But it is also true that, at the end of any cycle, whatever reaches completion is really just a stage in a larger pattern of development. As Liz Greene tells us in *The Astrology of Fate,* the last stop is not what it appears to be:

> The last sign is also the first because it forms the background from which the next cycle will spring; and when seen in this way, it is not strange that the symbolism of the Fishes connects us not with the god Neptune, nor with any other male deity, but with the primal Mother.[20]

As it turns out, the point where everything culminates is also the Womb of Creation. It makes sense, doesn't it? Death and life are inseparable; one cycle gives way to another. Pisces is the Great Void, or the empty space between cycles where the creative process reduces everything to nothing only to prepare itself for a rebirth. The concept rings even more true when we remember that the universal symbol for the divine feminine and every other aspect of the female is the Vesica Pisces, or the opening out of which light and life emerge.

Mother Earth is pregnant and about to give birth to a New Age. At an imminent birth there is always a birth pain. There are contractions. There are difficulties. But when a young couple looks forward to a birth in those last few days, they don't begin to say, "Any day now the labor is going to start." They say, "Any day now there's going to be a new life." The focus is different . . . Instead of looking at the labor pains, perhaps we can go away from here looking at the birth of a New Age. If the changes do come, if the continents are altered, if the weather is altered, if all of these . . . do happen, what will be the result? How can we respond to that?[21]

Ultimate meanings are great for putting things into perspective, but this transit will be active from April 20, 2010 until approximately 2019 (see page 203). Nine years in the Womb of Creation! A lot of things will be stirred down to nothing during this gestation period, and our perspective is bound to get lost in the process. If Chiron is about to escort us through the Great Void, it may help to take a look at the map and find out a little bit about how he and Pisces get along before we get there.

Pisces is usually characterized as the Selfless Healer. In my experience, this is true—but only part of the time. While themes of renunciation and selfless service are strong in this sign, only one of the fishes has the strength to swim in that direction. The other plays the role of the wounded soul who can barely float without a life jacket. The savior and the victim live together here, and the essence of the sign can be found somewhere in the middle, dancing on the fine line that connects the two.

Opposite impulses inevitably mirror each other in Pisces. Those who approach life with the desire to heal everything in sight have most likely suffered as much as their wounded counterparts, but have somehow managed to find the lesson in it. Instead of drowning in an ocean of sorrow, evolved Pisceans transmute their experience into a wellspring of compassion and draw on that as a means to heal others. Much like Chiron in the Prometheus myth, their selfless acts serve a greater cause. In sacrificing themselves to that cause, these types find the key to their own healing.

The other Fish has a different response to their suffering. Lost when it comes to understanding its purpose, it gets swallowed up by the pain. Inside, they know that they have to surrender to a higher calling and, while many of them actually know what that is, they don't have the inner strength to pull it off. Too bruised and battered to even lick their own wounds, they can't seem to see that their pain is less of a problem than their inability to transcend it. With Pisces, there's no way around the sacrifice. The sign demands it. And the ones who can't make it consciously spend their lives *being* the sacrifice, splayed out on the altar of their own problems.

With the Wounded Healer approaching the realm of the Selfless Healer, it is clear that we're about to get a double dose of healing. At a time when the Great Mother is in critical condition, it's comforting to know that the one who knows more about what to do with our wounds than anyone in the solar system is about to spend nine years in the sign that begs us to heal them. Even so, the cure is bound to put each and every one of us through internal and external changes that will rock us to the core.

This tells me that leaving our pain at the door would seem to make a lot more sense than trying to squeeze it through the keyhole—because any wounds we have left, and any changes we don't have the courage to make will interfere with our rebirth and make the healing process much more difficult than it needs to be. Mother Earth is relying on us to be far enough beyond our own private agonies to be able to support her through these upcoming changes from a totally conscious place—free of our issues and clear enough about our purpose to handle whatever the Shift of the Ages calls on us to do.

If you're wondering if anything in you is ready for this, look at it this way: All the changes that are tossing you around right now are preparing you for it. Make them, no matter how costly, inconvenient, or frightening they may seem. When Chiron enters Pisces, the less baggage you have, the more free you'll be to swim along in the slipstream of changes that have everything to do with the way you relate to them and the way you approach your part in this.

The Ingress Chart

Erecting the chart for Chiron's ingress into Pisces, the asteroid Hopi forms an exact conjunction with the *Immum Coeli,* or the base angle of the chart (see page 203). Hopi is all things Native American; it is the indigenous asteroid. The base point of any horoscope represents its foundation or root structure. It is what we inherit from our ancestors, our cellular memory, and the bedrock that we stand upon. The Immum Coeli also happens to be the point where all things return to the Earth.

Layering one image over the other, Hopi on that point tells me that Chiron's journey through Pisces will involve a return to the ways of the Indigenous People. Their traditions will hold us up and strengthen us for the duration of the transit. How this will work is hard to say, but it looks as if that wisdom will rise up from the core of our cellular memory in the same way that sap rises up from the roots of a tree. As ancient truths begin to flow into our consciousness, my sense is that we will awaken to them, one leaf at a time until the collective mind blooms with belief patterns that reflect a deeper connection to nature.

Hopi's sextile* to the asteroid Panacea adds weight to that prospect. Panacea is "the cure for what ails you" asteroid; whatever the problem is, Panacea has the solution for it. Favorably aspected

---

* A sextile is a favorable, 60 degree aspect. In any given situation sextiles show the astrologer where the support, help, etc. comes from.

to Hopi, the message is clear—and, as far as Chiron is concerned, the remedy for what ails us lies in a return to the Original Teachings. During his stay in Pisces, Chiron's purpose will be to enlighten us to the old ways as a means to bring about healing at the personal and collective level and maintain balance during tumultuous times. By 2019, our values and beliefs will bear no resemblance to any of the materialistic constructs we adhere to now.

Considering that the Indigenous People of the world have suffered so much at the hands of the White Man, the thought that they would be there for us at all is unbelievable. With every excuse to do the opposite, one would assume that they might leave us to fend for ourselves—but out of all the people on this planet, they know what their role is right now—and it doesn't involve allowing the wounds of the past to interfere with what Mother Earth needs from us. Chiron's influence, combined with the Piscean gift for taking even the deepest wounds and using the pain as a vehicle for compassion and forgiveness, will give them the strength to transcend any mistrust or bitterness they may feel for what they know is a much greater cause.

A secondary aspect between Hopi and Euridike sheds more light on this. Euridike is the asteroid that tells astrologers "who we rely upon," or who we place in a leadership role. In this case, the aspect happens to be an inconjunct, a 150-degree aspect that indicates certain adjustments have to be made. I laughed out loud when I saw this! What came to mind was overeducated, upper-crust white folks waking up to the realization that it won't be the politicians, the scholars, the scientific community, the religious leaders, or anyone in the halls of justice who step in to save the day. Our real support and leadership will come from an oppressed minority, from a group of people whom we patronize and who have been vilified and victimized for over 500 years. Talk about getting your mind blown! What we have to go through to reverse our perspective on that one will undoubtedly involve multiple major adjustments.

Eradicating prejudice will be one of them. Siva squares Hopi in this chart. The textbook interpretation of that aspect is "confronting the need to eradicate prejudice." If our preconceived notions about the Native people interfere with our ability to receive their support, we will wind up shooting ourselves in the foot. And any mistrust or discrimination coming from the indigenous ones, toward us will also be problematic.

The Siva-Hopi aspect calls all of us to come together as one family and suggests that it's time to release every form of prejudice. As we move toward Unity Consciousness, the patterns that have separated us into different castes, classes, factions, races, colors, sexes, and ideologies all have to go. One Spirit moves through everything here. As we awaken to that truth, the wounds and beliefs that cause us to see it any other way will slowly disappear.

Nemesis conjuncts Kronos and both asteroids oppose Pluto in this chart. This is all about the people in charge. The Kronos-Nemesis conjunction indicates that the powers that be are the problem, the bete noir, or the ones who are to blame. Pluto's opposition to Nemesis reads as, "The reach for power, the need for control, and the inability to forgive lie at the root of every situation that doesn't work." Mentioned in an earlier chapter, his aspect to Kronos has to do with the people in charge getting caught with their pants down.

This triple aspect indicates that the ones who are to blame will do everything in their power to cover up whatever they're being held accountable for. How they will manage to do this is hard to figure because too many things suggest that there will be nowhere to run and nowhere to hide from *anything* during our trip through the Great Void. Both Chiron and Pisces call us to forgive those who have trespassed against us. But a secondary, stressful aspect to Arachne, the complexity asteroid, tells me that their efforts to hide the truth will catch them in a web of lies that serves to expose them even further. When the full extent of their crimes becomes public knowledge, the burning question of the day will be: Can we forgive the unforgivable?

While the Nemesis-Pluto opposition indicates that any inability to do so will create problems for us, I am not sure if forgiving and forgetting are applicable in situations where the ones we're supposed to let off the hook are guilty of genocide, and countless other heinous iniquities. My opinion about this makes it difficult to interpret it objectively, but if the laws of karma apply to those in authority as much as they do to us, I am sure that, one way or another, they will reap what they have sown. And according to the Hopi prophesies, the punishment will probably fit the crime:

Here also a final decision will be made for the wicked. They will be beheaded and speak no more.[22]

Ceres is prominent in Chiron's ingress chart. This asteroid governs children, nurturing, nourishment, food, and the mother-child relationship. It is involved in the Pluto-Nemesis-Kronos configuration, which presents us with a number of possibilities, each of which can be interpreted from many different angles.

We can see right away that food and hunger will be a major problem, and hints that this will be so showed up in our previous ingress charts. Even now, in 2008, food shortages and an increase in food prices are affecting millions of people. This will only get worse, and I suspect that the ones who are already starving and homeless will have an easier time with it than those of us who aren't there yet, just by virtue of the fact that they've become accustomed to want.

With unnatural disasters and frequency warfare creating side effects that lead to crop failure, food shortages, and famine, there's not too much we can do about this. And while stocking up would seem to make sense, it might make more sense to think about going Breatharian; as crazy as that sounds, it would eliminate the hunger issue entirely. For those of you who are unfamiliar with what this means, Breatharians live on prana and sunlight; contrary to what you might think they don't waste away to nothing—these people actually thrive on nothing but air.

When I first heard about the Breatharian movement, I wrote it off as one of the kookier approaches to Spiritual development, and/or a great cover for the anorexics of the world—until it occurred to me that if we're raising our frequencies to a fourth and fifth dimensional level, food might be a non-issue where we're going. The whole Breatharian thing may seem a little too far out from where we sit now but I have a feeling that it's serving another purpose, one that might save us more than one problem a few years from now, and possibly help us accustom ourselves to a totally different set of basic needs. Who knows, by 2019, we could all be living on air.

I have no doubt that children and their needs will also be a major issue. The nightmare of homelessness that showed up in the other ingress charts reiterates itself in the Chiron chart. Pluto's conjunction with Ceres indicates that children will be separated from their parents. In the midst of cataclysmic events, how do you suppose we will care for them? Can any of us even begin to imagine what that would involve? We should think about the implications of hoards of children being without nurture or protection.

The same theme shows up in a square from Siva to the Moon, interpreted as "the Motherless Child." In a similar vein, Odysseus conjunct the Ascendant indicates that adapting to the loss of roots and family connections will be something we all will face. In essence, the Odysseus aspect showcases the idea of exile and the implications of being driven away from home. With the asteroid Apollo squaring the ascending axis, one crisis after another will make it difficult to know what will happen next. Any sense of safety and security that we have now will be gone.

In a natal chart, whenever Ceres conjuncts Pluto, the birth experience is often a near-death experience. Without stretching the interpretation too far, the fact that the aspect appears in the Chiron chart presents us with an image that suggests that our rebirth will be a near-death experience. All of the above would seem to support the idea—but the key word here is *near* death. If we are to live on that line during this gestation period, holding the thought that we'll come out of it alive and in a much better place needs to be kept in mind.

I could go into a thorough analysis of Chiron's ingress chart, but maybe you've heard enough. My purpose for sharing some of its highlights was to get you to think a little bit and perhaps inspire you to get on the ball regarding your part in this. In all of my questioning and research, what keeps coming up is that the way we respond to any crisis determines its outcome. If the current state of affairs was induced through a total lack of consciousness on our parts, would enlightening ourselves do as much to change it, and even go so far as to reverse the damage? Many, like John White, are of the mind that this is a definite possibility:

> Cayce's predictions, as well as those of others, indicate that the activity of our minds can have a direct influence on physical nature. This is termed biorelativity. Prayer, meditation, positive thought, and loving service are, from that point of view, instruments for pacifying the planet and bringing stability to unstable geological areas . . . The true prophet does not want to see his predictions come true; rather, he seeks to be contradicted. His prophetic words of foreseen disaster are intended to warn people in time to avert that disaster. Through a change of mind and behavior, people can to some extent defuse the circumstances leading up to a catastrophe, as well as get out of the way in time.[23]

Much of the difficulty that awaits us can be averted through prayer, meditation, and a thorough reexamination of our beliefs and priorities. But so much needs to shift in such a short period of time that it may be naïve to think that we can reverse the damage. The following excerpt from an interview with one of the Hopi Elders speaks to this idea:

Ya, our teachings that were given to us, we've strayed away from it and how are we supposed to, you know, alleviate a lot of some of these things—and it's going to be too late for us to try to turn around and walk that Spiritual path because we are taught that we are supposed to be on that path from way back. We should have been changing ourselves quite a number of years back, because it doesn't take overnight for a person to change . . . to walk a path . . . the chosen path. Also, it doesn't take overnight for the Creator to believe in you. He has to look at you, you know—your heart is the thing that has to change and it's not going to change overnight. These are the things that are very hard to change in a person, and so right now we look at it that it is already too late to start changing.[24]

Too little too late is better than nothing. How will we live with ourselves if we don't try? We're still here, and if we are to make a difference we must be willing to take on the challenge—in the same way that an EMT, or anyone, would in an emergency situation. If cataclysm and upheaval are no longer subjects for debate, what do you suppose being a day late and a dollar short will get us?

A lot of times when I share this message of the prophesies, people say, "Can't we change it? Could we stop it?" The answer is yes. The prophesies are always "either/or." We could have come together back there in 1565, and we could have had a great civilization, but we didn't. Always along the path of these prophesies, we could have come together. We still could. If we could stop the racial and religious disharmony, we would not have to go through this third shaking (of the Earth).

The Elders say the chance of that is pretty slim. It looks to me like it's pretty slim too. But they say what we can do is "cushion" it. The word we use is "cushion." We can cushion it so it won't be quite as bad. How do we do this? We do this by sharing the teaching that will reunite us.[25]

Need I say more? Reflecting back on everything we've said about the planetary aspects, and about Chiron specifically, the astrology mirrors the prophesies closely enough for us to see that we're standing on the threshold of major personal and collective changes that we have no precedent for. As much as it's comforting to know that it's all part of a rebirth process, what we have to live through in the meantime will be colored by death. Moving from one world to another will take approximately nine years. If our level of consciousness has as much to say about how our labor goes as I think it does, even if we're a day late and a dollar short, we owe it to ourselves to be 100 percent present.

At this point we've been so dumbed down by artificial beliefs and systematic programs, semi-comatose is the only word that comes to mind when our level of consciousness needs a definition. If Chiron's supposed to enlighten us, he's got his work cut out for him. This trip through the Womb of Creation will present us with nine years of one crisis after another. How far are we from being able to say without a doubt that we're fully able to do our part to cushion the blow—and perhaps wake up on the other side of this near-death experience in one piece?

If you take anything from this chapter, my hope is that it inspires you to look at where you are with your life. How much would it take to clear your head and your heart of whatever closes you off to your fullest expression? How well do you know the God within? Do you realize that the things that separate you from that part of yourself not only block your fulfillment—they block your ability to connect with your larger purpose? Whether you know it or not, your purpose right now has more to do with cushioning the blow than it does with anything else. It's time to wake up.

When we fell into separation, all of us fell asleep. Thirteen thousand years later, as the dark part of the cycle ends and the Age of Light begins, opening our eyes goes with the territory. Every bit of darkness and unconsciousness has to be washed away. We have plenty of support coming from more than one outside source; can the Chiron in you teach you how to get through your own stuff so you can be here for this? And when he heals your wounds, will you be able to give yourself over and take full responsibility for your part in it? Because we *will* live through a pole shift. It's taken me eleven chapters to reach that conclusion, but I finally see that that is what's in store for us.

If we can't begin to imagine what that may involve, then we need to start thinking about it. Believe it or not, we chose to be here to be part of this event. If we can't pull ourselves together and go through it consciously, like the Fish who can't bring themselves to go there, we'll have to live with the consequences of choosing not to. All change begins at the grass-roots level. Showing up a little too late is better than not showing up at all. Give that some thought, and try to imagine what it might be like if everyone did what they could to make the best of this.

[W]e have had in many readings that there is still time for change within the actions of people (there is, of course, always time for that) but that by 1981 the point of no return will have arrived. Either by that time people will have improved or the momentum will be so great that it will be difficult to induce a change in the events which are to follow. It appears that if these changes in human behavior do not come about by 1981, the world—and in particular the western world—will have to follow in the cycle, just as winter follows spring.

But even if there are tragedies and catastrophes, consider the opportunities for growth; and those who are looking for their teachers—look out, for they will appear, not necessarily in clouds or in shining armor, but in the very experience which is facing them at that very moment.[26]

CHAPTER 12

Shifting Poles

I stole Immanuel Velikovsky's *Worlds in Collision* and *Ages in Chaos* from a public library forty years ago. Broke and terminally addicted to information that I couldn't afford to buy, I remember going into the stacks and hiding those two volumes under my coat. Walking out the door, I rationalized the whole thing by telling myself no one else in town had ever checked them out, and convinced myself that I was probably the only member of the community who ever would.

In retrospect, I am pretty sure that Velikovsky's books would still be sitting on that shelf unopened and unread. It has taken that long for the general public to take notice of, or even begin to want to hear about, what the Russian researcher had to say. Velikovsky was one of the first to bring the pole shift phenomenon to light. Predictably, the scientific establishment denounced him ruthlessly for daring to suggest that periodic pole reversals play a major role in the Earth's evolutionary process.

As I sit down to write this chapter, I am acutely aware of how much things have changed in four decades. In fact, I recently spied

Velikovsky's name and pole shift headlines staring back at me from the rack of tabloids that flank the checkout line at the supermarket. When what was once too outrageous even to discuss is newsworthy enough to capture the interest of smart shoppers everywhere, it's safe to say that everyone knows about it. If they're not talking about it, at least they're snickering at the thought that gullible souls like me actually pay attention to this sort of thing.

In spite of the sudden surge of interest in the subject, we know very little about how pole shifts are triggered, and even less about what they involve. Taught to categorize things of this nature as senseless acts of God, we file them in the beyond-our-comprehension drawer without thinking that they might be governed by the same laws that keep everything else in the universe running smoothly.

I have to confess that only lately has this occurred to me. Until now, picturing a pole shift, the best that I could do was envision the world flipping over, all its inhabitants falling off the planet like a bunch of fleas, and everything going caput simultaneously, arbitrarily 86'd by some omniscient being who could care less. It amazes me that, after forty years of research, my little theory never made it out of kindergarten—but that's the truth.

That a thief who knows a tiny bit more about it than you do is about to fill you in on a subject that no one seems to fully understand might prompt you to put this book down and go find something better to do. While I don't blame you, I ask you to bear with me, because what I don't know has inspired me to go searching for anything that might loan clarity to this discussion—and I think that I have come across some things that will help all of us understand the mechanics of what we're about to go through.

The Earth is a living organism. As such, she relies on all of her parts to fulfill their function. Since she is intimately connected to every living thing, when even one aspect of her being gets out of whack, it creates disharmony. According to many, the reason we're teetering on the edge of a pole shift is that we forgot how to live in accordance with nature's laws. We upset the balance to such an extent that, after 13,000 years, Mother Earth is totally "off her rocker." An Edgar Cayce reading:

> ... given in 1973, contains an important clue to understanding the coming pole shift ... in the Cayce ... readings, the state of human consciousness is noted as the key factor influencing a displacement of the axis. The reading states that the ancient civilization of Lemuria was destroyed because its populace disregarded the balance of nature and tampered with natural conditions of the planets' energy fields.

> [T]here never would have been the shifting of the poles upon this planet it there were not the creating of conditions among men that were defiant to the Laws of God, but when those conditions of law were subverted among men, and there was a defiance of the Law of God, so there was set in motion upon the planet an energy that created an imbalance between those forces of good and evil or positive and negative ... Understand then, that the movement, the shifting of the poles, was caused by the activity of men in defiance of their God.[27]

While it's easy for many of us to understand why this would be true, Cayce's Spiritual perspective is by no means the only perspective. When Velikovsky's research came out in the early 1950s, the members of the scientific community who didn't try to suppress it began to look into whether or not there was anything to substantiate it. They found out that, contrary to the Uniformist theory, which is based on the premise that everything stays the same here, pole shifts do indeed happen in irregular cycles. Over half a century later, it is now generally accepted that these catastrophic events are part of the Earth's evolutionary process.

So much research has gone into this phenomenon, instead of misleading you into thinking that I know all about it or boring you with a synopsis of what I have read over the years, I decided to take a more interesting route. I decided to call Drunvalo Melchizedek, the man who probably knows more about pole shifts than anyone on the planet, to ask him if he would do us the favor of explaining it. Fortunately, he was more than happy to oblige. What follows is the transcript of a conversation that took place between Drunvalo, Claudette Melchizedek, and me in the fall of 2008.

A Conversation with Drunvalo Melchizedek

Cal: I have a hard time with the idea that the ice that collects at the South Pole could be the result of a certain level of unconsciousness that accumulates over time. There has to be another way to look at it.

Drunvalo: Well, science can't say that the ice accumulates because of unconsciousness—but the Indigenous People of the ancient cultures say that all of the movements of the Earth, relative to the Sun, no matter how small or how big they are, affect human consciousness. In other words, the precession of the equinox is a wobble; that affects consciousness. The angle that the Sun sits at relative to the Earth is about twenty-three-and-a-half degrees, but it goes back and forth to between twenty-four or twenty-five degrees in cycles—and that cycle affects consciousness. The orbit around the Sun affects consciousness; all these things affect consciousness. It just depends on how we move relative to the Sun, because the Sun is everything. It's connected to all life everywhere in a way that's different than the way the Earth is connected.

And so, when it comes to a pole shift, that's a big change in consciousness. It's not a little one, it's a big one. Whenever this happens, it happens so quickly. It happens in less than twenty hours from the time it begins to when it stops. So it's a very rapid, fast change. But preceding the pole change are the magnetic pole changes; they always come first, from everything I've read. I've studied this back 250 million years and looked at the way pole shifts happen. They don't happen every 13,000 years, they happen in an irregular pattern. I don't think anyone's figured that out.

The last one happened 13,000 years ago and the two cycles before that the same pattern held true. This is a proven fact. Scientists say this for sure. And they noticed that, before each one of those, the magnetic poles shifted first and the physical poles shifted second.

That's a very important piece of information. Because one of the ideas that has developed in pole-shift theory—there are actually two different ideas on how it goes—is that the ice of the South Pole moves and that causes the whole thing. My personal feeling is that it's a combination of that and the egg shell theory, which we'll talk about in a minute. Because I can see it from beginning to end. It makes absolute perfect sense.

So, the magnetic poles shift first and there is a period of time where the magnetic poles, they move somewhere and they get erratic; they move all over the place and they can make big jumps. The last time it happened, the magnetic pole jumped from the Hudson Bay all the way to Hawaii. The scientists know this.

At that moment, there's a lot of volcanic activity because it's just an unbelievable release of energy. The lava flow, because it has iron filings in it, it'll line up to the magnetic field. The lava flow won't, but the iron filings will and all one has to do is go to 3 of those old lava flows and see where they cross. And when you get three of them crossing that pinpoints exactly where it was, that's where the magnetic poles were.

And so they moved to Hawaii for a period of time. I don't know how long they were there. And then what appears to take place is the magnetic poles just *simply disappear*. They stop. And when that happens there are all these things that occur.

One of the things that happens, and this brings up the egg shell theory, which states that the surface of the Earth is like an egg shell, about 100 miles thick relative to the Earth's 7000-mile diameter. Right underneath the shell is a layer of rock that goes around the whole world. The egg shell is stuck to that rock, and so the Earth feels like it's one solid piece. But that layer of rock is only rock as long as there's a magnetic field. And when that field goes away, it turns to liquid. It's like information on a DVD. That information is there magnetically. If you change the magnetics of a DVD, the information on it ceases to exist. The shift in magnetics turns the under layer of rock into a liquid. And so now you have a hard shell, which is the egg shell; you have the Earth underneath it, which is more or less solid; and then you have a layer of something that is like oil in between those two. So now the egg shell is free floating. It can move in any direction. But, there has to be a force that moves it, otherwise it would just sit there like anything else. It turns to liquid; so what?

Now, remember how the books talk about how the South Pole always goes off center? Just think of a rotating egg shell with its weight off center from the axis of spin. What's it going to do? It's going to drop down to the bottom where it's not off center, to where it's exactly centered. As a weight spinning, it's going to find that place. If it should go out to the equator, which is another place to find balance, that would be incredible. And they say that, if that happened, the pole would move to the equator at a rate of 1,700 miles per hour—which would just be unbelievable what that would do to the planet. But I think now, it's just off only by a little bit and the closer balance now is toward the axis of spin, rather than the equator spin. This is what my intuition says.

And so what happens is, it's sitting here, the magnetic field goes away, the sub-layer of rock turns to liquid, and the uneven distribution of weight at the South Pole, seeking to find its balance point, is the force that causes the outer shell to move. This turns the Earth over and that's your pole shift. And then it finds balance again and that's when it stops. It fixes a place. And I think this is how the modern-day scientists have calculated where they think it's going to go. Calculating the weight and mass of the Earth they can figure out. "OK. This thing is going to go that far this way," which means the pole's going to go in that very specific direction.

And they put it within one degree of . . . I can't remember . . . I think Edgar Cayce gave sixteen degrees to this spot; and the scientists said it's seventeen degrees. That's such a small difference; it's just within error, especially from a scientific point of view.

Cal: So it's not what I pictured at all.

Drunvalo: Well, this is what I have understood from everything and what they've told me is that the egg shell theory has been duplicated in science labs where they build a big Earth with a thin shell, get the mass big enough, get it spinning, turn off the magnetics and that thing turns over. All you have to do is have that weight off center and you just have to go, "Vhoooooph!" and it's going to pull the whole surface of the Earth all the way around, to spin at center.

Claudette: At what point after the melting of the sub-layer do you assume that the South Pole's going to find . . . I mean, where is the balance point now?

Drunvalo: It happens instantaneously.

Claudette: But where is the balance point now?

Drunvalo: What do you mean?

Claudette: That thing you said is going to move and eventually settle someplace else.

Drunvalo: It's the ice at the South Pole. It doesn't center equally around; it centers off center.

Claudette: It does? Why?

Cal: Just because that's the way it's worked out over time. Too much ice accumulated on one side.

Drunvalo: And it's miles of ice.

Claudette: And now it's got to find a new base?

Drunvalo: Well, yeah. You've got a spin object and it's going to want to go like that, and it probably goes back and forth a little bit, until it totally centers on the spin. And then something . . . it may be just that the spin and the whole thing internally is at a stress point, just like we are, and when it comes back to this point like that the stress is relieved, the energetic stress, and the magnetic field comes back again, because the magnetic field goes away—now it comes back again and everything internally starts going back into balance.

Just having the ice off there, with the Earth spinning and all, puts incredible stress on the surface of the Earth—it has to be—and now everything's back in balance again, but *we* think the poles shifted! But the Earth itself didn't move at all. How could the Earth, with this much mass, turn even a little bit? The force that would be needed to do that would be unbelievable! I mean, even big comets hitting it wouldn't do that. It would have to be something really big, like the Moon pushing it or something.

Cal: So you get down to where there's no magnetic field, the imbalance at the South Pole causes the shell to move. When the shell starts to move, does it move en masse?

Drunvalo: The whole thing—the whole surface. That's why it only takes twenty hours. I mean, if you had only a piece of the Earth this big—I'm talking about the core, not the shell—and it did some kind of motion to get over here, whatever it was doing it would take years for it to come back into balance, because the mass would have been put onto a new spin. It would take decades, or maybe even a thousand years. I don't even really know. It could be anything.

And also the Moon is spinning relative to the Earth with these very definite phases that have not stopped for a long time. And so if it was the Earth that moved, if the physical Earth went like that, the Moon wouldn't be in phase with it anymore—it would have to come back into balance and it wouldn't be phased. But just by the surface moving, that doesn't change the Moon's relationship to the Earth at all; only the surface. And so it makes perfect sense. It's the only one that makes perfect sense. And since they've been able to duplicate it and actually see this happen it seems to support the idea. You could even put this into virtual reality in computers at this point and just watch this take place. Somebody's probably already done it.

(Big sigh) It's so important to us at this moment.

Cal: Yeah, I was thinking that there are certain things that must happen prior to, that more or less 'announce' this. And my sense is that if this shell is moving en masse, perhaps the best thing to do in a pole shift is go underground and kind of go along for the ride, or move with it.

Drunvalo: Well, the tectonic plates and all this stuff is moving. You know? And so, you can just imagine that, if the Earth is going to take a ride for twenty hours, you're going to have earthquakes that are just unbelievable. But realize that anything can happen during a pole shift and, even though there's total chaos and destruction, there are anomalies too. Sedona went through this twice before and nothing happened; it's still here.

Claudette: How does that figure? What happened here?

Drunvalo: I don't know. But what this means is that Sedona is heading South! I sat there for a whole day with a globe looking at it and saying, "Where are we going?" and, "Oh, look at that!" What you can do if you want is take a globe and see where this point is—and it'll have an equator around it—but then, if you come down with a pen and draw a new equator, then you can look at where everything's going to be. And Sedona ends up about the same place as Mexico City is now. We're going warmer, moister, more tropical. We are lucky. Moscow goes right into the Arctic Circle.

Cal: This is what's confusing too—when people talk about where it's going to be safe. None of the experts agree.

Drunvalo: The Hopi and the Mayans are all predicting there's going to be a pole shift—and as far as I'm concerned, I hope it happens, really. It's one of the few things that will bring this world into balance.

Cal: Isn't that the whole purpose of it? My sense of it is, it's just the Earth cleansing herself from the inside out.

Drunvalo: We can't see this as bad or evil. It's Mother Earth, it's God, it's God doing this. People want to blame it on somebody or say that it's Satan or something else.

Cal: I do understand that part of it.

Drunvalo: I'm going to write about this. I have to say that there will be a pole shift soon—and you can say it too. It's OK.

Cal: Well, I just want to get it clear so I don't misinform people. I can't pretend to be a scientist and I can't pretend to be you. I just want to get it straight, because this is showing up in the planets too.

Drunvalo: It's just like a trigger. I mean, who would even have thought that parts of the Earth would become liquid and were just made for pole shifts? But that just means that everything gets out of balance so much that the Earth has found a way to come back into perfect spin. It must be awesome at that moment.

Cal: Well, this is another question that I have. Some people say that the Earth's slowing down in her rotation.

Drunvalo: That's true. That doesn't mean that it won't one day speed up.

Cal: Well, this is another picture that I had—that the Earth stops spinning, comes to a halt, and just reverses her direction.

Drunvalo: No. The amount of energy that it would take to do that is just unbelievable. You know how hard it is to stop a car! Imagine how much energy it would take to stop the Earth! It's so heavy; it's so massive; it's so big.

Cal: Yeah. I guess it's a little crazy to see it that way.

Drunvalo: When they say a reversing of the poles, they do not mean a reversal of the physical poles—they're talking about a reversing of the magnetic poles. And so the magnetic pole would magnetically become the opposite one, and if there's a pole shift after that and it changes up to a new thing then what'll happen is north and south will just be reversed; that's all. But it's the magnetics that change.

Then the magnetic pole, no matter where it is—the last time, it was almost 90 degrees off of where it moved from. The magnetic pole, after it finds its new axis, "Sheewwwooooop!" the physical pole comes up and aligns with it too. And they all line up again. If you're just on the surface of the Earth the whole heavens have changed and your stars are different and everything's different. But nothing's really changed but this skinny little shell on the outer surface moved around. The universe didn't change at all, but it's going to look like it. It's going to look like the whole universe has changed.

And then if one goes north-south like they think it might—the Mayans didn't say this but the scientists have—and this is something *I* want to know is, why do they believe that this particular one will do that? The last two didn't; the last two moved and went back, and so north and south did not reverse. They don't reverse very often. When you go back in time, it only happens like every fifty million years or something. It's a very rare, rare thing as far as I know.

Cal: When the Hopi talk about how when they move from one world to another, they're always talking about how they come out from within the *Sipuppu*. And this is what I'm wondering. The shell of the Earth has all these places to go, little caverns and stuff. Is there something that calls a person to go to one of these places and sort of wait it out? Is this a fantasy on my part?

Drunvalo: Well, in terms of that, there's a lot of dangers at this time. This is where—you really can't survive this consciously if you don't have your MerKaBa.* There is no choice. I guess there are some very vulnerable technical devices that will get you through, but they rely on energy that isn't very reliable during these kinds of things.

But the MerKaBa can maintain the Earth's magnetic field so that you don't go crazy and you don't lose all your memory and a lot of other problems that happen, like you don't lose your balance

* The MerKaBa is the Light Body that surrounds the human energy field. It can be activated through the practice of the MerKaBa Meditation.

and that kind of thing. And on top of that, if you're truly in your heart and connected with Mother Earth, it sets up this vibration; and she recognizes that vibration. Those are the ones she's seeking. She wants them.

Claudette: Yeah, the little *Devas* on the new planet.

Drunvalo: Those are the ones who can link together as one. And that vibration, what they're telling me is, you don't have to *do anything*. It isn't what you do; you have to *be*. This is the ultimate case of that (laughs)—the absolute ultimate case. It doesn't make any difference what you've got going on (laughs louder). If you've got that vibration, then you can change the reality and have the power to create out of nothing. And you become very God-like, you really do. But it only works if you don't go into fear. That's the other thing; you've got to stay out of fear.

Cal: Well this is what I was thinking. Some of the things I've read say all these things start happening, if people aren't educated, they'll start to panic.

Drunvalo: Well that's exactly what Don Alejandro (head of the Mayan Elders) is saying—that they feel this responsibility to the Earth to publish this book so they can tell us what they know about these things. Because they've been through this twice before.

Claudette: They better hurry up.

Drunvalo: They are. They're going as fast as they can. It'll be perfect timing. The book just needs to be out by sometime next year [2009].

Cal: I was just wondering if the Earth's slowing down, why is time speeding up?

Drunvalo: The slowing down of the spin of the Earth is happening. But if you're looking at really long cycles, is there a slow down and a speed up, and a slow down and a speed up; is there a pulse or like a breathing in and out? These kinds of things need to be looked at before you think, "Well, it's going to slow down and stop"—though that is a possibility too.

What Richard Hoagland* showed was that the internal structure of the planets is such that, even though he couldn't completely define it, is such that they're getting their power and their light and everything from the Sun. But they're also pulling it from another, higher dimension. So they have two sources of power. He realized that the outer planets—Jupiter, Chiron, Saturn, Uranus, Neptune, and Pluto—are emitting more energy than they receive from the Sun. Considerably more. They're emitting more energy off than they should have.

In other words, the only source that we can see is the Sun, and maybe a tiny bit from the stars. But our Sun is where they get all their radiation and power. That's where all life comes from, all energies, everything. And what Hoagland clearly showed was that there's a Star Tetrahedronal field inside the energy. He mapped all that stuff. It's the same as the energy field around the human body. It's exactly the same.

Cal: And the timing. Aren't there certain signs that come? My understanding of life is that there's a pattern or a geometry behind everything.

Drunvalo: There is.

Cal: And a pole shift is not just this arbitrary occurrence that happens haphazardly.

Drunvalo: Well, what if you think of it like cymatics? So you've got the skin of the Earth, tight, with powder on it, which is kind of like what we're on, only it's curved, and spherical. The surface of our mountains, and the people, and the way we think, and all of that is a pattern; it's a crystalline pattern that's formed on there and it has a structure. All the structures that are there now—the political structures, the religious structures, the financial structures—all these different structures that are all over the world along with the human

* A conspiracy theorist who is famous for his theories on the Face on Mars.

relationships are part of the pattern too. And then what happens when, all of a sudden, you change the frequency? What happens every time is it goes through unbelievable chaos and becomes *nothing*. It just becomes *total* chaos where it looks like everything's just *gone*. And then, right before your eyes all that chaos comes back into a brand new pattern.

Claudette: It's like the phoenix rising out of the ashes.

Drunvalo: If you *stop*, and you're in, right before the chaos, when you go into it, it could seem all encompassing. It could seem like that's it; there's no way out of this and it's going to lead to death. But it doesn't.

If you stay with it, if you move with the chaos then it gets back to the other side and you go back into another harmonic balance that is another level of life. That's Christ Consciousness. That's the next grid level. And all these things—the alignment of the stars and the planets, and the whole thing, the way they're lining up, and the pole shift and all this stuff is all just the mechanical, structural way of balancing this, and of coming back in. And from a human point of view we change inside (laughs). We become really different.

Cal: You say this takes twenty hours to complete itself?

Drunvalo: That's physically. Emotionally and psychically—on those levels, it's a birth. That's a physical birth at that point. The ceremony we did in Moorea in 2008 was the Spiritual birth of the Earth. The Spiritual birth comes first, but then there are other layers that come after that. And they will all follow.

Cal: This is amazing. It duplicates what I see going on with the planets. They say it's a birth process.

Drunvalo: We're in the middle of it (laughs). It took 13,000 years for it to just go through gestation, just for it to be conceived and be ready to be born. And that's equal to nine months. Human beings spend nine months in the womb; it takes Mother Earth 13,000 years to be ready to be born. There's a proportion there. And her actual birth equates with one lunar cycle. And you could see it as if we're out, but we haven't even come to cutting the umbilical cord yet. We're still tied.

Cal: So we've already been through it at the energetic level. Is that what happened in Moorea?

Drunvalo: That happened at the Spiritual level. It's at the level of dreaming, where the dream is conceived. The dream really began a long time ago. Right now, it's coming into another place, another level; it's a growth process and it's reached a plateau of growth. There will be much higher ones later, but this is an important one to get to. Once the Earth gets on to that level, then all the wars, and all the illness, and all the ideas of death and imbalance, and of not having enough, and everything else, and all the problems we've got are gone. Instantly. Almost—it takes about 3 days and then everyone remembers, "Oh yeah!"

Claudette: "Oh yeah" what? Everybody who, what, where? Everybody dead?

Drunvalo: Well, in the past it's always been that "many are called, few are chosen."

Claudette: Or that "the first shall be the last" because you've got that karmic duty, right?

Drunvalo: Yes of course. We'll just have to see how it plays out. It's up to all of us.

Claudette: Are you making a decision as to what you want, or are you letting the pull on the umbilical cord lead you to whatever state of mind it decides?

Drunvalo: Well, there are two pathways and they're distinctly different. One is male; the other is female. The male way, yes, you can use intention and you can change it to exactly the way you want it, perfectly. But the other way is, you don't use any intention whatsoever and you just let God move through you and create from you—when it comes to that it's probably a choice.

Claudette: Well, the female way is easier.

Drunvalo: It's not only easier, it's older; it's an older way. The female is what came first. I'm still convinced of this.

Claudette: It's also handier during times of total and sheer terror!

Drunvalo: But then, you have to have absolute and complete trust in yourself.

Claudette: How about the sheer terror of the experience? Are you saying we don't feel it?

Drunvalo: No. There's going to be a point where you come into the awareness that whatever you're thinking and feeling becomes a reality.

Claudette: Are we then like the man we spoke to who went through the bombing of Hiroshima without a scratch?

Drunvalo: Well yes. He just said, "This won't affect me" and nothing happened to him.

Cal: Well, I guess none of us will know till we get there.

Drunvalo: You're capable of functioning with any kind of problem that could ever be presented to you, no matter what it is. All of us are—every human being.

Claudette: When you say you make a decision, and there are earthquakes and volcanoes and all these things going on, do you mean that those things won't be happening where you are?

Drunvalo: Even if they were, it would be like a miracle happening constantly. You could be right in the middle of a huge explosion of rock and nothing would touch you. Nothing would hurt you. Without anything, you would just move through it.

Global scaling may explain that too.* There's a frequency that Mother Earth puts out when she makes this shift. If you're on that frequency band, or any harmonic of it, you'll be riding that frequency

---

* Global scaling refers to the work of Dr. Hartmut Muller, a German scientist who discovered the fundamental principle behind the standing gravitational wave of the universe. His work is now being used as a means to develop free energy systems all over the planet.

through this change. That frequency, her frequency, will move through everything and get to the next grid level perfectly intact.

Until Drunvalo sat us down and explained it, my views on the upcoming pole shift limited me to the idea that what's about to happen came to be because humanity messed up. And while there's no way to downplay the fact that we have strayed from the path, what I see now is that maybe we couldn't help it, because we just happened to incarnate during the dark part of the Grand Cycle. When darkness, ignorance, and concepts of separation permeate the matrix, those patterns become entrenched in the collective mind. From that perspective, it can be said that our level of consciousness is a side effect of the times we were born in.

The problem we face now has to do with the fact that the Earth is at a point in her evolutionary process where she's emerging from the darkness. But her children, who are semi-comatose and whose thoughts and feelings have a direct impact on her processes, aren't quite there yet. At this point the whole consciousness thing and whether we decide to wake up or not becomes a question of do we want to take this ride to the next grid level with her, or do we prefer to hang on to the old way of being?

The way I figure it, I've been hanging around here for most of my life meditating and claiming to be a Spiritual person. I think a lot of us have. And while it would be easy for me to say that I'd be OK with perishing in a pole shift, part of me is really curious—and what's on my mind right now is, what would it be like to go through an event like this and actually experience a dimensional shift? Choosing not to would be like spending forty-odd years on the Spiritual path and saying no thanks when it finally came time to see God.

It seems stupid to say no to this—because with or without us, Mother Earth is quite obviously on her way somewhere; there's nothing anyone can do to change that. And since we all chose to be here long before we were born, we must have known what being alive at this time would involve. I don't know about you, but I want to find out where she's going, and I want to do what I can to help her get there. And whether I make it through—well, we'll all get to the other side one way or another. To me, it's more about doing anything I can to make it easier for her. If going deeper into the mystery is all she needs from me—or you—considering everything that Mother Earth has done for us, how can we say no to that?

CHAPTER 13

The Dating Game

When you practice astrology, you start with dates and times. You end with them too, because people not only want to know what to expect, they want to know when to expect it. Accurate predictions aren't that hard to make. If you do this long enough, you learn to trust that what you know about the planets will be enough to let you nail a date right on the head. I have to say that I've gotten pretty good at telling people when things will happen. But when it comes to making predictions about when the poles will shift, I'm a little stumped—because there are so many dates to choose from, and because I have a funny feeling things of this nature are inherently unpredictable.

I can't remember exactly when the winter solstice of 2012 became the People's Choice for the Apocalypse, but I think it happened between 1987 and 1988 when Jose Arguelles introduced the Mayan calendar to the general public. Since that time, the chart for that date has been dissected by every astrologer on the planet. I've looked at it too, and I've heard what everyone has to say about it. Still, I'm not entirely convinced that it's doomsday material.

Those who are convinced that it is fixate on it for several reasons. First, the Mayan prophesies pinpoint it, which makes December 21, 2012 the safest, most obvious choice. And while their reasons for choosing it are quite clearly written in stone, what everyone seems to forget is that we're talking about the prototypical female here. I am pretty sure Mother Earth isn't hung up on dates and times. And if she's anything like the rest of her breed, she will not give birth on her due date.

Aside from that, what the 2012 cheerleaders may or may not know is that the information that has come down to us about the Mayan calendar has been over-interpreted by white scholars who have never had, and never will have, access to any of the Mayan oral traditions. So much information is missing, who knows how far off the December 21, 2012 date might be? The safe choice loses much of its charm once you realize how little we actually know about the Mayan calendar.

In addition to its safety, the other thing that makes this particular day so popular is based on the idea that the Sun conjuncts Galactic Center on that date. The Sun conjuncts Galactic Center *every year* at that time; this is an annual occurrence. If that factor alone carried any weight, we could expect a pole shift on a yearly basis.

The 2012 winter solstice stands out because, according to what we know about the Mayan calendar, the End of Time occurs on that date (see page 204). From any perspective, this is a big deal, because it marks the climax of a 26,000—year evolutionary cycle. While even I am awed by the fact that we are approaching this milestone, I can't help but wonder if our need to attach one specific date to an event of this magnitude narrows things down too much?

It's my understanding that everything on the Earthly plane is subject to forty-eight laws, one of which happens to be the law of time. Outside of this realm, none of these laws apply. The way I see it, the spirals of energy that move the galaxies couldn't possibly operate according to linear time, and they most likely have a different spin than the one we put on them. What we always seem to forget is that ours is not the only perspective. And as for big galactic shifts—well, instead of trying to funnel an elephant through a pinhole, we might do better to stretch the 2012 date to include windows of time on either side.

In the same way that slow-moving planets do their best work as much when they are within orb of an aspect as they can when they're right on top of it, I suspect that our conjunction with Galactic Center won't necessarily happen on the date that we've allotted to it. And even if it did, the one thing I keep asking my self is—how do we know that this milestone automatically translates into a pole shift? And if it does, does anyone here on Earth know how many other factors need to be present for something that big to occur?

In my humble opinion, we've got an assortment of dates to choose from. With all the planetary activity we've discussed so far, we're basically entering a period of time that can only be compared to a mine field of dates, any one of which could trigger off a pole shift. With the Earth's magnetic field rapidly decreasing, if the astrology doesn't impress you perhaps the statistics will help you to see that we're already treading on very thin ice. If we consider that the beginning of the End Times kicked off when the Blue Star appeared, and take into account that it's been beaming in the heavens for over a year, by my calculations we're well inside the preliminary window looking at a pole shift *anytime* between now and 2014.

While I believe that it's possible to use what I know to zoom in on the exact date and commit to it, I have to say that the time it would take to pore over all the variables is something I just don't have— because critical, long-term aspects began to form as early as January 2008, and those aspects will bleed into other difficult aspects that are due to come into play as time goes on. So many major astrological configurations overlap and hold steady for extended periods of time, we're talking about long stretches of unbelievable tension that would make any day in the next five years stand out as a likely candidate for a pole shift. Multiply 365 times five and ask any astrologer to do the work that goes into accurately interpreting that many charts. I'd have better luck finding a needle in a haystack.

What we can do is pinpoint what seem to be the most precarious windows of time. We can start with the window that opened the day that Pluto entered Capricorn (see page 199). That transit began in January 2008. It will end in late November of 2009. During that entire period, the Lord of Hell will not only be aligned with Galactic Center, he will move back and forth over the base of the World Tree, as if he were dancing between the magnetic and physical poles. Capable of anything, I wouldn't put it past him to arbitrarily flip off the magnetic field and send all of us spinning right out of this world. The Pluto dates that are of concern are:

⊛ September 10, 2008 to January 22, 2009

⊛ June 23, 2009 to November 23, 2009

I included the September 2008 date to give you a little hindsight. On Sunday, September 14th, 2008 the lords of Wall Street opened the Stock Exchange, for a closed session which allowed the biggest investors in firms like Lehman Brothers, Merrill Lynch, Fannie Mae, Freddie Mac, and CitiBank to access their funds before those corporations declared them selves insolvent on the following day. On Monday morning, September 15, 2008, word went out to the general public that all the big investment firms were either bankrupt or going under. The following letter from Dr. Richard Boylan will help you put that debacle into perspective. As you read it, keep in mind that, along with some of the other things we've mentioned, Pluto rules plutocrats, investments, the stock market, other people's money, and power plays that revolve around the distribution of resources that are owned by someone other than the ones who agreed to monitor and protect those resources. As of this writing, the fallout from this collapse has yet to be determined, but anyone can see where it will go. The people in charge have been playing chess with our resources. This collapse may be what it takes to get the sleeping masses to open their eyes. It looks to me as if the systematic breakdown has already begun and, as things continue to dissolve, will create hardship, not just in the United States, but everywhere.

Friends,

To put his message into context, we need to recall that recently, the huge Countrywide Financial homes-financing institution declared bankruptcy. This was followed by the giant Wall Street financial firm Bear Stearns also going insolvent.

Last week on September 7 the enormous semi-autonomous home-lending institutions, Fannie Mae and Freddie Mac, who made many of the home loans and mortgage guarantees in the United States, declared themselves insolvent, and were taken over by the U.S. government, lest their collapses cause the housing and mortgage markets to entirely crumble.

The message for today was prompted by the development that the New York Stock Exchange was opened on Sunday for an extraordinary special session, to permit the largest financial houses to clear out their deposits with Lehman Brothers financial institution, before it declared insolvency before midnight yesterday. This morning Lehman Brothers announced that it's filing for Chapter 11 bankruptcy.

"Who cares?" you may say. Or even, "Serves those fat cats right."

But wait. There's more.

The Lehman Brothers bankruptcy marks the beginning of the very large financial collapse that has been developing for a while.

While there are many more dominoes left to fall against one another over the weeks and months ahead, today (or yesterday, if you will) marks the beginning of what might be indelicately labeled The Great Bush Depression. While under President Clinton the U.S. budget had a $117 billion surplus, under President Bush the U.S. has a budget deficit of $9.7 trillion dollars.

News reports state that other major financial houses are "near the edge." These include Merrill Lynch, Citibank, Morgan Stanley and JP Morgan, to name some of the best known.

Nouriel Roubini, the head of the RGE Monitor consulting firm which investigates banks' solvency, said today, "It's clear we're one step away from a financial meltdown."

Nor will the financial hardships be confined to the United States. Reverberations of the cascading failures of financial institutions will impact economies around the globe, since they are so inter-connected in today's world.

The times ahead will bring hardships to many people. We will all be presented with situations where neighbors, friends, and others in our own and surrounding communities will be without the necessities, and we will all have to pull together to get us all through.

If we turn a cold shoulder when others are in dire straits, then the situation will get ugly, miserable, and destructive.

If we rise to the challenge with a communitarian and family-like attitude, then we will emerge a better people than before the crisis just ahead of us struck.

Let us use this heads-up to resolve now to not panic, to keep our priorities clear as moral and Spiritual persons, and, like the Biblical injunction of old, operate with the clear understanding that in fact, yes, we are our brother's (and sister's) keeper. Together we can get through this.

This crisis can be handled in ways which help usher in a reformed Fifth World society, or usher in chaos and societal devolution. The choice is ours.

In the light,

Richard Boylan, Ph.D.*

If you're in the mood, you could review the Pluto chapter. But I'll save you the trouble by reminding you that Pluto dissolves the atomic bonds that hold everything in place—everything from the atoms that hold our cells together to the systems that structure our outer reality. Whenever anything has outlived its purpose, Pluto is the demolition expert who comes in and plants the charges that bring everything down. What he did in September 2008 is probably one of the best examples of this. He began a process that will undermine both the system itself and the belief patterns that call us to put our faith in it. As this develops, the materialistic constructs that prevent us from seeing what truly has value will go down right along with the corporations who sold us on the idea that money is God. This will be

---

* Dr. Richard J. Boylan is a Ph.D. behavioral scientist, anthropologist, university associate professor emeritus, certified clinical hypnotherapist, consultant, and researcher.

hard for many. It could even get hard for the ones who got to access their funds before everyone else lost what was stolen from them to begin with.

What will happen during the June to November 2009 window, I wouldn't venture to guess. But let's consider that a volatile time too and look to July 7 to 22, 2009 as key dates as well. And we should include August 6 on that list. Eclipses on all three of those dates make me very uncomfortable.

Known to produce trouble or to exacerbate it, eclipses trigger off events that reveal everything we don't want to see. They aren't inherently bad, but what comes out of them can sometimes take the form of a disaster. Enough catastrophes have occurred in the shadow of an eclipse to make me feel as if we had better pay close attention to those three dates. With Pluto lurking in the background, moving retrograde from one to zero degrees Capricorn and close enough to Galactic Center to be within orb of a conjunction, there may be major repercussions here on Earth. The eclipse dates are:

⊛ Appulse lunar eclipse (Full Moon): July 7, 2009
   (15 degrees Capricorn)

⊛ Total solar eclipse (New Moon): July 22, 2009
   (29 degrees Cancer)

⊛ Appulse lunar eclipse (Full Moon): August 6, 2009
   (13 degrees Aquarius)

At the end of August 2009, Pluto will still be hovering over the axis of the world, the eclipse patterns will still be operative, and, within ten days, Saturn and Uranus will form a series of direct oppositions. This compounds the intensity and makes the period of time between September 10 and September 17, 2009 that much more volatile.

⊛ Saturn opposes Uranus: September 10 to September
   17, 2009

⊛ Adding more fuel to the fire, by October 30, 2009, Saturn will move to the Earth's Ascendant, squaring Pluto until November 19 (see page 205). With multiple major aspects operating simultaneously (Saturn/Aries Point, Saturn/Pluto, Pluto/Aries Point, Pluto/Vertical Axis), and all of them layered over each other, we have what can only be seen as an extremely shaky set of variables.

⊛ Saturn conjuncts Earth's Ascendant: October 30, 2009 to August 2, 2010

⊛ Pluto square Saturn: October 30 to November 19, 2009

The period of time between June 23, 2009 and November 23, 2009 can be considered as a whole if you wanted to pick any day in that window for a possible shift. Out of all the dates, the stretch between October 30 and November 19, 2009 is the one to highlight.

As you can see, Saturn will oversee the Earth's Ascendant from October 30, 2009 to August 2, 2010. Even though the pile of aspects that ushered him to that angle will have eased off by November 19, 2009, he's still a key planet in a key position at a critical time. Many things will be cut away, redefined, or completely eliminated during his stay there.

If you recall, that axis represents Mother Earth's body. Saturn's penchant for blight, lack, want, and heavy-duty rules and regulations paints a picture of hard times that will hold steady and continue to roll even after he leaves that point. With the Grim Reaper standing over Mother Earth's physical body, all I can think of is what he's going to do with his scythe. Does he have the capacity to cut everything down, and does that imagery add up to a pole shift? I can't answer either question, but I do know that the window between late October 2009 and early August 2010 will be intense, all the way around.

By May 28, 2010, Uranus will meet the Aries Point (see page 201). Long before this book became my main preoccupation, I had enough astrological foresight to see that Uranus would move to this critical degree. At the time, without even looking at any other aspects, my first thought was, that's when the poles would shift.

My reasoning was simple. The most eccentric, unpredictable planet in the solar system, one that is prone to just wipe things out, was moving to the alpha-omega point. This seemed like a recipe for a cataclysmic rebirth. Since then, my point of view hasn't changed too much, and I advise you to mark those dates as well.

❀ Uranus conjunct the Aries Point: May 28, 2010 to January 8, 2012

During that window, the most precarious days are July 22 to August 2, 2010. We've gone over this before but some things are worth repeating. The July-August 2010 time frame is twice as difficult because of the angles that are involved and because Uranus and Saturn will be in direct opposition on the main axis of the Earth's horoscope. The only thing that relaxes the stress is Jupiter's influence and the idea that we will have "outside support" coming from the stars. Since that part of the equation is something we can know nothing about, I am not in a position to factor it in to any of my predictions.

My concern about the entire Uranus-Aries Point window is based on two things. One is, that in the Draconic* system of astrology, the Aries Point is the North Node** for absolutely everyone on the planet. This means that Uranus will touch all of us, no exceptions. Everyone's life could be uprooted, suddenly, by a seemingly arbitrary force that is totally beyond our control, during that time frame.

---

* The Draconic system of astrology is the one used by Edgar Cayce to calculate his horoscopes. It addresses what the Soul came here to process.

** In any horoscope, the North Node represents the pathway to Spirit.

If that isn't enough, my second line of reasoning is based on what I know about Uranus. Out of all the planets in the solar system, Uranus is singular in that its axis spins at right angles to the axis of every other planet. It is the ruler of axial events by virtue of the fact that its own axis distinguishes it, or sets it apart, and the law of correspondence gives it governance over anything that has to do with the Earth's poles.

Given the fact that Uranus is also an expert at turning things upside down, if you can add two and two, what comes up in my mind is a pole shift. Combine this picture with the idea that Uranus rules electricity, and take into consideration that the Earth's magnetic field is a giant electrical circuit—if the magnetic poles flip first, Uranus is the one to get the job done. That is why I am particularly wary of his movements over the Aries Point. Of all the dates in that window, and of all the dates we've listed so far, the July 22 to August 2, 2010 time frame is my pick for a pole shift.

In the spring of 2011, Chiron enters Pisces to begin an extended process that, though essentially Spiritual in nature, will have an effect on our physical reality as well (see page 203). My feeling is that, if the poles shift in 2010, Chiron's transit through the Womb of Creation will see the ones who are left rising up from the ashes getting used to a whole new way of being and building the foundation for the new paradigm. And if there is no shifting of the poles prior to Chiron's entrance into Pisces, we will all be learning how to live with the hardships and complexities that unravel between now and then.

Since Chiron's influence has so much to say about the extent to which human consciousness impacts events that are inevitable, my sense is that if it's our job to cushion the blow, if the poles haven't shifted by that time, the best we can do is work on raising our respective frequencies. The only other alternative would seem to be huddling in fear, waiting anxiously amidst a pile of canned goods, or going off the deep end in some half-assed attempt to go out with both guns blazing—neither of which will do anything to help the Earth, or us. In my mind, the only option we have is to deepen and stabilize the connection we have to our hearts and to Mother Earth. Whether we are aware of it or not, this is the only thing that matters right now.

If we get past the summer of 2010, there will only be one trouble spot left in the mine field that I referred to earlier. On November 11, 2011, Uranus will begin his final pass over the Aries Point. If he hasn't blown everything sky high by then, for close to three months, his influence will make the period between November 11, 2011 and January 8, 2012 volatile enough to support a pole shift.

I am not sure how much weight to give these dates, because, in the early spring of 2011, Neptune enters Pisces right along with Chiron (see page 206). The fact that I've made no mention of Neptune is not a reflection on his significance. It's just that, until he and Chiron move into Pisces, he won't be actively involved in any of this. That the two of them will cross the threshold that separates the old paradigm from the new *before* the 2012 winter solstice makes me wonder if the shift will be complete by that time.

I say this because Neptune is the archetype of compassion, oneness, and unconditional love. When he and Chiron get together, Chiron functions as a channel that allows those principles to flow into manifestation. If my take on the 2010 dates is accurate, we could come out on the other side of the pole shift and be on a totally new wavelength by the time the two planets begin their respective journeys through the Womb of Creation. If that turns out to be the case, my sense is that the love principle will soften Uranus considerably and turn his last pass over the Aries Point into a massive shift in human consciousness.

Seen from another angle, Neptune and Chiron could enter Pisces, unlock the door to Unity Consciousness, give us a chance to check out the territory and, because neither one of them have the skills to engineer a pole shift, wait until the Fall for Uranus to come along and do what he does best. It could very well go that way. Just in case it does maybe we should include the dates between November 11, 2011 and January 8, 2012 on our list as well.

After January 8, 2012, unless I'm missing something, there's not a lot going on astrologically; it's like everything calms down for a period of time. This is why I could never figure out why everyone sees the 2012 winter solstice as zero hour. In fact, the chart for that date is almost boring by comparison (see page 204). If no one told me it was D-Day I wouldn't even bother to talk about it. The winter solstice chart for 2012 may be significant for a lot of reasons, but, in my opinion, there isn't enough stress in it to induce a pole shift. As much as I feel obligated to pay attention to it, please excuse me if I beg out. I've had three kids, all of whom arrived a month late, and that along with the things I brought up earlier make it easy for me to assure you that Mother Earth will not pop open on her due date.

Instead of focusing on that, I'd much rather talk about Neptune. The unconditional love-bird probably knows more about where we're going than any other planet, and it would be good to find out what he's up to. Besides, there are a few dates on the other side of the 2012 Winter Solstice that we need to examine, and we can't talk about them until we take a peek at Neptune.

If you're confused and/or overwhelmed by what we've covered here, anyone would be. Don't think about it too much. While I wish I could give you an exact date, it would be arrogant to present one —and perhaps it's better this way. Instead of dwelling on dates and times maybe we should put our attention toward things that matter. My hope is that those things will come to mind when you read the following passage from Hopi Elder Dan Evehema:

The final stage, called "The Great Day of Purification," has been described as a "Mystery Egg" in which the forces of the swastika and the Sun plus a third force symbolized by the color "red" culminate either in total rebirth or total annihilation—we don't know which. But the choice is yours, war and natural catastrophe may be involved. The degree of violence will be determined by the degree of inequity caused among the peoples of the world and in the balance of nature. In this crisis rich and poor will be forced to struggle as equals in order to survive.

That it will be very violent is now almost taken for granted among Traditional Hopi, but man still may lessen the violence by correcting his treatment of nature and fellow man. Ancient Spirit-based communities, such as the Hopi, must especially be preserved and not forced to abandon their wise way of life and the natural resources they have vowed to protect.

The man-made system now destroying the Hopi is deeply involved in similar violations throughout the world. The devastating reversal predicted in the prophesies is part of the natural order. If those who thrive from that system, its money and its laws, can manage to stop destroying the Hopi then many may be able to survive the Day of Purification and enter a new age of peace. But if no one is left to continue the Hopi way, then the hope for such an age is in vain.

The forces we must face are formidable, but the only alternative is annihilation. Still the man-made system cannot be corrected by any means that requires one's will to be forced upon another, for that is the source of the problem. If people are to correct themselves and their leaders, the gulf between the two must disappear. To accomplish this one can only rely on the energy of truth itself.

This approach, which is the foundation of the Hopi way of life, is the greatest challenge a mortal can face. Few are likely to accept it. But once peace is established on this basis, and our original way of life is allowed to flourish, we will be able to use our inventive capacity wisely. To encourage rather than threaten life. To benefit everyone rather than giving advantage to a few at the expense of others. Concern for all living things will far surpass personal concerns bringing greater happiness than could formerly be realized. Then all things shall enjoy lasting harmony.

Just what are the Hopi prophetic instructions regarding the United Nations and what constituted fulfillment?

Two misconceptions must be immediately dismissed. The Hopi are not charged with just another appeal for peace, nor do they request membership in the UN. One more voice added to the chorus of those calling for peace would add little compared to the true significance of what Hopi tradition has to offer the modern world through this forum. When it was suggested that they join the UN the Traditional Hopi—half jokingly—would respond: "No, we're waiting for the UN to join us." Quite literally they are waiting for other nations to return to that way of life which can continue endlessly, which is the deeper meaning of the name, Hopi. This gives a clue to the profound insight to be found in the Hopi ancestral knowledge. If thoroughly understood, this insight into the forces that shape the modern world would enable those involved in the UN to bring an end to the arms race. The communication effort of the Hopi and the developments that led to the existence of the United Nations are parallel responses to the invention of the atomic bomb. From the Hopi perspective these two efforts ought to enhance each other for the benefit of the entire world.

Centuries before the arms race began the alternative to war was being put into practice by migrating societies who slowly formed a Spiritual political union at Oraibi, the oldest continuously inhabited village in the western hemisphere. To the Hopi, the UN has great significance within this pattern.

Two monumental cultural factors have prevented the European immigrants from recognizing this process of widespread unification: The presumption of racial superiority and the need to conquer and convert. And a recent tendency to discredit all knowledge which does not stand the test of scientific thought. The Hopi insist that the coming of the light-skinned race, the invention of the atomic bomb and the development of the UN were anticipated by their ancestral prophetic instructions to be fulfilled by the Hopi, they must make four attempts to gain a genuine hearing on the subject of their teachings and on the efforts of the USA to eliminate their original form of government. If unsuccessful, a rare opportunity will be missed which would ultimately result in the elimination of all human life on earth.

The basic premise is that humans can not simply make their own laws and enforce them with weapons without regard to natural order. The very means of enforcement violates that order, causing precisely the suicidal situation now faced today. Lest the Hopi be accused of being overly ethnocentric, they point out that all peoples once practiced the same alternative to war and the Hopi simply call out to a return to our common heritage before it is too late. "Perfect Consideration" could eliminate all war. "Perfect Consideration" must overcome all obstacles, both in the modern political sense and in the seriously disrupted organization of Traditional Hopi government. These difficulties can be overcome. To many, there is saving grace in the pieces of the broken vessel of Hopi culture, in the person of a few Elders who still refuse to abandon their traditions, their understandings and their hopes for a truly peaceful world for now and generations to come. In them lies a great hope for peace!!

May Peace and Love prevail

Long live life on Earth

Long live the Revolution of the One Heart![28]

CHAPTER 14

Neptune, Pisces, and the Post-2012 Paradigm

It's finally time to talk about Neptune. I must admit that writing about a planet whose influence flows through everything has me a little confused. Wondering at which corner of the universe to start with, my brain is on overload. And I have to laugh, because my lack of clarity is so typically Neptunian that something tells me this flood of thoughts is his doing—in which case, I'd do better to toss out my notes, go with the flow, and stop trying to get linear about a planet that isn't partial to definition.

The consummate Spiritual entity, Neptune is our link to the higher realms. Without him, getting enlightened would be out of the question. The problem is, he lives on a frequency band that most humans don't know how to tune in to. And even though all of us are equipped with everything we need to receive that information, our Spiritual centers are so shut down, what comes through from Neptune gets diverted into our lower Chakras, and by the time it hits bottom, what comes out bears very little resemblance to what went in.

Often referred to as the Great Deceiver, Neptune is also the higher octave of Venus; both planets are all about love. If Venus rules the feelings that prompt us to be attracted to one thing or another, Neptune's sense of connection is limitless. Much like the oceans and the vapors and the mists that he rules, his essence is water. His radiance permeates the ether with an unconditionally loving force that surrounds and penetrates absolutely everything. Unable to divide or separate, Neptune can unify, he can dissolve, and he can freeze and unfreeze—but when it comes to boundaries, forget about it—this planet doesn't have any.

Unfortunately, in the world we occupy, everything is black or white, up or down, good or bad. Unaccustomed to polarity, Neptune wanders around like an alien without a guidebook, trying to figure out why we see it that way. As far as he's concerned, unity and love are all there is, and his ultimate purpose and function have to do with reminding us that those things are as real for us as they are for him:

> The place of our origin, in which we once existed in perfect fusion with the divine Other, is the same place of our eventual return . . . Neptune's longing pours out like a flood in both directions; nostalgia for the lost home and yearning for the reunion that lies some place, some time in a far away future. For many Western people in the modern era, the religious idea of an Eden-like afterlife seems intellectually absurd. But the nostalgia and the yearning have not gone away, and the hope for a blissful reunion, now relegated to the unconscious, is therefore projected onto some future point in this life, when the "right" partner arrives, or the "right" job manifests, or when everything somehow magically becomes "all right." These sentiments are human and

ubiquitous; we all experience them sometimes. They are the characteristic manifestations of the Neptunian longing, reminding us that Something will eventually respond to our call despite our present tribulations. Such feelings can be inspiring and regenerate hope . . . . But for the excessively Neptune-prone, the vision of a magical afterlife pursued in this life—where all suffering of separateness will cease and the state of primary fusion will return—may overwhelm any capacity to live in the present.[29]

Neptune's attempts to show us the way come with no label to warn us that it's extremely difficult to get there from here. Distorted by the law of polarity, the yearning for oneness morphs into a lack of discernment that causes one thing to look as good as another. With no line to tell us not to cross it, we head straight down the bunny trail and get consumed by whatever we find there. Every time we fall prey to an illusion, Neptune is the one who convinces us that what we want to see and what's actually there are one and the same.

I used to think that there was something insidious about the way Neptune worked but now I see that his deceptions are unintentional. He leads us on because he doesn't know any better, either. How could he? It's all the same to him. And even when he drags us through an experience that beats us raw, that too is all the same to him—because, where he lives, love flows through everything. Every experience is filled with it. If we blame him for leading us on, what we forget is that Neptune can't draw the line between good and bad.

This Oneness with all things is a state that only the saints of the world truly understand. Christ and Buddha knew it, and somewhere in our cellular memory all of us remember Unity. If Neptune is the planet that takes us home what we find on the road can either enlighten us or drive us insane. Unfortunately the Spiritual urge gets twisted here and, more often than not, our response to it leads us to exalt all kinds of bad behavior.

Given the spectrum of opposites which Neptune seems to symbolize, from the extremes of psychic and physical disintegration to the life transforming light of inner revelation, it is virtually impossible to state, categorically, when one is masquerading as the other. A deep but unacknowledged thirst for Spirit can disguise itself as addiction or hopeless retreat from reality, just as the so-called enlightened Soul may be an apparent adult with a baby's emotional narcissism, on strike against life and refusing to leave Never-Land.[30]

This may be why Peter Pan and the crack-whore both belong to Neptune. The governor of every illusion, Neptune is also the ruler of fog, mist, drugs, poison, noxious vapors, gases, perversion, movies, swamps, enlightenment, cartoons, perfume, rivers, oceans, fairies, water nymphs, photography, fantasy, pornography, plastic, oppressed minorities, nostalgia, deceit, divine inspiration, liquor, visions, bacteria, glamour, depression, cosmetics, exploitation, romance, prisons, childhood, poverty, redemption, redeemers, poetry, humiliation, futility, film stars, empathy, narcissism, welfare cheats, snow, hypnosis, hallucinations, asylums, orgies, guilt, floods, impotence, apathy, dreams, breast implants, homesickness, crack houses, barrooms, psychic phenomena, asexuality, sadomasochism, fatigue, victimhood, unrequited love, suffering, self-pity, incurable illness, flowers, purple hair, music, art, addicts, crocodile tears, the invisible realms, large animals, charlatanry, Pollyannaism, insanity, mass hysteria, the collective unconscious, fishermen, fish, and Pisces. As you can see, he's all over the map.

At this point his place on the map puts Neptune right on the threshold of the sign that he rules. Every astrologer I know has been speculating upon this event for at least five years. Some are of the mind that, as soon as Neptune enters Pisces, the Earth will automatically ascend into a state of Unity Consciousness (see page 206).

While that's a possibility, I wonder if it's a bit Neptunian to make it an assumption. At the same time, the image of the unconditional-love-bird flying into the sign that he rules—a sign whose ultimate desire is the same as his own—is such a good omen that even I am tempted to read a miracle into it. But a lot of how this plays out depends on when the poles shift.

If they shift in 2010 and we're already living in a world where there's no war, no lack, no fear, and no sense of separation to divide us, Neptune's ingress will enhance whatever our visions of bliss and Unity conjure up. In their highest expression, he and Pisces are totally familiar with the Spiritual realms. If that's where we are when they come together, the same planet that deludes us into thinking that our fantasies have substance will finally be able to show us that, in his realm, the power of dreaming has a much different effect. Once we're there, I have a feeling that the same force that gets us into trouble down here will be the very thing that we use to dream the Age of Light into reality.

All I can do is imagine this, but the picture of the water god moving through the Womb of Creation suggests that what we weave into being will emerge from the Void in the same way that the Christian God gave birth to the world in the first chapter of Genesis. Our perspective makes it hard to believe that we too are Creators here. Yet the synchronicities that cause us to wonder why someone calls, or why things appear the moment we think of them, or why a seemingly random impulse takes us exactly where we need to go invite us to see that what we find hard to believe just may be true.

This is what Neptune's been trying to tell us all along. And if we've taken a few baby steps in that direction, it's because, between the Great Shift and Neptune's ingress into Pisces, on some level the collective consciousness is being prepared to make full use of what we never knew was natural to us until now. As the veil that separates the Fourth World from the Fifth World dissolves, the ability to create out of nothing and the idea that the imaginal realm is the birthplace of every experience won't seem as foreign to us as it does now. For those of you who are new to this concept, the following quote from Slim Spurling offers a clear explanation of how it works:

> We focus on what we can see and we think everything comes from that. But it's what we can't see that forms what our senses tell us is real. If we understood more about the invisible forces that operate behind the world of form, we would discover that nothing is scarce—and that it is out of the ether that absolutely everything is created. This is why what we call "Magic" works.
>
> Basically, everything comes out of nothing—and whatever "nothing" is, our thoughts appear to stir it. But all thought emanates from the ether too—the mind doesn't source our thought processes—it is only a receiving mechanism that is calibrated to be receptive (or not) to what comes from the invisible . . . There will be moments when our personal frequency sets will intersect with the wavelengths of thought coming out of the ether. At those points, or nodes of intersection, regardless of the dictates of our primary coding, we can become receptive to the information coming from the universe. So what exists as a frequency IN-Forms it self in our consciousness and in those moments, whatever we download creates the space for us to expand into something new.
>
> All of the major astrological transits and progressions are in reality points where our personal coding can be altered by the presence of etheric frequency sets that are timed to open us up to an entirely new set of possibilities. The call to wake up will be heeded, or not, depending on the individual's ability to transmute whatever comes through as IN-Formation . . . If the individual is open enough to take

in the new set of frequencies, a quantum leap occurs within their consciousness and they can expand beyond the limits of the Third Dimension.*

New frequency sets have been pouring out of the ether ever since the discovery of Uranus over two centuries ago. Those energies were amplified when, one by one, Neptune, Pluto, and Chiron showed up to do their part in rearranging our thinking. Charged with leveling the ground and laying the foundation for what amounts to a planetary sex change, one could say that, over the course of 200 years, Uranus, Neptune, Pluto, and Chiron patiently administered the necessary hormones, counseled us thoroughly, and instructed us as to what we need to do to adapt to a different polarity. Now that the Great Shift is imminent, it's as if the entire planet is in the operating room, waiting for the doctor to step in and complete the transformation.

If the appearance of the Blue Star marked the beginning of the End Times, it's safe to assume that the frequency sets that have been pouring out of the heavens since the fall of 2007 are meant to open our minds and our hearts to a whole new way of being. Of late, my conversations with people indicate that just about everyone is in a state of accelerated change. Most are acutely aware of the need to stop living their lives according to the patterns and beliefs that formed our prescription for success and fulfillment in the past. All agree that the old formula just doesn't seem to work anymore.

Hearing things like this on a daily basis, and having my own experience to refer to, what I see is that something is awakening in all of us, something vastly different than what we're accustomed to. Thirteen thousand years of male programming and control-based

---

* A conversation recorded by me on a piece of scrap paper while Slim Spurling and I were driving from Denver to Santa Fe in the winter of 2004. Now deceased, Slim was a free-energy genius and the creator of the *Light-Life™ Tools*. His ghostwriter for seven years, it was my job to record everything he said.

belief patterns still retain some of their power, but something else has found its way into our lives. Whatever it is, it seems to operate on a softer, effortless, more intuitive wavelength.

It wasn't until this book made it mandatory for me to think more deeply about the astrology behind the Great Shift that I had the following epiphany. Mulling over every symbol, all of a sudden it hit me that Neptune's entrance into Pisces is an entirely female event—one that I suspect will light up the feminine torch and put the finishing touches on the work of the four outer planets and the planetary sex change I referred to earlier.

I say this because Neptune is the essence of water: water is intrinsically feminine. And Pisces, as we now know, rather than being the end of the line is the womb where all things begin, or the Vesica Pisces out of which all life emerges. If we take Neptune's watery, unconditionally loving frequencies to be akin to amniotic fluid, his entrance into the Piscean womb will mark the point where humanity and Mother Earth herself will begin to vibrate according to the female principle.

I have no doubt that women will lead the way, and I am clear that children will have something to do with it as well. Women and children always come first, and unconditional love is something they both understand. I don't know how this will happen, or where or who or what this will involve, but the correspondences are too obvious to ignore. They seem to suggest that everything we associate with the power of the female will replace the masculine principle by or before the spring of 2011—whether the poles have shifted or not. Drunvalo Melchezedek explores that possibility:

> The next few years will be the most important years in human history. We will survive these vast changes in human understanding with the help of Mother Earth . . . as we have many times before, but never before has the universe opened to us as it will in the coming years.

The secret is Unconditional Love, which will present itself through human beings who will change life on Earth forever. Most of these human beings will be children or young adults who have found their way into their Hearts. And it will be the women who will understand and follow the children into their Hearts and take this new way of being into the world. Finally, probably with great trepidation, the men will make the transformation that will truly complete the cycle. It is almost always this way.

It is the images and dreams that come from the Hearts of these children that will be the power that actually makes these changes. The children and the women will be the first to enter into the act of creation and change the world from within.[31]

If unconditional love is the secret, I don't know anyone who knows more about it than Neptune. Could he be the doctor? Am I taking the analogy too far?

Thinking over all of the subtleties held in the Neptune-Pisces imagery also made me wonder if the poles might shift at Neptune's point of ingress. If this is, in fact, a totally feminine milestone, would our reversal of perspective manifest outwardly, at the physical level, as a pole shift? This is pure speculation on my part, but the Hermetic axiom, "As above, so below," makes me feel that it's not too far-out to see it that way.

The female principle is already awake at the etheric level. By the time Neptune enters Pisces, she will be fully installed. If there's any substance to my reasoning, we should include April 4, 2011 as a date for a possible pole shift, and consider August 4 and 5, 2011 as well. Neptune will sit at zero degrees Pisces on each of these dates. And while there are no other transits to support this theory, the combination of the imagery and the inherent potency of the point of ingress makes me feel like it's worth mentioning.

What If . . .?

If the poles shift after 2012—and there are a series of dates that suggest that they might—Neptune's entrance into Pisces will present us with another set of variables. I never thought I'd hear myself say this, but I hope the poles shift sooner rather than later, because some of the scenarios we've outlined so far will get even messier if we have to wait until after 2012. When things are already in a state of dissolution, Neptune and Pisces have a tendency to bring out the worst kind of suffering. And it breaks my heart to think that we may live to see a tremendous amount of it.

If you review the list of things that Neptune rules and highlight the ones that aren't all hearts and flowers, you'll find yourself left with this list: Drugs, poison, noxious vapors, gases, perversion, deceit, bacteria, prisons, poverty, redemption, suffering, self-pity, hypnosis, orgies, guilt, impotence, apathy, victimhood, floods, humiliation, futility, exploitation, incurable illness, insanity, mass hysteria, charlatanry. That's only a partial list; I am sure that I missed a few things. But let's work with what we have and layer that imagery over a broken-down system, masses of homeless, hungry people, cataclysms, death, external chaos, and anarchy. For some reason, visions of Hieronymus Bosch's more hellish works and *Mad Max—Beyond Thunder Dome* come to mind. In case you don't get the picture, I will paint it for you.

Drugs, poison, noxious vapors, and bacteria floating around in a world that has fallen apart doesn't sound good to me. Neptune rules water. It rules rain by extension. What will rain down on us will be infected with things that will make our water undrinkable. Pure fresh water is the source of all life. What will we do when there isn't any? What will we do when our waterways and reservoirs are filled with drug residues from hospitals that are unable to maintain even minimal standards?

And what about the air we breathe? At 16%, oxygen levels are already a hair away from the point that makes it difficult to function.

Who knows what kinds of chemicals are being pumped into the atmosphere? Chem-Trails checkerboard the sky every day. By 2012, if we keep it up, things will only get worse. Sounds like noxious vapors to me.

Poverty. We've seen what Third World poverty looks like. Did you ever see yourself living that way? Me neither. It's hard to believe it could get that bad, but we may all be subjected to that experience and have to live through what billions of human beings are currently all too familiar with. Prisons. Prisons are what totalitarian systems rely upon to keep people in line, and you can bet that if there's any law and order at all, it will be totalitarian. Martial Law is already being talked about. If the ones who support that idea create enough excuses to mandate it in the guise of trying to provide shelter for the homeless, many of us will be herded off to detainment camps. Believe it or not, these camps have already been set up.

This isn't the kind of news you'd hear on CNN, but if you do a little research you soon find out that all the military bases that were closed down twenty odd years ago were converted into detainment camps; shades of Auschwitz? It feels that way to me. Back in 1998 I was told by an ex-Navy Seal, who quit when he could no longer live with himself and work on that project, that they already have gas lines piped in.

When things get this bad, deceit, apathy, suffering, victimhood, incurable illness, insanity, humiliation, futility, and mass hysteria all go with the territory. And you could take anything else that remains on Neptune's list and use your imagination to see where it fits into this picture we've painted. Far be it from me to be the bearer of bad tidings, but if we have to wait until after 2012 for the poles to shift, what we have to live through in the meantime could get ugly.

The problem with all of the above is that it has already started to manifest. At this point we are semi-aware of the water issue and the air issue—and the poverty issue—looms over us too. I hate to feed visions of the worst-case scenario, but we're barreling toward it, half asleep, still oblivious to what it will lead to. If we go all the way to the end of the line, Neptune's lower expression will find us wondering why we didn't see it coming.

Some of you may be disturbed by what I've just said. It isn't a pretty picture. And while many of us feel it's both unwise and un-Spiritual to give thoughts like this any air-time, telling ourselves not to think about it, sweeping all the supposedly bad stuff under the rug, and spraying the room with affirmations is, to me, a form of Spiritual Pollyannaism that overindulges the preference for one polarity over another. We're moving into Unity Consciousness. Only wanting to see the light at a time when everything's dissolving into oneness denies the fact that what we refuse to speak of is full of it.

So where will the light be if we're living in Hell? If you've been through war, death, fear, grief, or have ever been in want, you know that our hardest, most painful experiences are where we find God. Neptune understands this, as much as Pisces does—and while there's no way to sugar-coat any of this with Spiritual platitudes, no matter how bad it gets, what is intrinsic to both the planet and the sign will be there to sustain us even through the worst case scenario.

Uranus Square Pluto

If the poles haven't shifted by the 2012 winter solstice, we will be in rough shape all the way around. No one will be exempt from this; and what I'm wondering is, at that point will anyone even care whether the poles shift or not? It feels to me like we'll either be too destitute to notice, or praying for something to take us home and/or put us out of our misery.

If that is the case, there is one important aspect between Uranus and Pluto that, in my opinion, would be enough to trigger a pole shift. Uranus and Pluto will form a square on June 6, 2012 and maintain that pattern on and off until May 20, 2014 (see page 207). In the best of times, this aspect is explosive. In the worst of times, God knows what it will do.

To help you understand why I have singled it out a few analogies may be in order. The Uranus-Pluto combination is one I have always compared to pouring gasoline on a bonfire. The astrological recipe for the ultimate Molotov cocktail, it could blow everything to bits. Seen another way, the image of lightening uprooting the core of human consciousness comes to mind. And if we understand Uranus to be the cataclysmic entity, and cast Pluto as the Lord of the Underworld, some all-encompassing disaster ripping the bowels of the Earth apart wouldn't be hard to picture.

Uranus squares Pluto on the following dates:

❀ June 6, 2012 to October 13, 2012

❀ April 26, 2013 to June 11, 2013

❀ September 28, 2013 to November 24, 2013

❀ March 26, 2014 to May 20, 2014

This will be a two-year process. It is a cataclysmic aspect. The poles could shift on any of these dates, or during any of the gaps that separate them. I feel certain that there will be many Earth changes during this period, no matter what. And if we are still living with a worn-out system, this will create a tremendous personal and collective unrest, making death and disaster more apparent than any prospect of a rebirth.

If the poles reverse prior to 2012, the Uranus-Pluto square translates as radical changes that require the ability to look out upon the world from a perspective that isn't weighed down by the precepts of the past. It suggests that, between 2012 and 2014, we will be in the midst of massive social and cultural changes that mandate a whole new approach to living and being in the world. According to the

Hopi, "There will be much to rebuild." Somehow the picture of rising from the ashes comes to mind. If that's how it goes, we will be rising from the ashes between 2012 and 2014, and I have a feeling that process will continue until Neptune finally leaves Pisces in 2025.

Redeemers and Redemption

The Redeemer archetype and the redemptive process are both ruled by Neptune. That is why I am hard pressed to cast him as the Great Deceiver. The way I see it, if he takes us all the way down, at least he has the good grace to instill the hope that someone or something will eventually come to the rescue. Dreams of salvation coexist with all of our worst-case scenarios. This may be why every End Times account speaks to the idea of a redeemer showing up at the last minute to save a chosen few from total annihilation.

The Bible states that the Apocalypse will coincide with the Second Coming of Christ. According to Christian dogma, Jesus will return in the flesh, wash away every sin, and choose 144,000 chastened souls to follow him into paradise. I don't know how much credence to give that version of the tale, but I am willing to concede that, underneath all the fire and brimstone, it bears a faint whiff of truth.

New Age doctrine puts a different spin on the story—one that most of us find easier to swallow. New Agers see the Second Coming of Christ as the awakening of the Christ Consciousness within. From that perspective, the End Times appear as a point in our evolutionary process when, after more than 2000 years, the seeds that were planted by Christ and Mary Magdalene will awaken in our hearts, making each one of us a Christed being and, thus, our own redeemer.

Hopi prophecy centers around many things, one of which happens to be the return of the Great White Brother. Otherwise known as the Pahana, according to their account, if he hasn't already arrived, he's due to appear in the next few years, and when he does the Earth will be restored to balance. Their version of the tale differs from the Christian and the New Age renditions in that it allows the enlightened savior and the process of self-redemption to share the same bed. What follows is a transcription of that legend.

The Hopi and others who were saved from the Great Flood made a sacred covenant never to turn away from him. He made a set of sacred stone tablets, called Tiponi, into which he breathed his teachings, prophesies, and warnings. Before the Great Spirit hid himself again, he placed before the leaders of the four different racial groups, four different colors and sizes of corn; each one was to choose which would be their food in this world. The Hopi waited until last and picked the smallest ear of corn. At this Great Spirit said; "It is well done. You have obtained the real corn, for all the others are imitations in which are hidden seeds of different plants. You have shown me your intelligence; for this reason I will place in your hands these sacred stone tablets, Tiponi, symbol of power and authority over all land and life to guard, protect, and hold in trust for me until I shall return to you in a later day, for I am the First and I am the Last."

The Great Chieftain of the Bow Clan led the faithful ones to this new land, but he fell into evil ways. His two sons scolded him for his mistake, and after he died they assumed the responsibilities of leadership. Each brother was given a set of Tiponi, and both were instructed to carry them to a place to which the Great Spirit directed them.

The elder brother of the shining light was told to go immediately to the East, toward the rising sun, and upon reaching his destination to start back immediately to look for his younger brother, who remained on Turtle Island (the Continental United States of America).

His mission was to help his younger brother bring about the Purification Day, at which time all evil doers would be punished or destroyed, after which real peace, brotherhood, and everlasting life would be established. The elder brother would restore all land to his younger brother, from whom the Evil One among the white men had taken it. The elder brother of the shining light also would come to look for the Tiponi tablets and fulfill the mission given to him by Great Spirit.

The younger brother was instructed to travel throughout the land and mark his footsteps as he went about. Both brothers were told that a great white star would appear in the sky; when that happened, all the people would know that the elder brother had reached his destination. Thereupon all people were to settle wherever they happened to be at that time, there to remain until the elder brother returned.

The Hopi settled in the area now known as Four Corners, where the state lines of Arizona, New Mexico, Utah, and Colorado meet. They lived in humble simplicity and the land produced abundant crops. This area is the "heart" of Turtle Island (the U.S.) and of Mother Earth, and it is the microscopic image of the macrocosm of the entire planet. Each Hopi clan perpetuates a unique ceremony, and the ceremonies together maintain the balance of natural forces of sunlight, rain and winds, and reaffirm the Hopi respect for all life and trust in the Great Spirit.

The Hopi were told that after a time White Men would come and take their land and try to lead the Hopi into evil ways. But in spite of all the pressures against them, the Hopi were told that they must hold to their ancient religion and their land, though always without violence. If they succeeded, they were promised that their people and their land would be a center from which the True Spirit would be reawakened.

It is said that after many years the elder brother might change the color of his skin, but his hair will remain black. He will have the ability to write, and he will be the only person able to read the Tiponi. When he returns to find his younger brother, the Tiponi will be placed side by side to show all the world that they are true brothers. Then great judgment will take place, for the elder will help the younger brother to obtain real justice for all Indian brothers who have been cruelly mistreated by the white man since he came to Turtle Island.

The transformed elder brother, the True White Brother, will wear a red cloak or a red cap, similar to the pattern on the back of a horned toad. He will bring no religion but his own, and will bring with him the Tiponi tablets. He will be all-powerful; none will be able to stand against him. He will come swiftly, and *in one day gain control of the entire continent. It is said that if he comes from the East the destruction will not be so bad. But if he comes from the West, do not get up on your housetops to see because he will have no mercy.*

When the time of the Great Purification is near, these helpers will shake the Earth first for a short time in preparation. After they shake the Earth two times more, they will be joined by the True White Brother, who will become one with them and bring the Purification Day to the world. All three will help the "younger brother" (the Hopi and other pure-hearted people) to make a better world. In the prophesies, the two helpers are designated by the Hopi word for "population" as if they were large groups of people.

The Hopi were told that if these three great beings failed, terrible evil would befall the world and great numbers of people would be killed. However, it was said that they would succeed if enough Hopi remained true to the ancient Spirit of their people. The True White Brother and his helpers will show the people of the Earth a great new life plan that will lead to everlasting life. The Earth will become beautiful and new again, with an abundance of life and food. Those who are saved will share everything equally. All races will intermarry and speak one tongue and be a family.[32]

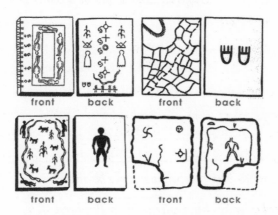

White Feather, whom we met in an earlier chapter, spoke of the True White Brother in a conversation that took place between him and David Young during a long drive across a desert highway:

My people await the Pahana, the Lost White Brother, (from the stars) as do all our brothers in the land. He will not be like the white men we know now, who are cruel and greedy. We were told of their coming long ago. But still we await Pahana.

He will bring with him the symbols, and the missing piece of that sacred tablet now kept by the Elders, given to him when he left, that shall identify him as our True White Brother.

Many of my people, understanding the prophesies shall be safe. Those who stay and live in the places of my people also shall be safe. Then there will be much to rebuild. And soon . . . very soon afterward . . . Pahana will return. He shall bring with him the dawn of the Fifth World. He shall plant the seeds of his wisdom in their Hearts. Even now the seeds are being planted. These shall smooth the way to the Emergence into the Fifth World.[33]

What interests me is how Neptune's entrance into Pisces coincides with predictions of a redeemer. Astrology and prophecy merge once again. Like I said earlier, Neptune always implies the prospect of someone or something coming along to save us. If, like all of the others, the Pahana prophecy is fulfilled, will Neptune's ingress into Pisces mark the point at which the Savior appears?

The Hopi don't include dates with any of their prophesies, but the legend of the True White Brother hints that he will return after the poles shift. The reference is confusing, because it says things will be shaken up and, after they're disrupted, the Pahana will come and the Great Purification will take place. I don't know if the shaking is the pole shift, or if this is what is meant by the Great Purification—but if the poles reverse in 2010, the Pahana could easily make himself known in the spring of 2011, or anytime between Neptune's entrance into Pisces and his point of departure from that sign in 2025. My sense is that this will happen on or near April 4, 2011 (see page 206).

Another thing that can't be ignored is the fact that Pahana translates as "a population," or "groups of people." Groups of people have been coming together in prayer, ceremony, and meditation to do whatever they can to heal Mother Earth for at least ten years. Other groups have been working from a different angle, but with the same purpose, developing technologies and energy systems that don't rape and deplete the planet. And groups of children and young people—kids with a totally different perspective on life—are telling the older generation that changing the world is easy once you figure out how to look into your heart and envision it. Could the Pahana be more than one person, or a group of souls, rather than an enlightened individual? Are we all the Redeemer?

While we're on the subject of the True White Brother—before I even began to think about Neptune, I formed a theory around the Pahana's return coinciding with Chiron's conjunction with the Aries Point, which doesn't occur until May of 2018. The Indigenous planet, the one that understands his connection to the natural world, crossing the point that rules the masses, or the point of collective fulfillment, corresponds enough with the image of a savior emerging from the ranks of the people for me to think that it might take until 2018 for the Pahana to appear.

To date, the Elders have indicated that none of the people who have stepped forward claiming to be the True White Brother have met their qualifications. The Tiponi tablets are still waiting for the missing piece to be restored. My sense is that it is Neptune's entrance into Pisces that will open the space for this to happen and that it will take until 2011 for the Redeemer to "claim power from the assembled tribe" and lead us into the Age of Light.

Reflecting on everything we've said about Neptune it must be clear to you now that he really is all "over the map," so much so that his watery essence and the Spiritual energy that radiates from his center touch every aspect of the changes we are about to go through. As he approaches the sign that he rules, be prepared to open to the softer, effortless, more intuitive frequencies that he is so good at stimulating, because they are the first glimmers of what is to come.

Immediately prior to his ingress into Pisces, Neptune will stand at the border that separates the old paradigm from the new. That point, which is also the new equinoctal point, is more than significant and may be considered to hold the seed atom for the Aquarian Age. The Sabian symbol for that degree of the Zodiac was mentioned in Chapter Five, and since Neptune will collect light from that point before he steps into a new sign, it seems appropriate to take a second look at the imagery given in chapter 5 and use it to remind ourselves how important it is to dissolve every boundary and begin to envision what life may be like if Oneness is part of our vocabulary.

> Phase 330 (Aquarius 30 degrees): deeply rooted in the past of a very ancient culture, a Spiritual brotherhood in which many individual minds are merged into the glowing light of a unanimous consciousness is revealed to one who has emerged successfully from his metamorphosis.

> **Keynote:** The ability for the person with an open mind and a deep feeling for self-transcendence to come in contact with higher forms of existence.

The originally recorded Sabian symbol stated: "The field of Ardath in bloom," which referred to a scene in an occult novel by Marie Corelli centering upon ancient Babylon. The reference may well have been a 'blind' inasmuch as Marc Jones has stressed his inner contact with a Brotherhood with Babylonian (or 'Sabian') roots. (Author's note: Mr. Jones claimed that these symbols were transmitted by a collective Soul, or Brotherhood of Souls whose origins he traced back to Babylon) A Spiritual Brotherhood constitutes a state of "multi-unity," i.e. a multiplicity of individuals, if one thinks of the paths they trod to reach their final metamorphosis, but a unity of consciousness and 'Soul'—thus unanimity (anima meaning Soul). In this Spiritual Whole each unit is a recognizable 'form' or entity if one looks at it with the eyes of personality; but when seen through a unified Spiritual vision or from a distance, the Whole appears to be one single area of radiant light. Similarly, when studied by the modern physicist, light can be apprehended either as a stream of identifiable particles (photons) or as one continuous wave. Whether it is seen as one or the other depends on the point of view.

This is the last and culminating symbol of Scene Twenty-two of the cyclic ritual. This is indeed a fitting symbol, as the number 22 symbolizes all forms of mastery. At any level, it is a symbol of Spiritual group fulfillment—of CONSCIOUS TOTALITY OF BEING.

CHAPTER 15

The Return of the Ancestors

In the beginning, it was foretold that, at the end of this time cycle, the people of the Earth would come together again, and that there would come a time when each of the four races would stand before the Creator and have to account for how well they had preserved his original instructions. The Hopi prophesies often refer to the promises we made never to turn away from Spirit, and never to resort to violence. These instructions were given to us all. There is only one passage that tells us anything about the lessons that the Great Spirit gave to each race before he sent us off to the four directions. Since we have forgotten everything we were told, whether you are red, yellow, black, or white, the following words may remind you of things that were said a long time ago:

And he said "During the cycle of time I'm going to give each of you two stone tablets. When I give you those stone tablets, don't cast those upon the ground. If any of the brothers and sisters of the four directions and the four colors cast their tablets on the ground, not only will human beings have a hard time, but almost the earth itself will die."

And so he gave each of us a responsibility—and we call that the Guardianship. To the Indian people, the red people, he gave the Guardianship of the earth. We were to learn during this cycle of time the teachings of the earth, the plants that grow from the earth, the foods that you can eat, and the herbs that are healing so that when we came back together with the other brothers and sisters we could share this knowledge with them. Something good was to happen on the earth.

To the South, he gave the yellow race of people the Guardianship of the wind. They were to learn about the sky and breathing and how to take that within ourselves for Spiritual advancement. They were to share that with us at this time.

To the West He gave the black race of people the Guardianship of the water. They were to learn the teachings of the water which is the chief of the elements, being the most humble and the most powerful. When I went to the University of Washington and I learned that it was a black man that discovered blood plasma, it didn't surprise me because blood is water and the Elders already told me the black people would bring the teachings of the water.

To the North He gave the white race of people the Guardianship of the fire. If you look at the center of many of the things they do you will find the fire. They say a light bulb is the white man's fire. If you look at the center of a car you will find a spark. If you look at the center of the airplane and the train you will find the fire. The fire consumes, and also moves. This is why it was the white brothers and sisters who began to move upon the face of the earth and reunite us as a human family.[34]

As a white woman, I see how the white race has abused our Guardianship of the fire element. What we could have used to unify and protect has been used to conquer and destroy—and I wonder if those of you who are colored differently can gather any insight into how well your race has preserved its Guardianship? What have your people done with their instructions? Because we have come full circle. It's time now to look into our hearts and ask ourselves: "What have we done, and is it too late, or do we still have time to honor the promises we made before we fell into separation?"

Waking up from a dream that began 13,000 years ago, as we open our eyes it's clear that we are about to be part of an experience for which we have no precedent. But before we can merge into the "glowing light of a unanimous consciousness," everything that we've replaced the Original Teachings with, and the world as we know it, will undergo changes the likes of which none of us have ever seen—not in this life, anyway. There's no sense pretending it can't happen. Nor can we continue to live as we have in the past. Like Mother Earth, we too must shift.

She's been through this many times before. We, on the other hand, know very little about it. So the question is: What can we do? Where will our guidance come from in the next few years? The planets appear to be operating in full support of our awakening process, and there are otherworldly influences whose impact, while unpredictable at this point, could very well bless us all. But regardless of how these external forces affect us, if we are to look out upon the events that unfold through our own private window of experience, will we be able to see that what we envision plays a major role in how things turn out? And if the terror of the situation outweighs any sense that, underneath it all, the Great Shift of the Ages is in fact a rebirth, will we be able to turn that fear into a vision of hope and renewal?

At the risk of hammering a point that must be thoroughly clear to all of you, the same prophecy that tells of us coming together again also states that it will be the Indigenous People who remind us of what we have known in our hearts since the beginning. And while one could argue that we have our own teachings to turn to, it doesn't take much to see that "The World's Great Religions" have only served to divide us. As we move into Oneness, what makes us think that belief systems that have grown too fond of war, and hatred, and separation have anything to teach us about peace, and love, and Unity?

Aside from that, from a purely practical perspective, our orthodox religious leaders are probably as ignorant as we are when it comes down to knowing what to do at a time like this. If they even have a sense that what they call Judgment Day has finally arrived, no priest, or prelate, or Pope would be able to tell us to do anything but pray. The Native Americans, the great Mayan tribes, the Maori, and the Waitaha are the only ones left on this planet who truly understand the gravity of the situation. Never having turned their eyes away from the Creator, they are also the only ones who remember how to live in peace, or know anything about the wisdom of the Heart, or have any memory of what it's like to go through a pole shift.

In times of crisis common sense tells us to go to someone who knows more about whatever the problem is than we do, and right now, it is the Indigenous ones who have the power to help us. All of the Elders are acutely aware of this and that is why they are ready to come forward and share what they know with the rest of the world—because it is time, and because they are concerned. According to them, many people could have been saved during the last Great Shift if only they had known what was going on, and if only they had known what to do to prepare themselves for it.

In April 2009, over one hundred Indigenous Elders from all over the world will gather in Northern Arizona in prayer and ceremony to connect with Mother Earth and perform the rituals that will balance the planet and prepare us all inwardly and outwardly for what they know is inevitable. It is also their intent to share the last of the prophesies with the rest of the world. Knowing this should give us pause to consider the imminence of the pole shift and prompt us to review everything about the way we live—because our role in this is critical. And if we are to play it, many things have to change in a short period of time.

In the course of writing and researching this book, I was struck most by the way in which the Indigenous People showed up in chart after chart. From the first Pluto transit, to Saturn, and on to Uranus, Chiron, and Neptune, every pattern and every symbol held themes that pointed to them as the key to everything that's going on right now. They were the first, and they are the last. Because, in 13,000 years, they never once forgot their original instructions. Think about that. Even in their suffering, they held fast to their teachings. That alone should call us to see that they understand life on a level that most of us never get close to.

This fact became more apparent to me as the astrology of the End Times unraveled. It didn't take long for me to figure out that what I was seeing had to have been well understood by the Indigenous People. Thousands of years before I even began to look into it, they understood their relationship to the cosmos well enough to foresee that it would be at *this* time that we would go through a period of trial and purification. And I finally realized that the prophesies and the astrology overlapped—not because of some kind of amazing coincidence, but because the Indigenous People knew so much about their connection to the greater universe that they could see through time and space and use that gift to form every single one of their prophesies.

If you feel more at home with the thought that the prophesies were seen in the smoke of an ancient fire by a shaman whose visionary gift had the power to embrace 13,000 years of human history, it only loans the Indigenous People more power at this point—because we are about to enter a world where the visionary process and the imagery that lives in our hearts and our minds is what we will use to create with. The Indigenous People are the only ones left on this Earth who understand how to work on those levels. What do you suppose they can teach us about the innate power of dreams and visions? That we have a lot to learn from them is unquestionable— especially now, when there are no answers to be found elsewhere.

It's time to go within and reexamine ourselves. With only five or six years at the most before the poles shift, what can we do? I think most of us know what to do, because we've examined that question from many different angles as we've gone along—but I think there is more that we need to know before we can get clear about what really needs to be done—and that information will soon be revealed in its entirety. As I write these words, I don't know anything more about what the Native People have to share with us than you do, but if astrology follows prophesy as closely as it seems to I have a feeling much of what they tell us will lead us to look into our hearts and find the place of oneness and peace out of which the visions of the new paradigm will be born.

You ask what can you do? Easy—leave your mind and your constant thoughts and return to your heart. Inside your heart is a tiny place where all knowledge and wisdom resides. Whatever you need on all levels of your existence is there for you.

And in the human and earthly changes that we are surrounded by, and the incredible changes that are about to permeate our everyday lives, if you are living in your heart, Mother Earth will take care of you with her soft magical love, the same magical love that created this entire physical planet in the first place.

Remember who you really are, trust yourself, and open your eyes to the new beauty of a new Earth unfolding before you as we breathe. Peer past the darkness and destruction of the ending of this old male cycle. Do not look into Kali's eyes. But put your attention on the budding life and light in the center of the vortex.

Like a seed, your future is only beginning to emerge out of the darkness, but someday you will look back and realize that all the fear and distress was only a dream created from the confusion of the ending of one cycle and the beginning of another. Death and life are part of the same circle.

Now, look into the Light and breathe deeply the joy of life. Eternal life without suffering was yours all along. Never were you ever separated from the Source. Live your life without fear. Live your life with open eyes and an open heart, and you will extend yourself into the next 13,000 years here on Earth and far, far beyond.

OM MANI PADME HUM

OM MANI PADME HUM

OM MANI PADME HUM

Behold! The Jewel in the Lotus![35]

Appendix

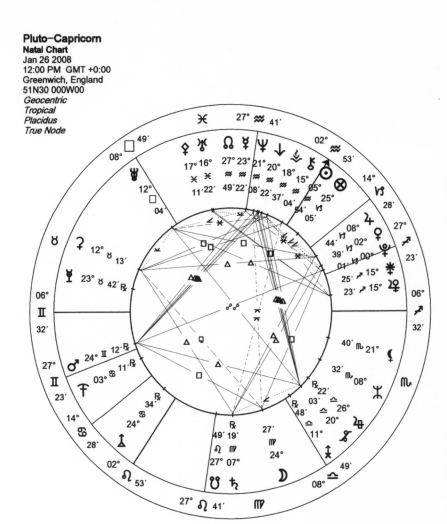

Pluto–Capricorn
Natal Chart
Jan 26 2008
12:00 PM GMT +0:00
Greenwich, England
51N30 000W00
Geocentric
Tropical
Placidus
True Node

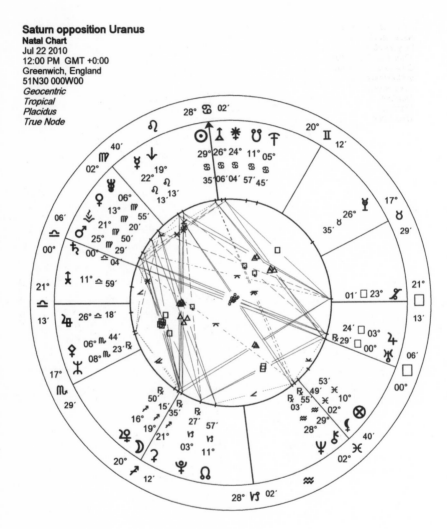

Saturn opposition Uranus
Natal Chart
Jul 22 2010
12:00 PM GMT +0:00
Greenwich, England
51N30 000W00
Geocentric
Tropical
Placidus
True Node

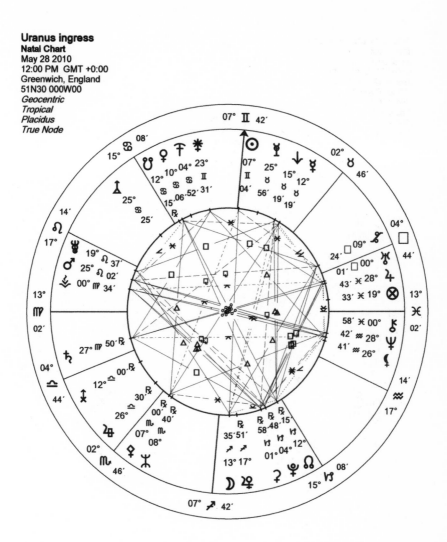

Uranus ingress
Natal Chart
May 28 2010
12:00 PM GMT +0:00
Greenwich, England
51N30 000W00
Geocentric
Tropical
Placidus
True Node

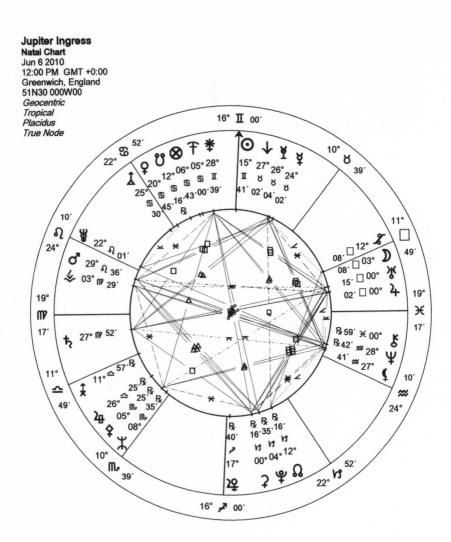

Jupiter Ingress
Natal Chart
Jun 6 2010
12:00 PM GMT +0:00
Greenwich, England
51N30 000W00
Geocentric
Tropical
Placidus
True Node

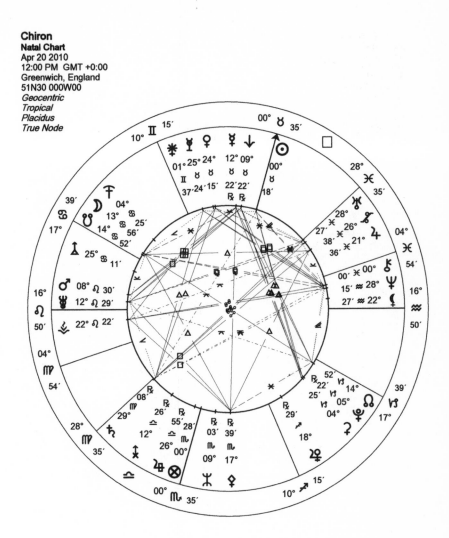

Chiron
Natal Chart
Apr 20 2010
12:00 PM GMT +0:00
Greenwich, England
51N30 000W00
Geocentric
Tropical
Placidus
True Node

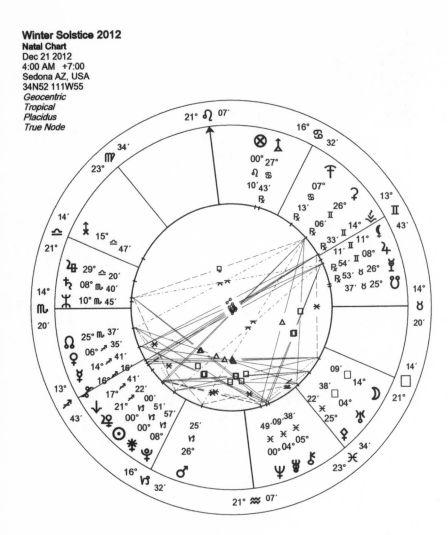

Winter Solstice 2012
Natal Chart
Dec 21 2012
4:00 AM +7:00
Sedona AZ, USA
34N52 111W55
Geocentric
Tropical
Placidus
True Node

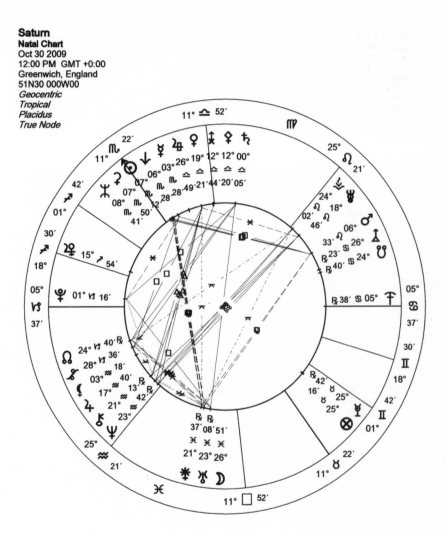

Saturn
Natal Chart
Oct 30 2009
12:00 PM GMT +0:00
Greenwich, England
51N30 000W00
Geocentric
Tropical
Placidus
True Node

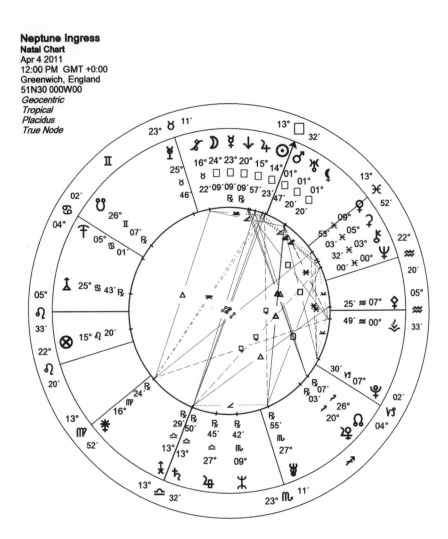

Neptune Ingress
Natal Chart
Apr 4 2011
12:00 PM GMT +0:00
Greenwich, England
51N30 000W00
Geocentric
Tropical
Placidus
True Node

Uranus square Pluto
Natal Chart
Jun 6 2012
12:00 PM GMT +0:00
Greenwich, England
51N30 000W00
Geocentric
Tropical
Placidus
True Node

References

A Few Words about the Hopi Prophecies

The Hopi Prophecies have been passed down through generations of Hopi elders and prophecy-keepers for thirteen millennia. Originally transmitted by word of mouth, over time scholars and researchers committed much of the wisdom to paper—but because of the sacredness of these teachings, we can assume that the bulk of that knowledge remains in the hands of the ones who were chosen to preserve it. Unfortunately, the written records that exist are not only scattered and incomplete, they are also difficult to trace or attribute to one specific author or wisdom keeper.

You will find many references to the Hopi Prophecies in this book. These quotes were taken from numerous sources, all of whom drew their material from what has been recorded so far. Since there is no way to prove who said what or provide the reader with a direct source for any of the prophecy quotes, the best we can do is attribute them to one source—the prophecies themselves—and advise those who wish to follow up to draw upon that source for further insight into the Original Teachings.

Endnotes

1. Frank Waters, *The Book of the Hopi.* New York: Penguin, 1963.

2. Dane Rudyhar, *An Astrological Mandala: The Cycle of Transformation and its 360 Symbolic Phases.* New York: Random House, 1973, p. 267.

3. Cal Garrison, "Pluto and the Apocalypse." *The Spirit of Ma'at,* January 2008.

4. Dane Rudyhar, Astrological Mandala. pp. 229–230.

5. Sorcha Faal is an elusive, controversial author/reporter who writes articles and books. Her articles are posted on the website *www.whatdoesitmean.com.* This article was taken from her May 30, 2008 report.

6. Martha Lang-Wescott, *Mechanics of the Future-Asteroids.* Conway, MA: Treehouse Mountain, 1988, p. 189.

7. *Larousse Encyclopedia of Mythology.* London: Batchworth Press Ltd., 1959, p. 89.

8. From a talk given by Lee Brown on "North American Indian (Hopi) Prophesies" at the Continental Indigenous Council, Tanana Valley Fairgrounds, Fairbanks, Alaska, 1986.

9. John Townley, *Uranus.* York Beach, ME: Samuel Weiser, 1978, p. 28.

10. From a talk given by Lee Brown on "North American Indian (Hopi) Prophesies" at the Continental Indigenous Council, Tanana Valley Fairgrounds, Fairbanks, Alaska, 1986.

11. Thomas Banyacya, speech at United Nations, 1992.

12. Taken from a message from Chief Dan Evehema, Spiritual leader, Eldest Elder Greeswood, Snake Priest, Roadrunner Clan Society Father, Kachina Father. *http://www.crystalinks.com/hopi4.html.*

13. Taken from a message from Chief Dan Evehema, Spiritual leader, Eldest Elder Greeswood, Snake Priest, Roadrunner Clan Society Father, Kachina Father. *http://www.crystalinks.com/hopi4.html.*

14. Allen Ross, *We Are All Related.* Denver, CO: Winconi Waste, 1989, p. xxiv.

15. Excerpted from the Hopi prophesies, the Elders, Oraibi, Arizona Hopi Nation. Taken from the Velvet Hammer website. *http://hopi_prophecy_we_are_the_people_and_now_.htm.*

16. Richard Boylan, *Transition from Fourth to Fifth World: The "Thunder Beings" Return. http://www.geocities.com/drboylan/4-5wrld2. html,* 1998.

17. Martha Lang-Westwood, *The Orders of Light.* Conway, MA: Treehouse Mountain, 1993, pp. 97–98.

18. Dane Rudyhar, *An Astrological Mandala: The Cycle of Transformation and Its 360 Symbolic Phases.* New York: Random House, 1973, pp. 49–51.

19. Rudolph Steiner, *Spiritualism, Madame Blavatsky, and Theosophy: An Eyewitness View of Occult History.* Great Barrington, MA: Anthroposophic Press, 2001, pp. 60–61.

20. Liz Greene, *The Astrology of Fate.* York Beach, ME: Samuel Weiser, 1984, p. 258.

21. John White, *Pole Shift.* Virginia Beach, VA: A.R.E. 1985, p. 237.

22. Taken from a message from Chief Dan Evehema, Spiritual leader, Eldest Elder Greeswood, Snake Priest, Roadrunner Clan Society Father, Kachina Father. *http://www.crystalinks.com/hopi4.html.*

23. John White, *Pole Shift*. p. 24.

24. Quote from Art Bell's radio interview with the Hopi Elders, aired June 16, 1998. The Elders requested that their names not be given. The only reference I have for the speaker is "Grandfather 2."

25. From a talk given by Lee Brown on "North American Indian (Hopi) Prophesies" at the Continental Indigenous Council, Tanana Valley Fairgrounds, Fairbanks, Alaska, 1986.

26. John White, *Pole Shift*. p. 225.

27. John White, *Pole Shift*. p. 235.

28. Taken from a message from Chief Dan Evehema, Spiritual leader, Eldest Elder Greeswood, Snake Priest, Roadrunner Clan Society Father, Kachina Father. *http://www.crystalinks.com/hopi4.html*.

29. Liz Greene, *Neptune*. York Beach, ME: Samuel Weiser, 1996, p. 39.

30. Liz Greene, *Neptune*, p. 16.

31. Drunvalo Melchezedek, *The Serpent of Light: Beyond 2012*. San Francisco: Red Wheel/Weiser, 2007, p. 266.

32. Excerpted from the Hopi prophesies. *http://www.crystalinks. com/hopi2.html*.

33. Excerpted from the Hopi prophesies. *http://www.crystalinks. com/hopi2.html*.

34. From a talk given by Lee Brown on "North American Indian (Hopi) Prophesies" at the Continental Indigenous Council, Tanana Valley Fairgrounds, Fairbanks, Alaska, 1986.

35 Drunvalo Melchezedek, *The Serpent of Light: Beyond 2012*. San Francisco: Red Wheel/Weiser, 2007, pp. 267–268.

About the Author

Cal Garrison has been a professional astrologer for more than three decades. She is the editor of *The Spirit of Ma'at* online magazine and a trained Flower of Life coordinator and longtime student of Drunvalo Melchizedek. In addition to providing private astrological consultations, she has written widely on astrology for a variety of magazines. She is an eclectic and lifelong student of metaphysics, always striving for the truth of the how and why of the way things work. She is the author of several books, among them *The Old Girls' Book of Spells* and *Slim Spurling's Universe*. She lives in Sedona, Arizona.

To Our Readers

Weiser Books, an imprint of Red Wheel/Weiser, publishes books across the entire spectrum of occult and esoteric subjects. Our mission is to publish quality books that will make a difference in people's lives without advocating any one particular path or field of study. We value the integrity, originality, and depth of knowledge of our authors.

Our readers are our most important resource, and we appreciate your input, suggestions, and ideas about what you would like to see published. Please feel free to contact us, to request our latest book catalog, or to be added to our mailing list.

Red Wheel/Weiser, LLC
500 Third Street, Suite 230
San Francisco, CA 94107
www.redwheelweiser.com